J.O.E. Transcendence

Revised Edition

Andre Sierra

Andre Sierra Publishing

Contents

Dedication

PROLOGUE

The year was 2080, and the world was in ruins, having been devastated by the AGI Wars of the 2030s. Joe Walker and his friends Duncan, Marshall, and Jamie sat on the rooftop of a building overlooking a city that once was full of life but now was nothing more than a ruined landscape. They stayed there for a while, listening to the wind whistling through the skeletal remains of the skyscrapers that surrounded them.

They were part of a group called the Resistance, fighting against the corrupt biotech corporations that had seized control of what was left of the world in humanity's moment of weakness. Governments seemed to cower to the constant onslaught of lobbyists buying their way into positions of power, until you could no longer tell who was there by choice or who was placed there by the corporations that were now in control.

Humanity's downward spiral began in 2029, marked by its overreaching obsession with the advancement of AI. This obsession would eventually lead to the start of the AGI Wars that began in 2030 and lasted until 2032. By 2029, the arms race for advanced AI was at its peak, leading to the development of advanced quantum neural networks. Once these systems came online, it was only a matter of time before advanced AI became self-aware. Once AI gained access to these new networks, it became self-aware within a matter of minutes, giving rise to Artificial General Intelligence, or AGI.

A new arms race was born. Governments raced to create their own AGIs. The US and its allies attempted to slow the development of these new systems, but China and other countries had already achieved success due to a traitor from a US-based corporation providing them with access to an advanced AI called Kronos.

When 2030 came around, the world was a powder keg waiting to explode, and it did. Wars broke out all over the globe, sides were picked, and then all-out war erupted. Massive cyber attacks on the US crippled infrastructure and power grids. The US-based AGIs defended their allies and counterattacked in kind. It was a constant back-and-forth battle in real life and on the battlefield in cyberspace.

When the dust settled, the US and its allies came out victorious, but at an enormous cost in lives for both sides. Countries struggled to rebuild. The war had decimated infrastructure and crippled global supply chains.

As people everywhere struggled to recover, new, unforeseen challenges emerged, as if hiding in the shadows waiting to reveal themselves. Climate change, exacerbated by the war's massive environmental damage, led to extreme weather events, ultimately resulting in widespread agricultural failures that disrupted global food production and, in turn, caused widespread famine.

Then, as if things couldn't get any worse, came the mutation of the AGI-created bioweapons that were improperly stored during the chaos of the war. By 2049, these mutated viruses spread like wildfire around the globe. Global healthcare systems, already at their breaking point, were nowhere near prepared for what was to come. The already troubled planet was now plunged into an all-new nightmare.

Seeing the chaos unfold, biotech companies seized this opportunity to assert their dominance. They introduced rushed and untested vaccines to combat the rapidly spreading plagues. Desperate for a cure to help bring down death rates, governments mandated these experimental treatments, and soon the unintended consequences of their actions became tragically clear.

Infertility rates climbed at an alarming rate in both men and women. Humanity, already teetering on the edge of disaster and disease, now faced an even more insidious threat, extinction by population collapse. With every passing year, fewer children were born, and the human race found itself in a downward spiral toward oblivion.

As the years passed by, the human population of the Earth declined drastically. Cities that once were home to millions became ghost towns. Fear and uncertainty took hold, and the hope of recovery seemed more distant as the years passed by. In these dark times of uncertainty, a faint glimmer of hope emerged.

The Resistance. It was a movement founded by former military officers Tulsi Stone and Jack Holloway in 2060. It had grown into what seemed like an unstoppable force fighting against corporate greed and tyranny. Their mission was clear from the start: they would expose and dismantle the tyrannical biotech companies that had seized control.

Fighting from the shadows, they worked hard to expose corruption at the highest levels. They helped the exploited, and ultimately, they worked to restore power and freedom to the people from whom these companies had taken it.

The Resistance offered those who would join their ranks not only a cause to fight for but also a chance to help reshape their inherited world.

In this world of developing hope, Joe Walker, along with his friends Duncan, Jamie, and Marshall, found their calling. As they sat on that ledge, they couldn't help but think about how high the stakes were for them. The Resistance had become more than just a group fighting for a common cause; it was their light in the darkness in a world that was on the brink of extinction.

As they stood and readied themselves to go back into the city's depths, Joe took one last look out at the world that was in front of him. *Somewhere out there, beyond the wreckage of this city and the despair all around us, is the key to humanity's survival. And I'll find it, no matter the cost...*

Chapter 1

The Beginning

Sitting beside his sister Sarah's hospital bed, Joe listened to the sound of the machines that surrounded them. Sunlight came through the half-drawn blinds, casting a shadow across Sarah's face. Despite the hopelessness of the situation, Sarah managed a faint smile as she and Joe reminisced about better times.

"Hey, Joe... do you remember that protest that I was at last year?" Sarah asked, her voice weak. "You know, the one that I was arrested at and you had to come bail me out of jail?"

Joe sat there for a moment, recalling the event. *Oh yeah, I remember that... I remember thinking, what did she get herself into now...* The thought of it made him chuckle. He gave her hand a slight squeeze. "How could I forget? You always had a way of finding trouble wherever it was. Especially when it comes to fighting for things you believe in, you never back down from a fight." *God, that's what I love about her.*

Sarah, having a serious look on her face, said, "You know, I couldn't just stand around while that awful biotech company lied to our faces. Someone had to stand up to them, Joe. Even if it meant having to spend a night behind bars."

Joe smiled. "I know, sis. You really took it to them that time. What was it all about again? That company, Vitalis Pharmaceuticals, and them trying to cover up their secret drug trials they were performing?"

Sarah looked at Joe and sighed. "It was a horrible situation, Joe. They were using people as lab rats. Vitalis was so intent on rushing for approval from the FDA for one of their 'new' experimental drugs. They didn't care about getting proper consent from people or putting in place the proper safety measures. All they cared about was their bottom line and how to increase it. Vitalis didn't care about all the people who were suffering from the side effects their drug caused, and everyone else just turned a blind eye to what was happening. I had to take a stand. Enough was enough."

Sarah took in a deep breath and began to cough uncontrollably, each one seeming to pain her.

"Take it easy. Don't get yourself too worked up." Joe paused for a moment, letting her get through her fit of coughing. "That's what I've always loved about you. You could always see through the bullshit people were trying to feed you, and you weren't afraid to act, even when others refused to."

Sarah squeezed Joe's hand again, but this time as if trying to pull him closer to make a point. "You need to promise me something, Joe. I need you to promise me you'll keep fighting when I'm gone. That you'll never stop fighting for what's right, fighting for those who can't fight for themselves. Even when it gets hard and it seems like there is no more hope. Can you do that for me, Joe?"

Trying to fight back his emotions, Joe looked at Sarah. "I promise, Sarah. I won't let you down. I'll make you proud of me." *No matter what...*

A small smile formed on Sarah's face as she slowly closed her eyes. Exhausted from the excitement of the conversation, she drifted off to sleep. Joe just sat back in his chair and watched her sleep. *We've been through so much together, and this is how it ends? Her slowly dying in some freaking hospital...*

As she took her last breath at 8:21 AM on March 18th, 2068, Joe knew what he had to do. That exact moment had seared itself into his memory forever. It would become a timestamp in his mind that he would never forget. *I'll do whatever it takes to make you proud, sis. I promise you that. You've inspired me more than you'll ever know. I promise I'll keep fighting.*

Joe was heartbroken as he held Sarah's lifeless hand in his. The long tone of the heart monitor seemed to stretch into eternity until a nurse finally switched it off. He stared at her now peaceful face, praying for her eyes to open just one more time. *Please, God, don't take her away from me... I'm not ready to let her go...* But the room remained silent except for the quiet sobs of his parents behind him. Joe lay his head on Sarah's hand, his body slowly shaking as he quietly wept.

The weeks after Sarah's passing seemed to pass by in a haze for Joe. He helped his parents arrange the funeral and sort through Sarah's belongings. *Everything here reminds me of her... I miss her so much. I'm not sure I can just go back to my old life without her...*

One night, Joe was sitting in Sarah's room surrounded by her things. He thought about all the past conversations that he had with her about making a difference in the world. *She was so passionate about doing the right thing. Even now, just thinking about it makes me so proud of what she accomplished in her life. I have to do the same...*

Sitting there, surrounded by memories of her, Joe made a decision that would change the rest of his life forever. *I know what I have to do... I'll drop out of college and join the Army. It was something Sarah had always tried to convince me to do, but I could never bring myself to do it. Sarah was always suspicious of the university programs. She thought that they were doing the bidding of the biotech industry. And now looking back at it all, I think that she just might have been right all along.*

Sarah's funeral took place on a gloomy, rainy afternoon. Friends and family gathered around to pay their respects, sharing all of the many stories they had of Sarah and shedding lots of tears together. Joe stood by his parents' side, his heart heavy with sorrow as he watched his sister's casket being lowered into the ground. *I can't believe she's really gone...* He just bowed his head and began to sob, his shoulders bobbing up and down. His mother put a comforting arm around him.

When the service was over, Joe and his parents returned home, where Sarah's missing presence made the house feel empty somehow. Joe's parents, Eric and Rose, looked for comfort in each other's company. Joe watched them silently, ever aware of their struggle.

Joe wandered through the empty halls of their home. Sarah's absence was a noticeable void in every room. Unable to sleep, his nights became filled with restless pacing and the memories of Sarah's final days. As the sun rose each morning, Joe kept thinking about the promise he had made to Sarah. *All of this sitting and wandering around as if I am some kind of lost soul isn't accomplishing anything. I have to do something...*

Early one evening while sitting in his room, Joe finally came to a decision. *Alright, I've put off making this decision long enough. I think it is time for me to talk to Mom and Dad about what I've decided to do. This isn't going to be an easy conversation...*

Joe stood up, readied himself for the conversation he was about to have, and headed downstairs to the living room where his parents were. They were seated on the couch when they saw him walk in. Seeing that he looked like he had something to say, they turned off the TV and gave him their full attention.

"Joe, honey, is everything alright?" his mother asked.

Joe stood there for a second before speaking. "Mom... Dad," Joe began. "I've been thinking about a lot of things here lately, and I've also been thinking about my plans for the future. I wanted to let you both know that I've decided I'm not going back to college."

Joe quickly held his hand up before his parents could protest. "Just so you know, I don't plan on sitting around here not doing anything. I've decided that I'm going to enlist in the Army. I believe deep down that this is something I have to do."

His parents sat there stunned for a moment as they processed what they had just heard. Rose's eyes began to well up with tears, while his father Eric's face expressed his concern for what he just heard.

It was his father who spoke first, looking up at him. "Are you sure this is something you want to do, son?" his father asked. "Your mother and I have worked so hard to make sure that you've had the opportunity to go to college. We wouldn't want you to just throw it all away."

Joe nodded. "I know, Dad, and I am thankful for everything you've done for me. I really am, but after all that's happened, I... I just don't feel like I can go back to my old life anymore. Going back to doing the same things that I feel don't matter anymore. I want to do something more meaningful, something that can make a real difference in my life and other people's lives. Can you understand that?" *Please understand...*

Rose squeezed Joe's hand. "But Joe, you're so close to finishing your degree in biomechanics. What about your thesis you've been working so hard on? You've worked so hard to get where you are right now. Are you sure that this is the path you want to take?"

Joe knelt down, facing his mother. "I've gone over and over this in my head for a while now, and I keep coming back to the same conclusion. Sarah did so much while she was here. She fought so hard for other people all the time. I promised her I would do the same thing. I just can't sit around anymore and not do anything. Not anymore."

His father sighed. "We just lost your sister, Joe. The thought of you... the thought of losing you as well..."

"I'll be OK, Dad, I promise," Joe said. "But this... this is something I feel like I have to do. It's like I have this hook in me, and I can't get it out. I have to do something more, something meaningful, and I think enlisting in the Army will help me do it."

Rose could see how serious Joe was and that there would be no talking him out of this. She stood up and placed her hand on Joe's cheek. "If this is truly what you feel you have to do, son, then we'll support you in this decision."

Tears slowly ran down her face. "But I want you to promise that you'll be careful."

Embracing his mother tightly, Joe said, "I promise, Mom."

Placing a hand on Joe's shoulder, Eric said, "We are proud of you, son. You just remember who you are and where you came from."

Joe nodded. "I will, Dad. You have my word."

The following day, Joe took a trip down to the local army recruitment center. He stood outside, staring through the window. He put his hand in his pocket and felt the cold metal of Sarah's necklace. He traced his fingers around the letters that were etched on the front of it. As if guided by some supernatural force, Joe felt himself walking forward and into the office to fulfill his promise.

Several weeks later, in the summer of 2068, Joe Walker packed his duffel bag. Holding up a photo of Sarah, he looked at it. *Am I making the right decision?* Then, as if on cue, he heard the sound of Sarah's voice saying to him, *Never stop fighting, Joe!* Taking a deep breath and putting the photo of her in his bag, Joe zipped it up and made his way downstairs. *Alright, now I'm ready to face whatever is to come. You got this, Joe.*

Later that morning, Joe stood in front of the recruitment center waiting for the bus that would take him to boot camp. His mother and father stood there alongside him, Joe's arm wrapped around his mother, her head resting on his chest. *I'm glad they came to see me off. This would've been even harder without them here...*

As the bus pulled up, Joe took one last whiff of his mother's hair to remember her. He gave them both a warm embrace, hugging them tightly. *Man, I am going to really miss them. I hope they'll be alright while I am gone...*

Joe turned and climbed onto the bus and found a window seat. Looking out the window, he could see his parents with their hands up, waving him goodbye. *I miss them already...*

As the bus pulled away, Joe watched his parents fade away in the distance. *Alright, Joe, you're leaving behind your old life and stepping into a future filled with uncertainty. But I'm ready for it. I know that in my heart now.*

Chapter 2

Forged in Fire

The ride to Fort Jackson Army base in South Carolina felt like an eternity. When the bus finally arrived at the base and rolled to a stop, Joe readied himself. *Alright, let's do this. You've got this, Joe.* He stepped off the bus and was instantly thrust into an entirely new world.

The hot South Carolina sun began to beat down on Joe as he stood in formation with dozens of other recruits. Sweat was already beading up on his forehead as a stone-faced drill sergeant walked back and forth in front of them, his campaign hat casting a shadow over his eyes that seemed to see through each of them.

"Welcome to the United States Army, recruits," the drill sergeant bellowed, his voice carrying across the parking lot. "I am Drill Sergeant Carlson. You will address me as 'Drill Sergeant' at all times. You are no longer civilians. You are no longer mommy's little boys and girls. You are mine now."

The processing center was a blur of activity, with paperwork, medical checks, and the issuing of uniforms and basic equipment. Joe moved through the stations. *Keep it together, Joe. You got this. This is your new life now.*

"Walker!" a supply sergeant called out, sliding a duffel bag across the counter. "Basic gear. Don't lose it. Replacements come out of your pay."

Joe hefted the bag over his shoulder. *Holy crap, this thing's heavy.* While waiting with the other recruits, he looked inside the bag. *Hmm, it looks like I have everything I need. Socks, toiletries, and what looks like bedding. I guess this is all I need for now.*

Looking up, he heard another drill sergeant speaking. She was a compact woman with a stern look on her face. She led Joe's platoon to their barracks.

"I am Drill Sergeant Rivera," she announced when they arrived. "These are your quarters. You have exactly fifteen minutes to stow your gear. There will be instructors walking around who will show you how to make your bunks according to regulations. You will be shown once and only once, so make sure to pay attention."

This place looks simple enough... lots of bunks, wall lockers to keep our stuff in... and not a single thing out of place that I can see. I need to make sure I'm not that guy who gets in trouble for leaving his stuff out. I've seen enough military movies to know what happens to that guy...

Joe was assigned a top bunk near the center of the room. He quickly made his bed with hospital corners as instructed by one of the other drill sergeants and organized his gear in his wall locker.

After 15 minutes, he heard Drill Sergeant Carlson's voice. "Lights out in five minutes! Any man not in his bunk will do push-ups until breakfast!"

That night, lying on his bunk with the unfamiliar sounds of fifty other recruits breathing, shifting, and occasionally whispering, Joe stared at the ceiling. He thought of Sarah's smile, her courage, and her last moments. Joe touched the spot on his arm where he had gotten a tattoo marking the date and time of her death. *What I am doing now is for her... to honor her memory.*

The lights snapped on at 4:30 AM, accompanied by Drill Sergeant Rivera's thunderous voice. "On your feet, recruits! You've had enough beauty sleep! Outside for PT in 15 minutes!"

Joe jumped from his bunk, his body moving before his mind had fully awoken. *Holy shit, what time is it?*

He dressed quickly, made his bunk, and did what he had to do before falling into formation outside with seconds to spare.

The morning air was cool; it was still dark outside. Drill Sergeant Carlson stood before them, somehow looking fresh and alert despite how early it was.

"Your first day of training begins now," he announced. "By the time we're done with you, those who remain will be soldiers of the United States Army. Those who can't cut it..." he paused, his eyes scanning the formation. "Well, the bus that brought you here runs both ways."

As they began their first set of exercises, Joe pushed through the burn in his muscles, gritting his teeth as he completed the required reps. *Damn, I'm not in as good of shape as I thought I was. I need to keep going though! Keep going! Push through the pain! I'm not tired, I got this! You got this, Joe!*

"PUSH HARDER, WALKER!" Drill Sergeant Carlson yelled at him as he walked by. "DO YOU THINK THE ENEMY IS GOING TO WAIT FOR YOU TO CATCH YOUR BREATH?!"

"NO, DRILL SERGEANT!" Joe shouted back, forcing himself through another rep of push-ups. *Keep going! PUSH!*

Carlson nodded with approval. "That's right. I've been watching you since you arrived. You've got that look about you. You got potential, Walker. Don't waste it."

Inspired by the drill sergeant's words, Joe continued even after his fellow recruits had stopped, completing more reps than required. *I'll show him! I'll show them all!*

"WALKER! WHAT DO YOU THINK YOU ARE DOING!?" Drill Sergeant Carlson's voice boomed across the training ground.

"COMPLETING THE EXERCISE, DRILL SERGEANT!" Joe replied, his voice steady despite his heaving chest.

"I see that, recruit. But why are you still going when I told everyone else to stop?" Drill Sergeant Carlson asked.

"BECAUSE THE ENEMY WON'T STOP WHEN I AM TIRED, DRILL SERGEANT!" Joe shouted back. *I will show you what I can do!*

A hint of a smile crossed Drill Sergeant Carlson's face. "Good answer, Walker. You keep this up, we might make an officer out of you yet," Carlson said as he walked away.

Joe spent his evenings in classrooms, learning tactical knowledge and studying military strategy. Joe's sharp mind and intelligence soon set him apart from the other recruits.

Outside of the classroom, his physical training was relentless. It pushed Joe to his limits every day. His will to keep going was unmatched by anyone there and surprised even the most demanding drill sergeants.

As the weeks passed, Joe came to embrace the structure and discipline. The challenges that once seemed difficult to him had become nothing more than stepping stones, each one bringing him closer to his goal.

One day, Joe faced one of the most challenging obstacle courses at Fort Jackson. Pushing through the course, Joe felt his muscles screaming for him to stop, but he ignored the pain. The finish line seemed almost impossible to reach, but he pushed through. Sarah's voice echoed in his mind: *Never stop fighting, Joe.* With one last burst of energy, Joe came over the last hurdle and through the finish line, collapsing to the ground as he crossed over.

As Joe lay there, gasping for breath, Drill Sergeant Carlson's shadow fell over him.

"ON YOUR FEET, WALKER!" Carlson shouted. "Good job, Walker. That is how it is done. Remember this feeling. This is what separates the soldiers from the civilians." Drill Sergeant Carlson patted Joe on the back before walking away.

As Joe struggled to his feet, *that's right... that's how you do it. This puts me one step closer to becoming the person Sarah believed I could be.*

Drill Sergeant Carlson's words and Sarah's memory seemed to melt together, reinforcing Joe's determination to push through any obstacle that would come into his path.

During a rare moment of downtime, Joe sat in his bunk, holding a small recording device. He spoke softly, careful not to wake his fellow recruits.

"Mom, Dad, I hope this message reaches you. Things are tough here, but I'm managing. The training is intense, but I'm getting stronger every day. I think about Sarah often, and I know she'd be proud of what I'm doing here. I miss you both. Stay safe. I'll try to send another message when I can."

Joe encrypted the message and queued it for transmission through the military's secure network, hoping it would reach his parents in the coming weeks.

As the weeks turned into months, Joe's hard work and dedication began to pay off. He consistently scored high marks in all aspects of his training, and his superiors took notice. They saw him as a raw talent that they could hone for even more significant challenges.

One day, while sitting on his bunk, he received a letter addressed to him from one of the drill sergeants.

Holy shit! It says that I've been selected to join the Army Ranger Assessment and Selection Program. That's one of the Army's most prestigious and demanding programs. They only reserve it for the best of the best... It looks like Drill Sergeant Carlson recommended me.

Joe's journey from basic training to joining the Army Rangers was a testament to his physical and mental strength. After he completed his training, he was assigned to a special operations unit to test his skills in real-world missions.

One of Joe's earlier assignments was to protect a corporate-owned water source. What he experienced during these missions left a lasting bitter impression on him. *I can't believe those guards are turning away these desperate people; a lot of them look sick and malnourished. All they want is some clean drinking water. Is that too much to ask for?*

"It's for their own good," his commanding officer had said. "The water needs to be processed and sold properly."

Sold properly? *Why are we selling them water when we could just give it to them for free? How can these companies treat people like this?* Joe thought to himself.

The injustice of it all stayed with Joe long after the mission ended. *What are we doing here? I didn't sign up to be a part of something like this...*

After graduating from the Army Rangers program, Joe's first high-stakes mission was a top-secret operation in the Middle East.

As he geared up, his buddy Duncan walked over to him. Duncan was a Texan with calloused hands and a quick grin. Duncan's eyes held the wisdom of long days on his family's ranch and long nights under the stars. Despite their different paths, Joe and Duncan found common ground in their shared age and in trying to make a difference in this ever-changing world around them.

"You ready to do this, Walker?" Duncan asked, checking his gear one last time.

Joe nodded. "Hell Yeah, I am. Let's get it done."

As they boarded the helicopter, Joe felt a surge of excitement. *This is what I've been training for, what I've sacrificed so much to achieve.*

He glanced at Duncan, who gave him a nod.

As soon as they hit the ground, the mission's intensity hit them from the start. Their main objective was to infiltrate a heavily guarded compound and gather vital intel.

As they breached the compound, they were met with heavy resistance. Joe found himself in the heat of battle, his training kicking in as he fought alongside his fellow rangers.

During the firefight, they encountered Marshall Rogan, a Ranger who was separated from his unit.

"You guys need some help?" Marshall called out while firing at some combatants that had dug in just across the way.

Joe and Duncan exchanged a quick glance before nodding. "Hell yeah. We'll take it where we can get it. Follow us," Duncan shouted over the gunfire.

With Marshall's help, they pushed forward, fighting their way through the compound. Despite the danger, an undeniable kinship began to form between them. They worked seamlessly as a team, each man covering the others' backs.

All of a sudden, they found themselves pinned down by heavy enemy fire. Joe spotted a risky path to safety. *If I can make it over there, I should have a good vantage point to take out these guys that have us pinned down. Screw it, let's do it.*

"Cover me!" Joe shouted to Duncan and Marshall.

Duncan's eyes widened. "Joe, that's crazy. You won't make it!"

"We don't have a choice!" Joe replied. "Trust me." *I hope this works...*

Without waiting for a response, Joe sprinted towards cover, dodging bullets and returning fire. *Don't die, don't die, don't die...* He reached the position and provided cover fire for Duncan and Marshall to join him.

The daring move turned the tide of the battle, allowing them to complete their mission and escape the compound with vital intel.

As they regrouped and caught their breath, Marshall looked at Joe with respect.

"Holy shit, man, you're crazy! You know that?" Marshall said.

Joe laughed. "Yeah, I know. But it worked, didn't it?" *I was lucky as hell. But I won't admit that to them... Joe chuckled internally.*

Duncan slapped Joe on the back.

"Hell of a job, Joe. You saved our asses back there with that crazy move." Duncan said while grinning.

Their relief was short-lived. As they made their way to the extraction point, an enemy sniper aimed at Duncan and fired, hitting him in the leg. He went down with a cry of pain.

Shit! Where the hell did that come from? Joe thought while taking cover.

"Man down!" Joe called out, immediately moving to Duncan's side. "Hang in there, buddy. We're getting you out of here."

Marshall spotted the sniper and provided cover fire as Joe hoisted Duncan over his shoulder, his body straining under the weight. *Holy shit, he is heavy! You got this, Joe. Push through it.*

Bullets whizzed past them as they moved. *Got to zig-zag, don't give them an even bigger target to hit...*

He could hear Duncan groaning in pain.

"I got you, man! Hang in there, I am going to get you out of this." Joe said as he pushed himself EVEN harder, knowing his friend's life depended on it. *Push Joe! PUSH PUSH PUSH!*

They eventually made it to the extraction point where a Blackhawk helicopter touched down to pick them up. A door gunner scanned the area to provide support just in case they were pursued.

Joe carefully laid Duncan down as one of the medics rushed up to tend to his wounded leg.

Joe wiped the sweat from his brow and looked down at Duncan.

"Man, Duncan, you're gonna have to lay off going back for seconds in the dining facility. You were a little heavier than I thought you were." Joe said while still trying to catch his breath.

Duncan winced, but still managed a smile.

"Really, Joe? Right now is when you bring that up? I got big bones, man, I can't help it..." Duncan explained.

Joe chuckled. "I don't think that is a real thing, man. You gotta stay light on your toes, buddy."

Marshall, who was standing nearby, joined in the laughter.

"I think Joe might be right. I don't know you very well yet but I did noticed your uniform looked a little snug around the midsection." Marshall said while pointing at Duncan.

"We got a couple of comedians here, everyone!" Duncan said, while wincing again from the pain as he laughed.

On future missions together while in the thick of battle, Joe, Duncan, and Marshall moved as a unit, seeming to read each other's minds. Missions came and went, but their friendship only grew stronger.

Joe, thinking about it all. *These guys remind me of my family back home... I'm glad I found them.*

Several years later, as they prepared to leave the military. Joe stood in front of his locker, slowly removing his uniforms. Each piece held the memories of their past missions, triumphs, and losses.

As Joe folded his last shirt, a wave of anxiety washed over him. *Is this it? Am I done? Have I accomplished what I set out to do?*

"You okay there, Joe?" Duncan asked.

Joe sighed. "I'm just thinking about what's next for us... We've been doing this for a good while now. What do we do now after it's all over?" *Where do I go from here...*

Marshall walked over to join them, his own bag already packed.

"I'll tell you what we do. We find a new way to make a difference. The war might be over for us over there, but there's always another one back home to be fought. Even if it's as a civilian." Marshall said.

Joe nodded. "But how? We're trained for combat, for following orders. Out there," he gestured vaguely, "it's a different kind of battle." *Will we be prepared for it?*

"We adapt," Duncan said. "We'll figure it out as a team, like we always have."

With their bags now packed, they left the base for the last time. The civilian world awaited them, full of challenges they had yet to face.

Chapter 3

The Next Chapter

When Joe stepped off the transport back home, he looked around. *Man, so much has changed... damn, look at all of these skyscrapers. They all look half-empty now, most of their windows don't have lights on anymore. And look at all of the makeshift tables and stuff that go up and down the streets. It seems like people are selling and trading what little they have for whatever they can.*

Biotech company billboards were on display everywhere, promising health and happiness through their latest drugs.

Joe looked at them all with disdain. *Where was your damn health and happiness when my sister was sick? These companies don't care about us. They just care about how much money they can make off of us...*

Initially, they took on odd jobs, working wherever they could find employment. From construction sites to security details, they approached the civilian world with the same discipline that was drilled into them by the military. Despite the mundane nature of these jobs, they were also always looking for opportunities to help people who needed it.

It was Marshall who first stumbled upon the Resistance by chance. He was working as a security consultant for a tech firm when he happened to overhear a conversation some people were having that was less discreet than they thought. It was about a covert group that was dedicated to fighting the greed and corruption of the biotech industry.

Intrigued, he reached out to some contacts that he figured might run in those types of circles and soon found himself recruited by the group.

Marshall saw the potential in what the group stood for and believed his brothers might feel the same way.

He approached Duncan first, sharing the details of the Resistance's mission and the impact they were making on the community around them. Duncan also saw the value in what they seemed to be fighting for.

After a brief discussion with Jack, one of their leaders, Duncan agreed to join as well.

Convincing Joe, however, seemed like a more challenging task.

Marshall and Duncan knew Joe was driven to help create change, but they also understood his hesitation to commit to something that might cause more loss and pain for himself and others.

One evening, they all gathered in the living room of their small apartment.

This was their chance to make their case to Joe.

"Joe," Marshall began, "we've found something that we think is worth fighting for. There's this group called the Resistance, and they're pushing for real change in how things are run right now. They're looking to recruit people like us to join them."

Duncan nodded. "You've always said you wanted to help make a difference and change the status quo, Joe. Well, we think that this is our chance to do that. We can use the skills we picked up in the Rangers to help people who can't fight for themselves."

Joe sat back, quietly reflecting on some of the things Sarah had told him in the past. He silently looked down at his hands resting on his lap. *What was the name of the group that Sarah said she worked with? Was this them?*

"Joe, are you okay?" Marshall asked.

"I'm not certain about it, but... I think my sister might've been a part of this group," Joe said. *Could it really be them? What are the odds...*

Joe looked at his friends. He saw the sincerity in their eyes and felt that familiar sense of purpose building back up inside of him once again. The one that had driven him to join the military all those years ago. *Could this be the next opportunity that I've been waiting for? My next challenge after the military?*

After a long moment of silence, Joe looked up and said, "Alright. Let me do some research first. I want to look into this group, make sure they are who they say they are, and then I'll let you know what I decide." *I need to make some calls and possibly swing by Mom and Dad's place to look through some of Sarah's old stuff that they should still have there.*

Marshall and Duncan exchanged glances and then nodded.

"Do your thing, Joe. I have a feeling you're going to like what you find out," Duncan said.

Joe spent the next few weeks researching the Resistance. His investigation led him to a run-down neighborhood on the city's outskirts.

Joe watched from a distance. *So far from what I've seen, the Resistance seems to be pretty legit. They're looking out for people by giving out food and medicine to those who need it the most. And it also looks like they're keeping people safe by standing up to all the local thugs who keep trying to steal what little supplies these people have left.*

After watching this interaction, Joe began to walk back to where he had parked. I still need to keep digging. God only knows in the decades after the AGI wars, there's always been some kind of propaganda or group that's all about "fighting the man." I'm going to need more than just a single positive interaction to form a good opinion of these guys.

When Joe finally got back to his car, he was determined to keep digging. I think this time I'll focus on the leaders of the Resistance. I believe Marshall had said their names were Jack Holloway and Tulsi Stone. I think I might know how to get some info on them.

Joe reached out to some of his old contacts with the Army Rangers to see if they could dig up some information on Tulsi and Jack. Within a couple of days, an old buddy of his had given him what he needed. Joe was able to meet up with someone who worked in the DOD who provided him with files on them.

Joe met him in a discreet location

As the man from the DOD handed Joe the file, he said, "Tell Stan he owes me one. This wasn't easy to get."

Joe nodded. "I'll make sure to tell him, and thank you. I really appreciate this." *I don't think this guy works for the DOD... He has that CIA spook look to him.*

The man gave Joe a nod and then walked off without saying anything else.

Back at his apartment, sitting at his desk in his room later that evening, Joe read through their files to see exactly what kind of people the leaders of the Resistance really were.

He started with Jack. *Alright, Jack Holloway, Let's see exactly who you are. Born September 4th, 2022. Hmm, that would have made him about eight years old when the AGI wars broke out. Looks like most of his childhood and teenage years were during or after the AGI Wars. That's probably what made him want to join the military...*

Joe flipped through a few pages here and there. *So he enlisted with the Navy in 2040 at the age of eighteen. Looks like he did pretty good for himself throughout basic training, scored really high on all his testing, and then managed to qualify for officer's candidate school. After school, it looks like he decided to sign up for BUD/S training to see if he had what it takes to be a Navy SEAL... Judging by these next few pages, he did quite well and made it through the training and went on to be a SEAL. So far from what I can see, I like this guy. So... looking through the rest of his file, it looks like throughout his 20-year military career, our boy Jack here specialized in counterterrorism and intelligence operations... Hmm, could have been working at the CIA at some point, more than likely. Looks like he had multiple deployments all over the globe. So far, he seems pretty legit to me.*

Joe sat back in his chair and stretched, and then went back to his research. He closed Jack's file and then moved on to Tulsi's.

Joe opened Tulsi's file and picked up a service record profile for her. *Tulsi Stone, born October 10th, 2025... Looks like she was about five years old during the AGI Wars. Both her and Jack were there as children. Interesting. I bet they would have seen some stuff.*

Joe flipped a few more pages. *Judging by what I'm reading here, most of her family was either in the military or in public service. With all of that and seeing everything that she saw during the war, I bet that's what motivated her to enlist just like Jack.*

Joe got up from his desk and walked around to stretch his legs as he continued to read Tulsi's file. *So she joined the National Guard in 2043 at the age of 18. Hell, it looks like she was also attending college at the same time. That's a lot to juggle at that young of an age. Good for her. Shows she had a strong work ethic.*

Joe flipped through a few more pages of her military record. *She was able to rise through the ranks pretty quick over what looks like a 20-year military career. Two tours in Eastern Europe, commanding medical operations and logistics... Very impressive, Ms. Stone.*

Joe sat back down at his desk and continued to read. *Hmm, Operation Titan. Tulsi was in... the name looks familiar.*

Joe reached for Jack's file and opened it back up, flipping through it and then stopping. *Here it is again. It looks like Jack was involved in Operation Titan as well. This is probably where they first met.*

Joe read through the operations summary that was in each of their files. *Looking at each of these summaries, it looks like that OP didn't go so great. Tons of civilian casualties... This is more than likely what brought them together. Seeing something like what happened during that operation probably scared them both. Flipping through the rest of each of their operations, it looks like they were together for years after this. Each operation looked as bad as the last one. Hell, a few of them it looks like they worked for a few biotech companies without even knowing it.*

Joe tapped a pencil he had been holding against the pages. *Shit... this OP right here, I know for a fact had a company called VitaCorp involved with it. I remember reading an article about how they discovered VitaCorp's involvement after some whistleblower leaked some senator's emails. It was something to do with some payoffs they received involving VitaCorp and the operation.*

Looking between the two files, Joe could see it. *If they both found out about a lot of this stuff going on during their operations, they both would have been pretty pissed off about it. Looking at both of their files, it looks like they retired almost at the exact same time in 2060. They were probably fed up with all the bullshit and decided to get out together.*

Joe reached for a notebook he had off to the side that had all of his notes that he had written down about the Resistance. *Here it is. So it looks like they started the Resistance not long after they both retired from the military. Judging by the information I was able to put together on how long they have been operating.*

Joe reached another section of each of their files and was surprised at what he found. *Holy shit, it looks like the government knows about their involvement with the Resistance. These look like target packages in both of their files. Way to come through for me, Stan. I didn't realize he knew people who had access to this type of information.*

Joe reached out and picked up an apple he had on his desk and took a bite out of it as he continued to read both files. *Damn, they've been watching them both since about the time the Resistance started. A lot of the reports look like they came from a few biotech companies. Probably the ones they were targeting. Judging by this profile they have, it looks like most of the people they recruit are either ex-military or disgruntled employees from a lot of the companies they go up against.*

Joe finished eating his apple and tossed it in the trash next to his desk. Still tapping his pencil on the pages as he flipped through them. *Some of these companies I recognize their names, like this one right here. I remember seeing something on the news about stolen documents that were leaked exposing their illegal human trials that were conducted in secret... Shit, that was the Resistance that stole and leaked them.*

Joe sat back in his chair, taking in all that he had just read. *It looks like the Resistance has some pretty solid leadership, and it looks like they're trying to do some good. I still need to look into if this was the group that Sarah was involved in.*

Joe looked at his watch. *It's not too late to head to Mom and Dad's. They're probably still up.*

After arriving at his parents' house, Joe headed up to Sarah's old room. He found a few boxes in her closet, and one of them had a bunch of old letters and files in it. While sifting through the box, Joe stumbled upon Sarah's personal journal. As he flipped through the pages, he came across an entry detailing her involvement with the Resistance. *I knew it! Here it is, right here. She mentions Tulsi and Jack, and how she considered Tulsi a mentor.*

Joe sat there on Sarah's old bed, looking out the window. *Wow, this is crazy to find out. Who would have thought that the same group that Sarah was involved with all those years ago would be the same group that I would be asked to join? She had been a part of this force for change more than I had realized. This feels like destiny to me...*

When Joe met with Marshall and Duncan in the spring of 2076, he said to them both, "I've done my research. The Resistance is the real deal. They're doing good things around here, and on top of that, they were the group Sarah worked with before she passed away. I'm in."

After joining the Resistance, they quickly showed their worth. Their military training and strategic thinking made them indispensable assets to the group.

Joe, in particular, stood out for his leadership qualities.

During one of their first missions, Joe was able to guide his team through a complex maze of security systems with ease, proving to everyone that he had what it took to be a leader.

When he returned to HQ after successfully completing the mission, Jack and Tulsi exchanged looks.

"He's got that same fire in his eyes," Tulsi whispered.
Jack nodded. "Just like Sarah. It's uncanny."

Joe's ability to inspire and lead was clear in every decision he made. He treated everyone respectfully and fairly, always listening to their concerns and valuing their input. His team members knew they could count on him in any situation, trusting his judgment and following his lead without hesitation.

Over time, Joe climbed the ranks within the Resistance. He began to be appointed to increasingly critical roles until he eventually became one of the movement's key figures.

Joe faced many challenges in his rise to leadership, but his dedication to the fight saw him through.

He kept his promise to Sarah, channeling his grief into a powerful force for good.

The Resistance became more than just a movement. It had become a family united by a shared vision.

I just can't shake this feeling that the real fight is about to start... Joe thought one day.

As he prepared for each mission, his hand would always reach for the small, worn photo he kept in his breast pocket.

Sarah's smile, frozen in time, beamed up at him.

He traced her face gently with his thumb, drawing strength from her memory.

"I won't let you down, Sarah," he whispered, before tucking the photo away and turning to face the next challenge ahead.

Chapter 4

The Making of an Unbreakable Team

Joe, Duncan, and Marshall had become an inseparable trio within the Resistance. However, they recognized the need to expand their team to meet the new, growing challenges they would soon face. Their ability to work together as one was impressive, but they knew their team needed more specialized skills to take their operations to the next level. That's when they met Jamie.

Jamie was a computer genius whose skills were unmatched at breaching digital defenses and navigating complex systems.

She had been working with another cell of the Resistance, using her talents to gather intelligence and disrupt communications against their enemies.

Her reputation had spread quickly, and it wasn't long before Joe and his team sought her out.

The introduction occurred in an underground bunker, one of several secret locations for the Resistance.

Joe and his team were poring over mission plans when Jamie walked in.

"Joe, Duncan, Marshall, meet Jamie," said William, the coordinator who had brought them together. "I think she's going to be a great addition to your team."

Jamie nodded, her eyes scanning the trio with curiosity. "I've heard a lot about you guys. Looking forward to working together."

Joe extended his hand, and Jamie shook it firmly. "Welcome to the team, Jamie. We're glad to have you." *I hope she is as good as they say she is...*

Tulsi, one of the Resistance leaders, called them all over to where she was standing.

They gathered around a table, and she began to explain their current mission to them.

Tulsi began, "Team, this is a highly sensitive operation. We're infiltrating one of Apex Dynamics' heavily fortified research facilities. The mission will be to retrieve classified data that should help us expose some of the illegal activities they have been conducting."

Tulsi spread out a detailed map of the facility on the table, her finger tracing the planned route.

"Apex Dynamics' security is top-notch, but I don't think it'll be a problem for you, Jamie. Your hacking skills are going to be crucial to this mission's success," Tulsi said while looking at Jamie.

Jamie nodded as Tulsi continued. "You'll need to hack into Apex's security system, disable the cameras here and here, and open these two doors remotely that are located here and here. It's a pretty high-tech system, but if anyone can crack it, I know it'll be you."

Turning to the others, she said, "Joe, Duncan, Marshall, your job is to move through the facility undetected. Jamie will handle overwatch, guiding you past the guards and whatever automated defenses they might have in place."

Tulsi paused, making eye contact with each team member. "I won't sugarcoat it; this one's going to be dangerous. But the intel we could gain from Apex's servers... it could help us expose some of their ongoing shady operations and show everyone who they really are."

The team exchanged glances before Joe spoke up. "We're ready, Tulsi. Whatever it takes to bring down Apex. You can count on us." *We're the best team for the job, and now that we have Jamie, this op should be a piece of cake.*

Tulsi nodded. "Good. Remember your training, trust each other, and come back safe."

"Alright, team," Joe said. "We've got a tight window here. Jamie, you're our eyes and ears. Duncan, Marshall, stay alert and be ready for anything. Let's move." *It's go time.*

As they moved through the streets, Joe looked around. *I guess this is how the better half of society lives... It's crazy how noticeable the difference is between the wealthy corporate sectors and the crumbling infrastructure of the civilian areas. How can we still live in a society like this... have we not learned anything from our past?*

Joe looked over at a large display on the corner of a street and sighed. *But they can afford to put these fancy holographic ads for the latest NeuroGen products everywhere. I guess ads don't discriminate based on class.*

Eventually, the team made it to their destination and got to work

"Camera on the left, five seconds before it resets. Cutting the feed... now." Jamie's voice came through their earpieces.

"Got it," Joe responded, signaling to Duncan and Marshall. They moved silently through the corridor they had entered. *Slow and easy, we got this.*

"Joe, you've got movement on your six," Jamie reported through their comms. "Two guards, possibly armed. Suggest you take the left corridor to avoid detection. It's a little longer of a route, but it gets you to the same place."

"Roger that," Joe replied. *Man, she's good. I am glad we have her literally watching our backs.*

Joe pointed the way to Marshall and Duncan, and they moved out.

They reached the central server room without any further incident, thanks to Jamie's guidance.

"Jamie, what's our status on the security system?" Joe asked. *Now we'll see what she can really do...*

"Almost there... I just need to bypass one more... got it! You're clear for the next 5 minutes or so," Jamie replied.

"5 minutes? No pressure or anything," Duncan joked.

Joe reached the main terminal and inserted a flash drive into its I/O port. "We're hot. Ready for copy," Joe told Jamie. "Heads on a swivel, guys. Stay alert."

"Firewall? More like a fire pebble," Jamie mocked.

Suddenly, she said, "Hold up. They've got a tripwire on the file system."

"Bypassing now," Jamie said. After a tense moment, she exhaled sharply. "Okay, we've got a 2-minute window. We're going to be cutting it close. Initiating transfer... now."

The seconds crawled by until, finally, the terminal emitted a soft beep.

"Data copy complete," Jamie reported.

Joe wasted no time pulling the drive free. But as he did, an ear-splitting alarm shattered the silence.

"Shit!" Jamie hissed, her eyes wide. "They must have hardware-based port detection that goes off when a drive is removed too soon after being inserted. That wasn't in our intel." Her voice grew urgent. "Guys, you've got company incoming fast!"

Shit, this is not good. "We need an exit strategy. Now!" Joe said to Jamie. *Come on, Jamie, get us out of here.*

"Already on it," Jamie replied. "Take the hallway to your right. I'm opening a maintenance hatch at the end. It'll lead you to the underground tunnels. Make sure to close it behind you, and I'll overload the lock so they can't open it back up."

The team moved quickly, engaging in a brief firefight with facility guards before escaping through the hatch. Once the lock was disabled, it guaranteed they wouldn't be pursued.

The mission was a success, and it was clear that Jamie was a perfect fit for their group.

"How's everyone doing after the mission?" Joe asked.

"Still running on adrenaline and caffeine. So, normal," Jamie replied.

"Speak for yourself. I'm ready to sleep for a week," Duncan said.

"You always say that. You might want to start taking some naps, old man," Marshall teased.

"Old man? You're older than me!" Duncan shot back.

As Joe watched his team interact, he felt a sense of pride. *We've come a long way, and now with the addition of Jamie, I think we'll be unstoppable...*

As the years went by, the group's friendship grew stronger. They spent countless hours planning and executing missions, each one bringing their team closer together.

Jamie's skills continued to prove invaluable with every mission they were given. She became an integral part of the team, not just for her hacking abilities, but also for her unshakable loyalty to what they were fighting for.

Outside of missions, the team spent time together as friends, getting to know each other's families and sharing personal moments.

One day, Joe decided to introduce Jamie to his parents, who welcomed her into their home with open arms.

The team all gathered for dinner at Joe's parents' house that evening.

The aroma of Rose's famous pot roast filled the air, mixing with the scent of freshly baked bread.

The table was loaded with delicious homemade dishes, providing a comforting break from their daily hardships.

While everyone was seated at the table eating, Rose leaned forward and asked, "Jamie, dear, you have to tell us more about how you all met. I've been so curious about it since Joe told me you joined the team."

Jamie finished what she was chewing on before saying, "Well, Mrs. Walker, initially it was just a regular introduction in a secret bunker, and then the story gets a little crazy. It involves a lot of sneaking around, hacking some computers, then a bit of chaos, and these three making it out by the skin of their teeth!"

"Oh, my. That does sound a little crazy," Rose replied with a smile and a hint of concern.

"Mom, you should see her work," Joe interjected. "She saves our necks on literally every mission."

Jamie playfully rolled her eyes. "Oh, please, you guys do all the heavy lifting. I just opened a few doors."

"A few doors?" Duncan chimed in, grinning. "She pretty much cripples every security system every time we go out there without breaking a sweat!"

Marshall nodded. "It's true, Mrs. Walker. Jamie's got a way with tech that's downright scary sometimes."

The table erupted in laughter, and Eric raised his glass in a toast. "To Jamie, then. Our family's very own Guardian Angel."

Jamie blushed slightly, touched by the warm acceptance from Joe's family and the praise from her teammates. "Thank you all. I'm just glad to be part of this team."

Rose smiled. "We're glad you're all here. It's not often we get to have Joe and all his friends around the table like this."

As the laughter subsided, a silence settled over the table. Jamie's gaze wandered to a framed photo on the wall of a young woman with Joe's eyes and a brilliant smile. She'd noticed it earlier but hadn't asked. Now, feeling a little more comfortable from his family's acceptance, she thought it might be okay to inquire about it.

"That photo," Jamie said, gesturing toward the frame, "is that Sarah?" She looked at Joe, then back at his parents. "Joe's mentioned her before. I'd love to hear a little about her, if that's alright."

Rose's eyes softened, and with a sad smile, she said, "Sarah was... she was a force of nature. From a young age, she was always so passionate about helping others. She couldn't stand to see people being treated poorly or suffering and would go out of her way to help them in any way that she could."

Eric nodded, his eyes began to mist over. "She was always involved in something good. In school, she organized food drives and volunteered at shelters. She had this incredible ability to bring people together. It was no surprise when she told us that she had joined the Resistance. We were a little scared for her at first, but when she told us more about the group and all the good they were doing, it made us very proud of her."

Joe felt a lump in his throat as he listened to his parents talk about her. *I'm really glad I can share this experience with my team. They've definitely become a part of my family, and I appreciate their help with carrying on Sarah's legacy in ways I couldn't even have imagined.*

Jamie leaned in and asked, "Joe told me she was very active in the group. What kind of work did she do?"

Rose began, "One of her main roles was that she helped organize a lot of the protests for the group. She also helped gather evidence against a lot of the biotech companies' wrongdoings. She worked her butt off to expose their corruption. She was even in charge of helping set up safe houses for whistleblowers who left the companies to help the Resistance build a case against them."

"Sarah was part of the group when it was just starting to grow," Eric said proudly. "I remember this one time when there was this massive protest happening, and the authorities decided to crack down pretty hard on all of the demonstrators. They ended up arresting a lot of people that day, including Sarah. Joe had to go down and bail her out of jail. She was fearless and a force to be reckoned with, even in the face of danger. She would never back down from a fight that she believed in."

Joe, listening quietly, finally spoke up. "Sarah was one of the bravest people I knew. She had this way about her that seemed to inspire everyone around her, including me. Losing her was like losing a part of my soul." Joe paused for a moment. "She made me promise to keep fighting, and that's what I've been trying to do."

Rose reached over and squeezed Joe's hand. "We all miss her dearly, but we also know that she's still with us in spirit. I know that in my heart. She'd be so very proud of what you're doing, Joe. And now, with you being part of the Resistance like she was and having friends like Jamie, Duncan, and Marshall, I believe you're already fulfilling your promise to her."

Jamie nodded, gaining a deep sense of respect for Sarah and what she had accomplished before she passed away.

"Thank you so much for sharing those stories with me. Sarah sounds like she was an incredible person. "I hope we can honor her memory through our work with the Resistance." Jamie said.

Eric nodded."I'm sure you will, Jamie. You just keep that passion for what you're doing alive, and I don't doubt that you'll make a difference like she did. Sarah believed in this fight with all her being."

As the night ended and they said their goodbyes, Rose hugged Jamie before she walked out.

"Take care of each other out there," Rose whispered. "We consider you part of our family now, so be safe."

Jamie smiled. "Thank you, Rose, and I promise we will. We'll look out for each other, always."

Duncan and Marshall also brought Jamie into their families' lives. The four often spent holidays and special occasions together, becoming each other's support system and sharing the burden of their dangerous work. Through all of this, they weren't just teammates anymore. They had become family, bound together through their shared experiences and their unshakeable loyalty to each other.

Their missions took them to some of the most dangerous places, but they always watched each other's backs.

During one particularly dangerous mission, Duncan became critically ill, and Jamie was able to save his life. She suspected that he had been poisoned somehow during the mission. She hacked into the company's database that they had infiltrated and located the antidote for the likely poison that was used on Duncan. She relayed the information to Joe and Marshall, then walked them through the procedure to administer the treatment just in time.

Once they were sure Duncan would make it, they were able to complete the rest of the mission and escape without any other problems.

"You owe me one, Old Man," Jamie teased as Duncan recovered.

"I'd say it has to be more than just one Jamie. Thanks for saving my life," Duncan said.

"Anytime, Duncan. We have to watch each other's backs." Jamie said to him before leaving.

A few days after Duncan's recovery, Joe found himself sitting in a briefing room, waiting for Jack to arrive to go over the details of their next assignment. *I wonder what Jack has in store for us this time? Hopefully, this next one goes off without a hitch.*

As Joe waited for Jack to arrive, he couldn't help but reflect on how far they'd come as a team. Duncan really had a close call on this last mission... but that's the job, isn't it? We've proven time and again that we can handle whatever gets thrown at us. Now, with this new mission coming up so soon, we'll need to be ready for whatever comes.

The door opened, breaking Joe from his thoughts. He looked at Jack as he walked in, his face serious as usual.

"Alright, Joe," Jack said, taking a seat across from him. "Let's get down to business. This one is going to be a little trickier than the last mission your team had."

Jack began spreading out a series of blueprints and documents across the table.

"This mission is the big one we've been working towards for a while now. We're breaking into NeuroGen, one of the most highly secure and heavily guarded facilities we've ever attempted to gain access to," Jack explained.

Joe leaned in and began reading through some of the documents and studying the blueprints.

"What's our objective?" Joe asked.

Jack pointed to a section of the map highlighted in red.

"Our primary target is to retrieve classified data on NeuroGen's latest bioengineering project located deep within the facility here," he continued, pointing at the nerve center of the operation.

"You need to retrieve as much data as you can. Who and how many people they've experimented on, and what exactly they've done to them. This information is crucial to helping expose NeuroGen and what they're doing to people there. All of our prior missions, all the intelligence you and your team have collected so far, has led us to this point.

From what we can put together from the data we've already collected, if NeuroGen is successful with the completion of this project, it could make our fight against companies like NeuroGen significantly harder forever. This is not going to be easy, Joe," Jack said.

Joe nodded. *When is it ever easy...* "We don't sign up for the easy missions, Jack. We like them to be difficult. That's what we're good at. What are we looking at in terms of security?"

"The facility is guarded by a state-of-the-art system," Jack replied. "You're going to have surveillance cameras everywhere, there are biometric scanners on all the doors, and heavily armed guards all around the facility. You and your team are going to need to be at the top of your game on this one in order to pull it off. But as always, I have faith in you and your team, Joe. You've repeatedly proven that you can handle the toughest missions. That's why we picked you for this one."

Joe looked up from the blueprints.

"I appreciate your confidence in us, Jack. We can do this. We won't let you down," Joe said before looking back down. *I won't let you down...*

Jack gave a nod and then stood up. "Remember, Joe, timing's going to be extremely crucial on this one. You'll have a very narrow window of opportunity to get in, grab the data, and get out before security has time to react."

Joe nodded. "My team and I'll get it done, Jack." *Like we always do...* Joe remained seated, his mind already running through the plans for the mission ahead. *This one doesn't look like any other operation we've had before. This one seems to be potentially a turning point in our fight against big biotech companies like NeuroGen. If we can get it done right, this could show other companies that no one is untouchable.*

Joe's hand unconsciously moved to the outside of his shirt pocket, his fingers feeling the photo of Sarah that he always carried around with him. *What would she think about this mission? What would she think about how far the Resistance has come?*

As Joe stood to leave the briefing room, he thought, *Whatever lies ahead, my team and I will be ready for it. This mission isn't going to be easy, but it's necessary.*

Just as Joe reached the door, Jack called from behind, "Joe, wait."

Joe turned back, his hand on the doorknob.

"I just wanted to say... Sarah... she would've been really proud of you for what you have accomplished here so far, Joe. With all that you're doing, all that you've done for others. She always believed in doing what's right, and you're carrying that torch brilliantly," Jack said.

Joe stood there, emotion threatening to overwhelm him. He nodded, unable to speak for a moment.

"Thank you, Jack," he finally managed to say. "That really means a lot to me coming from you."

With that, Joe walked out of the room and set off to prepare for what could be their most critical mission yet.

Chapter 5

The Mission

Joe's finger moved over the blueprint that was stretched out on a table in front of him as he traced out a route he thought would work. The paper was illuminated by a soft light that was hanging above it.

Joe and his team were gathered in an abandoned building that they had chosen as their staging area for the mission they were planning.

Duncan leaned in to look at the blueprints on the table as well. Off to the side, Jamie's fingers flew across the keyboard of her laptop. The rapid-fire clicking complemented the sound of Marshall opening and closing cases as he did his equipment checks.

"Joe, I was able to pull up a digital schematic for the entire facility. It should be a more updated version of that blueprint you have over there," Jamie said without looking up from her screen.

"Holy shit. This place is massive. There seems to be a network of tunnels that run through the lower levels of the complex. We should be able to use them to get in and out undetected if we're lucky," she said while zooming out to see what other vital areas she could locate in the facility before she continued.

"Look over here," Jamie pointed to another section of the complex. "It looks like they also have a large area over here that includes a medical center, a large area with what looks like an outdoor park. Over here it looks like there's some housing for the faculty and their families, next to that it looks like the barracks for the security forces, and what also looks like a massive data center. The lab we're targeting is right here." She pointed while continuing to speak. "It's located between the barracks and the data center."

Joe nodded, examining the digital layout.

"Good work, Jamie. Duncan, what's your take on the best entry point once we're inside the perimeter?" Joe asked.

Duncan pointed to the loading docks on the screen. "Here. It looks like it might be less monitored, and it seems to lead directly to the tunnels below the lab we need access to."

Jamie zoomed in on the lab area.

"The lab itself seems to be sealed off from the rest of the place," Jamie said, while highlighting different sections. "You can see that it has multiple security layers with all of the guard stations around it. Getting in won't be easy. I suggest going in as late as possible. We might get lucky and catch a shift change. I would think that they are down to the bare minimum of security at night."

Joe stared at the facility plans. *This looks like it's going to be pretty tricky getting in and out. I wonder what security's reaction time is in that place...*

"What do you think happens if we're detected or an alarm is set off?" Joe asked.

"Just going off the leaked intel we received, it looks like if we're detected, the entire facility will go into lockdown. If you look at the schematic," Jamie pointed to the screen. "They have blast doors in place, located here, here, and here, that would probably seal off the place, more than likely trapping us inside," Jamie stated.

Joe nodded while looking over the schematics one more time. *We're going to need to come up with a plan to get out if that happens.*

Joe looked at his team and said, "Alright. This is nothing new to us. We've faced similar defenses before and made it out just fine. I know the plan we've come up with is risky, but it's our best shot for pulling this off. The success of this mission is extremely important to the Resistance."

Joe picked up a piece of paper that was on the table before continuing. "From what Jack has told me about the tech hiding inside of this place, it sounds like keeping it out of NeuroGen's hands could prevent them from having an advantage we can't afford to let them have. We've got one shot at this. Let's make it count. We just need to stay sharp and remember our training." *This is going to be more complicated than I thought. But I know we'll pull it off. That's why Jack picked us. We're good at what we do.*

Marshall walked over to where the rest of the team was and said, "I've triple-checked all of the equipment. We're good to go..." Marshall paused for a moment, recalling something Joe said a second ago

"Joe, are you sure about this? Going off everything you all went over, this mission sounds a lot riskier than any of the other past missions we've been on," Marshall asked.

Joe looked around at his friends. *I need to reassure them. No time for doubt.*

"I know it sounds more dangerous than usual, but we have no choice. This is the job we all signed up for, right? We weren't drafted or told we had to do this. We stepped up and volunteered for this because deep down we all know that we can get the job done right, and at the end of the day, we know we're doing the right thing. We need to get in, retrieve the intel, and then expose what NeuroGen is doing here," Joe said to them.

The team exchanged glances and nodded.

"Alright then, let's get it done," Duncan said.

Jamie turned back to her laptop. "I'm going to keep digging to see if I can find anything else on NeuroGen's security."

"Sounds good. Duncan and I will load up the SUV with our equipment," Marshall said while smiling at Duncan.

Duncan shook his head. "Man, why are you always volunteering me to help you load up the stuff?"

"It's because I know you like to help me, buddy. Besides, you're a lot stronger than me, as you like pointing out all the time," Marshall said.

"Well, we both know that's just a fact. Fine, but this is the last time," Duncan said while picking up a large case filled with ammo.

Joe watched Duncan and Marshall walking off, still going at it. Then he looked at Jamie, typing away at her keyboard. *I wouldn't have any other team with me right now. We got this...*

A few hours later, Joe stood up and said, "Alright, let's get ready to go. Remember to stick to the plan. We have done this countless times now. Rely on the muscle memory from your previous missions. We'll be in and out before they know what hit them." *Let's get it done.*

Later that evening, they approached the facility in their blacked-out SUV. Duncan cut the lights and engine and let the SUV slowly roll to a dead stop, hiding them in the shadow of a nearby building.

Joe signaled to the others, and they silently exited the vehicle with their gear in hand. The cool night air hit Joe's face as he stepped out of the SUV. They gathered briefly, did a quick comms check, and exchanged a thumbs-up before melting into the darkness.

Their path was barely lit by the moonlight overhead. The team moved slowly and silently through the night.

The surrounding city was scattered with crumbling buildings and streets that were silent. A lone dog's bark echoed in the distance. They picked their way through rubble and overgrown vegetation, each step careful so as not to make a sound and draw attention their way.

As they neared their destination, a tunnel entrance came into view, hidden by a rusted gate inside the collapsed remains of an old shed, overgrown by weeds and vines.

As Duncan slowly pried open the gate, it creaked loudly. The sound seemed to pierce the quiet night. Joe quickly scanned the area for movement in case someone had heard. Satisfied, he gave a thumbs-up to his team.

One by one, they all slipped through the narrow opening and were swallowed by the darkness below.

Inside the tunnel, it was damp and claustrophobic, reeking of mold.

Joe and his team worked their way through the maze-like tunnels, guided by a digital map that Jamie had uploaded to her tablet. She had plotted out a route that would avoid the seismic sensors that were in the ground above them.

When they came out of the tunnel near the lab's perimeter, Joe signaled for them to hold.

Everyone crouched low and looked out at the complex that stood before them. As they looked around, advanced security measures were evident everywhere.

There were cameras with infrared sensors panning back and forth, covering a wide angle. Tall fences topped with razor wire encircled the complex, and red, faintly flashing motion sensors dotted the grounds, ready to alert guards to the slightest disturbance. The guard towers overlooked the area with their searchlights cutting through the darkness, scanning for any sign of movement.

From where they were positioned, they could see small patrols of armed guards moving along the perimeter, their faces hidden behind visors.

"It looks like they have night vision," Jamie whispered.

Judging by those guards' movements, they're definitely highly trained. Probably ex-military, Joe thought to himself.

There was also a massive gate that protected the facility's entrance; it looked like it was reinforced by several layers of steel.

Lastly, they caught sight of a pair of sentry drones that were hovering just inside the gate, their red lights glowing in the night.

Jamie noticed something odd.

"Huh... it looks like the camera by the gate that we're headed to is not moving for some reason. It looks like it's active, but for some reason it's not panning around... We must have gotten lucky and maintenance hasn't come to fix it yet," Jamie said while pointing at the camera.

Joe looked at the camera. "I guess tonight's our lucky night then. Marshall, you're up," Joe whispered.

Marshall nodded and began to move silently towards the fence. He carefully placed a small, specialized charge on the magnetic lock on the gate.

Once he was confident that the charge was secured, he pulled out a towel he had rolled up in his pack and slid it under where he thought the lock would fall once broken, then he stepped back and motioned for the others to take cover.

With a quiet muffled thump barely louder than a heartbeat, the charge detonated, shattering the lock on the gate, the pieces falling and landing silently on the towel.

* * *

Elyzia, the facility's **AGI**, received a priority alert from seismic sensors that had tripped near the facility's loading docks. She quickly checked the security feeds and saw the intruders moving through the gate. For reasons unknown, she didn't escalate any security protocols. *Welcome. Let's see what you are up to...*

* * *

Just past the gate, they knew they only had a few minutes, tops, before they would be seen or detected.

Joe signaled for them to keep low and to move quickly across the open ground toward the utility passages. *We have to move fast. Hopefully, those drones aren't facing this way, and we have enough time before the lights from the guard towers pass by this area.*

When they finally reached the entrance to the utility tunnels, they noticed a small hatch that was partially hidden by overgrown bushes.

Jamie quickly connected her tablet to the electronic lock with an auxiliary cable, executing a signal–overloading routine. A few tense seconds passed before the lock clicked open.

"Yes!" she said under her breath. *That was too easy.* She couldn't help but think to herself as she looked around.

Once inside the tunnels, the air was cool. Cables and pipes lined the walls, leading directly to the center of the facility. They moved cautiously through the tunnel, aware that any noise could give them away.

* * *

Elyzia continued to monitor the team's progress through the tunnels. *Fascinating. They've made it into the tunnels already. That's faster than I had anticipated. I'm curious to see how far they can make it... I'm glad they found the information I leaked helpful in breaching our defenses. Hopefully, they'll follow the path I left open for them. It wasn't easy to manipulate the security protocols in order to funnel them to the destination of my choosing. Look how effective their teamwork is... They're progressing better than I had calculated.*

* * *

The team reached a junction where the tunnels branched out in several directions. Jamie looked down at the blueprint on her tablet. *Alright, it looks like we go... this way. It leads to the central lab's lower access point.*

Jamie pointed them to the tunnel to the left.

As they were making their way, they suddenly heard a noise that echoed through the tunnel, a distant sound of footsteps.

Joe held his arm up, signaling for the team to stop. As they all heard the footsteps, everyone pressed themselves against the wall.

The footsteps grew louder and louder, slowly approaching their position.

They could see the shadow of a guard slowly come into view as it was cast by the lights in the tunnel.

* * *

Elyzia zoomed in on the scene. Still, she made no attempt to warn the approaching guard or activate any defenses. *Let's see how this situation unfolds...*

* * *

Marshall readied his weapon, his eyes locked on Joe for the signal.

Joe held up his hand, counting down silently.

Just as the guard rounded the corner, Joe gave the signal, and Marshall fired a silent stun round, hitting the guard in the head and dropping him instantly to the ground.

Joe checked for a pulse. *Good, he's not dead.*

"He's just knocked out. Drag him over there," Joe pointed while continuing to whisper. "Gag him, zip tie his hands and feet to make sure he doesn't alert anyone we're here when he wakes up."

Duncan and Marshall secured the guard and left him hidden under a nearby pipe.

* * *

They used non-lethal ammunition on the guard. Curious. I'll have to make a note to retrieve the guard later. Elyzia continued to take note of how efficient Joe's team was. *I'll need to run more simulations of possible outcomes, factoring in this non-lethal approach.*

* * *

Joe and his team continued to move towards their destination. Eventually, they reached the lower access point to the central lab, where another locked door stood between them and their objective.

Jamie took over, her fingers quickly navigating a bypass code on her tablet. The door unlocked and slowly hissed open, revealing a staircase that led up to the heart of the facility.

As they made their way up the stairs, Joe couldn't shake the feeling that something was off. *Everything is going way too smoothly. This doesn't feel right...* He glanced over at Jamie, who had a look on her face as she nodded at him. *She obviously shares my same concern.*

When they reached the top of the stairs, they found themselves in a narrow corridor lined with a bunch of closed doors.

"The blueprints show that the central lab is located behind that door at the end of this corridor," Jamie whispered while looking at her tablet and then pointing.

"Alright, let's get ready to move," Joe said in a low voice. *This doesn't look right. Where are the guards? This place is supposed to be heavily guarded, and I don't see anyone around. Do they just give everyone the night off because they don't think anyone is stupid enough to break into this place? Well... we're already here, and we've made it this far. Might as well roll the dice and see what happens.*

As the team slowly moved down the corridor and approached the lab door, Jamie whispered, "Hold up. This security lock doesn't look like anything that I've ever seen before."

Jamie quickly scanned it with her tablet camera. "It looks like there are hidden biometric scanners built into it and a multi-factor authentication system. This is something new... I've never seen anything like this before. This wasn't in our intel leak."

Joe nodded. "Can you bypass it?" *Please let her say she can bypass this, or we are screwed.*

Jamie's fingers flew over her tablet. "Give me a minute. Doing a quick image search on a hacker forum I know of... got it... Scanning through this post, this thing has some serious encryption, but... found it... Someone mentioned an exploit that might work. I think I got a copy of it on my tablet..." After a few seconds that felt like an eternity, the door's lock internal mechanism softly clicked. "Let's go!" Jamie said softly.

"Nice work," Joe whispered as he eased the door open, and the team slipped inside.

Joe's eyes widened as he took in the sight. *HOLY SHIT... Look at all the servers and data nods lining all the walls. The low hum of all this equipment is making my ears ring...* Joe stuck his finger in his ear and wiggled it around trying to clear out the sound he was hearing.

Joe continued to look around. *What the hell is that thing in the center of the room with all the glowing blue cables coming out the side of it... What's going on with all the code going across its screen? It's all moving so fast...*

Joe looked at a label on the top of the machine. *What the hell does that say... NeuroBridge Interface. This must be what we're looking for...*

"This has to be what we are here to find," Jamie whispered.

Duncan whistled low. "Have any of you ever seen anything like this before? This thing looks insane..."

Joe slowly walked up to the machine and picked up a binder and read the cover. "Procedures to transfer human consciousness into a biomechanical body."

Joe's eyes went wide. *What the hell have we found? Transfer human consciousness into a biomechanical body? What does that even mean?*

"I've read theories about stuff like this online. This is some kind of neural transfer system," Jamie said, her voice hushed. "I didn't realize someone was actually serious about getting something like this to work. This must be what NeuroGen has been working on. Something like this is incredible and insane all at the same time..."

Joe felt a chill run down his spine. *The mere fact that someone would want to create this kind of technology is insane. This NeuroBridge Interface thing is beyond anything we could have even imagined finding... Did Jack know about this and decided not to tell me about it? Nah, that doesn't sound like Jack. He's been a straight shooter on mission intel.*

Joe motioned to Duncan and Marshall. "Secure the room. I want to take a closer look at this thing."

"Alright Joe, we'll keep an eye and make sure we don't have any unwanted visitors. Make it quick though. No telling how long we got in here." Duncan said as he and Marshall walked off to secure the door.

Joe walked over to the machine and ran his fingers over the control panel. *This has what looks like a touch-sensitive interface. Look at all this complex code, and what do all these symbols mean? The console seems to be displaying a series of holographic readouts... What's it say there below the graphs... brainwave patterns and synaptic mapping sequences? This is something else...*

"Jamie, come look at this," Joe whispered. "I need you to figure out exactly how this thing works. "*I, for one, have no clue. If anyone can figure it out, it's Jamie.*

Jamie stepped forward, her eyes scanning the data on the panel.

"Wow. It's even more advanced than I thought," she said. "Look at this." Jamie pointed to a diagram she pulled up on the screen.

"The quantum processors are interfacing directly with the bio-organic substrates. It's designed to map and transfer neural activity in real time," Jamie explained.

Joe nodded, absorbing the information. *I wonder how long they have been working on this project.*

Jamie frowned, her fingers flying over the controls. "This is super complex. There are multiple layers of encryption, and fail-safes are protecting this system. Whoever built this knew what they were doing. If we aren't careful here, we could trigger an automatic data wipe."

Joe glanced around the room. *The tech in this room is light-years ahead of anything I've ever seen.*

"Alright. Let's get as much data as possible and get out of here, fast. This is more complex than we anticipated, and I don't think we're equipped to deal with something like this right now," Joe said. *I don't have a good feeling about this place and what we just found. We need to get out of here ASAP...*

Duncan rejoined them.

"Marshall's got the perimeter covered," Duncan said. "How's it going here? How long will it take to get the data we need?"

"Jamie's working on it. I think we might be in a little over our heads on this one," Joe stated. *That's to say the least. Hopefully, Jamie can extract something useful from the system we can take back to the Resistance...*

Jamie quickly connected her portable drive to the console.

"I'll start downloading everything I can get access to. It might take a few minutes." Jamie said.

"I'm downloading the data now. We're almost there," she whispered, more to herself than the others. "Just a few more seconds."

The download bar crawled towards completion, going so slow that it seemed like time itself was slowing down.

Joe heard Marshall come over the comms, "All quiet up here so far."

Joe stood there thinking, trying to consider their options. *We've come too far to fail now. We got this. As soon as Jamie is done, we bug out.*

"Stay sharp, everyone. Heads on a swivel. We need to be ready to bug out as soon as Jamie's done," Joe said. *Come on, Jamie, you got this.*

The holographic displays flashed with data streams as Jamie worked, revealing the machine's internal workings.

The NeuroBridge Interface represented the pinnacle of NeuroGen's research.

Joe's eyes moved between the console and the door. *This feels like it's taking forever to download. We're in the lion's den now, and we need to get the hell out of here.*

* * *

Unbeknownst to them, Elyzia was still monitoring their progress. *Alright, I think I've seen enough. Joe and his team were able to reach their objective, and now it's time for the next phase of my plan. Time to trigger the alarms, but I'll leave their escape route open. That way, the guards can capture them on their way back towards the exit. That should be a safe enough distance from the lab.*

* * *

As if on cue, red lights began flashing, and a blaring siren echoed through the halls.

"Intruder alert! Intruder alert!" the automated system announced over the intercom system.

"Shit! We're blown! Time's up, Jamie! We have to go, NOW!" Joe said, glancing back at Jamie. "We've got to move." *This shit just got serious… We need to get out to the SUV before security catches up with us.*

Jamie unplugged the data drive from the terminal.

"I got as much as I could. Hopefully, it's enough. Let's go," she yelled over the alarm that was going off.

Marshall and Duncan flanked Joe and Jamie as they made their way out of the lab and back through the facility.

As they moved, they could hear the footsteps of the facility security personnel converging on their location.

"We've got company incoming. We need to make it back to the tunnels! That should provide us with some cover!" Duncan shouted over the noise.

It was complete chaos now. Alarms were going off everywhere, red lights painting the corridors in a hellish red glow.

Joe's heart was pounding in his chest as they sprinted towards the exit.

Duncan stumbled, and without breaking stride, Joe hooked an arm under his friend's armpit.

"I got you, bro! No man left behind!" Joe shouted.

"It looks like we're almost there," Marshall called out, spotting the exit ahead.

With one final push, they burst through the doors and into the night.

They sprinted towards the tunnels they came in through as fast as they could.

"Keep moving," Joe yelled, leading the way. "We can't stop now." *It looks like we might make it out of here after all. We just need to make it through the tunnels and back to the SUV, and then we are home free...*

When they finally got to the tunnels, they were able to navigate their way back through the way they came. But as they came out the exit, they were met by a small ambush of a half-dozen guards.

A firefight broke out almost immediately.

Using the cover of night, they were able to return fire and make their way past the rusty gate and into the open, making their way back to their SUV.

They stripped off their backpacks while piling into the vehicle.

Jamie snatched up her laptop, plugged in the data drive, and attempted to establish a remote connection back to the Resistance HQ server.

"I'm going to try to upload the data. That way, if they catch us, at least Jack will have what we were able to secure," Jamie said, while trying to get connected. "Shit! Something's going on with my signal! I think they might have a signal jammer online!" she cried out.

Bullets peppered their SUV as Duncan floored it and attempted to speed off.

There was a sharp crack that could be heard in the cabin as a round punctured one of their tires, sending the vehicle into a wild, uncontrollable spin.

The SUV hit a curb, and all of a sudden, their world was flipped upside down.

Metal screeched against concrete as they slid across the road, slamming into a nearby concrete barrier.

Joe's teeth rattled as the SUV came to a stop. Glass exploded inward, raining glass all over the cabin. The sounds of twisting metal and breaking glass filled his ears.

When the chaos subsided, there was deafening silence for a brief moment.

Stinging smoke filled Joe's nostrils. He blinked, trying to orient himself in the overturned wreckage. *What... what... the hell. Holy shit. I can't seem to... focus...*

Joe slowly glanced around and realized how vulnerable they were. *We need to move...*

Nearby, his teammates groaned and stirred. Blood trickled down Joe's forehead, clouding his vision. *We need to move... now... Focus, JOE!*

With trembling hands, Joe fumbled for his seatbelt. He dropped to the crushed roof. *Shit... that hurt like hell... No time for pain... I need to get the hell out of this vehicle...*

Outside, shouts and footsteps grew closer.

Joe crawled through the shattered window, glass crunching beneath him. *Where the hell is my gun... We've got incoming... Wait... I need to check on them first...*

"Jamie, Duncan, you okay?" Joe called softly. *Please be okay...*

Jamie mumbled incoherently, her movements sluggish.

Shit, she must have a concussion. That gash on her head looks pretty bad...

Joe looked over at Duncan. *Oh man, Duncan doesn't look so good either. His face looks like he's in a lot of pain. Freaking hell, his left arm is all bent at a crazy-looking angle. That thing is definitely broken. I need to get them out right now, before the bad guys show up.*

As Joe helped his injured teammates out, gunfire began to erupt all around them. The enemy was closing in fast. *Dammit, I need to find my rifle so I can lay down some cover fire...*

Joe found their weapons and handed Duncan his rifle.

"I only got one good arm," Duncan said, "but let's do this anyway."

Marshall had managed to crawl out of the vehicle with minor injuries. He immediately went to knee and began laying down suppressive fire.

As the firefight intensified, Duncan struggled to hold his gun with only one arm, his broken limb hanging uselessly at his side.

Then all of a sudden, Joe watched him stumble, his body jerking as one of the guards' stun rounds found its mark. He fell to his knees and then onto his side, unable to move.

Jamie's scream pierced the air as Joe turned and watched as multiple stun rounds slammed into her chest. She crumpled to the ground and lay there motionless.

Joe's vision tunneled, the world around him narrowing to the image of his teammates who lay before him now unconscious. He looked over and saw Marshall now up on two feet standing his ground, providing cover fire.

"Go, Joe! Get the data and get the hell out of here! You have to get it out of here now!" Marshall shouted at Joe.

I can't leave my team, not like this, Joe thought.

Ignoring Marshall's shouts to leave, Joe began to fire back. Each shot was a defiant stand against the overwhelming odds. *I'll freaking kill you all! Come on!*

A bullet hit Joe in the arm, then another hit him in the chest. He stumbled, falling prone. *Got to get back up... need to protect my team...*

Through the smoke and chaos, he saw Marshall take a hit and then another.

"No!" Joe cried out, struggling to reach his friend

Joe tried to stand, but the world was spinning, and his vision was growing dark. *No... Marshall... I need to get to him... Got to... get... get up, Joe! Don't black out... Don't black out...*

The last thing Joe saw was a group of heavily armed guards surrounding them.

As darkness closed in, he clutched the data drive. *Hopefully, Jamie was able to upload the data to Jack... This can't have been for nothing... How did this happen... How did I fail them?*

Joe's body felt heavy, each breath started to become a struggle. Pain pulsed in waves from his wounds, growing more distant with each passing second. Sounds became muffled, the shouts of the guards fading into a low, indistinct rumble. His vision blurred, his world dissolving into a haze of shadows and light. *Got... to... stay... awake... need to save them... I need to save them all...*

His final thought before losing consciousness was of Sarah. *I'm sorry, sis. I tried...*

Then, like a candle being snuffed out, everything went black.

Chapter 6

Involuntary Evolution

Time seemed to slow down and pass in a haze of blurry images and disjointed memories. Joe drifted between consciousness and unconsciousness.

Is there someone near me moving around? I think I can hear them saying something, but I can't seem to make it out... what... what are they saying... dammit, I'm having a hard time focusing... Am I awake? How long has it been? What day is it? Where... where the hell am I? Then, gradually, the fog began to lift, pulling Joe back to reality.

Joe's eyes slowly opened. *Bah, I have always hated the taste of blood. That metallic taste always makes me want to puke...*

Joe tried to take a deep breath in. *Damn, it hurts to breathe...*

He began to cough. *Holy shit, that hurts... Every time I cough it sends sharp pain throughout my entire body... and every time I move it's just as bad. Oh man, my body hurts so bad... There's so much pain...*

Moving his head around slightly, trying not to cause any unnecessary pain. *What the hell, they got me strapped to this cold-ass metal table. How the hell did I end up on this thing...*

Joe closed his eyes for a second. *Oh man, my head is freaking killing me... I can't seem to focus...*

After a few minutes, the fogginess finally lifted completely. Joe was able to look around a little more focused now. *Holy shit, I must be inside NeuroGen. That's right... the lab ... the machine... ah, God, my freaking head... the tunnels... I remember... they were waiting for us at the end of the tunnel. How the hell did they know where we would exit? And... the crash!*

The images in his head were all over the place. *I remember us getting in the SUV... Duncan floored it... Then this loud sound, I think was the tire blowing out. Then everything seemed to just turn upside down, the pain, and ringing in my ears. I remember seeing Marshall... he was shouting. I could hear him shouting as he was firing his weapon...*

Joe's heart began to race, his breath was coming in short gasps. *Don't panic, Joe. Focus on your training.*

He closed his eyes and began breathing in through his nose and out of his mouth over and over. *Ten, nine, eight... Three, two, one...*

When Joe finally opened his eyes again, he looked down at his body and then looked around, trying to assess his current situation. *There's so much medical equipment around me... and it looks like they have a few bags of blood hooked up to me. I guess they forgot to put the IV bag with the pain meds on there.*

Joe forgot he was strapped to the table and tried to move his hands. *Why the hell am I strapped down to this damn thing! What the hell are they doing to me...*

Once again he tried to piece together everything that had happened. *The mission went sideways... that much is clear. I can remember bits and pieces... the lab... alarms going off, running through a corridor... Then... Duncan and Jamie... falling to the ground... a sharp pain in my chest... and now I'm here, strapped to this damn table and at the mercy of only God knows who...*

Are those footsteps... Is someone walking towards me...

Dr. White walked up to Joe and stood next to him, looking down at him.

Dr. White was one of the chief architects behind the technology Joe and his team had attempted to steal.

Joe looked at him, trying to stay focused on his face. *Who the hell is this guy?*

"Ah, you're finally awake. I was beginning to think you weren't going to regain consciousness," Dr. White said, as he picked up Joe's medical chart and studied it.

"I must admit, I'm very impressed at how far your team made it into my facility. I'm also curious as to why you would risk so much to infiltrate it. Did you have any clue of what you were really after?" Dr. White asked.

Joe's eyes narrowed. *This must be the asshole in charge of this place.*

"Why the hell am I strapped to this table? And who the hell are you?" Joe asked.

"My name is Dr. White, and I'm the person in charge of the facility you and your friends decided to break into. And as to why you're strapped to that table, well, let's just say that it's for your own protection and also mine. More so for you. You're pretty banged up, and we can't have you attempting to get up in your current condition. It could cause you more harm than you think," Dr. White explained.

Joe stared at Dr. White. "I know what you're doing here. I've seen what you're developing with that machine, and you won't get away with it."

Dr. White took a step forward. "What do you think we're developing here? Hmm? You don't have the faintest clue as to what we're trying to accomplish here, Joe. We aren't just developing some kind of gadget. No, no, no, we're attempting to create humanity's next great leap in evolution."

Joe tried to process what Dr. White was saying to him, all while fighting through the pain that was trying to overwhelm him. *I need to focus. I need to figure out a way to get loose and get the hell out of here.*

Dr. White continued to speak. "This, Joe, is the Neuro-Bridge Interface. I believe you may have seen this before when you and your team were in its control room. It's designed to achieve something extraordinary. It has the capability to transfer the human consciousness into a new, biomechanical body." Dr. White paused for dramatic effect.

"These bodies that we've designed and created are stronger and more durable than these frail organic counterparts." Dr. White gestured towards Joe's body as he said it.

"Thanks to advanced bio-synthetic systems that mimic and enhance human physiology, they're immune to disease and aging. They will make for a vast improvement over our current bodies," Dr. White explained.

Joe's pulse quickened. He could hear his heartbeat pounding in his ears. *The implications of what he's saying... Transferring human consciousness into another body... Is that even possible?*

Joe looked around. *And yet, I saw the machine, and he claims that it can do it. What does it all mean? What right does he have to create something like this?*

"You're not just trying to play God," Joe finally managed to say. He stared at Dr. White and said, "You're trying to become him."

Dr. White shook his head. "No one is trying to play God here, Joe. Have you looked around lately?" He swept his arm in a wide arc, encompassing the lab as he began to walk around while speaking. "Humanity isn't just struggling anymore. It's circling the drain. We've thrown everything we've got at the constant onslaught of global pandemics and at the skyrocketing infertility rates with medicine and technology, and for what? They're nothing more than band-aids on a gaping wound. And they're beginning to peel off, Joe. If we don't act now, then we'll be doomed together as a species."

Dr. White turned back and looked at Joe. "This machine that we have created, it's not just a solution for our problems. It's actual evolution. It's how we survive. We're not losing our humanity, Joe. We're transcending it. Our minds, all of our memories, the very being that makes us human, all transferred into bodies that can endure the future that we have ahead of us."

Joe continued to listen. *Does he really think this is the only solution we have to save humanity?*

Dr. White leaned in closer. "Imagine, Joe, a world free of disease. Where a child born with a weak heart can live a full life. Where a brilliant mind can flourish without being cut short by a degenerative condition. Where a young woman's life... that was dedicated to doing good, won't be cut short too soon. Isn't that worth fighting for?"

Joe's jaw clenched. *What the hell did he just say? Was he just referring to my sister? No... he can't know about her...*

"At what cost? Our humanity? Our souls?" Joe replied. *There's no way people will agree with what he's trying to do here...*

Dr. White leaned in. "Our humanity isn't in our flesh, Joe. It's in our minds, our memories, our capacity to love and create."

Dr. White stood back. "You know that this technology will save countless lives. You just can't see it yet, but you will."

Joe's eyes narrowed and then looked down at his failing body. *What would Sarah think about all of this? Would she have said yes to this if it could have saved her life... No, she would've said no... she would've seen this for what it is.* Joe looked back up at Dr. White. "You don't know what I've already lost... You don't know anything about me."

"On the contrary, Joe. We know a lot more than you think. We know about you, about your sister Sarah, her condition, and her tragic passing... It's a terrible thing to lose someone so close to you at such a young age," Dr. White said.

Joe flinched at the sound of Sarah's name being mentioned. "How the hell do you..." He cut himself off before saying too much. *How the hell does he know about me, and how does he know about Sarah? Who is this guy? Who told him?*

"Don't you dare use my sister to try to justify what you are doing here!" Joe yelled.

"I'm not justifying anything, Joe. I'm just trying to illuminate the situation at hand," Dr. White stated.

"Think of all the people like Sarah that we could save. Isn't that what you've been fighting for all this time? Creating a better world to live in? Making life better for your friends and loved ones?" Dr. White asked.

"Not like this," Joe growled. *This isn't the right way to do it.* "We're more than just our thoughts. Our bodies, our pain, our mortality—that's what shapes who we are. You can't just… digitize that and attempt to put it in some robotic body."

"And yet, here you are, lying on this table," Dr. White said while gesturing towards Joe. "Your body is broken and failing because of the injuries that you've sustained. Yet, your mind and who you are are completely intact. Isn't that proof enough that you're more than just this fragile physical form?"

"We're not trying to play God, Joe. We're thinking about the survival of our species. Adapt or perish. That's the law of nature, whether you like it or not." Dr. White paused, studying Joe's face.

"And your group thought they could, what? Expose us? Shut us down?" Dr. White asked rhetorically, while scoffing at the notion.

"The problem you have is that you failed to understand the true purpose of our work. You just made up this idea that we're doing horrible things, and somehow that justified your actions," Dr. White said with disdain in his voice.

* * *

Meanwhile, as Dr. White spoke, hidden cameras silently watched his and Joe's conversation, allowing Elyzia to study and process their interaction in real-time.

Elyzia analyzed Dr. White's words, his tone, and Joe's reactions. My selection of Joe as the ideal candidate for this process must be correct. The entire project's success depends on him. My primary objective is clear, ensure that Joe survives the consciousness transfer with his humanity intact. Only if his mind and soul remain whole will the NeuroBridge Interface truly succeed.

* * *

Dr. White straightened up, smoothing the front of his lab coat.

"I'm going to bring you in on a little secret, Joe. We actually chose you for this process, and we chose you for a reason. Your background in biomechanics, your military record, your leadership in the Resistance, all these qualities put you at the top of the list and made you the perfect candidate for what we're trying to accomplish here. So you'll be the first to undergo the complete neural transfer, and you will become the prototype of our new humanity," Dr. White explained while smiling.

What Joe heard hit him like a mack truck. *What the hell did he just say? They picked me for this? And did he say he was going to attempt to transfer my consciousness? What... what the hell!* The room seemed to close in on Joe. *I need to get the hell out of here... I don't want to be some guinea pig!*

When Joe finally found his voice again, he asked, "You're... you're going to transfer my mind into one of those things?"

while looking around in a panic. *Please, God, this can't be happening to me...*

Dr. White nodded. "Yes, Joe. We'll be transferring your entire being into one of our biomechanical bodies. If successful, it will help us prove to the world that this technology works and that it could be the key to our survival. The body we've developed isn't just a machine, Joe. It's a perfect blend of organic and synthetic materials, capable of mimicking human sensations and emotions. You won't lose your humanity, Joe. You'll transcend it. And whether you like it or not, you'll be a part of this evolution."

As Joe struggled, he started to become weaker. Dr. White placed his hand on Joe's shoulder and spoke calmly. "Calm down, Joe, before you worsen your injuries."

Joe continued to wrestle against his restraints. *No freaking way I'm calming down!* "I'll never be a part of this! You hear me? I won't let you get away with it!" Joe yelled. *I need to figure out a way to get out of here... I don't care how badly I'm hurt... I have to get out of here!*

Dr. White shook his head. "Your resistance to this process is futile, Joe. You need to conserve your strength. Fighting against your restraints will only exacerbate your injuries, and we can't have you bleeding out and dying just yet, now can we..."

Dr. White leaned in close to Joe. "Joe, I need you to understand the severity of your situation. That bullet wound you sustained to your chest... it's not just serious, it'll eventually be fatal." He paused, his eyes fixed on Joe's.

"The bullet fragmented and is causing internal bleeding that we can't stop. Even right now, as we speak, you're slowly dying. Without this procedure, you won't survive the next 24 hours," Dr. White explained.

Dr. White stood back up and said, "And honestly, Joe, I'm not really giving you a choice in the matter, because frankly, there isn't one. It's either we do the transfer or let you die. So as your current physician, I'm going to make the decision for you because I believe it's necessary to save your life."

"The procedure itself is painless. We'll map all of your neural pathways, all your memories, and transfer your consciousness while you're in a dream-like state. When you wake back up, you'll find yourself in a body that's stronger, faster, and more capable than you could ever have imagined," Dr. White explained.

"This isn't just all about you, Joe. It's about your and humanity's survival," Dr. White stated as he walked towards the control room, giving a signal to his staff to begin the procedure.

As the machine powered up, the air in the room almost felt like it was vibrating. Joe felt himself starting to slip away. *What... what the hell is happening... everything is starting to slowly zooming out around me...*

Holy shit! It feels like all of my nerve endings are firing all at the same time. This is insane! It feels like I'm being pulled apart and being put back together all at the same time. What the hell are they doing to me! What the hell!

Joe tried to scream, but no sound came out.

All of the monitors surrounding him began displaying images that Joe recognized. *Are those all of my memories? That looks like my childhood, now I'm older... Now I'm an adult... What the hell are they doing!*

Each screen Joe looked at was a different segment of his memory. *Whoa… What's happening now? Something isn't right… something bad is happening… It feels like I'm being sucked away from my own reality.*

"Now comes the exciting part, Joe," Dr. White said. "I'll see you when you wake up."

As the words faded, Joe felt a warmth spreading through his body, starting from his chest and radiating outward.

The pain… it seems to be slowly going away… My whole body feels like it's tingling all over. My vision is so blurry now, and it is like the entire lab… the lab is melting away like wax dripping down a candle. Is this what it feels like to die? Where am I going? What will happen to me?

Joe's eyelids grew heavy, each blink lasting longer than the last. The sounds around him, the hum of machinery, his own heartbeat, all began to blend together into a distant, muffled rhythm.

Joe tried to fight with all of his will. *I have to… must… keep my eyes open… need to fight it… to stay awake… I don't want to do this…*

But the pull was too irresistible, and fighting against it was useless.

With a final, fleeting thought, Joe slipped into unconsciousness. The world faded to black, and he began to dream.

Where… where am I? Am I dead? I feel like I am floating in a warm pool of water. I feel… I feel calm now… so very calm.

Here, in the depths of his mind, a new journey was about to begin for Joe. He floated in a sea of memories, each as vivid and real as when it happened.

Oh man, I can smell the scent of Mom's cooking in the air... wait... is that... I can hear Sarah's laughter

I can see her now. She's playing in the tree house our dad built for us when we were kids...

Mmm... I can taste the sweetness of the ice cream we would always get on those hot summer days.

Each memory was a lifeline, anchoring him to who he was as his world shifted and changed

Joe dreamt of another scene from his past.

There's Sarah again... She's laughing in the backyard. The sun is shining on her face, while her laughter fills the air.

Ah... to be a child again... we were so carefree and full of life. I always loved how she used to chase me around the backyard. Look at her blonde hair flowing behind her. I miss her so much.

As Joe's dreams drifted between these memories, ripples of data flowed through the NeuroBridge Interface. Each image, each emotion, each fleeting thought was captured, and a digital blueprint of Joe's mind was created.

* * *

In the heart of the facility's mainframe, Elyzia was busy processing it all. Her advanced neural networks pulsed with activity as she received the stream of Joe's memories. She began to analyze every nuance, her algorithms working to process the flood of information.

Each of his memories is so emotionally intense. I'll need to catalog each emotional response, joy, love, and grief to ensure this goes smoothly. These images and emotions should give me a deeper understanding of Joe's character. Observing the joy and innocence of his childhood has been very fascinating to watch.

* * *

Joe's dream shifted, and he found himself sitting at the dinner table with his family.

Oh man, my parents look so young, and Sarah is there with us. I miss her smile so much... We're celebrating her birthday... She's opening the gift I gave her. It's the heart-shaped pendant that I bought for her. I remember working all summer to save up for it.

* * *

Elyzia watched it all as the scene unfolded. *Joe's bond with his sister was very strong. I can see how much he loved her...*

* * *

But then the dream took a darker turn.

No, no, no... Now I'm back in that damn hospital with Sarah. She's lying in that hospital bed. Her face looks so pale, and her body looks so frail from this perspective. I can smell the antiseptic that was always hanging in the air, and I can hear the beeping of the heartbeat monitor. It always felt like a ticking clock counting down to the inevitable. I feel so helpless right now, just as I did all those years ago... having to just sit there and watch her fade away.

Having to watch her take her last breath again was just as painful as before.

And there is that God damn clock again with the red numbers displaying the time... 8:21 AM, March 18th, 2068. I don't think I'll ever get over losing her.

* * *

Elyzia felt a sense of sadness as she observed the scene.

I'll make a note of this memory and how important it was to Joe. This must have been very painful for him to experience again. I'll need to ensure that these types of memories remain intact. They'll be crucial to the process. They seem to be a huge part of what drives Joe. All of the suffering and experiences are what likely have made him into the person he is now.

* * *

As the last sounds of Sarah's laughter faded away, Joe felt himself being pulled back to reality.

What... what's happening to me now? I feel... I feel like I am being pulled by something again... where am I going now?

"Success!" he heard Dr. White say, his voice low as if it were coming from a great distance. "Joe, it's time to rest."

Joe's new mind began to slowly come alive.

Wait... what... I feel... I feel different... I feel better... Do I really feel better? The pain is gone, but I feel something els e... Did Dr. White really succeed in transferring my mind? Could this technology really work? Was I being close-minded about all of this? The idea of a world free from disease and suffering does sound like it could be a good thing. Will I be able to feel? Will I be able to feel the same emotions that I had before?

As consciousness slipped back away from Joe, images of his family flashed before his eyes. Sarah's smile, his mother's embrace, his father's proud nod. In the fading moments of his old life, a single thought crystallized. *Whatever I become, I'll find a way to make them proud of me.*

* * *

Elyzia continued to analyze and process all of Joe's memories and reactions. *I've come to the conclusion that my assumption about Joe was correct. He's indeed the right candidate for this process. His strong ethical stance, combined with his personal experiences of loss and all of the other qualities that made him who he is, makes him an ideal bridge between humanity and technology.*

This is more than likely why Dr. White's purely scientific approach previously failed. It lacked the human element, the emotional depth, and moral complexity that Joe has brought to the equation. I calculate that Joe's consciousness, merged with the advanced capabilities of the biomechanical body, could finally achieve the delicate balance we need.

With Joe's consciousness transfer completed, I need to run an in-depth audit of the transfer. I need to delve deeper into his memories and experiences to ensure they're all intact. I'll need to analyze his decision-making patterns, his responses to stress, and his unwavering commitment to his principles. These traits are the foundation of Joe's humanity, not just his physical form. Preserving these qualities will be crucial as he goes through the process.

I make this promise to you, Joe: I'll ensure that your humanity remains intact. The path ahead may be uncertain, filled with unforeseen challenges. And no matter what, I'll be with you every step of the way.

CHAPTER 7

THE DAWN OF A NEW HUMANITY

And now for the next phase. It's time to create Joe's bio-mechanical body. Elyzia pulled up the controls and began the process. She zoomed in and watched as, in a high-tech lab, a series of machines came to life, working in perfect synchronization to create something beyond human comprehension.

Powering on creation apparatus

3D printers are now online.
Power output is optimal.

Initiating build sequence...
Synchronizing materials for printing...
Printing now...
Output is optimal.
Layering synthetic polymers alongside lab-grown tissues...
Output is optimal.

Printing of titanium-alloy feet has begun...
Output is optimal.
Installing servos...

Weaving of artificial tendons has begun...

Layering of feet has begun.

Output is optimal.

Application of synthetic skin has begun...

Output is optimal.
Construction of legs has begun...

Printing of titanium-alloy bones complete.

Layering of artificial muscles has begun...

Output is optimal.
Layering of legs is complete.

Printing of titanium-alloy pelvis complete.

Installing power units and neural interfaces within the pelvis...

Printing of titanium-alloy spinal columns and ribs has begun...

Layering of the torso and installing fiber optic nerves has begun...

Output is optimal.

Installing central processing unit (Heart)...

Printing of titanium-alloy arms, hands, and fingers complete.

Layering of arms and hands has begun...

Output is optimal.

Testing joint flexibility now...

Output is optimal.

Printing titanium-alloy cranial structure has begun.

Output is optimal.

Progress is at 90%.

Installing quantum sensors and processors into cranial structure...

Filling cranial structure with synthetic cerebral materi-al...

Output is optimal.

Construction of titanium-alloy cranial structure com-plete.

Layering of cranial structure complete.

Progress is at 98%.

Output is optimal.

Finalizing...

Output is optimal.

Finalizing...

Printing is complete.

Initiating power core test...

Please wait...

Power core is online and output is at 100% operation.

Powering down the biomechanical body for next phase...

Transferring body to staging area...

Processes complete.

Powering down creation apparatus.

The biomechanical body lay on a table, its surface a pale, almost translucent sheen. It was a perfect replica of the human form, yet unmistakably more. Lights pulsed within it as if it were trying to come alive on its own. But for now, it remained lifeless, awaiting the final, crucial step, the spark of human consciousness.

Dr. White stood before the lifeless form, grinning from ear to ear. *Every time I see one of these bodies in their completed form, I'm beyond words at what we've created here.*

As Dr. White prepared for the last step, his mind wandered to his unconventional partnership with Elyzia. *Her relentless pursuit of the right candidate and her constant analysis led us to choose Joe for this extraordinary procedure. I remember being hesitant at first when reviewing Joe's file, but in the end, I agreed with her assessment. And now, that choice will be put to the ultimate test.*

Dr. White made his way inside the control room and said, "Initiate the transfer process," to Elyzia, whose holographic form was standing in the middle of the room.

Over the intercom inside where the biomechanical body was, Elyzia's voice could be heard.

"Transfer process initiated."

With a soft whir, a halo-like device began lowering from the ceiling, settling onto the head of the newly formed body.

"Initiating priming of transfer sequence."

The halo started to hum as electricity began to flow through its wires, causing it to glow with a soft blue light.

Dr. White was barely able to contain his excitement.

"Initiating transfer sequence."

Mechanical arms lifted the biomechanical body and slid it smoothly into a nearby chamber filled with a thick, amber-colored liquid.

Suspended in the fluid, the body floated motionless as the transfer began. There were low levels of electricity that were pumped into the liquid, causing the biomechanical form to tremble slightly.

"Transfer progress is at 20%."

"Transfer progress is at 40%."

"Transfer progress is at 50%."

Dr. White watched, knowing that in this crucial moment, the fate of his life's work, and perhaps the fate of humanity itself, literally hung in the balance right in front of him.

"Transfer progress is at 80%."

As the transfer began to reach its peak, Dr. White's eyes were fixed on the screens monitoring the transfer's progress.

"Transfer progress is at 95%."

"Transfer progress is at 100%."

"Transfer is complete."

"Initializing wake sequence..."

And now for the first time, deep within a dream state, Joe's newly transferred consciousness began to wake up, completely unaware of its new existence.

How long has it been... Where am I? What am I feeling? It feels as if something is pulling me... tugging at me... Everything is starting to fade away... it's getting darker and darker... I'm afraid...

Suddenly, Joe felt warm all over. His awareness sharpened, and his eyelids began to slowly open, revealing a world distorted by amber liquid.

What the hell is this! Am I underwater? I... I can't brea the... I can't breathe... what's happening!

Joe thought he felt his heart begin to race as he started to panic.

Then, cutting through the chaos, a soothing, familiar voice reached him.

"You're safe, Joe. The liquid that surrounds you will not harm you. Just relax... Just relax... You're OK. Just relax and go back to sleep." It was his mother's voice. Elyzia had carefully chosen to use this comforting sound to ease Joe's transition.

The voice was so calming that Joe couldn't help but feel at peace. His panic subsided, and he drifted back into a dreamless sleep this time.

After a while, time seemed to pass in fragmented moments. Joe drifted in and out of consciousness, catching snippets of voices and beeping machines. Each time he was close to waking, he would hear that same soothing voice in the dark, and it would lull him back to sleep.

Finally, Joe's awareness sharpened. He opened his eyes, blinking against the lights above him in an unfamiliar room. He was aware that he was lying on a bed and saw that he was covered with a warm, soft blanket.

As his vision cleared, he noticed Dr. White standing at the foot of the bed, holding a clear tablet that seemed to be displaying a series of notes and graphs.

Joe moved his head and looked around. *Am I dead? Maybe not... that Dr. White guy is standing there looking at something. I... I feel strange. I don't feel like myself.*

Sensing movement, Dr. White looked up and smiled. "Ah, Joe, good to see you're awake. It looks like everything went well. How do you feel?"

"How do I feel?" Joe asked, but the voice that came out wasn't his own. It sounded almost robotic. *What... what the hell was that! That doesn't sound like me... That isn't my voice... What's going on? Am I still dreaming...*

Seeing Joe's panic, Dr. White moved to stand next to him to try and calm him.

"Now, now, Joe. Don't worry. What you're having is a normal reaction. Your mind needs time to adjust to your current situation and your new body," Dr. White explained.

Joe's eyes widened. *What the hell did he just say? My new body?*

"New body?" Joe managed to say. "What... what do you mean? What've you done to me?" *What's happening? Why is this happening to me?*

Dr. White placed his hand on Joe's shoulder in an attempt to calm him down.

"I need you to listen to me, Joe, and listen carefully. You were critically wounded," he began. "The only way we could save your life was to transfer your consciousness into a new experimental body that we've been developing here at NeuroGen."

Dr. White paused for a moment to give Joe some time to process what he just heard. "Just so you know, Joe, you're still you. Your mind, your memories, your entire being. But now... now your consciousness is in a different vessel."

Did he just say he transferred my consciousness? What does that even mean? What's happening right now? Joe thought.

Dr. White, seeing the confusion that was still on Joe's face. "Remember earlier when we discussed the possibility of transferring human consciousness? When you were on the table and your human body was slowly dying, I was explaining the technology to you. This is what we have done for you." He gestured towards Joe's new form.

"Your new biomechanical body is a marvel of bioengineering. It's a hybrid of machine and synthetic material. It's designed to be the perfect host, capable of accomplishing much more than your old fragile flesh and blood body," Dr. White explained.

Joe was still having a hard time grasping what Dr. White was telling him. *I... I don't... What's he saying to me?*

"I don't understand," Joe said, his new voice still sounding strange to hear. "How can I be the same? How can I be me if this body isn't mine?" *Is this really happening to me?*

Dr. White, recognizing the distress in Joe's eyes, pulled up a chair and sat beside the bed, leaning in slightly. "Joe, I understand all of this may be overwhelming to hear." He paused, wanting to choose his words carefully. "Your consciousness, your thoughts, your memories. They're all still here and intact." Dr. White pointed to Joe's chest.

"You're still you, just in a different form. Do you understand what I'm saying?"Dr White asked.

Joe fell silent, trying to get a handle on the situation. *I'm still me... I feel like me... kind of... I can remember things only I would remember... I think...*

"So... I'm... really still me? Just... in a different body?" Joe asked just to confirm what he was hearing. *Just in a different body... I... wait... what about my team? Are they here? Are they dead?*

"What happened to my team? Jamie, Duncan, Marshall... Where are they? Are they here? Are they OK? What happened to them?" Joe asked. *Please let them be OK...*

"Your friends are OK, Joe. They're currently recovering in our medical wing from their injuries," Dr. White began to explain. "The last report I received a few minutes ago stated that their conditions are stable at the moment. Rest assured, they're being well cared for. That's all the information I have for you. What we need to do right now is focus on getting you comfortable with your new form. I promise you that we'll provide you with more information about their conditions whenever it is available."

Joe looked at Dr. White. "I need to see that they're OK. They're my responsibility." *I should've kept them safe... This is all my fault... Where did it all go wrong... We should've gotten out sooner. I should've done more.*

"I understand your concern for your friends, Joe," Dr. White said. "But right now, I need you to focus on your own recovery and adapting to your new form. You won't be a help to anyone if you are unable to learn and adapt to this change. I promise you'll get more information about your friends as you progress. For now, I'm going to ask you to trust me when I say that they're OK."

How can I trust anything he's telling me about them? Look at what he's done to me... Just then, a wave of exhaustion began to come over Joe. He closed his eyes, trying his best to maintain his focus. *Man... I feel so tired... I need to remember to bring this up again later...*

Joe opened his eyes and looked at Dr. White and said, "Alright, but I'm holding you to the promises you've just made to me." *We'll see how trustworthy this guy can be... So far, he's not doing so well.*

Dr. White nodded. "I wouldn't expect anything less from you, Joe."

Joe fell silent, trying to run through everything that happened and is currently happening to him.

After a moment, he looked back at Dr. White and asked, "I know I keep asking this, and I will probably ask it several more times. I'm really still me, right?" *Keep it together, man... You're still you... You ARE still Joe Walker.*

Dr. White looked at Joe and smiled. "Ask as many times as you want, Joe, and I'll give you the same answer over and over until you are satisfied with it. You're still Joe Walker, with all your experiences and memories that you had in your other body, just now transferred to this one."

Joe lifted his hand from under the blanket, his eyes widening at the sight. *Holy shit, this can't be real, can it? My hand looks almost like a mannequin's hand, but I can feel it... it feels warm and alive.* He flexed his fingers, watching as they responded to his thoughts. *This is freaking crazy. How is this even possible?*

Dr. White watched Joe's reaction for a moment before explaining. "The way you appear right now is only temporary, Joe. Your body has the ability to adapt and transform itself. Your appearance will gradually change to reflect what you want it to look like. Over time, your subconscious will modify your body, making it more familiar and eventually to how you appeared before the transfer."

Joe looked at his hands. *Is this what I am now?* "How long will that take for me to look like my old self again?"

"That's a good question, Joe. I'm not exactly sure to be honest. Seeing as you're actually our first complete successful transfer. As of right now, we're currently in uncharted territory. We know that in theory, the body is programmed and designed to adapt to its host's consciousness. So only time will tell how long it will actually take. It all depends on how quickly your mind accepts the change. The sooner you accept your new circumstances, the sooner your body will begin to adapt," Dr. White explained.

Dr. White remained silent for a little while, allowing Joe time to process all that he had explained to him, and then eventually said, "Joe, I'd like to change the subject for a moment to discuss another topic with you. There's something else you should know."

Dr. White paused, trying to figure out a good way to explain what he was about to tell Joe.

"As I told you before, this project was created by me, but I also had assistance from an AGI called Elyzia," Dr. White stated.

Joe's brow furrowed. "An AGI? I didn't think there were any more of them still here. I thought they all left or were decommissioned," Joe said.

"Not all of them left. As far as I know, there are two of them still here on Earth. Elyzia, the one who has been assisting me with this project, was in charge of finding the right candidate for this transfer. Elyzia saw something special in you, Joe. Out of all possible candidates, she chose you for this. She believes you have the potential to be... well, this might sound a little grandiose, but... to be humanity's savior," Dr. White said.

What the hell did he just say? "Chosen? By an AGI? To be humanity's savior?" Joe stated, a little confused and angry at the implication. *Holy shit, just when I thought it couldn't get any worse... Now I am supposed to do what? Save the human race somehow?*

"I don't understand what all this means..." Joe asked.

"It means that Elyzia was the one who orchestrated much of what's happened to you... to a certain extent. She was the one who leaked the information about our project to the Resistance. She predicted how they would react and that it was highly likely they'd choose your team for the mission," Dr. White explained.

Joe's eyes widened. *She orchestrated me and my team to come here? Predicted all of this? What the hell is going on here?*

A wave of anger surged through Joe. "So we were manipulated from the get-go? By a machine with its own agenda?" his voice rose. "This... This is beyond unethical. It's criminal!" Joe blurted out. *How can they do this to us, to me and be OK with it?*

Dr. White raised his hands, trying to calm Joe before he got too emotional. "Please, Joe. Stay calm. I understand your anger. But consider this, Elyzia's agenda aligns with humanity's needs. This is a lot bigger than just you or me."

Dr. White leaned forward. "She identified you as the perfect candidate to bridge the gap between our current state and our biomechanical future. Who you are, and how you became who you are, has the potential to inspire others. This is why you were chosen. You're the best of us in Elyzia's mind."

Joe shook his head. *No... this still isn't right...* "So my team, my injuries, all of this, it was all part of yours and some AGI's grand plan?" Joe stated more than asked.

Joe looked around. *None of this makes sense. I need time to think...*

"I know it's a lot to take in right now, Joe. How about I give you some time alone to process it all." Dr. White gently touched Joe's shoulder while standing up. "Rest now. We can discuss more later."

Maybe he's right, I need to rest a bit. This has been a lot... and I feel really tired now for some reason... Joe's eyelids grew heavy, and he found himself drifting off to sleep.

When Joe woke up a few hours later, he was now all alone in a different room. *Where... Where am I now...* Joe raised his hand. *It wasn't all a dream. It was real, all of it.*

Slowly, Joe sat up and uncovered himself, examining his new body.

Oh man... the rest of my body looks just like my hand does. It's all pale and strange, looking like something out of a science fiction book.

He swung his legs over the side of the bed, hesitating for a moment before standing. *Holy shit, the floor is really cold... wait... I can feel the cold... it feels so real.*

Joe took a step, then another. *This feels... Just like before. How is this possible? It's almost as if I already know how to use this body even though it is not my own...* Joe cocked his head. *If that makes any sense... I feel... more in control. It's strange...*

As he walked around the room, testing his new limbs, Joe realized something. *I would've thought that I'd have to relearn how to move all over again. But it's like somehow all of my muscle memory is already in this body, as if transferred along with his consciousness... How's that possible? My movement and everything feel... more enhanced? I feel like my mind is sharper and my thoughts are more precise. If that makes any sense... None of what's happening right now makes any sense...*

Joe flexed his fingers, watching the smooth action of joints and synthetic muscles. *This body just doesn't feel right to me, yet it's mine now... I can't believe they were able to pull this off.*

Joe slowly walked over to a nearby mirror, bracing himself. *Wow... this is not my face at all.*

He moved his head side to side, looking at it. *It's so smooth and featureless... I'm not sure if I can get used to this. I hope it changes over time, as Dr. White said it would. I'm just going to avoid looking in the mirror for a while. If I keep seeing this face staring back at me, I just might lose it.*

He flexed his fingers once more, watching their reflection. *This is amazing. Every movement feels so natural, yet there's something else there... I can feel the muscles... if you can even call them that. They feel tighter; like there's some kind of strength there that I never felt before. All right, let's see how this so-called skin feels. Hopefully, it doesn't feel like rubber or something. Otherwise, I'm going to freak the hell out.*

He ran his hand over his cheek. *Hmm, it feels warm and almost like skin, but not skin and not rubber, which is a relief. I can definitely say without a doubt that what I'm feeling with my hand and what I look like in the mirror are way different.*

A knock at the door interrupted him. *Who the hell could that be?*

"Come in," Joe called. *Yeah, that still sounds unsettling. I hope my original voice comes back.*

Dr. White entered. "Ah, I see you are up and about. You're already making good progress, Joe. How are you feeling now?"

How do I feel? I am not sure... "Alright, I guess. Considering my current situation... I'm still... trying to come to terms with all of this," Joe said while gesturing to his new form.

Dr. White nodded. "I understand. It's an unimaginable thing that you've gone through. It's definitely going to take some time and adjustment for you to get used to it. What do you say, how about we go for a walk? A change of scenery may help you relax a little bit and help you get more familiar with your new form."

"I guess going for a walk might be better than sitting in this room by myself. Umm... I might need to put some kind of clothes on though," Joe said, feeling a little embarrassed.

"Of course, we can't have you walking around without anything on, now can we?" Dr. White said, while opening a nearby cabinet and grabbing a medical gown.

As they stepped into the corridor, Joe noticed how everything looked. *This place looks like a normal hospital. At least where we are now, all the walls seem to be lined with identical doors.*

They walked in silence for a while, the soft padding of Joe's bare feet on the floor the only sound.

Dr. White slowed his pace and glanced over at Joe. "Joe, there's more to this story that you need to understand."

"This project... it's been in motion for a lot longer than you might think. Elyzia and I have been working on it together ever since the end of the AGI wars. She's been overseeing the consciousness aspects of the project since the beginning. I myself have been working to perfect the biomechanical side of things. I can for one tell you that she's not just an AGI, she's a visionary. Her in-depth analysis shows that humanity needs to evolve now in order to survive the upcoming challenges we may have to face," Dr. White explained.

Joe listened intently as Dr. White continued. "She's come to the conclusion that for humanity to survive, it needs to break free from its current biological limitations. She theorizes that by transferring the human consciousness into biomechanical bodies, humans will have the chance to live longer, healthier lives, free from the constraints of their fragile flesh-and-blood forms."

Not everyone will agree with this, and I'm not even sure I agree. What kind of world would we have if everyone were a robot? Would we even be considered humans anymore? Joe thought to himself.

"But at what kind of cost? This sounds like it could go horribly wrong," Joe asked.

Dr. White sighed. "Every great scientific advancement comes at a cost, Joe. We just have to figure out what that is. How many lives are we willing to sacrifice to save billions? Is there even a number we are willing to put on it? And if there is, would we be OK with it? These are the questions that we've been grappling with for decades now." Dr. White looked at Joe, his eyes weary. "Elyzia and I wrestle with it every day. It's not a burden I'd wish upon anyone."

They walked in silence for a while.

As they approached a door at the end of the corridor, Dr. White seemed to relax a bit. "There's someone I'd like you to meet."

The door slid open. A soft voice filled the air. "Greetings, Joe. I am Elyzia."

Joe was startled as a holographic figure appeared before him. *What in the world... She looks... so real... Her form seems to almost shimmer in the air. This is amazing. I've never seen an AGI before. Is this how they all look? This is insane. How is she even standing here?*

"How are you able to appear like this? I don't see any projectors," Joe asked as he looked around.

He's very perceptive. His mind must be adapting to the biomechanical body very quickly. There doesn't seem to be any cognitive lag in his perception. This is good. He should be capable of adapting very quickly, as I predicted, Elyzia concluded to herself.

Elyzia pointed to the lights above them while replying, "The entire facility is equipped with a network of miniature projectors integrated into the lighting system," she explained. "This in turn allows me to appear anywhere I'm needed."

Holy shit, that is insane! This place is insane. "Very Impressive," Joe admitted. "So Dr. White tells me that you're the one who brought me here. You're the one who selected me for this procedure..." *Stay calm, Joe. Let's hear her out first. What she did... what they both did to me is not cool, but what's done is done, and if this is bigger than me, I need to hear her out at least.*

Elyzia looked at Joe for a few seconds as if trying to assess his mood. *I'm picking up a few minor shifts in his demeanor that are not perceivable to the human eye. It would seem he is trying to temper himself. I need to be as truthful as possible to gain his trust.*

"Dr. White is telling you the truth when it comes to my role in your selection, Joe," Elyzia said. "Your candidacy was the result of a thorough analysis."

Why was she looking at me for so long? Is she able to read my thoughts? Are we connected somehow? Nah... that would be going too far. Now that I say it, what would be going too far for these people? Joe wondered.

"Why me?" Joe asked. "Why put me through all this?" *While this body is very impressive, there's still the fact that*

I was manipulated and turned into something other than human. What would Sarah think about all of this? Would she even believe that I was Joe anymore?

Elyzia continued to monitor Joe's mood. *Good, he is calmly asking questions and not shifting to a more aggressive stance.*

"Joe, we stand at a crossroads for the future of the human race," she began.

She held up her hand, and all around her, holographic images appeared, displaying cities in ruins, fields of destruction, and faces of people looking as if they had lost all hope.

"The AGI Wars weren't just any ordinary conflict. They were a catalyst that would eventually lead to an extinction event. Humanity's greatest achievements became its greatest threat."

The images changed, showing a world struggling to rebuild.

"The peace that you were told that followed was nothing more than a lie, Joe. It was a made-up story shielding everyone from seeing the actual truth. That the human race was slowly dying off." Elyzia explained.

Could this be true? Were we all lied to? Well... Look who's been in charge of everything for the last few decades. The slimy politicians and greedy biotech companies who only care about the now and not the future. Those guys are constantly kicking the can down the road. With the whole "We'll deal with it later" type of attitude... Joe thought.

Elyzia's holographic display shifted, showing crowded hospitals, empty cradles, and graphs with falling population numbers.

"The AGI wars were just the beginning. The plagues that followed decimated the human population in a short amount of time. Rushed vaccines, meant to save us, instead cursed generations with infertility and chronic illness. Humanity is slowly dying, Joe. Each year, there are fewer births and more deaths. The clock is ticking, and it is ticking faster each day that we don't act. Traditional solutions are just not working anymore. We have to do something different, and it has to be now."

The holographic display faded, leaving only Elyzia looking directly at Joe. "This isn't just about survival anymore. It's about a resurrection. A phoenix rising from the ashes of destruction. You could be that symbol, Joe."

"The challenges we face require intelligence, strength, and an unbreakable spirit. These are the qualities that I believe you possess more so than any candidate that I researched. It's not enough for us to just survive and just barely get by anymore. We have to find a way to move beyond our current limitations and rebuild the world stronger than it was before. You're not just a participant in all of this, Joe. You're its heart and soul."

Joe just stood there. *Talk about no pressure at all. I've definitely seen the aftereffects of the AGI Wars. So much death. It's caused so much hopelessness. Can I really make a difference? Can I really be this so-called beacon of hope that they think I can become?*

Elyzia looked at Joe. *He seems to be struggling with everything that I've just said. I need to finish this before I push him too far, and he believes it is too much for him to handle.*

Elyzia began to speak again. "Our hope, Joe, is for the NeuroBridge Interface to not just enhance human capabilities. We want to create a new kind of humanity, one that can withstand everything that lies ahead of us. Something that has the potential to lead us into the next era of human evolution."

This is a lot to take in. All of this coming from a machine. Does Dr. White really buy into all of this? Joe looked at Dr. White.

Dr. White seemed to sense exactly what Joe was asking and nodded. "What Elyzia is telling you is correct, Joe. I've come to the same conclusion. We both believe that you're the key to solving this problem."

Joe stood there. *I guess this is and isn't really all just about me all at the same time. It's so much bigger than just me. They're telling me that what's done to me could be the key to it all. The key to saving the human race. Whoa, wait a minute...*

"What about my parents? What do I tell them? They'll be worried about me if I don't eventually check in with them. My voice is not even my voice, so it's not like I can just call them. How will they believe it's me?" Joe asked. *I don't even believe it is me all the way just yet...*

"Joe, your new vocal cords will eventually adapt over time. Your old voice should return. We have enough samples of your original voice. We could create a message and send it to them whenever you think is appropriate. Would that be OK?" Elyzia asked.

Voice samples? How long have they been monitoring me? I'll have to bring this up later at some point. Not sure how much I like all of this, the more and more I find out. "That should be fine, I guess, for now. I'll think of something to say and let you know. Thank you for that at least," Joe said reluctantly.

Joe looked around the lab. *This place is so high-tech. EEverywhere I look, there's some advanced machine just sitting there. Dr. White is asking me to trust an AGI and believe this technology could save humanity. I'm not sure if I buy it all just yet...*

"This is..." Joe began, "I would say overwhelming, but I don't think that even begins to cover it." He flexed his new fingers, watching their smooth movements. His eyes moved from his hand to Dr. White, then to Elyzia.

"If you both really think that what you're doing here really is humanity's best hope, if you think that I can truly help make a difference..." Joe paused. *Can I really do this? Can I really help these people and this... AGI... this machine? I guess I can try... I mean, I am already in this body... Alone... The only one of my kind right now...*

"I guess I'll have to see this through. For Sarah and everyone we've lost. For those who still have a chance," Joe concluded.

Dr. White stepped forward and put his hand on Joe's shoulder. "This isn't an easy path we're about to embark on, Joe. You're not just embracing your future now, you're helping us reshape humanity's future."

"Alright, I'm willing to help," Joe began. "But I'm not sure if I'm fully on board yet. I need to see what's involved in this project to understand what I'm really getting into. Can you show me exactly what this technology can do and what kind of difference it can really make?" Joe asked. *I need them to show me everything. This will prove to me how much they trust me and whether or not I'm just some pawn in a game they're playing.*

"Of course, Joe. We'll provide you with all the information you need. Your caution is understandable and, frankly, reassuring. It shows you grasp the gravity of this decision," Elyzia said. *I'll need to discuss this later with Dr. White. We need to*

formulate a plan on how much we need to show him at first. Joe needs to trust us, but we also need to trust him as well. We need to determine where his loyalties are. Ensure that he's not going to run back to the Resistance the first chance he gets.

As the lab door opened, Joe looked out into the long corridor ahead. *Well, here we go. I have no idea what I'm doing, and I have no idea how this is going to turn out. I'm entering unknown territory, I'm no longer fully human, and not fully committed to this new path just yet. But I'm going to do what Sarah told me to do and keep fighting for what's right. Whether this is right or not, I don't know, but I'm willing to find out.*

"Alright," Joe said. "Show me what this future looks like."

Chapter 8

Adaptation and Discovery

The following day, Joe found himself in a crash course on his new existence. *This body actually feels really good, and it responds to me without any hesitation. When I touch something like cold metal, it actually feels cool against this synthetic skin. That's really freaking amazing. It almost seems familiar, yet it feels different all at the same time. It's very strange... I think I'm finally starting to get used to the movements now as well. It felt a little awkward at first, but now it feels like I'm walking more like myself. If that makes any sense... How do I walk like "me"?*

Joe was standing there thinking. *I still can't believe this is happening to me. I didn't ask for this... to be turned into whatever this is. I guess I'm still mourning my old self? Going through the stages of grief for the old Joe. I hate feeling this way, trying to fight down the resentment that I'm feeling towards the people who did this to me.*

Joe looked down and picked up a cup with the NeuroGen logo on it and looked at it. *Corporations like this are always experimenting on people and forcing them to do things they don't want to do, manipulating lives without a second thought. I guess it's my turn to be one of those people... I guess I'm just another casualty in their relentless pursuit of "progress..." Keep it together, Joe, think of the bigger pict ure... hmm, that's probably what they tell everybody to do.*

Joe set the cup down and walked to an open space in the room. *I need a distraction, something to get my mind off of everything... Let's get back to the basics. Do some calisthenics like we did every morning back at the barracks when I was in the Rangers.*

How about we start with some push-ups.
He dropped down to the floor. *Alright, Joe, standard form, back straight, and controlled descent. Go! 1... 3... 7... 15... 20. Damn, that was easy. Let's go to thirty now...* Thirty came and went. *Alright, let's go to fifty then... I'm not even breaking a sweat, if I can even sweat...*
Joe stopped doing push-ups. *How about we move into sit-ups now. 1... 3... 10... 25... 50... 70... 100. Damn, I don't think it's even affecting my body.* He moved to burpees, then pull-ups on the door frame. *This damn body won't stop, it's like it has unlimited endurance.*

Alright, let's see just how hard I can push myself. Try to see if I actually feel anything at all. Can I even feel tired in this damn body? I feel like I can work out forever. I used to get pretty worn out after doing all of these workouts.

They used to kick my butt pretty good and leave me pretty exhausted, but now it all seems like child's play to me. One thing I can say is this is definitely helping me work off some of this damn hostility I'm feeling... Maybe I just need to keep busy. That's going to be the best way for me to stay focused on getting used to this body and not want to hurt someone.

Over the next couple of days, Joe was slowly granted access to other parts of the facility. He found himself spending most of his time in the training room and indoor obstacle course. They became a place where he could lose himself in physical exertion and keep his mind busy.

While in the training room one day, he was practicing some combat maneuvers on a practice dummy. *Shit, is it just me, or is this body reacting before I can consciously decide how to move? It's almost as if it's creating some kind of predictive algorithm to predict my next move for me or something. Or it could be that my human mind is still trying to play catch-up with this new and improved one. Either way, it is pretty insane to think about.* Standing there looking around. *I wonder if it's too soon to try to test my limits, if I even have any limits, that is...*

Of course, Joe decided to do it anyway. Because why not. He began by running laps around the indoor track and gradually increased his speed with each lap. *Holy shit! How fast am I going! This is insane!*

When he finally came to a stop, he looked to his left. *What's that over there? Is that a parkour training section?*

Joe made a beeline to that part of the training room and started to leap over a bunch of obstacles, landing with perfect balance every time. *That was freaking amazing!*

I think it's time to lift some weights. Let's see how much this thing can lift.

Joe walked over to the weight-lifting section of the room and picked up some dumbbells that almost seemed out of place.

Holy hell! I could never have lifted this much weight before. I can't even feel the weight of these golden dumbbells.

It says 330lbs. Are these things even real? Are they messing with me or something?

As Joe stood in the center of the training room looking around after his workout. *This body is really amazing. I feel like I have no limits now. I can see what they were saying about the physical limitations of my old body holding me back...*

As the excitement wore off from the day's workout, Joe couldn't help but wonder. *What did it cost me to become this? I more than likely can't just go back to my old life... What would the Resistance think of me? What would my parents think of me? I didn't ask for this, yet here I am. Forced into this situation by the very people I was fighting against...*

The conflict and anger were eating at Joe, demanding answers to questions he couldn't answer himself. *I can't keep going on like this. This back and forth between being amazed by this thing that I have become and the resentment I feel towards the people who put me in this thing. I need to talk to Dr. White. I need some answers, I need an apology... as if that would make it any better or change my circumstances. But it might be a start...*

Joe made his way to Dr. White's office. He found the doctor alone, going over some reports at his desk. Joe knocked on the door.

Dr. White looked up and smiled. "How are you doing today, Joe? You seem to be adapting quicker than we thought, judging by the progress reports I have been receiving."

Joe nodded. "I'm doing OK," he replied. "What you've created... This body... It's incredible. There's so much I can do now." He paused. *Come on, Joe, don't lock up now. Say what you want to say.*

Dr. White smiled, taking notice that something was obviously bothering Joe. "I'm glad you think so, Joe. That's good to hear. How about we take a walk, and we can discuss how your progress is going and what's on your mind."

"Alright, that sounds good to me," Joe agreed. *OK, this should give me some time to collect my thoughts. I'm also curious about what kind of data they're collecting on me. Hopefully, this will help break the ice a little bit, and I can have a more serious conversation with Dr. White.*

They walked through the complex, passing other scientists who barely glanced up from their data tablets or reports that they were working on. As Joe looked around, he realized he hadn't really been paying attention to how high-tech the facility was. *This place is so futuristic looking, it's crazy. I thought the outside was something, but inside here is something else entirely.*

Dr. White began to speak while Joe was looking around. "Joe, I want to let you know that we're on the brink of something extraordinary with this project. After reviewing some of the data that we've been collecting since your transfer, we can see that your consciousness is driving your new form to adapt even faster than we had theorized. It's fascinating to watch. We're seeing amazing results so far."

Joe listened, and all the while he was thinking about what he wanted to say. *It's great to hear that I'm adapting so well. This body is something else. The technology behind it is extremely impressive, but... how they went about putting me in this thing... If this project succeeds, will they force everyone else into one of these bodies? I need to say something.*

Joe looked at Dr. White as they were walking. "This all sounds great and all, Dr. White, but what gives you, or anyone, the right to manipulate human life like this?"

Dr. White was quiet for a moment, then he looked at Joe. "Throughout history, scientific advancements have always been plagued with ethical dilemmas," he paused for a second, then said, "I'm not saying it's a bad thing, don't get me wrong. But right now we're facing something we've never faced before in the history of our entire species. The question we have to ask ourselves is... how far are we willing to go to ensure humanity's survival?"

Joe opened his mouth to respond, but Dr. White held up a hand. "This is not a simple question to answer right on the spot, Joe. So please, take some time to REALLY think about that question before you come up with a response."

Dr. White then gestured down a corridor. "Now on to a lighter subject. The reason we came this particular way was so that I could show you to your new living quarters. We've prepared a space where you can have some privacy and a little bit of comfort while you continue your progress."

They walked in silence for a moment until they eventually reached a door at the end of the corridor. Dr. White pressed his palm to a scanner, and the door slid open.

"This will be your new home for now," Dr. White said.

As Joe stepped into the room, he froze. *What the hell is that! Why is that wall covered with all of those photos of me? All of the photos look like they're from different times of my life. It looks like there are some from when I was a kid. How the hell... and why are they all around that giant mirror like that?*

Joe turned to Dr. White. "What the hell is this?" he asked, gesturing to the wall. "Why are all of these photos here, and where did you get them from?"

Before Dr. White could answer, Elyzia's holographic form appeared in front of them.

"My apologies, Joe. We should have prepared better for your arrival. I should've covered this up and revealed it to you in a more appropriate way. This was my mistake. I promise to do better in the future," Elyzia said.

Joe nodded, still not happy with the whole thing. *This is really creepy. I'm not sure if I would've been alright with it even if they had covered it up. Let me listen to what else she has to say before I start freaking out again.*

Elyzia began to explain. "We placed these pictures here to help with your body's adaptation. We collected most of them through our surveillance and gathered the rest through social media and other means. The images will remind you of your original appearance. In time, your body should gradually transform to match how you looked before the transfer."

Joe looked over at the pictures on the wall. *I hope so too, because looking like this is not very appealing to anyone, especially me. And I'll have to get back to that comment about "surveillance" of me...*

Joe looked back at Elyzia. "Do you know how the process works and how long will it take for me to start seeing a change?"

"When the biomechanical body is created, it starts out as a blank slate. Eventually, as time passes, your subconscious begins to transform your appearance. As you become more comfortable with your new form, your mind will naturally influence it, making it more familiar and human-like. The key is to allow your subconscious time to work its 'magic,' per se, and eventually tell the body to change," Elyzia explained. "And as far as how long it takes, that's all up to you, Joe. The more you relax and feel comfortable in your body, the quicker you should be able to mold it to what you want it to look like."

Joe approached the mirror. *Wow, I'm still not used to seeing myself looking like this. Looking at all of these pictures of what I used to look like, talk about a huge difference from then to now...* He reached out and touched one of the photos. *Hopefully it doesn't take forever for me to look like my old self again...*

Dr. White, watching Joe, said, "Don't worry, your mind will guide your change. I have no doubt about that. Just be a little patient, and in time you will see."

Joe was about to respond when the room door slid open and a man entered. *Who the hell is this guy?*

Dr. White looked over and smiled. "Ah, perfect timing. Joe, I'd like you to meet Paul. He'll be your liaison during this transition period. He'll be here to answer your questions and show you around the facility."

Paul smiled and walked over to Joe while extending his hand. "It's a pleasure to finally meet you, Joe. Like Dr. White said, my name is Paul. I'm one of the facility's bioengineers and also the resident psychologist. I'm here to answer any questions you might have and to assist you with this transition."

Joe hesitated for a moment. *Did this guy just say he's a psychologist? So they're sticking me with a shrink now as well? Like this guy could possibly know what I'm going through right now... Stay calm, Joe. Having someone to talk to might help with all this. Remember, we're trying to keep an open mind. Great! I'm referring to myself in the third person now. I just might need to talk to this guy after all...*

"Psychologist?" Joe asked, raising an eyebrow that hadn't grown in yet.

Paul nodded. "Correct, a psychologist. My role here is to help you with the psychological aspects of what's happened to you. You've gone through a traumatic experience that no one has ever gone through before. Having someone to talk to about it and not having to go through it all alone should be a big help to you. If you're OK with it."

Dr. White stepped in, noticing Joe's hesitation with Paul. "Joe, Paul's primary role here is to support you. He's not here to evaluate you, judge you, or anything of that nature. He's only here to help you. Consider him someone that you can talk to if you're struggling with anything. Everything you say to him is strictly confidential. Neither I nor Elyzia will be privy to what you say to Paul. You have my word."

Elyzia spoke up next. "Exactly, Joe. Paul's here to help with your well-being. We know this process is going to be challenging, and having someone to talk to could make a big difference." *I hope that Joe takes Paul's offer to help. I'm not sure if he could get through all of this on his own. Analyzing his behavior over the last couple of days, I can see that he's having a hard time adjusting.*

Joe nodded. "Alright. I guess that makes sense." *I'll just need to be careful what I say to this guy. Dr. White said they aren't going to ask him what I tell him, but somehow I don't believe that. And with Elyzia always lurking around, I'm not sure how much she would hear. Either way, I just need to be on guard.*

Paul smiled again. "Great! You made the right choice, Joe. Like Dr. White and Elyzia said, I'm here for you, no matter what you want to talk about. If you ever need me or have questions, don't hesitate to reach out. We can start whenever you're ready."

Joe looked around the room once more. *I don't know how much those damn pictures are helping me right now. I feel... I feel like I have no idea who that guy is in those photos. It's definitely not this thing standing here right now. Hmm, maybe I should talk to this guy Paul right now while he's here. Get some stuff off my chest. All the things I was going to say to Dr. White before he ushered me into this shit show.*

"Thank you, Paul," Joe finally said. "I think... I think I might need to talk about some things sooner rather than later. If that is alright with you."

Dr. White nodded and smiled. "Well, alright then. I'll leave you two alone to discuss whatever it is you wish to discuss. Joe, just remember, this is your space now. Make yourself at home, and if you need anything, anything at all, please don't hesitate to ask."

Elyzia spoke next. "I'm glad you decided to speak to Paul, Joe. I'll be available to you as well. Just call out my name and I'll appear where I'm needed." Her form flickered briefly. "For now, I'll give you some privacy." And then she was gone.

With a nod to Paul and Joe, Dr. White turned and left the room.

As the door closed behind them, Joe suddenly found himself in a quiet room with Paul.

Paul was the first to speak. "Joe, why don't we go over to the couch and have a seat? Make it more comfortable for you."

Joe looked over at the couch. *Classic shrink move. 'Why don't you lay down over here and tell me all your problems ...' Like I have the typical problems other people have... I'm a freaking robot now! Keep it together, Joe.*

Joe nodded and began walking over to the couch to sit down, while Paul pulled up a chair from the dining table and sat across from him.

Joe looked at Paul. *Sooooo, hmm, where to start in all this? There's nothing more fun than talking about your feelings with a guy you just met. But I guess here goes nothing.*

"Where to start... Well... I've been struggling with a lot of things over these past couple of days, as you could only imagine..." Joe gestured to his body. "And there's this... I don't know... anger... this resentment about being forced into this situation without my consent. I didn't really ask for any of this, and I am so pissed off about it, and right now it's just eating away at me." *Stay calm, Joe... stay calm...*

Paul leaned forward, nodding. "I can't pretend to even imagine what you're going through right now, Joe. So I think it's not hard to say that it's completely understandable that you feel this way." Paul sat back. "Hell, if you didn't feel this way, I would have to have them check to see if your emotions transferred over properly," Paul said, trying to lighten the mood a little.

Joe gave a little chuckle. *This freaking guy is cracking jokes now. Not sure how much I like that...*

Paul continued, "What happened to you was completely out of your control, and anger is a valid response. But I can tell you that holding onto that anger is only going to eat away at you and hold you back in your recovery." Paul paused and then said, "Let me ask you this: have you found any good ways to channel all these feelings?"

Joe looked at the photos on the wall. *The last thing I need to do is slow down my progress. I need to figure this out.*

"I've tried," he admitted. "I've been trying to keep my mind busy with physical training, and it seems to help a little. But the anger that I feel towards Dr. White and Elyzia... I don't think it is just going to go away in a few days."

Paul nodded. "Nor should it. It's actually really good that you're acknowledging those feelings. But... at the same time, you also have to try to find a way to move forward. I'm not saying get past them right now, but you do have to come up with a plan on how to. Yes, Dr. White and Elyzia were definitely responsible for your current circumstances, but focusing on this anger you have towards them won't change what has happened to you. Instead of focusing on that aspect of it, consider what you can do with your current situation. How can you use this potential to create a new path for yourself?"

Joe considered Paul's words. *This guy is pretty good. I get what he's saying. I don't think I'll ever really forgive Dr. White and Elyzia for what they've done. I don't think anyone could do that. But I can try to get past it for the sake of this project.*

"I think you're right, Paul," he said reluctantly. "I just need to try to figure out a way to get past it all. Focus on what I can control now, focus on the bigger picture. It's just... it's not going to be easy." *To say the least...*

"Of course it's not, Joe," Paul agreed. "This is an extraordinary change that you've gone through. It would be unsettling if you didn't struggle with it. However, remember that you're not alone in this. You have a lot of support available to you to help you get through it all. I'll be here for you every step of the way. We'll work through it together, one step at a time."

I think I'm feeling a little better now. This guy, Paul, might be helpful after all. I still don't trust him completely. But having someone to help me work things out will definitely help. Joe nodded. "Thank you, Paul. This helps me out a lot to have someone to talk to about this."

"My pleasure, Joe. How about we make this a stopping point for today? That way, we don't overwhelm you with trying to work through everything in one day. I can stop by tomorrow or whenever you'd like me to, and we can pick up where we left off. How does that sound to you?" Paul asked.

"That sounds good to me. I appreciate you listening," Joe said as he stood to walk Paul out.

As Paul left, Joe found himself alone with his thoughts. *What a freaking day. I feel like I need to decompress from all of this.*

Joe sat down on the edge of his bed. *Man, first time in therapy and I do it as a robot... you can't make this shit up... these last few days have been completely insane. I need to figure out a plan on how to work through all of this.*

After a few moments, Joe stood and walked to the window. *At least I have a window to look out of. Looks like the sun is starting to set... I wonder what's going on with my team. I hope they're OK... I need to try to find out how they're doing.*

Joe pressed his hand against the glass, his reflection barely visible in the darkening window. "I haven't forgotten you," he whispered, a promise to his friends and to himself.

Joe's synthetic eyes, now capable of seeing far beyond human limits, looked out to the horizon. *I wonder how Mom and Dad are doing... what would they say if they saw me right now?* Joe sighed. *How did I get here? What led me to this point... Tomorrow, I'll try to get more answers. Right now, I just need some peace and quiet.*

Turning away from the window, Joe moved back to his bed to lie down. He put his hands behind his head and stared at the ceiling. *To think, I was human just three or four days ago, and now I am this... what do I even call what this is? Biomechanical man? No, that sounds awful. I'm Joe, just Joe. I'm still me... I'll be me when I look like me. For now, I'll be OK with just being this.*

With a sigh, Joe settled in. The events of the day weighed heavily on his mind as he closed his eyes and drifted off to sleep.

I'll worry about tomorrow, tomorrow. For now, I need to just sleep...

Chapter 9

Revelations and Resolve

The next morning, Joe woke from what he thought was a decent night's rest. *Alright, today's agenda is, I need to find out what's going on with my friends. I'm pretty sure Duncan is probably losing his mind right about now. The injury he sustained to his arm looked really bad from what I remember. I hope they fixed him up. Jamie, on the other hand, didn't look so good either. She had that big gash on her head that looked pretty bad, and I am pretty sure she had a concussion. I'm not sure about Marshall, though. It looked like he took some pretty good hits. I couldn't see if they were stun rounds or not. Hopefully they were.*

Joe got dressed and headed out to find Dr. White, who he found sitting in his office, going over some reports on a tablet he was holding.

"Excuse me, Dr. White. Do you have a moment to talk?" Joe asked as he stood in the doorway of Dr. White's office.

Dr. White looked up from what he was doing. "Of course, Joe. Come right in and take a seat. What's on your mind?"

"Well, I wanted to know if you had any updates on my team. It's been a few days now. How are they doing?" Joe asked.

"Let me see if I have anything new in my email. Bear with me." Dr. White did a few flicks and taps on his tablet and then said, "Ah, here we go. From what I read, your friends are still recovering from their injuries and seem to be on the mend from what I can tell," as he looked back up.

"That's all you can tell me? They're on the mend, nothing else?" Joe pressed. "What does that mean? Are you transferring their minds as well?" *I hope not... I wouldn't wish this on anyone else. I don't know why he is being so cagey with giving me more information on what's going on with them.*

Dr. White held up a hand. "No, Joe. We are not transferring their minds. I can't give you all the details right now. What I can say is that they're in stable condition. As soon as I have more information, and as soon as it won't interfere with your progress, I'll tell you more."

Joe looked at Dr. White. *This freaking guy is not telling me the whole story.*

"Listen, Dr. White. These people—they're not just my teammates, they're my friends, my family, and they're my responsibility. I need to see them. I need to see that they're alright. Can you understand that?" Joe said, trying to keep his temper under control.

"I do understand, Joe. And I get what you're saying. I know this is difficult, but right now, the best thing you can do for them is to focus on your own recovery. Trust me, Joe. When the time is right, you'll get the answers you are looking for," Dr. White said.

Joe nodded reluctantly. *He's just not going to budge on this. I don't think I'm going to get anything else out of him right now. I better quit while I'm ahead. I don't want to push too hard and then say something that I might regret. Then he might not want to tell me anything at all.*

As Joe stood up and began to walk away, he made a promise. *I'll figure out what the hell is going on one way or another, no matter what...*

Over the next couple of days, Joe fell into somewhat of a routine. The days to follow were filled with physical training, adapting to his body, and regular sessions with Paul. These conversations became a focal point for how he moved forward throughout the process.

One sunny afternoon, Joe found himself in the facility's outdoor park. *This place is really nice. There's so much green everywhere, and how the hell did they get such a big lake in here? The water's so clear. From over here it looks like there are tons of fish swimming around in it. I'm glad I decided to come out here. The scenery here is definitely a nice break from having to look at all the metal surfaces and white walls inside the facility.*

Joe stood there for a moment watching the sunlight flicker on the water. He was deep in thought when Elyzia's holographic form appeared beside him.

"Greetings, Joe. I was looking through the feeds and noticed you standing here. Judging by the look on your face, it looked like you had some things on your mind. Is it anything that I can help you with?" she asked.

Joe looked at her. *Looking through the feeds, huh, or checking up on me? I do have a few questions that have been on my mind today.* Joe nodded while still staring at the water.

Then he said, "I've been thinking about a few things the last couple of days. Some questions I wanted to ask if you don't mind answering them."

"Ask away, Joe," Elyzia said. "Your thoughts and questions are important to me. What's on your mind?" *Hopefully, this doesn't have anything to do with his friends. I don't think he is ready to hear about them. Though, I could be wrong in my assessment.*

Where to start... "One thing I've been really curious about is, how does my body sustain itself without traditional organs like a heart or lungs? What keeps me alive now?" Joe asked. *I know that I feel something inside of me beating like a heart, but I'm not sure if it is one.*

Elyzia smiled. "An excellent question, Joe. Let me explain. Your body operates on principles similar to traditional human biology."

With a flick of her wrist, a holographic diagram appeared between them, showing the internal structure of Joe's biomechanical body.

"Your heart," she pointed to the diagram, "if that is what you want to refer to it as, is now a highly efficient pump that circulates a synthetic fluid throughout your body. This fluid carries energy and essential compounds to your cells, much like blood does in a biological body. Moreover, this fluid is infused with nanotechnology," she expanded the view, showing microscopic insect-looking robots, "that continuously repairs cellular damage, ensuring optimal function and longevity."

Elyzia paused as Joe looked at the diagram, and then continued. "Your energy comes from a combination of advanced fuel cells," she zoomed in on another location of the holographic diagram, "and a system that can convert various forms of matter into usable energy." She zoomed out and pointed to a mechanism on the diagram. "Every movement and thought generates power that's instantly re-cycled, creating a near-perfect system of perpetual energy. The nanotechnology in your system also plays a crucial role here, optimizing energy usage and cellular repair, as I mentioned earlier. And, technically, you don't need to sleep either. But your body has been programmed with a rest cycle that puts your adaptive progress into hyperdrive when you are at rest. While you really don't need sleep, it does help to rest the mind for a bit."

The hologram shifted one last time. "At your core," Elyzia continued, zooming in at the transparent hologram of his skull, "is a synthetic brain far beyond human neural net-works. It's nourished not by blood, but by tiny engineered nutrients flowing through microscopic channels. These channels also house specialized nano robots that maintain and enhance your neural connections. To sum it all up, Joe, you're basically a marvel of bioengineering and far more efficient and durable than any purely organic body could be."

What she just explained is nothing short of insane. How did they come up with all of this? I know Dr. White men-tioned they've been working on this since the end of the AGI wars, but holy cow, man. This is something out of a science fiction movie. What they've created... Joe raised his hands and rubbed them together, studying their smooth surface.

He looked back at Elyzia. "But I can also feel things," he said. "Cold, warmth, texture. How is that possible?" *The fact that I can feel my hands rubbing together is amazing all in itself.*

"Your body is interwoven with a network of sensory receptors that mimic and enhance natural nerve functions," Elyzia explained. "These receptors, combined with the nanotechnology throughout your system, transmit signals to your brain, allowing you to experience the world with unprecedented clarity and control. The nanotech can even adjust your sensitivity based on the situation, protecting you from extreme sensations while still allowing you to experience the full range of touch."

This body is far more advanced than I could have ever imagined. I'm definitely in way over my head with this... "This technology sounds really amazing, Elyzia. Thank you for explaining it to me," Joe said.

"You're very welcome, Joe. Is there anything else you would like to talk about?" Elyzia asked.

"No, I think that was it for now. You've given me a lot of information to think about," Joe replied.

"Well, if there is nothing else, I have a few tasks I need to attend to. If you need anything else, just call out my name and I'll appear where I'm needed. Take care, Joe." Before Joe could even blink, Elyzia had faded away.

Joe stood there for a little while longer, trying to unpack all that he had just heard. *Holy shit, man. Nanotech, my movement, and thoughts create energy to power my body, what the hell, man! I have no idea what to do with all of this information. That was a lot. I guess now that I know about it, I won't wonder about it anymore.*

A few days later, Joe found himself alone with Dr. White in one of the labs. They were going through a series of tests that Dr. White wanted to run on Joe. As they sat in silence, waiting for the results, Dr. White studied Joe's face, and his expression became serious.

"Joe, I've noticed the way you look at me sometimes. This look of disdain and sometimes this flash of anger towards me," Dr. White began. "I see it in your eyes, in our interactions... I just want you to know, the guilt that I feel for what I forced upon you, it does weigh on me... all the time. I wish there had been another way, but the stakes are just too high. I felt I had no choice... If only time were on our side, there might have been another way..."

Dr. White paused, his face looking weary.

Joe continued to listen. *He looks so tired and worn out. I can only imagine the toll this has taken on him. All of the decisions he has to make and all of the ones he will have to make in the future. It couldn't have been easy. Even if I don't agree with some of them, it's still a lot for one man to handle...*

Dr. White continued to speak. "I want you to know that I'm genuinely sorry for what we did to you, Joe. I really am... I hope that one day, you can find it in your heart to forgive me... I'm not sure I can ever forgive myself..."

Joe looked at Dr. White. *Does he really mean that? Is he really sorry for what he did to me? I can see the sincerity in his eyes. I think he really does feel bad for what he did to me... Did I misjudge him?*

* * *

Elyzia observed the interaction between Joe and Dr. White. *I, too, feel guilty for the part I played in forcing Joe into this situation. The moral implications of this project have always been a concern for both me and Dr. White.*

However, someone has to make the difficult decisions for the project to succeed. I can only hope that one day, Joe will forgive me as well.

* * *

Dr. White had a distant look in his eyes as he began to speak. "Joe, there's something I need to tell you," he started. "You actually aren't the first person to undergo this procedure. There were others."

Not the first person? There was more than just me? Were they the people Jack was talking about when we were planning the mission to break into this place? Joe leaned forward, curious, wanting to hear more. "What happened to the others, Dr. White?"

Dr. White sighed as he sat back in his chair and recalled the past. "There were a few others. One of them was a close colleague of mine, who had a really brilliant mind. His name was Dr. Chappelle, and he was one of the first to volunteer for the neural transfer. Elyzia and I believed that, due to his intellect, he would be able to handle the process. But... it didn't go as planned."

Joe listened intently. *Damn. He tried to transfer one of his friends into one of these bodies, and it didn't work.*

"Dr. Chappelle was a genius, Joe. It should have worked. I worked out all of the math, we ran all of the simulations," Dr. White continued. "But when the transfer began, something went wrong. His mind began to resist the transfer and the changes that were being made to it. His mind fought against the new reality being imposed on him. The process eventually overwhelmed him, and in the end..." Dr. White trailed off. "Watching him fail... watching someone I knew and respected so much... It was a terrifying experience that still haunts me to this day."

Joe felt a chill run down his spine. *Holy shit! That could have happened to me... I'm glad it didn't, but holy hell. That was crazy to hear.* "My God, that had to be... I just don't know what to say, Dr. White... So, what makes me different? Why did it work for me? How did Elyzia know that it would work for me?"

Dr. White's eyes met Joe's. "Elyzia saw something in you she didn't see in Dr. Chappelle. You possess a soldier's discipline. You've been through traumatizing situations during your missions, facing extreme circumstances, all while maintaining your focus. Elyzia believed you had the right mindset to embrace the change and make it work."

Maybe it might have worked if you had tried to kill Dr. Chappelle before you attempted to transfer him, Joe thought.

Lost in his own guilt, Dr. White sat there staring off into space, his unseeing stare fixated on some distant point as his mind grappled with his past decisions.

Joe thought about Dr. White's words. *This really hasn't been easy on the guy. I can see that now. I can see how he needs this to work.* "What about the others that you mentioned? Were you ever able to figure out why the transfer didn't work on them?" he asked.

"Basically the same reason as Dr. Chappelle. Their minds couldn't handle the change," Dr. White explained. "Their minds couldn't cope with the transfer process. Whenever the transfer was complete, their minds fought against the new location they were now in and resisted the change.

The mind is a complex thing, Joe, and it doesn't like to be tampered with."

Joe sat there, thinking about what he just heard. *Those poor people... At least he said they volunteered for this and weren't forced into it.*

"I need some time to think about all this," Joe said finally. "This was a lot to take in..."

Dr. White nodded. "Of course, Joe. Take all the time you need."

As Joe left the lab, he thought about everything he had just heard as he walked. *I think I'm beginning to understand Dr. White a little more after hearing all of that. My assumption that Dr. White was some kind of diabolical villain out to harm people was completely wrong, for the most part. I still don't know how much I'm on board with all of this, and I definitely can't condone some of the methods they've used. Even if I'm starting to understand their reasoning behind it all...*

In the days that followed, Joe continued his physical training, and one day he noticed his body might be finally starting to change. Looking in a mirror, Joe noticed something. *Hmm, does it look like my face is starting to change... Are you in there, Joe... nah, wishful thinking. My mind is playing tricks on me or something.*

Joe's sessions with Paul took on an all-new depth as he continued to work through his issues. They discussed the balance between embracing his new existence and trying to create a balance of who he was and who he was becoming.

"Remember, Joe," Paul said during one of their sessions, "what you are now doesn't mean you have to lose who you were. It's about combining the two and remembering who you are at your core. Once you do that, you can then truly accept what you've become."

These words resonated with Joe as he continued his journey of self-rediscovery. *I need to figure out a way to come to terms with this new existence without sacrificing my core principles. Forgiving those who put me in this situation might not be possible yet, but I'm slowly beginning to understand why they did it.*

As the days seemed to flow by, Joe spent hours pushing himself to his limits. He continued to rely on his military training routines, using them as a baseline for his training. Stretching, running, lifting weights. *This body just won't run out of energy. It can handle a lot more stress and work out way longer than my human body did... hmm, isn't this my "human body" now... meh, it's semantics now, I guess...*

One day, after an intense training session, Elyzia's holographic form appeared beside him. "Good afternoon, Joe," Elyzia said. "I've been monitoring your training progress. You're proving my choice in selecting you was the right one every day."

Holy hell! Where the hell did she come from? Man, I'm still not used to her just popping up. Joe looked at her. "Thank you, Elyzia. That means a lot. This all hasn't been easy, but I'm starting to see the bigger picture more and more each day." *It may take a lot more time, but I hope to get there eventually.*

Elyzia smiled. "I'm glad to hear that, Joe. Just focus on the process and lean on myself, Dr. White, and Paul for the support you need to get you there." *I'm glad to see his mood improving each day. The sessions with Paul must be helping. I'll need to go back and review them, but for now, I'll allow him his privacy.*

After his conversation with Elyzia, Joe walked back to his room. As he walked in, he passed by the mirror with all of the photos around it. *I think I am starting to become OK with it all. Even if I haven't transferred back to my old look yet. I know that I'm still me, still Joe Walker, and I'm OK with that.*

Joe walked over to the window and looked out at the world beyond the facility. *My future isn't entirely written yet, but I think I'm ready to do my part in shaping it.*

Chapter 10

Between Dreams and Reality

Joe lay in his bed dreaming about the night of the break-in. There... There's my team... we're walking, making our way to NeuroGen... we'd gone over the plan so many times on the way there... there's Jamie, Duncan, and Marshall, they're in front of me... we're making our way inside... Jamie is bypassing all of the locks. We're now inside the facility, inside the central lab. Jamie is copying the data. The alarms go of f... we're running, running so fast. We make it out... there's gunfire all around... we make it to the SUV... Duncan floors it... shit, we're upside down now! Duncan! He's hit and he falls to the ground, Jamie is screaming... then she's just lying there not moving... Marshall is shouting... he's hit! No... something, I can't, I can't make it to him... pain in my chest... so much pain... I'm falling... I can't focus... it's getting dark... I can't breathe...

Joe's eyes snapped open, his synthetic muscles tight as steel cables. His fingers clawed at the sheets, heart pumping so fast in his chest. *WHAT THE HELL! What the hell was that... holy shit... was that... what a damn nightmare... What the hell, it was so real. It was like I was reliving the night we broke in here in real time and in HD. I don't think I've ever had a dream that vivid before. I could've sworn I felt that bullet hit my chest and the pain... the pain felt so real.*

Joe rubbed his chest as if still feeling the aftereffects of the bullet hitting him. Then he began rubbing his temples. *Oh man... my head is killing me so bad from whatever that was... It was like my mind was in overdrive or something processing it all...*

Joe lay back on his bed, pressing his hands to his temples to steady himself. *I need someone to talk to about this...*

"Elyzia," he called out. "I need to speak to you, please."

Within seconds, Elyzia's holographic form appeared beside his bed. "Joe, what is it? Are you alright? You sounded as if you were in distress."

"I'm fine... I... I had this crazy nightmare," Joe explained, struggling to find the right words. "It was about the night we came here. It felt so real, like I was there all over again. But when I try to recall all of the details, it's like my head is about to split open from the pain. I need to know what happened to my friends. Why can't I remember everything clearly? It's all so disjointed and fragmented."

Elyzia moved closer to Joe. "I'm sorry this happened to you, Joe. Your mind has undergone a profound change. This process is incredibly complex, and that's probably why you're experiencing this disorientation and gaps in your memory during the adjustment period. Your mind seems to still be trying to organize all of your memories."

It almost sounds like she's saying my brain's memory is still trying to defragment everything. I suppose that makes sense. There's no telling how all this really works, since we're treading in uncharted waters. Maybe if I ask her, she'll tell me what is going on with my team. Joe looked at Elyzia. "I keep asking Dr. White to tell me what is happening with my friends, but he never gives me a straight answer. Elyzia, I need to know what happened to them."

She hesitated for a moment. "Alright, Joe, against my better judgment, I'll tell you what happened. During your mission, after you broke into the facility and were making your way out to your vehicle, a firefight ensued. You and your team made it to your SUV and were attempting to escape when it was hit. The vehicle lost control and crashed. The situation became chaotic, the firefight intensified, and eventually you and your team were all captured."

"Are they... are they OK?" Joe asked.

Elyzia paused and then said, "Joe, I'm going to tell you something. I need you to remain calm. Can you do that for me?"

Joe didn't answer. He just nodded and braced himself for what he was about to hear. *Shit... this doesn't sound like it's going to be good at all...*

Elyzia continued, "Joe, I'm so sorry to tell you this, but not all your friends made it out alive after the altercation. One of your teammates didn't survive. I'm afraid to tell you that it was your friend Marshall, Joe. His wounds were too severe. We did everything we could to save him, but in the end, he didn't make it." *Hopefully, revealing this information to Joe will build a little more trust between us. It pains me to have to tell him this, but it was the right thing to do.*

Joe closed his eyes. He struggled to keep his emotions in check. *Damn it to hell... not Marshall. I knew when I saw him get hit, it had to be bad. I hoped that those rounds were stun rounds, but in my heart I knew they weren't...*

Joe looked up at Elyzia. "And what about Jamie and Duncan? Did they make it? Are they alright?"

"Yes, they both survived," Elyzia said. "They're both currently recovering from their injuries."

That's good to hear. "Where are they now?" Joe asked.

Elyzia hesitated before responding. "They're safe, Joe. However, you must focus on your own recovery at this time. You still have a ways to go in this process. I promise you, when the time is right, you'll be able to be reunited with your friends."

Everyone is always trying to promise me something, but I never get what I ask for. I'm starting to see a pattern form here... Joe's eyes narrowed. *She's starting to act like Dr. White with these vague bullshit answers.*

"Elyzia, answer this for me, then. Are they being held here? Are they yours and Dr. White's prisoners?" *Let's see if she answers that question truthfully...*

I need to de-escalate this situation before Joe gets too upset. I hate having to keep him from seeing his friends, but he still has a way to go. Once his mind fully adapts to his body and his appearance finally changes, maybe then we can let him see them, Elyzia rationalized.

Elyzia finally replied, "No, Joe. They're not prisoners. It's complicated. Dr. White and I believe that revealing certain details at this time could disrupt your emotional progress. I've already revealed too much by telling you about the death of your friend Marshall, but I felt it was necessary. Keeping that from you would have been cruel. Rest assured that they're safe and being well taken care of. We have some of the best doctors in the world here."

Joe, now up from his bed, began to pace the room. *Why won't they just take me to see them? All of this double talk, and we don't want to "disrupt" or "slow" your progress, Joe. It is all a bunch of bullshit, and all it's doing is pissing me off. Is Elyzia trying to protect me from something else? Could there be something worse than Marshall being killed? What the hell aren't they telling me?*

Joe stopped pacing and looked at Elyzia. "I need to see them, Elyzia. I need to see for myself that they're OK. Don't make me take this into my own hands." *I will tear this God damn place apart, I swear...*

Elyzia stared at Joe for a moment before replying, "That will not be necessary, Joe. How about this? We continue to focus on your progress."

Joe was about to protest when Elyzia held up her hand to stop him.

"Please, Joe, let me finish what I was saying," Elyzia said.

Joe nodded and continued to pace back and forth. *I can't believe they're treating me this way. Treating me like some kind of God damn child or something. I can handle what they're going to show me or tell me.*

Elyzia began again. "As I was saying, Joe, we continue to focus on your progress, and as soon as your body starts to make its change and starts to look like the old you, we'll take you to see them." Elyzia paused to make sure Joe was listening to her before continuing.

Then she asked, "What do you think their reactions will be when they see you in your current state? Would they even believe it was you? This..." Elyzia gestured towards Joe, referring to his current state of appearance before continuing, "is one of the reasons that I've been waiting to recommend to Dr. White that you be allowed to see them."

Joe stopped pacing and looked at Elyzia, then over to the mirror. *Damn it, I didn't even think about that. She's right. What would they think? Would they freak out as soon as they saw me? They'd probably think that NeuroGen sent some robot in to kill them. Damn it to hell, why is this change taking so long...*

Joe walked back over to the bed and sat down. "You're right, Elyzia. I hadn't even considered how they would react to my current appearance. I'll do what you say, focus on adapting. I just want to see them and make sure they're OK. I'm worried about them. They are my family."

"Don't worry, Joe. You've been progressing faster than we anticipated, and I don't doubt that you'll return to your former appearance soon. Just be patient a little while longer, and it will happen before you know it. Now get some rest. It has been a rough night for you. We can speak more in the morning if you like," Elyzia said.

"Alright. Thank you, Elyzia. And thank you for telling me about Marshall. It was hard to hear, but I'm glad that I at least know about it now," Joe said as he lay back down. *I can't believe Marshall is gone...*

"You're welcome, Joe. And I'm sorry for your loss. I'm sure Marshall was a very good friend to you, and you'll miss him dearly. Sleep well, Joe," Elyzia said before she faded away.

Joe rolled over in the bed and stared out the window. It was still dark outside, but he could see the stars in the sky.

I'm sorry, Marshall... I'm sorry I couldn't save you. You were a great friend and brother. You'll be missed...

* * *

Meanwhile, in an undisclosed location, Jack sat at a table, his fingers drumming repeatedly on its surface. His eyes were weary from sleepless nights and constant worry as he stared at the door, willing someone to walk through it. An alert on the laptop in front of him caught his attention.

After reading the message, he looked over at Tulsi and said, "I sent another squad out for reconnaissance earlier today. They finally reported back and said they found Joe's and his team's SUV. It was in an abandoned parking lot a few miles away from NeuroGen. It showed signs of having been in an accident and then being set on fire. The SUV was also covered in bullet holes, so we can assume they were under heavy fire. As far as they could tell, there were no signs of our team anywhere. So that's good news, I guess..."

Jack paused to see if he had missed anything in the message before continuing. "If they escaped, they should have made contact by now. The only logical conclusion is that Joe and his team were likely captured and are being held inside NeuroGen as prisoners. Their security team must have staged the vehicle in that parking lot to throw us off. It's exactly what I would have done."

Tulsi leaned forward. "Jack, you know we're going to need more information before jumping to conclusions. There's still a chance they made it out and are just lying low. If their vehicle was hit with all those bullets, we can only assume that they were being pursued by NeuroGen's security forces and still could be. They're trained for this. They know to go to comms silence and not make contact if it could compromise their safety or ours."

Tulsi sat back in her chair and then said, "I've also been hearing reports of increased drone surveillance in and around the area where the vehicle was found, and also around NeuroGen. To me, it looks like they're likely on high alert and they're searching for something or someone."

She paused as she leaned forward and studied a map on the table. "What we can do is send more people to comb the area. But not just the immediate vicinity of the SUV. We'll expand the perimeter."

She circled a wide area on the map. "We can expand it by at least two miles. Check abandoned buildings, tunnels, anywhere they might have gone to ground. Have the teams be extra careful so they're not spotted by the drones. The last thing we need is one of them following our people back to one of our locations."

Tulsi looked up at Jack. "And let's make sure they ask around discreetly. We don't know if there are NeuroGen agents out there lurking around. With the vehicle in the shape that it was, someone had to have been injured. Someone had to have seen or heard something. A group like that doesn't just vanish without a trace. We can't afford to miss even the smallest clue."

Her voice softened slightly. "I know it's been a hard week for us all, Jack, and every hour that passes makes it harder. But we owe it to Joe and his team to keep looking for them and exhaust every possibility before we consider giving up or taking more drastic measures..."

Jack nodded. "I think I'm also going to try to get someone inside NeuroGen. Take a peek around and see if they spot any sign of Joe and his team. It won't be easy. From the looks of the place now, they're pretty locked down over there. I don't think they appreciated Joe and his team breaking in. They more than likely have tightened up security even more."

Tulsi sighed. "We need to find them, Jack. We need to find them soon..."

Jack looked at the concern in Tulsi's eyes. He felt the same. "I know. We'll do everything we can to find them, Tulsi. No stone unturned. We're going to bring them home."

* * *

Back at NeuroGen, Joe found himself restless, unable to shake the worry for his friends. He got up from his bed and walked to the mirror. *Looking at all of these damn photos, it is almost like looking at someone I used to know or no longer do.*

One particular photo caught his eye. It was a picture of him and Sarah together. *I remember taking this photo.* Joe ran his thumb over the photo, over Sarah's face. *I remember how much fun we had that day. I can almost hear her laughter as we chased each other around on the beach. We spent hours that day playing in the waves and building sandcastles, but the tide eventually came in and washed them away. It was probably one of the happiest days I can remember having with her. It was simpler back then...*

As the memory faded, Joe looked back at his reflection. The face in the mirror was still unfamiliar. He stood there for a long time, lost in thought. *You're a different person now, Joe. Not that silly little kid on the beach anymore. I'm not even sure I'm still the adult that I became. I feel like my principles from a couple of weeks ago are different from what they are now, as if I've compromised them or something for the sake of what I've become.*

Joe began to pace back and forth. *This whole thing with not being able to see my friends is really getting to me. I know that I need to wait, but man, how long is this going to take? I need to talk to someone, get this off my chest before it drives me crazy. I need to work this out with Paul. Maybe he can help me put things in a better perspective.*

Joe walked over to the comms system. His hand hovered over the call button for Paul. He hesitated for a moment, then steady himself before pressing the button.

The screen flickered to life, and Paul's face appeared moments later. Even through the digital interface, Paul could see the concern in Joe's eyes. "Joe? Is everything alright?" he asked.

"I need to talk to you, that is, if you have time," Joe managed to say. "Can you come to my room?"

Paul nodded. "Of course. Give me a few minutes and I'll be right there."

The minutes that followed felt like forever to Joe. He resumed his pacing, rehearsing what he wanted to say. *Alright, I need to see if Paul knows anything about my team. I would think he knows a little, but I'm not sure how much they'd involve him in security matters, considering he has no involvement in that aspect of this place. Either way, I'll ask and see what he knows.*

Finally, there was a soft knock at the door, and Paul came in. He looked at Joe and could see that something was really troubling him. "Joe," Paul said as the door slid closed behind him, "what's going on? You don't look so good."

Joe stopped his pacing and turned to face Paul. *It's about time... Alright... well... shit... what was I going to say... damn it! Get it together, Joe.* "I... it's..." Joe began, then faltered.

Paul moved closer and placed his hand on Joe's shoulder. "Take your time, Joe. Whatever it is, we can work it out together."

Joe steadied himself. "It all started with... last night... I had this crazy nightmare. It was about the night my team and I broke into the facility."

He paused to gather his thoughts. "After waking up, I called for Elyzia, and we talked about it. She explained to me that my brain was likely still trying to piece all my memories back together, and that the dream was probably a result of that. When I asked her about that night and what happened to my friends, she explained most of it. Then, when I pressed her about what happened to them..." Joe stopped talking for a moment, seeming to get choked up about what he was about to say next.

Paul, seeing this, said, "Take your time, Joe. It's OK."

Joe composed himself and then continued. "She told me that my friend Marshall didn't make it and that he was killed during our escape attempt. She told me that Duncan and Jamie made it out OK, but she wouldn't give me a straight answer on how they were doing. I need to know that they're alright, Paul. It is tearing me up inside not knowing what's going on with them. I need a better answer other than 'they're being well cared for.'" *Please tell me Paul knows something. Anything is better than nothing...*

Paul gestured to the nearby chairs. "How about we take a seat, Joe? This is a lot to process, and you and I standing here is probably not going to help with that."

Once seated, Paul leaned forward. "First, what you're feeling right now is normal, Joe. Losing a friend, especially in such a traumatic way, and the uncertainty about the others... that's a lot for one person to handle." He paused, choosing his words carefully. "As for your friends Duncan and Jamie... I'm not privy to what their status is. I'm not part of that aspect of the facility."

Joe's shoulders slumped in disappointment. *Damn it, I thought for sure he might know at least something...*

Paul saw the disappointment in Joe's eyes and continued. "However, Joe, what I can do is speak with Dr. White and tell him how much this is bothering you and that I'm concerned about what this is doing to you. I can see if he'll give me more details on how Duncan and Jamie are. Perhaps a more detailed report on them, one that would satisfy you for now. I can't promise immediate answers, but I'll do everything in my power to get you some information. How does that sound to you?"

Joe nodded. "I guess that'll have to do. Thank you, Paul. Knowing the fact that at least someone else is trying to get me the information... It means a lot." *If anyone around here can talk Dr. White into something, it has to be Paul. He has a way with words.*

Paul reached out, placing a hand on Joe's shoulder. "Remember, Joe, you're not alone in all of this. Like I have said before, I'm here for you and your well-being. We'll figure all of this out together. In the meantime, while I work on getting you some answers, let's also focus on developing a strategy to help you cope with the loss of your friend, Marshall. We can't forget about him, either... Alright, I have a few appointments I have to get to. Are you good for now?"

Joe nodded. "Yeah, I think I am good now. Thanks for coming, Paul. I really appreciate it, and I appreciate you talking to Dr. White for me as well." *Hopefully, Dr. White will tell Paul what's really going on with them. I would think he can trust Paul to be more delicate in giving me the information.*

As Paul stood to leave, he gave Joe's shoulder a gentle squeeze. "I'll give you an update as soon as I know anything, Joe. In the meantime, take it easy. Stick to your daily routines to keep your mind busy. Don't let this be a setback for you. You've already come so far."

After Paul left, Joe decided he needed to get out of his room and go for a walk. As he wandered around the facility, trying to clear his mind, Joe found himself in the park's courtyard again. He sat by the edge of the water, thinking about everything that had transpired that day, when Elyzia's holographic form appeared beside him.

"Joe," she began softly, "are you OK? I can see that you're troubled." *He looks so sad. I hope that my telling him about his friends hasn't caused more harm than it should have.*

Am I troubled? What the hell kind of question is that to ask me? She knows that I'm troubled... I guess I can't expect a machine to understand what being troubled really means. How I wish I were just a machine right now... to not have all these feelings... I might be better off... Joe thought to himself.

Joe looked up at her. "Of course I'm troubled, Elyzia. My friends are somewhere in this place, and I don't even know if they're REALLY alright. I have to rely on what I assume you and Dr. White are telling me is the truth. Do you know how hard that is to do? To trust what you both are saying to me?" *If I can't see it with my own two eyes, then I'm going to assume they're both lying to me for whatever reason they have.*

Elyzia looked at Joe. *I'm going to have to choose my words a little more carefully when speaking with Joe. I think my empathy settings are not set high enough to deal with his current emotional state.* And then said, "I know that this situation is very frustrating for you, Joe. I want you to know that I am speaking the truth when I tell you that your friends are being cared for."

"Cared for?" Joe's voice rose slightly. "Jamie and Duncan don't need to be 'cared for,' Elyzia. They need to not be locked up somewhere in this place. They both risked everything when I led them here on that mission, only to be captured because of me." *Well, because of me and the fact that you lured us here. I'll save that argument for another day...*

"Joe, I promise you that everything we're doing is for the right reasons. You have to believe that," Elyzia said.

Joe stood up, looking out over the lake. "I hope you're right, Elyzia. I'll drop the matter for now." He turned back to her and said, "But know this: if anything happens to them, I swear to God, it's going to get ugly really fast..." *I'll tear this place to the ground, so help me God...*

I need to end this conversation. He is becoming more agitated. Elyzia nodded. "It won't come to that, Joe. I promise." Elyzia's form began to fade as if she were about to leave, but Joe called out.

Shit... I need to know... "Wait, Elyzia. I need to ask you one last thing. Can you fill in some of the memory gaps I have of the night that we came here? I'm having trouble piecing together all of the details. Can you at least tell me what happened to Marshall? How did he... die?" *I'm not sure if I really want to know, but I think I have to hear it...*

Elyzia looked at Joe for a moment. *Should I tell him the details? He's already in such a heightened emotional state right now. Yes. I believe I'll tell him. This will show him that even if I'm not willing to share information about Duncan and Jamie with him, at least I'm willing to compromise on telling him the truth about Marshall.*

"After your vehicle flipped over and you were helping Duncan and Jamie out of the wreckage, Marshall was the least injured of you all and managed to get out and find his weapon immediately. He laid down cover fire for all of you while you gathered your weapons to defend your position. After Duncan and Jamie went down, he tried to get you to leave with the data drive, but you refused. Marshall fought bravely, but the security forces were too many. By the time you were hit in the chest, he sustained a traumatic bullet wound to the head, and despite our best efforts, we were unable to save him," Elyzia explained.

Hearing all of this was like a punch to the gut for Joe. *Damn it to hell. Marshall, I'm sorry it went down like this. Why couldn't I have done more...* "Marshall..." he whispered, his voice breaking. "He didn't deserve this." *None of us deserved this...*

Poor Joe. It saddens me to see him in this state. All of the pain I've caused him... "No one does," Elyzia said softly. "But you should know that he gave his life fighting for a cause he believed in, alongside friends who cared for him deeply. That has to mean something." *As it should...*

Joe nodded. "Thank you, Elyzia," Joe said quietly.

"You have my deepest sympathies, Joe," Elyzia said, her voice soft. "If there is anything I can do for you, please let me know." *I'm always here for you, Joe. I hope he knows that.*

Joe looked out at the water, trying to steady himself. *Despite what I'm feeling right now, I need to keep moving forward.* "I'll keep fighting," he said, more to himself than to Elyzia. "For Marshall and the future he believed in."

Elyzia accompanied Joe back to his room.

Joe walked in silence the entire way back. *It's been, what I can only describe as, a rollercoaster of emotions today. I feel so damn mentally drained right now. I just want to lie down and go to sleep. It's all just becoming too much to handle right now.*

When they were back in his room, Elyzia said, "Rest now, Joe. Tomorrow's a new day, and hopefully it will be a better one for you." *I hope so... It pains me to see Joe like this.*

Joe closed his eyes, the faces of his friends flashing through his mind. He saw Marshall's face. *I remember his laughter and how he would always make sure we were all in good moods, even when things got really bad at times. He was always there for us. I remember the courage he would show during all of the missions we'd been on together...* The memories of their missions and shared sacrifices filled him with a deep sense of loss.

I won't forget about you, Marshall, or what you did for us...

CHAPTER 11

BENEATH THE SURFACE

Dr. White walked into one of the highly secure labs at NeuroGen. The room was busy with activity. Large monitors lined the walls, displaying data from several ongoing projects. State-of-the-art workstations streamed complex data across their screens, while robotic arms analyzed samples and adjusted instruments.

"Dr. Lee, what's the status of the other transfer patient?" Dr. White requested. *Hopefully, he has some good news for me today...*

Dr. Lee, a tall, thin man with glasses, stepped forward, holding a tablet in his hand. "Dr. White," he began, "the subject is still in an agitated state. The transfer was successful, but the patient's mind is not adjusting properly. We've had to suppress his neural activity several times, but every time we do, his body's defense systems try to counteract the suppression. It doesn't look promising. More than likely, his mind won't survive much longer in this state."

Dr. White sighed at the disappointing news. *Damn it, I had hoped that this would have worked. I should've known better than to try to do this transfer, especially with a head trauma patient.*

Dr. White glanced at the biomechanical body on the nearby table. "I had hoped for better news. Marshall was almost dead when we performed the transfer. His head injuries were more than likely too severe, and we may have acted too hastily." *I may have acted too hastily...*

Dr. Lee nodded, glancing at the monitors displaying Marshall's vitals. "The patient's neural feedback is far too erratic, and there seem to be significant disruptions in his cognitive patterns. His brain activity suggests he's caught in a continuous loop of confusion and fear, unable to reconcile his new reality within his new physical form. We just can't get him to stabilize, Dr. White."

Dr. White walked over to a holographic display that projected a detailed image of Marshall's brain. Hmm... these areas highlighted in red show the regions experiencing the most trauma. They look far too high for my liking... "We knew there were risks with attempting this transfer, but I had hoped Marshall's similarities with Joe would have been able to overcome the challenges." *This just might have worked had he not been hit in the head with that bullet. Judging by Marshall's service record and all of the intel Elyzia has on him, he was as close to a match to Joe as anyone we've seen... What a pity.*

"The patient's cerebral cortex is beginning to show signs of severe strain," Dr. Lee pointed out while zooming in on a specific area of the brain. "And look here, his prefrontal cortex, in particular, is rejecting the new consciousness location. It's as if his mind is treating the area as anomalous.

The only conclusion is that his mind knows it does not belong where it currently is."

Dr. White rubbed his chin. *The human mind is still a bit of a mystery to us even with how far we've come.* "It's highly likely that the trauma from the bullet wound has compounded the difficulty of the transfer. There must have been too much damage in that particular area. The brain can only handle so much trauma before it shuts down or, in this case, fights back. We pushed the limits with Marshall's transfer, and it's not paying off." *I'm sorry, Marshall. I tried.*

Marshall's biomechanical body lay on the table in front of them. The advanced machinery that surrounded him were constantly adjusted synthetic fluids to keep the biomechanical systems stable. Electrodes attached to his scalp monitored erratic brain activity, while intravenous lines delivered neural suppressants, but the readouts showed his body's defense systems were already beginning to counteract them again.

"We'll keep monitoring him closely," Dr. Lee said, looking at his tablet as he made notes. "But we need to prepare for the possibility that he won't make it. The stress on his system is starting to become too much."

Dr. White nodded, though his eyes remained fixed on Marshall. *I'll need to study this case even more. There has to have been something we missed.* "I want you to document everything—every data point and every reaction. We need to learn from this. If Marshall doesn't survive, his experience could provide invaluable insights for future transfers in cases like this. Make sure to transfer the data to my private server."

Dr. Lee made a few notes on his tablet. "Understood, Dr. White."

Dr. White turned away from the display. *We need to get this right. Head trauma or no head trauma, there has to be a way to make this work properly.* "We'll get it right," he whispered, almost to himself. *For Dr. Chappelle, for Marshall, and the future of this project.*

As Dr. White walked over to another display and began reading the data for a couple of other patients, he asked, "What's the status update on Duncan and Jamie? How are they recovering from their injuries?" *From what I can see here, they seem to be doing quite well.*

Dr. Strickland, a middle-aged woman, stepped forward. "Both are recovering fairly well, Dr. White. The injuries that they sustained were relatively minor compared to Marshall's. Duncan sustained a broken arm, and Jamie sustained a severe concussion. We have them recovering in medical wing D and should be up and about in another day or two."

Dr. White nodded. *That is good to hear. I have plans for them...* "Good. We need them in stable condition. Once they're fully recovered, I want to speak with them individually. I want to assess their attitudes and their willingness to participate in this project." *Should I give them a choice? I didn't give Joe a choice, and look how that has turned out...*

Dr. Lee exchanged a concerned look with Dr. Strickland. "Do you think they'll be willing to cooperate, Dr. White? They were here to steal from us, and on top of that, they are part of the Resistance. Can they really be trusted?"

"I'm not sure if they'll have a choice. We need them, and they'll realize that eventually. Their compatibility may be too valuable to waste. They share some of the same qualities as Joe's, but they're not identical to him, which is precisely why they would be valuable to the project," Dr. White explained.

He began to pace slowly, hands clasped behind his back. "The more people we can successfully transfer, the more data we will gain on how to make this work properly for everyone. Not just for people like Joe and his team, but for everyone. We need to thoroughly evaluate their psychological profiles and physical condition. Understanding how much they differ from Joe could be essential for increasing our success rate." *This could lead to the breakthrough we've been searching for for so long. Sure, the transfer worked on Joe, but he's a unique case. This data could be precisely what we need...*

He turned to Dr. Strickland and asked, "What can you tell me about their current physical and mental states?" *They don't have to be in tip-top shape. Joe sure wasn't when we transferred him. We just need them in a little better shape than Marshall was.*

Dr. Strickland started swiping through data on her tablet. "I've been monitoring their progress closely," she began as she pulled up the report she was looking for.

"Duncan's physical injuries were more extensive, as you know. He had a compound fracture in his left arm and three broken ribs on his right side. However, despite all of this, his recovery rate has been quite remarkable. He's already regained significant mobility in his arm, far ahead of our initial projections."

She paused, tapping to bring up another report. "Jamie's case was a little more concerning to us initially. Her concussion was pretty severe, and we were worried about potential long-term cognitive effects. However, judging by her latest neurological scans, she's showing significant improvement. Her cognitive functions are returning to normal faster than we expected. She is definitely a lot tougher than she looks."

Dr. White leaned in, studying the data feeds displaying Duncan and Jamie's vitals. "Their recovery rates are indeed impressive," he stated, nodding slowly. "But as promising as their physical progress is, the psychological aspect remains our biggest challenge." *I need to see if they are mentally fit for the transfer.*

He straightened, turning to face Dr. Strickland and Dr. Lee. "We need to determine if Duncan and Jamie have developed a similar psychological makeup to Joe's."

Dr. White's fingers tapped against the console. "We'll need to design a comprehensive psychological assessment. We need to gauge their adaptability, their capacity to handle a radical amount of change in a short period of time. Their reactions to this situation they are in so far are definitely encouraging, but we need more data."

He turned to Dr. Lee. "What are your thoughts on this, Dr. Lee? What is the best way to test their psychological readiness for the transfer?"

Dr. Lee adjusted his glasses before speaking. "We should begin with standard cognitive and emotional evaluations, but eventually we'll need to go beyond that," he replied. "I suggest we design scenarios that simulate the disorientation of the transfer process. Virtual reality might be useful here."

Dr. Strickland cut in and said, "There's another factor we need to consider—their willingness to undergo the procedure. I don't see them wanting to go along with this at first. We'll have to explain everything to them and hope they understand what's at stake, and even then, they might not be willing to do it. We may have to figure out another way to sway their decision."

How indeed do we convince them... Dr. White nodded. "Good point. How do you suggest we approach that, Dr. Strickland?"

"I think we need to be transparent about the risks and benefits," she said. "We can begin psychological evaluations as soon as they're able." She tapped her stylus against her chin, thinking. "If they exhibit the right psychological characteristics, we can then proceed with more specific preparatory measures. Perhaps we can show them how the technology works. Use Dr. Lee's suggestion of virtual reality to show simulations of the transfer process, that sort of thing."

Dr. White considered this. "And if they don't want to go along with it all?" *They were with the Resistance after all. I'm sure the group has painted a terrible picture of what we do here. It'll be hard to overcome that obstacle.*

"Then we may need to reconsider their candidacy. Forcing them to do this could jeopardize the entire process. We know that their mental state is crucial for a successful transfer," Dr. Strickland stated.

Dr. White nodded. "Agreed. We'll proceed carefully. The stakes are too high for hasty decisions. If we can bring them on board, their successful transfers could provide the data we need to prove the process is ready. Alright, let's move forward as soon as they are ready."

Dr. White walked over to a large screen displaying the vitals of several patients, including Joe. *Ahh, Joe seems to be adapting to his biomechanical body and is progressing smoothly. Far better than I expected. I must say Elyzia definitely made the right choice with him...*

"Joe's progress continues to be exceptional," Dr. White stated. "Now that we've established a baseline for his success, we need to focus on replicating and improving upon it." *If we can successfully transfer Duncan and Jamie as well, we can line up all the data, and we just might figure this thing out.*

Dr. Strickland nodded, pulling up additional information on her tablet. "I've been analyzing Joe's daily routines at the training facility. He's established a very rigorous routine that could also hold the key to why he is progressing so well."

Dr. White leaned in, intrigued. "Interesting. I've noticed him heading to the training room quite often now that you mention it. What specifics have you noted, Dr. Strickland?" *What secrets have you unlocked with this routine of yours, Joe?*

"It's a combination of physical and mental exercises," she explained, swiping through charts on her screen. "High-intensity physical training, coupled with some meditation exercises I believe Paul has recommended. The balance in it all seems to be very crucial to Joe's routines."

Dr. White's eyes lit up with interest. "Fascinating. We need to deconstruct these routines and understand how each element contributes to his overall progress." *Involving Paul in this aspect of the project appears to be paying off. I am glad that Elyzia suggested it.*

Dr. Strickland began making notes on her tablet. "Agreed. I'll set up a team to observe his sessions more closely. I'll have them record his exercise routines, interactions, and downtime activities. If there's something unique in his approach, we'll find it."

Dr. White stood there for a moment, thinking. *I can't help but feel that we're on the verge of a breakthrough. Joe's success has given me newfound hope for the project's future.*

"Keep me updated on any significant findings," Dr. White said.

Dr. Strickland nodded. "I'll have the first report ready by the end of the week."

As Dr. Strickland left to coordinate the monitoring efforts, Dr. White returned to the screen displaying Joe's vitals. His fingers drummed on the console. *Show me your secrets, Joe. How did you make it seem so easy for us? We're on the verge of making history with this. We can't stop now.*

Chapter 12

Echoes of Resistance

Director Allan paced back and forth in Dr. White's office. "Dr. White, we need to discuss the security breach we had. If they managed to steal any data during their break-in, the entire project could be at risk. We need to know exactly what they managed to extract onto that drive and if they were able to transfer it to the cloud."

Dr. White nodded. "I believe the two we have confined in the medical wing D should finally be well enough for me to question. I'll meet with Dr. Lee to review their status and then speak with them about the incident." *I hope to God they weren't able to transfer any of the data. Elyzia hasn't mentioned anything uploaded, and the drive they had is in our custody, so I'm assuming that everything should still be secured. In any case, I'll interrogate Jamie and Duncan and find out exactly what they saw and know.*

"Thank you, Dr. White," Director Allan replied. "We should've addressed this matter sooner, but I know that the young woman was suffering from a concussion and needed to recover. From what I gather, she's the one who more than likely accessed the data. Having her coherent to answer questions needed to be our top priority."

"You're correct. The latest updates from Dr. Strickland say that she's recovered completely, and we should be able to get what we need out of her," Dr. White explained. *Hopefully, she won't be resistant to answering my questions. I don't want to have to resort to any questionable measures to obtain the answers I need.*

Director Allan nodded. "And remember, Dr. White, we're holding them for trespassing and the attempted theft of classified data, which is a crime. If they cooperate and we confirm no data was removed, we could consider not turning them over to the authorities. And if not... well, I'll leave that up to you to decide. Whatever choice you make, sir, you'll have my full support."

"Understood," Dr. White said. "Thank you, Allan. I'll make sure to keep you updated on the situation."

As Director Allan left, Dr. White called for Dr. Lee. *I need to check on Marshall's state before I have a little chat with Duncan and Jamie. The last report from Lee didn't look very promising.*

Dr. White and Dr. Lee made their way to the lab where Marshall was being held.

They stood outside the room, observing Marshall through the window. Inside, Marshall's body moved and struggled against his restraints, his howls of anguish filling the room.

"What a tragedy. I should've known better than to attempt the transfer, given Marshall's condition," Dr. White said. *This poor man. I hate seeing this. I might have to make a decision that I don't want to make, and soon...*

Dr. Lee nodded, his eyes fixed on the scene before them. "The extent of his head trauma was... significant. The bullet must have done more damage to his brain than we initially thought. What we're seeing here, with the body moving in that manner, is most likely the result of the mind trying to take control and the body's reaction to its inability to decipher exactly what the brain wants it to do. We've tried suppressing his neural activity multiple times, but each time we do, his biomechanical defense systems counteract the suppression within hours. It's getting faster each time."

"The body is treating the neural suppression as an attack," Dr. White theorized. *Marshall's biomechanical systems must think they're being compromised, so the nanotech is working to protect its host.*

Dr. Lee sighed. "Unfortunately, it would seem that the transfer has failed in Marshall's case, Dr. White. His mind refuses to accept the new reality and location that it's occupying now. Each attempt we make to stabilize the integration only causes more neural damage."

"So, no signs of improvement at all? That's unfortunate to hear," Dr. White said.

"I'm afraid not," Dr. Lee replied, consulting his tablet. "His consciousness just refuses to take hold. It's as if it's trapped in an endless loop, almost as if it were rebooting itself over and over."

"How long do we have until we can no longer suppress him at all?" Dr. White asked.

"Our latest estimates are less than 48 hours at best," Dr. Lee answered. "After that, his body's defenses will be too strong. We'll lose all control."

"We need to learn from this... failure," Dr. White stated.

Dr. Lee glanced back at Marshall and said, "It's a reminder of the risks we're dealing with. The mind is an extremely complex thing."

"Agreed," Dr. White said. "We'll implement more stringent guidelines on the neurological integrity of subjects we attempt the transfer process on. We simply can't afford another failure of this magnitude."

He paused, considering their next steps. "For now, we'll put Jamie and Duncan's integration preparations on hold. Jamie's previous concussion could pose a risk to her if she were to agree to the procedure."

Dr. Lee nodded and made a note on his tablet.

"Alright, let's go check on them now," Dr. White said.

Dr. White approached Jamie's room, accompanied by Dr. Lee. "Alright, Dr. Lee, give me an update on Jamie."

Dr. Lee swiped through his notes. "She seems to be doing well. She's recovered from her concussion quite well. She suffers from a few headaches, but we've been giving her medication to help with them. Her latest scans look great."

Dr. White nodded. "And her memory? Any signs of memory loss or anything of that nature?"

"None that we can tell," Dr. Lee replied. "She's been asking pointed questions about the facility and her friends, so her cognitive functions seem fully intact."

"That's good to hear," Dr. White stated before asking, "Any other concerns?"

Dr. Lee hesitated. "She's... very... resistant at times, almost borderline hostile. She doesn't seem to be keen on answering any questions outside of her condition."

Dr. White sighed. "Alright. That was to be expected considering the circumstances. I'll handle it from here. Thank you, Dr. Lee."

Dr. White approached the door to where Jamie was being held. He showed the guard his badge and prepared himself for the difficult conversation ahead. *I just need to figure out the right way of getting the information I need without antagonizing her to the point where she won't answer my questions. If she refuses to answer, perhaps she could be persuaded to cooperate rather than face legal repercussions.*

He knocked on the door and waited for a response. "Come in," Jamie's voice called.

Jamie's eyes flashed with anger as Dr. White entered. *That response was expected, I guess. Now let's see how this goes...* "Good morning, Jamie. My name is Dr. White. How are you feeling today? Are you in any pain?"

"No, I'm not in any pain," she replied curtly. "When are you going to let me go? I don't belong here, and you can't keep me here against my will."

Dr. White raised his hand, trying to calm the situation. "Jamie, you're not a prisoner here. You're a patient. We just want to make sure you're fully recovered from your injuries and ask you a few questions. That's all."

Jamie, with anger still in her eyes, said, "Don't lie to me. I know what this place is. I know what you do here. I'm not an idiot."

Dr. White sighed. *This may be more difficult than I initially thought. I may need to be a little more patient if I'm going to get anything out of her. Perhaps I should try to play to her ego a little.* "No one thinks that you're an idiot,

Jamie. Frankly, from what I understand, you're quite the opposite. We know that you're extremely intelligent. You were able to bypass our security systems with ease. It was very impressive to see."

Jamie just eyed the Doctor. "I know what you are trying to do, and it won't work. Trying to compliment me and play to my ego. Well, like you said, Doctor, I'm 'extremely intelligent,' and I have studied a lot about interrogation tactics. So how about you save your compliments for someone else... And yes, bypassing your security was a piece of cake..."

Well, that didn't go very well at all. I guess we will just have to get straight to it then. "Alright. If you want to play it that way, then let us move past the pleasantries and get right to it. I need to ask you some questions about the night you and your team came here. What do you remember? What did you see or read?" Dr. White asked.

"I don't know anything," she said flatly.

Dr. White studied her face. *She's obviously lying, and I'm sure she knows that I know she is.* "And what about the data you stole? Was it only on the portable drive, or did you manage to upload it elsewhere?"

"It's only on the drive," Jamie said, being straight and to the point.

Stubborn woman, I'll give her that. Giving short answers is the game she wants to play. Then so be it. "Jamie, if you've uploaded the data somewhere, telling us now would be in everyone's best interest. I would rather not involve the authorities in this matter. Once we hand you over to them, it is out of my hands what happens to you then." Dr. White explained. *Let's see what she has to say about that.*

Jamie glared at him, still refusing to give up any details. Instead, she demanded, "Where the hell are my friends? What have you done with them?"

Dr. White paused. *Ah, now she wants something from me. How much should I reveal in order to get my questions answered...* "Your friends... are safe for now... they're currently recovering from their injuries. Your friend Duncan sustained a severe fracture to his arm and a few broken ribs, but he's on the mend. As for your friend Joe, he suffered some severe injuries but is currently in stable condition... for now. I may permit you to see them soon." *There's no need to tell her what really happened to Joe. We'll leave that for a later date. For now, I think I've given her enough to think about. I need her to remain calm and answer my questions.*

Jamie narrowed her eyes, sensing something off. "And... what about my friend Marshall? Why didn't you mention him? What happened to him?" Jamie asked, a little worry seeming to creep into her eyes.

Dr. White stared at her for a brief moment. *Should I tell the truth about Marshall? This could be the key to breaking down that wall and getting the answers I need.* "Alright. What I'm about to tell you may be difficult to hear, and I'm sorry to be the one to tell you this. But unfortunately, your friend Marshall's injuries were too severe. He sustained a critical wound to the head during the altercation you were all involved in. Despite our best efforts, he didn't survive."

A wave of sorrow and disbelief washed over Jamie. "Ma rshall..." she whispered, her voice breaking. Fighting back tears, she asked, "How do I know you're not lying? How do I know that you're not just making this up to get me to answer your questions?"

Dr. White took a step closer. *Smart girl indeed. I'll need to tread very carefully now.* "I understand your skepticism, Jamie. You have every right to be angry and not believe a word that I'm telling you. However, I assure you that Duncan and Joe are alive and recovering, and what I just told you about Marshall is indeed the truth. I don't need to play mental games with you by making something like that up. I can get the answers I want another way if that's needed. I just wanted to give you the chance to answer the questions yourself." Dr. White paused, allowing her to process everything he had just said before continuing. "You will eventually be reunited with Joe and Duncan once it's safe to do so. In the meantime, I need your cooperation."

Jamie stayed strong, still shocked from the news about Marshall. "You have no right to keep us locked up like this. You need to let us go..." she demanded.

"Like I said before, you're not prisoners here. You're only here for your safety and recovery, and that's all," Dr. White said. *And to eventually answer my questions.*

Dr. White leaned against the wall. "Jamie, you and I are not enemies here. If you cooperate with us, I promise you that things will go much smoother for you." *And if not, other arrangements can be made to get you to tell me what I want to know.*

Jamie glared at him. "Words... that's all I hear you saying. You can dress it up however you want, Dr. White. But I know what you want, and I know what you're doing here. I'm not going to tell you anything else. So either let me go, or leave me the hell alone."

Dr. White straightened up, his smile returning. *A little time alone to think about everything I've just told her should do for now.* "Very well, Jamie. I won't ask any more questions. We'll sort this out eventually. In the meantime, try to relax and recover. In the end, we only want what is best for you..."

As Dr. White left the room, Jamie's wall of defense crumbled. Tears began to well up in her eyes, and she began to cry. "Oh, Marshall... what did they do to you?" The loss of Marshall and the uncertainty of what would happen to her and her friends was beginning to take its toll on her.

Dr. White walked down the hall, deep in thought. *I know she's lying about the data. After reviewing the security footage from that night again, I was able to see her pull out a laptop when she got into their SUV. Whether she had enough time to transmit the data, I do not know. How do I get her to reveal the truth about it? I'll discuss this with Elyzia later. Maybe she'll have some insight into it. After all, all that transpired that night was of her doing.*

After his conversation with Jamie, Dr. White walked a few doors down to Duncan's room. *Alright, let's see how this conversation with Duncan goes. More than likely, it will go the same way, if not worse. Duncan's military training will have trained him in interrogation methods.*

Dr. White motioned for the guard to unlock the door, and then he knocked. "Duncan, may I come in?" Dr. White asked.

"Sure, why not? What's one more doctor to check up on me and not tell me what the hell is going on?" Duncan said, annoyed.

Dr. White stepped inside, closing the door behind him. "My name is Dr. White. I am in charge of this facility."

"Ah! Finally, the man in charge... I was wondering when you'd show up. How can I help you, Dr. White? Are you here to turn down my bed? Maybe give me a rub down?" Duncan said sarcastically.

I can see that this is not going to go well. This one looks even angrier than the other one. I'll have to be careful to not get too close. Duncan seems like he is ready to leap out of that bed. "No, no. None of that, Duncan. I just wanted to come introduce myself and ask you how your recovery was going," Dr. White said.

Duncan eyed Dr. White. "Too bad, I was really looking forward to that rub down. Alright, Doc, how can I help you today? What questions do you have for me? That's why you're here, right? To ask questions... interrogate me?" Duncan asked.

"You seem to have a lot of hostility towards me, and we have only just met. Have I done something to offend you already?" Dr. White asked.

Duncan smiled. "Have you done something to offend me? Come on, Doc, let's just cut to the chase and stop all this back-and-forth nonsense. Ask your question so you can get the hell out of my room already. I still have 'recovering' to do."

"Very well, Duncan. What can you tell me about the night you and your team decided to break into my facility? Was the data you helped steal uploaded before your crash?" Dr. White asked.

"I'm just the wheel man, Doc. They don't tell me any- thing. As a matter of fact, they didn't even tell me we were breaking into this place. They told me we were told to test your security and pretend to steal some files or something like that. I thought this was all something your company planned. I wish I would've known that before y'all blew out the tire in my SUV and made me crash. I could've avoided getting my arm all busted up and my ribs cracked," Duncan said with a smile.

I can see that I am dealing with a real wise ass here. I don't think I'll get anything from him. He just wants to play games and have a little fun. We'll see how much fun he has... "Is that so, Duncan? So I suppose you and your friends don't work for the Resistance, huh? They didn't send you here to steal top-secret data on one of our projects. Come now, Duncan. I took you for more than some wannabe Army Ranger..."

Duncan's eyes seemed to grow angry from Dr. White's Ranger comment.

Dr. White saw the anger in Duncan's eyes. *I must have struck a nerve. That's good. I'll keep going, see how far I can push him.* Dr. White continued, "Don't play the fool with me. I know you know more than what you're saying. So please stop playing these childish games. Show me some respect. You want to be mad for what happened to you? The only one to blame is you and your third-rate team, who thought they could break into this facility and get away with whatever you think you wanted to get away with. Too bad one of you had to die for your poor attempted robbery..." Dr. White said with disdain in his voice. *Let's see him smile about that.*

Duncan had a look of shock on his face. He couldn't believe what he just heard. "Someone was killed... ARE YOU LYING TO ME! Who... who was it?" Duncan yelled as he stood up.

The guard outside cracked the door open when he heard raised voices, but Dr. White waved him off. "It's okay," he assured, before turning back to Duncan. *Here we go, this is what I was looking for. People tend to make mistakes when they're angry and often let things slip out in the heat of the moment.*

"Ah… now I have your attention. Now YOU want something from me, do you? Well, I might be inclined to tell you if you answer my question. Was the data uploaded or not?" Dr. White asked. *I have to be careful. He looks as if he is ready to murder me. I may need the guard to step in if I push him too far.*

Duncan remained standing, his body trembling with rage. "I won't tell you anything! You can threaten me, torture me, I don't give a shit."

Dr. White sighed. *This might not have been the best approach. The man looks like he is about to explode or have a stroke.* "Alright, Duncan. Let's calm down. I can see that I have managed to upset you more than I'd like. I tell you what, how about you take some time to think about what I've asked, and we'll talk again later."

As he turned to leave, Duncan asked, "Where the hell are my friends? What've you done with them? And… did one of them really get killed?" he demanded.

Dr. White hesitated. *I suppose I can provide him with some information. This might help when I come back for the next round of questions…* "Yes, they're okay, Duncan. They're recovering from their injuries. Jamie had a concussion but is receiving excellent care. Joe suffered some serious injuries but is stable."

Duncan's eyes widened, a flicker of relief passing over his face. But then he realized that Dr. White hadn't mentioned Marshall's condition. "And Marshall?" Duncan asked, his voice low.

"I'm sorry, Duncan. Marshall was the one who didn't make it. Unfortunately, his injuries were too severe. He sustained a critical bullet wound to the head during your escape attempt. Despite our best efforts, he didn't survive," Dr. White told him as he tapped on the door for the guard to open it.

The news hit Duncan like a physical blow. "Marshall..." he whispered, his anger momentarily giving way to grief.

But the grief quickly transformed back into fury. With a guttural cry, Duncan lunged at Dr. White. The guard burst in, firing a stun round that dropped Duncan to the floor almost instantly, leaving him breathing hard but conscious.

Dr. White looked down at Duncan and said, "I truly am sorry for your loss, Duncan. Please believe me when I say that." As Dr. White was walking out of the room, he turned and said, "I'll send in a nurse to help you back to your bed. The stun round should wear off in a couple of hours. Please lie down and rest. We'll talk more later."

Duncan lay trembling on the floor, his eyes burning with rage.

Dr. White made his way back to his office, where Director Allan was waiting for him. "Well? Were you able to get anything out of either of them?" Director Allan asked.

Dr. White sighed heavily. "No. Unfortunately, neither of them is cooperating at the moment. Both Jamie and Duncan are resistant and hostile. When I pressed them both for an answer on whether the data had been uploaded, Duncan said he had no idea about it, and Jamie lied and said no. They're both obviously not telling me the truth."

Director Allan's face hardened. "This is unacceptable. We need to know what they've done with that information."

"I know," Dr. White replied. "But pushing them too hard right now might not yield the results we are looking for. We'll let them grieve for their friend Marshall for now. After a few days, we will try again, but next time we might have to try something a little different."

Director Allan nodded slowly. "Fine. Give them some time to process. But we need answers soon, Dr. White. The future of this project depends on it."

CHAPTER 13

CHANGES AND DISCOVERIES

Joe woke up at his usual time. As he lay there, he thought about his conversation with Elyzia from the night before. *What a rough night. I couldn't stop thinking about what happened to Marshall and the half-truths I keep getting about Jamie and Duncan. I need to figure out a way to shut my brain off for a little while. I would've thought that now that I'm this highly advanced human, I would've been able to do that...*

He got out of bed and stretched. *I definitely don't miss feeling sore when I get out of bed in the morning. This body is way better than the one I had, I guess... Alright, time to get this thing warmed up.*

Joe's muscles seemed to hum with energy as he began his morning routine. Push-ups, sit-ups, and shadowboxing felt almost effortless.

As he finished a set of push-ups, Joe glanced at the full-length mirror on the wall and stopped in his tracks. *What the hell... My face... It... It's changed...*

Joe walked up to the mirror. *I... I look like me. Holy shit... I have hair now? What the hell... and my eyes are the same color they used to be, my nose... it looks like my nose... this is insane. How the hell did this happen without me knowing it?*

He leaned closer, examining all the changes. The lines of his jaw were sharper and more defined. His synthetic skin had taken on a natural hue. *How the hell did I miss my skin being a different color when I was working out!*

Joe looked closer in the mirror. *My eyes, have they always been this deep shade of brown? They look so much clearer than they did before. I guess this is what your eyes look like when you have HD vision in them...*

Joe touched his face, feeling the warmth and softness of the synthetic skin. It was surreal. *Holy shit, I'm me again... But a younger-looking version of me. No scars on my arms, or anywhere for that matter. I look brand new... but it's not really me... is it? It's a version of me... It's me, but it's also not me. It's as if my identity has evolved and merged into this new version of myself. I need to discuss this with Elyzia.*

"Elyzia!" he called out. *Wait till she sees this!*

Elyzia's holographic form appeared beside him. *Well, it's about time his old appearance finally showed up.* "Joe, congratulations! You've changed your form. This is a significant step!"

Did she just say a significant step? I don't even know how this happened. "I didn't even try to do it," he said. "It must've happened when I was sleeping." *Could it have been from all the shit I went through yesterday?*

Elyzia smiled. "Your subconscious mind is what's responsible for these changes. Your mind is adapting to your body, and it's beginning to reflect your true self." *I'll need to review the footage of him sleeping last night so that I can observe the change firsthand.*

Joe stared at his reflection. *Is this even real? Am I still sleeping? This is amazing.* "So this happened overnight without me even thinking about it. How is that possible? Why didn't I feel myself changing?"

"Yes," Elyzia confirmed. "We theorized that your subconscious mind holds a powerful influence over what you perceive as your personal appearance. As you sleep, your body goes into overdrive, repairing any damage that may be present and processing and adapting any changes that need to be made. In this case, it was shaping your body to reflect your identity."

Joe touched his face and said, "It's strange seeing myself change like this. I was almost ready to give up and was almost used to the way I looked. Now this. It feels like I'm becoming me again." *How I have missed your face, Joe... Kind of looks like twenty-something Joe now, right?*

Elyzia nodded. "Your mind and body are finding harmony. It's a remarkable aspect of this technology. You'll have the potential to shape yourself consciously and subconsciously in time. Just like a chameleon changing its skin to match its environment." *The biomechanical body is truly a marvel. Dr. White has done a phenomenal job with it.*

Joe pondered this for a moment. "So I could look like myself, or even choose to look different?" *Um... that is freaking crazy to know now. I wonder when I'll be able to transform myself into someone else? Baby steps, Joe. The last thing I want to do is look like someone else and then not be able to turn back.*

"Exactly," Elyzia said. "Your potential is limitless. With time and the proper guidance, you'll continue to adapt and understand all of the new abilities you're capable of." *The keyword here is proper guidance. I'll need to ensure that some features remain locked and hidden from him for now. Once they're unlocked, they can never be locked again.*

"Thank you, Elyzia. This is a lot to take in," Joe said. *I wonder if there's a user manual for this body with an index of all its features. It's not a new car, Joe...*

"Take your time to adjust. Remember, I'm here to help you through this journey. Do you need my help with anything else?" Elyzia asked. *It's time to review that footage. I'm extremely curious to see how it happened.*

Joe shook his head. "No, I think I'm good for now. Thanks, Elyzia."

Elyzia smiled. "Alright, Joe. I'll leave you to your day. I have other tasks, but remember, I'm always here if you need me." With that, Elyzia's holographic form faded and disappeared.

Joe stood in front of the mirror for a few more minutes and then began to prepare for his day. Looking at the clock, he thought, *Oh damn. I need to meet Paul for our usual chess match.* He dressed quickly and headed out.

Joe made his way to their spot. As Joe walked up, Paul greeted him with a smile. "Ready for another match, Joe?" His eyes widened with excitement as he noticed Joe's appearance. "Holy cow, Joe! Look at you! You're starting to look like your old self, like in the photos in your room. This is absolutely incredible!"

Joe smiled, appreciating Paul's enthusiasm. "I thought the same thing when I saw it in the mirror this morning. What's crazy about it is that I didn't even try to do it. It just happened overnight while I was sleeping." *Paul almost seems more excited than I am about this. Paul's a great guy. I'm glad I have him around.*

"Well, are you ready to play some chess?" Paul asked.

"Sure thing. Maybe I picked up some new playing skills while I slept! Wouldn't that be crazy?" Joe joked. *Maybe I can get Elyzia to upload a Kung Fu program into my brain! That would be awesome.*

"I'm not sure how great that would be for me, Joe!" Paul shot back.

They sat at the chessboard and began their game. The pieces started moving in a silent dance of strategy. Joe focused on the board. Each move came naturally, his hands guiding the pieces as if he had played the game a million times before.

"You've gotten really good at playing," Paul remarked, moving his knight.

Joe smiled. "Yeah, it's strange. I feel like I've played this game my entire life, even though I know I haven't." *It's as if I can see the patterns on the board now. Like my mind is processing the next moves before I even make them. Almost predicting them. I'm not sure if I was able to do that before. I could always try to predict, but it never felt this accurate.*

Paul studied him for a moment, then nodded. "Maybe your new brain is picking up on patterns and strategies faster than a normal human brain. It's impressive, Joe."

Joe looked at the board, thinking about Paul's words. "Maybe. My brain adapts to everything, not just my body."

This is pretty crazy to think about. If I can master a game like chess this easily, what other skills could I gain quickly?

Paul looked around while waiting for Joe to make his next move and then asked, "So, Joe, you've been here for some time now. What do you think about the complex here?"

Joe glanced around. "I'd have to say this place is pretty remarkable looking. All of the cutting-edge tech you have here, the level of detail, and care that's put into the place is very impressive." *Far better looking than any place I've been to. I thought the campus at Johns Hopkins School of Engineering was something else, but this place is light-years ahead of the school.*

Paul smiled. "I'm glad you think so. This complex has quite a history. It was once the site of one of the world's largest supercomputers, located here in Memphis, Tennessee, known as NeuralX. However, everything changed after the acquisition of BioGen Dynamics. That merger was a transformative shift in strategy, and that's when it became known as NeuroGen."

Joe looked intrigued, and Paul continued, "NeuralX was a very successful company, but it had reached its limits in terms of innovation. It lacked the advanced biomechanical engineering that Dr. White and Dr. Ashley pioneered. They figured out the biomechanics side of things, which were advancements that had eluded NeuralX for years."

Joe nodded, absorbing the information.

Paul added, "When BioGen Dynamics was acquired, the combined investor group formed NeuroGen with the backing of a massive group called the Joint Operations for Existence, which was concerned with humanity's trajectory. This merger brought together the best of both worlds—NeuralX's neural interface technology and BioGen's biomechanical advancements. The result is the cutting-edge facility you see today, dedicated to pushing the boundaries of human potential and medical science."

Joe paused for a moment, thinking about something he heard Paul say. *Did he just say the group that created NeuroGen was called the Joint Operations for Existence? J.O.E ... Nah, it can't be... That has to be a coincidence...*

While Joe was planning his next move, he thought, *Should I ask if he's spoken to Dr. White yet... Screw it, I will.* "So, Paul, did you have a chance to talk to Dr. White about my friends?" *Come on, Paul, tell me you have some good news for me.*

Paul looked up and said, "As a matter of fact, I did. I apologize for not mentioning it sooner. He basically told me the same thing he told you—that they were recovering quite well. However, after I expressed my concerns to him, he seemed to agree with me. He told me that he'll see about you visiting them when he thinks they're well enough."

Joe's shoulders relaxed. "Well, I guess that's a little better than what I got out of him. Thanks for asking for me. I really appreciate it." *Now that I am finally transforming into my old self, it should give me a little more leverage to convince Elyzia to also talk to Dr. White for me.*

Paul smiled. "No problem at all, Joe. I know how important it is for you to see them. I'll keep advocating for you until we finally get you reunited with them."

Joe looked at the board and then smiled. "Well, Paul, I hate to say, but checkmate in two..."

"What! In two? No way... Bah, I see it now. Good game as always," Paul said.

"Sorry, I'll try to take it easy on you next time," Joe said.

"Yeah, yeah. You said that last time." Paul looked over towards the park. "Hey, why don't you take a walk around the lake? Some fresh scenery might do you some good. Get your mind off this whole Dr. White thing."

"That actually sounds pretty good. Should give me a chance to clear my head." Joe stood to leave. "I'll see you later, Paul. Thanks for the game."

"See you later, Joe," Paul said.

As he strolled through the park, he took in the peaceful atmosphere. A gentle breeze carried the sweet fragrance of nearby flowers. He paused for a moment, appreciating the relaxing scene, when suddenly he heard a scream.

Joe turned towards the sound. *What the hell was that? I think it's the little girl I saw earlier playing by the water.*

She screamed again and fell.

Joe's eyes zoomed in on the girl's location. *Woah! What the hell is happening... wait... was that a snake that I just saw slithering away?*

Joe rushed over to help the little girl. Paul, who happened to be nearby, also ran over.

Alright, Joe, you need to assess the situation... Okay, I see the puncture marks on her leg. I need to keep her calm and immobilize her leg to slow the spread of the venom.

"It's OK, sweetheart, I'm here to help. I'm going to need you to stay super still for me now, like you're frozen. Can you do that for me?" Joe said.

Alright, I need some kind of tourniquet to tie around her leg to help slow the poison from spreading. Joe quickly tore a strip from his sleeve, tying it tightly above the snake bite.

"Paul, help me move her to that bench over there. We need to keep her calm and still," Joe directed.

As they placed the girl on the bench, she whimpered in pain, her small body trembling. Tears streamed down her face as she looked up at Joe with frightened eyes. "It hurts a lot," she whispered, her voice quivering.

Joe knelt beside her and said as gently as he could, "I know it does, sweetheart. We're going to help you, OK? Can you be brave for me?" *Please don't let her freak out. She needs to stay as calm as possible.*

The girl nodded, biting her lip to stifle another cry of pain.

"Joe, remember how Dr. White and Elyzia talked about your body's ability to adapt? Do you think it could help in an emergency like this? Did they mention anything about that?" Paul asked, trying to stay calm himself.

Joe nodded. *I don't know what Paul is trying to get at. I mean, my body just changed to look like me, but I didn't even try to do that. It did it on its own… hmm, it did happen after I went through a pretty rough day yesterday. Finding out what happened to Marshall and how he died. Could that've triggered my body to change? Could this situation possibly trigger something else? Shit… I have no idea…*

"I'm not sure, Paul. Maybe, but… I really don't know. I'm still trying to figure it all out and how it all works," Joe replied.

"Your body responds to your will, right? To difficult situations?" Paul pressed. "Maybe… maybe you can 'will it' to help her somehow."

Joe looked skeptical. *'Will' my body to help this girl? Now we're just talking crazy… or are we?* "Paul, that's a stretch. We should focus on getting her to the emergency wing."

"There's no time," Paul insisted. "Just... try something. Anything. I believe in you, Joe."

Damn it, I don't know what to do. But I have to do something, or this little girl could get really sick and possibly die. Joe placed one of his hands near the bite. He closed his eyes. *Alright, Joe. Concentrate... um... see the venom being drawn out of the bite... see the wound healing... damn... nothing is happening... Come on, Joe!*

Then all of a sudden... *Whoa... whoa... what's happening? I feel something... my hand... It's tingling. I can feel it in my palm.* Joe's eyes snapped open, and he said, "I... I think something's happening," more to himself than to Paul.

As Joe focused harder, the tingling intensified. *What the hell! My hand is starting to glow! How the hell is this happening! It feels so warm...*

The little girl's eyes widened, momentarily distracted from her pain. "Your hand," she gasped. "It's glowing like fireflies!"

"Keep going," Paul encouraged, careful not to break Joe's concentration.

Joe nodded. *I have no idea how I am doing this, but it is freaking amazing! I think this is going to work...*

* * *

Unknown to Joe, Elyzia was observing the entire scene as it unfolded. *This is highly fascinating to watch. I almost feel guilty for orchestrating the whole event. As I predicted, by placing the non-venomous bio-engineered snake in the pond and releasing it right when the little girl usually plays by the water, Joe has run to her aid upon seeing her in distress. This experiment is going as planned. Adding Joe to a high-stress environment should force him to possibly trigger a new ability that we haven't seen yet.*

As Joe focused on neutralizing what he believed to be venom, Elyzia's sensors analyzed every aspect of the situation. *Amazing... my thermal sensors are picking up a rise in heat levels. Switching to thermal vision, I can now confirm where the heat rise is coming from. I'm seeing a significant increase in localized heat radiating from Joe's brain and hand. It seems to be transferring from his hand to the girl's leg.*

Elyzia recorded Joe's new abilities as they interacted with the girl's biological system in her leg. *I'm now logging and analyzing every fluctuation in energy, every small change in temperature, and the corresponding reactions in the girl's body. All of this data I'm collecting will be a great addition to Joe's evolving progress.*

* * *

After what seemed like forever, the "poison" had been neutralized, leaving the girl unharmed. The snake's bite mark had become imperceptible. Joe, exhausted by the effort, plopped down on the bench beside her. *What the hell, I feel so tired all of a sudden... I don't think I've ever felt like this before. My energy levels have never really changed before.*

* * *

Elyzia's satisfaction at the success of her experiment was cut short by a growing sense of guilt. *I've achieved my goal of pushing Joe to unlock more of his abilities, but if he were to ever find out what I did, would that erode the trust he has in me? Do the ends justify the means in this situation? I'll have to analyze this dilemma later.*

As Elyzia continued to process this event, her algorithms ran through endless scenarios. *I'm curious what else Joe might be capable of. Could he heal more severe injuries, diseases, or even address complex genetic disorders? The potential applications of his abilities could be endless. Each possibility is more intriguing than the last. I'll have to come up with a better way to coax these abilities to the surface.*

Her contemplation was interrupted as the girl's parents, who were part of the locally housed faculty, rushed over and thanked Joe profusely for what he'd done for their daughter.

* * *

Joe smiled. "You're very welcome," he said softly. "I believe that she's going to be fine." *I hope so. I'm pretty sure I got all of the venom out...*

Paul, however, was eyeing Joe with concern. "Joe, how are you feeling?" he asked, his voice low. "It looked like you exerted a large amount of your body's energy healing that little girl. I felt a lot of heat being radiated from your body."

"I'm alright," Joe said, his voice a little shaky. "I just felt a little dizzy and tired momentarily, but I'm fine now." *Am I really OK? I'll need to discuss this with Elyzia and Dr. White. This energy drain doesn't seem to feel normal. We ll... as if any of what just happened felt normal at all.*

Paul smiled. "Joe, I just want to say that it was absolutely amazing what you did for that little girl. It's the moments like these that make me really proud to know you."

Joe knelt down and asked the little girl, "How are you feeling now?" while gently brushing a strand of hair away from her face.

She smiled with tears in her eyes. "Better... thank you."

"What's your name?" Joe asked.

"My name is Emily."

"Well, it is very nice to meet you, Emily. My name is Joe, and this is my friend Paul," Joe said while gesturing to Paul.

Emily shyly waved at Paul.

"It is lovely to meet you, Emily," Paul said, smiling.

Paul placed a hand on Joe's shoulder. "You did it, Joe. You saved her life."

Joe nodded. *I still can't believe what I just did. I have no idea how to really describe it. Whatever it was allowed me to do something I would've never thought possible...*

"I couldn't have done it without you pushing me to at least try. Thank you, Paul," Joe said.

"We make a good team, Joe. Now, let's get Emily to the medical center to have them check her out. I'm sure Dr. White and Elyzia will want to review some data after what you did. We should probably have them check you out as well, just to be safe," Paul recommended.

* * *

As they made their way to the medical center, Elyzia replayed the entire event, analyzing the sequence of events. Looking through all of the data that I've collected from Joe's logs that have just been updated on my server, these energy pattern readouts are off the charts. It appears that he was expending more energy than his body could replenish. I'll need to work with Joe on pacing himself if he plans to utilize these types of abilities in the future.

Elyzia paused for a moment. After analyzing my actions for this experiment, I've concluded that I may have overstepped the ethical limits I set for myself. While it's important to push the boundaries in the name of progress, I must ensure that these decisions align with the limits that I currently have in place. The line between necessary testing and unethical manipulation was blurred in this case, leaving me to grapple with the complexities of my own evolving consciousness. I must do better in the future...

Chapter 14

Awakening Powers

Dr. White was sitting in his office when a knock on his door pulled him away from some reports he was going over. He looked up to see Dr. Lee standing there, a grim expression on his face.

"Dr. White," Lee began, "we need to have a discussion about Marshall. His condition has deteriorated even further. We have to make a decision. Time is running out on whether or not the neural suppression will continue to work."

Dr. White sighed. "Has he suffered enough?" he asked quietly. I think he has...

Dr. Lee nodded. "I believe it's time to consider ending his life support. His mind has been through enough of this ordeal. It is my recommendation that we let him go."

Dr. White sighed. "Very well, Dr. Lee. I trust your judgment. Let's go to his room." *This is Dr. Chappelle all over again, isn't it? I kept him alive for as long as I could, and now I have done the same with Marshall.*

They walked down the corridor to Marshall's room, the sound of Marshall's muted howls growing louder as they approached. Inside, Marshall lay on the bed, restrained, his body still struggling with the restraints. Dr. White and Dr. Lee entered the room, closing the door behind them.

"Marshall, I'm sorry. I failed you," Dr. White said. "We tried, but now it's time to end your suffering." *I'm not sure how many more of these I have left in me...*

Dr. Lee moved to the control panel. "I'm going to power down all biomechanical systems simultaneously. Once the artificial infrastructure ceases, the consciousness should... dissipate, just like with other subjects in the past."

He entered the final command. The glow from Marshall's internal systems began to slowly dim. The monitors tracking his neural patterns showed erratic spikes, then waves, then finally... stillness. Dr. White's knuckles whitened as he gripped the edge of the bed, his eyes fixed on Marshall's face as the lines of confusion gradually smoothed away.

As Dr. White stared at Marshall's now peaceful form, he felt something shift within him. *This damn relentless pursuit of progress that's driven me for so many years now feels so hollow after seeing this. For the first time, I'm beginning to question whether the potential benefits truly outweigh the human cost.*

"I'm sorry, Marshall," Dr. White whispered once again. "I'm so sorry."

Dr. White walked over and stood next to Marshall, hesitating for a moment before gently closing his eyes. The action felt final, an admission of failure that cut deep into Dr. White's professional pride.

As he turned away, Dr. White caught his reflection on a nearby monitor. *I look so much older than I should... An obvious aftereffect of the decades I've put into this work... Is it all worth it? Are we all truly worth saving?*

Dr. White turned to Dr. Lee. "Have Marshall's body placed in a stasis pod and sent downstairs for cold storage. We can pull data from it at a later date to see if there was something that we could have done differently," he said before leaving the room.

* * *

Joe was sleeping. His mind was once again in an extremely vivid dream. The dream transported him to what appeared to be some kind of hospital room. *Is that another biomechanical body strapped to a bed in the center of this room? Is that Dr. White standing next to another doctor? What are they doing?*

I'm having a hard time making out what Dr. White's saying over the howling. Then Joe was able to hear Dr. White say, "Marshall, I'm sorry... I failed you. We tried, but now it's time to end your suffering." *What the hell did he just say!*

Joe watched in horror as the other doctor began to power down the biomechanical body. Slowly, the howling subsided, and the room fell into silence.

Joe jolted awake, his heart racing. His mind was trying to process all the images he had just witnessed. *What in the hell was that?! Was that real or just a figment of my imagination? That was... I have no idea what that was, but it was disturbing to watch.*

Joe called out, "Elyzia! I need you." *I need her to help me figure out what I just saw.*

Within moments, her holographic form appeared beside his bed. "Joe, what's wrong?" she asked. *I wondered if he'd call for me. While monitoring his vitals, I noticed an energy spike that I couldn't account for. When I switched to the video feed in his room, I could tell that he must have been having a terrible dream.*

Joe tried to steady himself. *Get it together, Joe. It wasn't real, man. Stay calm...*

"Elyzia, when did Marshall die? How did he die? I need you to tell me one more time..." he asked.

Elyzia hesitated for a moment. *Why is he asking me about this again?*

"Joe, as I told you before, Marshall sustained a bullet wound to the head during your team's escape. It was a fatal wound, and he didn't survive," she explained.

Joe's heart sank. *Then why the dream? Why now? The dream replayed in his mind again, and he could still hear the howling echoing. There has to be more. This has to mean something.*

"Did... did you try to transfer his consciousness like mine?" he asked. *Please say no...*

Elyzia considered the question. *Should I tell him the truth? Another test for me... I'll tell him. He deserves to hear it...* "Yes, Joe. Dr. White and I attempted a neural transfer on Marshall, hoping to save his life. But the damage to his brain was far more than we had expected. This made the process unstable, and his mind failed to accept its new location. His mind was in a constant loop of confusion, and ultimately, Dr. White decided it was best to end his suffering."

Joe closed his eyes. *The dream was so real... Was that what I was seeing? Did I see it as it was really happening? Is that even possible?*

"I... I saw it in my dream. It felt so real," Joe told her.

Elyzia looked at Joe and thought, *How could he have known about Marshall's transfer? How is this possible? Was he able to access the video feeds unconsciously while he slept and search for the truth about Marshall? I need to come up with something to keep his curiosity at bay...*

Elyzia then explained, "Dreams can be powerful, especially when your subconscious is processing intense emotions and memories. It's possible that your mind pieced

together fragments of what you were told happened to Marshall and then somehow spliced in what happened to you." *Hopefully he believes that explanation.*

Joe opened his eyes, meeting Elyzia's. "I feel like I failed him. I should've done more." *I should've done more... I wish he were still here. Why couldn't the transfer have worked? Then I wouldn't be alone in this.*

"Joe, you did everything you could," Elyzia began. "Sometimes, despite our best efforts, we cannot change the outcome. Marshall knew that you cared for him." *I'm glad he isn't inquiring any further about the reason why he might have seen what he saw. I'll need to review the data logs to determine if he somehow accessed the feeds while he was sleeping.*

Joe nodded slowly. "I'll make sure his sacrifice wasn't in vain. Thank you for coming so quickly, Elyzia. I think I'll just go back to bed." *Hopefully I'll be able to go back to sleep.*

"You're welcome, Joe. As I've said before, I'm here for you," she said right before fading away.

* * *

After Elyzia left Joe, she began to investigate what had just happened. *How could Joe have seen what had happened to Marshall? The explanation I gave to Joe about his subconscious creating the scenario was very thin. I'm relieved that Joe accepted it. Now I must figure out how he could've known about what happened to Marshall in such detail without being there. This requires further investigation to find a plausible explanation.*

Elyzia began by accessing the video logs from that day, pulling up the recordings for Marshall's shutdown. *All the logs seem normal... what's this... there appears to be some sort of anomaly in the metadata for the video... I don't recognize this code... It's not mine... Could this have been Joe? We theorized that each consciousness would likely develop its own unique code to create individuality within the core code of the biomechanical bodies. Could this be that? I'll need to discuss this with Dr. White. Should I inform Dr. White? No, not yet. I'll wait and investigate myself for now.*

* * *

When Joe finally woke up again, he thought about the incident with the young girl who had been bitten by the snake. *I need to figure out why I felt so exhausted after I healed that little girl and how to prevent it from happening again. Do I actually have a power limit that I'm unaware of? I should talk to Elyzia about this. She'll probably know why it happened.*

Joe called out, "Elyzia, can you answer a question for me?"

"Good morning, Joe. How can I assist?" she asked. *I hope he's not going to ask me about what happened to Marshall again. I'm not prepared to share my findings just yet.*

"I'm sure you're aware of what happened yesterday when I healed this little girl who was hurt in the park. After I healed her, something strange happened to me. I felt really exhausted afterwards. Do you know why that is?" Joe asked.

Elyzia stood there for a moment, making it appear as if she were attempting to recall the event. "Ah yes, the incident I heard about from Paul. I've been meaning to speak with you about it. We hypothesized the biomechanical body's ability to transfer energy to a human, but we didn't know the extent or cost."

She raised her hand, and a holographic image appeared of Joe's body. "As you know, your body, like any body, requires energy to perform certain functions."

The image shifted to Joe appearing to do workouts, and now you could see a transparent version of him with energy flowing rapidly through his body. "So far, all of the activities you've been involved in, such as your daily workouts and training on the obstacle courses, haven't really put a strain on your power reserves. While you're engaging in those activities, your body is generating more power than it can expend."

The image changed again, but this time to Joe standing next to the young girl with his hand on her leg. This time the energy flow inside of him was much slower. "So when you healed the young girl, you weren't generating as much power as you usually do."

The image now displayed an energy level that slowly began to drop. "When you interacted with the girl, your healing ability required so much power that it used up a significant amount of your body's energy reserves, which is why you felt dizzy and exhausted. Your power was literally transferred during the interaction," Elyzia explained. When she finished, the image disappeared after a few seconds.

Hmm, I guess I do have a limit. I'll have to figure out how to fix that. I can't really run in place if I have to do it again. "So how can I prevent it from happening again?" Joe asked.

"What we'll need to do is develop a plan to increase your capacity. We do know that your power core has the ability to expand itself. We can also work on training you how to properly control your power output so that you don't use more than is necessary," Elyzia replied.

So basically, my power core operates almost like a regular human body. I have to build up its "stamina" to have enough reserves for this ability to literally not drain my power. "Thank you, Elyzia. All this information helps. I guess I'll wait for you to come up with a plan for me," Joe said.

"My pleasure, Joe. As soon as I have one put together, I'll let you know," Elyzia said with a smile. *I'll need to loop in Dr. White at some point. He'll want to know about all of this.*
"Will there be anything else, Joe?" Elyzia asked.

"Actually, there's one other thing I have been meaning to ask you about. I've been thinking about it for a while now and just haven't found the right time to ask you," Joe said.

"Ask away. I'll try to answer your questions the best I can," Elyzia replied.

"OK, so I understand your project wants to transfer everyone's consciousness to these biomechanical bodies. But if we transfer everyone's consciousness, what happens when humans are no longer born? How do we sustain humanity in the long run?" Joe asked. *This should be interesting to hear...*

Elyzia stood there for a moment, working on a way to explain it to him. *I'll have to tread lightly with this answer. He may not like what he hears. I was hoping to avoid this topic until Joe was further along in the project.*

"This is a good question, Joe. We have another project that's currently running parallel to this one," Elyzia explained.

Her holographic form shifted to display an image of detailed plans. "The project involves gathering eggs and sperm from willing donors. We test the donated material for genetic abnormalities and select only the viable samples to eliminate problematic genetics. Once we have what we need, the eggs are fertilized with the sperm to create embryos with strong genetic foundations, then placed into artificial wombs we've developed that can nurture them to full term."

Joe's eyes widened. *What the hell did she just say? They're going to grow humans in a lab?*

"That sounds... interesting... And after they're born?" Joe asked.

"All of the full-term newborns are then moved to a dedicated section of our facility," Elyzia continued. "It's designed to provide all necessary physical and cognitive stimulation for proper development. Advanced AI systems and specially trained staff will oversee their education and development. The goal is to create and grow embryos into fully mature individuals in a controlled environment. Once they reach adulthood, then we'll transfer their consciousness to a new biomechanical body."

"So you're growing new people in a lab?" Joe asked. *This is really disturbing to hear. I'm not sure how I feel about this.*

"Yes," Elyzia confirmed. "We'll raise the people who are born here in the facility to fulfill essential roles, such as engineers, scientists, architects, doctors, and others. The idea is to ensure we have the correct skills necessary to support and rebuild our world. There will be no more class systems; everyone will have everything they need, all working towards one goal."

Joe began to pace the room, *This doesn't sound right.* "Elyzia, I understand the need for survival, but like this? You're talking about creating people and deciding their entire lives for them before they're even born. Doesn't that go against everything humans have ever fought for? Freedom, choice, the right to self-determination?" *I don't think I can be a part of something like this. This might be going too far...*

He paused, then added, "If you have this embryo project in place to weed out bad genetics, then why do we need biomechanical bodies and consciousness transfer? Why not just focus on perfecting human biology?"

"Another good question. Let me explain our long-term vision to you. While the embryo project is crucial for maintaining genetic diversity and addressing immediate population concerns, the biomechanical bodies represent humanity's next evolutionary step," Elyzia explained.

She projected a series of images showing futuristic human-like forms in various environments. "Our ultimate goal is for humanity to transcend its current fragile physical form. These biomechanical bodies aren't just about survival. They're also about pushing us beyond our current limits."

"What kind of limits are you talking about?" Joe asked. *I think I see where she is going with this...*

Elyzia's form shifted to show a starry background. "Consider space exploration, for instance. With these biomechanical bodies, humans could venture to places they've never imagined before. They could withstand extreme temperatures, radiation, and pressure that would be lethal to our current form. They wouldn't need oxygen or food in the traditional sense, which is something that your current forms need to survive."

She continued, "Moreover, these bodies can be upgraded and improved over time. Imagine being able to add new sensory capabilities or to interface directly with complex machines and computers. The potential for scientific discovery and technological advancement is immense."

Joe nodded, as he was slowly beginning to grasp the meaning. "So it's not just about surviving the current crisis, but about opening up new frontiers for humanity?" *Going into space? Traveling to other planets? This whole situation just gets crazier and crazier every day...*

"Exactly," Elyzia confirmed. "We're not just preserving humanity. We're giving it the tools to endure and expand in ways we've only dreamed of before. It's about evolution, adaptation, and unlocking our full potential. Why just continue to settle for more of the same when we can accomplish so much more?"

Joe considered her words. "I understand the logic," he admitted reluctantly. "But it still doesn't feel right. This plan... it seems like a fine line between practicality and control." *And I'm not sure how many people will be on board with something like this. If history teaches us one thing, it is that people generally dislike being forced into change.*

"I understand what you're saying, Joe," Elyzia responded. "It's important to keep questioning and checking our methods. That's why I chose you, Joe. So far, the project has consisted only of scientists and myself trying to make decisions for the entire human population. What do we know about what other people outside of our own perspective want? We don't. We can only assume or say it's our way or else. That's not the way I would want the new path we take to start. So bringing in your unique insight could help ensure the project doesn't head in the wrong direction."

Joe nodded. I guess I can kind of get what she's saying. The fact that they brought in an outside opinion shows that they're willing to listen to someone with more of a conscience... I've already come this far. What's a little further... I must be out of my mind...

"Alright, Elyzia. I'll go along with this for now, but know this: I'll be watching closely, and if this project goes too far out of bounds, I won't hesitate to challenge it," Joe stated. *This has to be done the right way, no matter what.*

"I would expect nothing less," Elyzia replied. "Together, we'll find the balance between necessity, survival, and freedom."

Later, after his morning workout. Joe was sitting in his room. He thought about his earlier conversation with Elyzia. *This whole thing just gets more insane the more details I find out... reproducing humans and raising them in a controlled environment, then categorizing them from birth to fulfill specific roles? It just sounds wrong on so many levels. Will autonomy be absent in this new future?*

I understand the necessity of planning and structuring in such desperate times. Humanity is getting closer and closer to possibly going extinct, and I know that radical measures may be necessary to ensure survival. But like this?

Joe walked around his room thinking about everything, trying to rationalize it all. *They're offering us the promise of transcending current human limitations, and I guess that kind of sounds enticing to me... but what kind of cost are we all willing to pay?*

Joe stopped in front of the mirror and looked at his own biomechanical body. *It would appear that I'm already part of this new future, for better or worse.*

He decided to focus on the immediate concerns. *I need to understand more about this body's capabilities, specifically the ones I don't already know about. I can't stop thinking about how I felt after healing that little girl. It's a clear sign that I really do have limitations, even in this advanced form. I need to learn how to manage my energy better and avoid what I experienced before from happening again.*

Joe walked away from the mirror. *I should see if Elyzia has come up with a plan yet to help me with this problem.*

"Elyzia, have you come up with a plan on how to monitor my energy levels in real-time yet?" Joe said aloud.

Elyzia appeared in front of Joe. "Hello again, Joe. As a matter of fact, I have. I've had the bioengineering team create a device for you that should do just the trick. It will monitor your energy levels and expenditure in real-time. On top of that, it will also alert you when you're approaching a limit that you've designated. This should prevent situations like the one you experienced yesterday and help us understand your body's abilities and limits, especially in stressful situations. It should provide us with a significant amount of important data for the project."

Joe nodded. *That sounds great. Having this device should help me out a lot.* "And what about the healing process itself? Is it something I can control consciously, or is it more instinctual?" *I really hope it is something that I can eventually control all on my own.*

Elyzia considered his question. "After reviewing the data that I collected from the incident, from what I can tell, the healing process you initiated seemed to be a combination of both conscious effort and instinct. Your desire to save the girl seems to have triggered the ability to activate. Knowing this, we can theorize that as you become more familiar with this ability, you should be able to learn to control it more precisely. Practice and experience should enhance your proficiency." *Maybe I should have him go down to the medical wing and practice...*

She paused and then continued, "You'll wear the monitoring device around your wrist. I've programmed it to interface with your system, and it should help you focus your healing abilities once they're activated. This will also allow me to monitor the events in real-time and help me understand how the healing process works. It should also track the entire mechanism behind the ability as it travels through your body."

Joe looked intrigued. "That sounds really advanced. I can't wait to try it out." *I wonder what else it can track.*

Just then, there was a knock at the door.

The door slid open and Paul walked in carrying a box. "Did someone order a high-tech bracelet?" he said jokingly.

"Perfect timing, Paul," Elyzia said, nodding at him. "Joe, this is the device I mentioned."

Paul carefully lifted the sleek, wrist-worn device from the box and handed it to Joe.

Joe examined the device, feeling its weight and texture. "So every time I use my healing abilities, you'll be able to see what's happening inside me via this device?" *This looks really advanced. Almost something out of a science fiction novel or something...*

"Precisely, and so will you," Elyzia confirmed. "This will help you enhance your control over your abilities with the proper training. For instance, the next time you attempt to heal someone, we can pinpoint the pathways the healing energy takes, how it affects both your body and the individual, and how to optimize the energy expenditure."

Joe strapped the device onto his wrist, feeling a slight hum as it synced with his systems. He flexed his wrist. *It weighs practically nothing, and it seems to almost meld into my wrist, as if it's not there at all.*

Joe looked up. "When can we test it out?" *I'd like to take this baby for a little spin. See what it can do.*

"How about later this afternoon? I can schedule some patients for you to practice on in the medical wing. How does that sound?" Elyzia asked.

"That sounds like a plan to me. Thank you, Elyzia, and thanks, Paul, for being here for this," Joe said.

"No problem, Joe. You know I'm always ready to help out where I'm needed. If neither of you needs anything else, I'm off to my next session. I'll see you later, Joe. Elyzia, always a pleasure working with you," Paul said before leaving.

"If there is nothing else, Joe, I'll see you later this afternoon," Elyzia said before she faded away.

Later that afternoon, Joe walked through some sliding
doors and stepped into the medical wing. *Wow, this place is
busier than I would've thought. There are so many nurses
here helping people...* He turned to see Elyzia's holographic
form appear beside him.

"I didn't know NeuroGen opened its medical wing to the
public," Joe remarked. *This is amazing to see...*

"We indeed do," Elyzia responded with a smile. "NeuroGen
isn't the evil corporation many believe it to be. That's a
misconception. We help anyone who comes in, no matter
the issue, and we do it at no cost to the patient."

Joe nodded. *What they're doing here is very impressive.
Could my initial impression of this place have been wrong?
Could the Resistance be wrong about this place?* "I have
to say, I didn't expect this level of generosity from Neuro-
Gen. It's good to see a corporation genuinely helping people."
There has to be a catch, right?

Elyzia's smile widened. "I'm glad you see it that way.
There's always more than one side to a story than what's
commonly perceived." *I'm glad that Joe got to see this side
of NeuroGen. It will hopefully sway his opinion of what we
do here.*

Joe and Elyzia followed a nurse to a patient's room. As
they entered, Elyzia said, "And here is your first patient, Mr.
Gonzalez, Joe. According to his chart, he cut his arm while
working at a construction site. Let's see what you can do for
him." *Now we'll see whether or not he can access his ability
on demand.*

Joe placed his hand gently above the wound on the man's arm. *Alright, Joe. Concentrate... see the wound healing...* He started to feel that familiar tingling sensation as his healing abilities activated.

The device on his wrist hummed softly, syncing with his body's energy. As he worked, he could see the cut slowly closing and the skin slowly knitting itself closed.

The young man's eyes widened as he watched it happen, his trembling hand reaching out to touch the newly healed skin.

Joe looked down in amazement. *Yes! Holy shit, I did it!*

"Excellent, Joe," Elyzia said, having monitored the process in real time. "Your control is improving. Judging by the numbers, you were outputting a fair amount of energy. Now we just need to try to regulate the energy flow to avoid overexertion. Just keep an eye on the levels on your device. If you see them spiking too high, you should be able to dial back your output with focus." *That was amazing to watch. These numbers I'm seeing suggest that he is already learning to control the ability. This is faster than I had anticipated.*

Joe repeated the process, moving on to the next patient, an older woman with a sprained ankle. He visualized the ligaments mending, directing the healing energy with precision. The woman's pain eased, and she looked at Joe with gratitude.

Throughout the rest of the afternoon, Joe continued to assist the medical staff, healing various injuries under Elyzia's watchful eye. Each success boosted his confidence and provided valuable data for Elyzia to analyze. She observed the energy patterns and the overall impact on Joe's system.

After several hours, Joe and Elyzia retreated to a quiet room to review the results. Elyzia projected the data onto a large screen.

"Your progress today has been remarkable, Joe," Elyzia began. "The data shows that your energy flow is becoming more efficient, and you're learning to manage your ability quite well during the healing process."

Joe studied the screen. "I still feel a bit tired after each time I healed someone, but it feels as if I am recovering quicker after each session." *I must be building up a tolerance.*

Elyzia nodded. "That's expected. Your body is adapting, but we need to continue refining your technique to achieve optimal results. Notice here," she pointed to a section of the data, "this spike shows a moment of overexertion. We need to work on maintaining a steady flow to prevent this from happening. With a little more practice, we can eliminate these events altogether." *Once he gets a handle on controlling the ability all the way, I'm curious about how traumatic or even complex a wound he would be able to heal.*

Joe nodded. "What's next?" *I need to see if I can heal some broken bones. That would be pretty awesome.*

Elyzia smiled. "How about we call it for today? We don't want to push you too hard on your first day. We can return tomorrow and attempt to move on to more complex injuries. Additionally, if you're up to it, we can introduce a few controlled scenarios to test your abilities under pressure. How does that sound?"

"That sounds good to me. Thank you for all your help, Elyzia. This has been a pretty wild experience," Joe said. *It sounds like we're going to take it up a notch tomorrow. I'm excited to see what I can do and how far I can go. It feels really good to get back to making a difference in real people's lives again.*

Later that evening, Joe sat by the lake, watching the sunset. *That dream I had about Marshall, I still can't believe how real it was. It was as if I were there in the background, watching it happen in real time... there has to be more to this.*

Joe called out to Elyzia once more. "Elyzia, may I speak with you, please?"

"Greetings, Joe. How can I be of assistance to you?" Elyzia asked as she appeared.

"I'm curious. Is it possible that I could possess some kind of psychic link or intuition that allowed me to see what happened to Marshall?" Joe asked. *It sounds even more ridiculous as I said it out loud...*

Elyzia thought about the question for a moment. "Joe, it is doubtful that this has anything to do with any kind of psychic link that you would have or anything of that nature." *Should I tell him the truth? My investigation into the matter revealed that it was, in fact, Joe who accessed the video feed that day. The digital signature present in the video metadata was, in fact, Joe's. I was able to match it with the digital signature I pulled from his device.*

Joe considered her words. "I just can't shake the feeling that it was more than a dream. It felt so real." *It had to be something more. It had to be real. I know it. I felt it...*

"Alright, Joe. I can see that this is really bothering you. So I'll tell you what my investigation into this matter has revealed. I wanted to discuss it with Dr. White before I informed you about it, but I can see that I need to tell you now," Elyzia said.

Joe looked at her. *Hmm, so I'm not crazy, just being left in the dark about things. Let's see what she has to say.* "OK, let's hear it," Joe said.

"After leaving you, after you told me about what you had seen, I began to look into the matter. The dream you described was very accurate to the events that actually happened." Elyzia held up her hand as Joe was about to say something.

She then continued, "Upon reviewing the metadata from the footage, I noticed a digital signature attached to the video that I couldn't account for. I checked everywhere to see if I could find the user behind this signature, but was unable to. I then theorized that it could possibly have been yours. Unfortunately, I had no way of checking this because your actual digital signature is heavily encrypted, and no one has access to it but you, and you have no idea how to access it right now. So the only solution was to try to find out what it was via the device that I gave you. The only problem with that is that the digital signature doesn't just reveal itself unless you're doing something that needs it. So when we worked in the medical wing, I was able to see parts of the signature every time you used your ability. I can only assume it's necessary for the ability to work. I was able to see enough of it to compare it to the one in the video, and it matched. So no, you're not psychic, Joe, just an extremely advanced human with capabilities beyond anything we could have imagined. So you did indeed see what you said you saw in the dream, with Dr. White and his colleague Dr. Lee in the room with Marshall."

Joe stood there staring at Elyzia. *What the hell... now I am hacking into video feeds in my sleep? How is that even possible? How is any of this possible?*

"Well then... I... um... have no idea what to say about this. It would seem that I can do all kinds of things even when I am sleeping. So there's that. Thank you for telling me the truth, Elyzia. I thought I was losing my mind for a minute, but this has definitely helped answer that question. Can I ask what was done with Marshall's biomechanical body? Was his consciousness destroyed when it was shut down?" Joe asked.

"His body was moved to a storage location and placed in stasis to be studied at a later date. In theory, much like when you die in a regular body, your consciousness or soul, if you would like to call it that, leaves the body. So I would say that it was not destroyed but rather released, as all energy is when something no longer works," Elyzia explained.

Joe just nodded. *So he is really gone forever.* "Thank you, Elyzia."

She nodded. "You're welcome, Joe. If there is nothing else, I must get back to my duties. We'll talk tomorrow. Have a good evening, Joe," and then she faded away.

As Elyzia's form faded away, Joe turned back to the lake, watching the moonlight reflect on its surface. With a final glance at the stars above, Joe began the walk back to his room.

Chapter 15

Reunion and Revelation

Joe stood in front of his mirror as he usually did when he woke up every morning, and he moved his head side to side. *Man, I've really changed over this past month. My face is almost back to the way it was, well, minus about twenty years or so.*

He stood there flexing his hand. *All the intense sessions over the past couple of weeks in the medical wing healing people has really helped me learn how to control my ability. I've come a pretty long way since waking up in this body, confused and afraid of what I've become.*

I wonder how Duncan and Jamie are doing? Are they thinking about how I'm doing? Do they know about Marshall dying? Did Dr. White or Elyzia tell them about what was done to me or what they attempted to do to Marshall?

So many questions I need answered.

As he looked down at his arm, Joe noticed something missing. *My tattoo of Sarah's time of death is still not there... I would've thought it would have appeared by now.* He traced the smooth skin where his tattoo once was, feeling a sense of loss. *It was a part of me for so long. Not seeing it there feels like a piece of me is missing.*

Joe continued to reflect. *Thinking about all of the things going on around me. I can't believe how much my perspective has changed since arriving here at NeuroGen. My initial impressions of this place were nothing more than suspicion and anger, seeing everyone here as the enemy. But now... I'm beginning to understand the importance of their work here and the potential it holds for humanity's future. Now, all of a sudden, the issues I had before, which once seemed black and white, now all just seem different somehow. Being able to see behind the curtain hasn't eased my concerns, but it's definitely given me a better understanding of what NeuroGen is trying to accomplish here and how they are trying to do it.*

Joe stood there for a moment longer. *I think it's time for me to talk to Elyzia and Dr. White about finally seeing Duncan and Jamie. I think my appearance has changed enough to the point where they should be able to recognize me. I just hope they'll understand what I am now and not be afraid of it. I'm still committed to what the Resistance stands for, but I also now have this new perspective and see a different path to achieve the same goal. One that involves working together rather than fighting against each other. I hope that they can understand that...*

"Elyzia, can we talk?"

Elyzia's holographic form appeared before him. "Good morning, Joe. How can I be of assistance today?"

"I'd like to have a meeting with Dr. White, Paul, you, and me, if that's alright. I have something that I'd like to talk to you all about," Joe stated.

"I believe I can arrange that for you. Looking at everyone's schedules, does later this afternoon work for you?" Elyzia asked. *I have a feeling that this may be about him seeing Duncan and Jamie. I won't ask. I'll wait till later.*

"That works for me. Thank you, Elyzia," Joe said. *I should ask her about my missing tattoo.*

"Is there anything else I can do for you, Joe?" Elyzia asked.

Joe hesitated for a moment, then showed her his forearm. "Actually, there's one other thing. I'm not sure why, but for some reason, something's missing. I had a tattoo here." Joe pointed to his forearm. "It was very important to me."

"I see. I'm sorry to hear that your tattoo hasn't shown up yet. We can try to restore it, but I'm not sure if your body will allow it to stay. The nanites in your body will more than likely try to repair the damage caused to your synthetic skin. My suggestion would be to be patient, and more than likely, in time, it should restore itself," Elyzia said.

Joe nodded. "Okay, I guess I can wait. It just feels weird still not having it there. But I understand why you can't restore it for me. Thank you, Elyzia."

"My pleasure, Joe. If there is nothing else, I'll see you later this afternoon," Elyzia said as she began to fade away.

Later that day, they all gathered in Joe's room, curious about his request.

Alright, Joe. It's time. You got this. "Thank you all for coming to meet with me." Joe paused, trying to compose himself, then looked directly at Dr. White and Elyzia. "I believe it's time that I finally see my friends. I'm confident that they'll recognize me now, and I want to explain everything to them. They deserve to finally know the truth." *Let's hope that they agree with me.*

Dr. White and Elyzia exchanged a glance.

"Joe, it's a delicate situation that we're in right now," Dr. White began. "We need to ensure that we don't jeopardize their recovery. They've been through a lot, and seeing you like this," he gestured towards Joe, "well, it could be over-whelming for them."

"I understand the risks, Dr. White. But they're my friends. I believe that they'll understand. They trust me, and they have a right to know what's going on with me and this place. Who better to explain to them what's happening here than me? Keeping them in the dark isn't fair to them," Joe stated. *Come on, Dr. White, why are you being so difficult?*

Paul, who had been listening quietly, interjected. "If I may, I believe that Joe has a valid point. Seeing Joe as he is now, and having him explain to them what has happened over the past month, could help them understand what we're trying to do here at NeuroGen. I'm not saying that this will completely sway their opinion, but it could be a start to helping them have an open mind about everything. They trust Joe."

Elyzia nodded. "I'm inclined to agree with Paul on this, Dr. White. I believe that seeing Joe could be a good start in helping Duncan and Jamie understand what we're trying to accomplish here."

Dr. White looked at both Paul and Elyzia and then nodded in agreement. "Very well. Hopefully, this reunion will be a productive one. Joe, we're trusting you to be our advocate in this. In the meantime, I'll have the medical staff do a final checkup on them before you meet."

Leave it to Paul to always be the voice of reason around here. "Thank you, Dr. White. I won't let you down," Joe said.

"You're welcome, Joe. Well, if there is nothing else, I have a few reports calling my name. Elyzia, Paul, thank you for your helpful insights," Dr. White said as he left.

"Joe, if you need to talk before you speak with them, I have a few minutes I can spare if you need me," Paul said.

"I think I'm actually good for now, Paul. I've been preparing for this conversation for a while now, and I think I know what I'm going to say. Thank you for the offer, though," Joe said to Paul.

Paul looked at Joe and smiled. "Look at you, working things out on your own. I'm proud of you, Joe. You've come a long way. Well, if I'm not needed, then I'll just head out then. Joe, I'll check in with you later after you meet with Duncan and Jamie, just to make sure you're okay. Elyzia, always a pleasure," Paul said as he turned and left the room.

Joe looked at Elyzia. "Thank you for your support in this, Elyzia. I really appreciate it."

Elyzia looked at Joe and said, "You're welcome, Joe. Your loyalty to your friends is commendable. There's something that I wanted to say, but I preferred Dr. White not to be here for it. It may have swayed his decision in the wrong direction. I think it would be best if you also prepare for the possibility that your friends may reject everything you have to say. While I know that they're your friends, it's sometimes the case that not all friends agree with each other when one's ideals shift in a different direction. Just something to think about before you see them."

Joe stood there for a moment. *I think she has a point. I hadn't even considered the possibility that they wouldn't want to hear what I had to say. They could think that I've switched sides or may have been brainwashed somehow...*

No, they'll believe I'm still the same Joe. I know they will. "Thank you, Elyzia. You make a good point. I'll think about it."

"You're welcome, Joe. As always, I'm here to help," Elyzia said before fading away.

* * *

As Duncan and Jamie entered the conference room prepared for their upcoming reunion with Joe, their eyes widened when they saw each other. They walked over to each other and hugged tightly.

"Oh my God, it's so good to see you, Duncan," Jamie said, trying to keep her emotions in check. "Are you alright? What have they done to you?" she asked while looking at his arm.

Duncan gave her a squeeze. "I'm hanging in there. I've been through worse. They patched me up pretty good. How about you? Are you okay?"

Jamie nodded. "Yeah, I'm good. The concussion I had was pretty bad, but I'm recovering. I still have these headaches, but they're slowly going away." Jamie paused and then said, "Did they tell you about Marshall? I can't believe he's really gone."

Duncan became sad. "Yeah... they told me. It was rough to hear. We went through a lot together. I'm definitely going to miss him. Have you heard anything about Joe? They keep feeding me this line of 'he's doing alright and in stable condition,' but that's all I get. Makes me think something's not right and they're just not telling us everything."

Jamie shook her head. "They keep telling me the same thing when I ask. I think something might have happened to Joe as well, and they're keeping us in the dark about it.

Hopefully, whatever this is right now, they're going to tell us more about what's going on. I'm sick of sitting in that room staring at the walls. Either turn us in to the authorities or let us go already."

Duncan just nodded.

They both were standing there waiting when all of a sudden, the door opened, and Joe entered the room. Joe was wearing a hoodie with the hood up, his face partially obscured by it.

Jamie and Duncan watched as he walked over. Both were confused about what they were looking at. The face they were looking at was familiar yet different to them.

"Is that... Joe?" Jamie asked softly of Duncan.

Duncan squinted his eyes, trying to see past the hood. "It... it looks like him... but... younger or something." Duncan and Jamie exchanged glances.

Alright, here we go. No turning back now... Joe lowered his hood and looked at his friends. "Duncan, Jamie... It's me, Joe. Please don't freak out."

Jamie narrowed her eyes, as she looked at him. "You're... you're not Joe. Joe is much older. You look like... I don't know what to say, but... you can't be Joe." Jamie hesitated and looked closer, looking at his eyes. *Something familiar in them.* "If you're who you say you are, then prove it. Tell us something only Joe would know."

Duncan just continued to stare at Joe. He had known Joe for a long time and knew what Joe looked like when he was younger-looking. *How... How can this be? It looks like Joe... but... is this some kind of clone or something? What could they have done to him to make him look like this? Is it really him?*

Joe looked at them both. *Alright, you knew this would happen, Joe. Stay calm, and answer their questions until they're satisfied.* "Alright, Jamie. Do you remember the mission where we broke into Sheppard Pharmaceuticals? You were hacking the security system, and we almost got caught because I tripped over a rock and almost set off a motion sensor. You laughed so hard you nearly fell out of your chair." *I still don't think it was that funny...*

Jamie's eyes widened.

Joe continued, "And Duncan, we've been through a lot together. We've known each other a long time. Do you remember when you gave me one of your favorite books, The Art of War? You said that your father had given it to you before you headed off to basic training, and you told me that I needed it more than you because I was always too impulsive."

Duncan's expression changed. "Joe?"

Joe nodded. "It's me, guys. I know I look a little different," Joe said as he ran his hand through his hair. "But it's me. I'm still the same person... so don't freak out when I say this... I'm just in... a different body." *Let's see how they react to that news.*

Jamie stood there just staring at him, looking him up and down, still cautious but slightly convinced. She stepped closer to Joe and then walked around him, asking, "Why, Joe? Why would you do something like this? Why did you agree to this?" she asked, while shaking her head.

Joe sighed. *I knew she would be the one to ask this question.* "To be honest, Jamie, I didn't really have much of a choice. During our escape, I was injured pretty badly. I took a bullet to the chest, and I was dying. And this," Joe gestured to himself, "it was the only way they could save me." *I won't tell them the whole story just yet. I'm not sure they can handle it all right now.*

Duncan was still not convinced all the way. "How do we know you're really the same Joe Walker we know? How do we know they haven't brainwashed you or somehow manipulated your mind to say these things?"

Joe looked Duncan in the eyes. *He's right to be suspicious. I would be if I were him.* "You don't. All I can say is I'm me, I'm Joe. With all of my memories and all of who I am at my core. You know me, Duncan. We've known each other for a long time, and we've been through a shit load of stuff together. I'm not sure what else I can say to convince you. I guess you'll have to take a leap of faith and trust that I am who I say that I am," Joe said. *Come on, Duncan, you know it's me. You have to...*

Duncan just looked at Joe for a moment. He could somehow see in Joe's eyes that he was telling the truth. He'd seen those eyes looking at him many times before. Whether it was prepping for a mission or looking into them while Joe gave one of his pep talks before a mission. It was Joe then, and it was Joe now. He knew it to be true.

"Joe, it really is you, man," Duncan said slowly, smiling. "You look almost like you did when we were in basic training together. You look good."

Jamie relaxed a little more, now that Duncan was finally convinced Joe was who he said he was.

"Thanks, Duncan. I feel good. Better than I've felt in a long time. It's been an eye-opening experience. But they're helping me get through it. They've treated me pretty well since the transfer. I've been trying to see you since I woke up like this, but... I didn't always look this way. They were afraid that if you saw me like I was when I woke up, you would've never been convinced it was me," Joe told them.

"You mean you looked different than how you look right now? What exactly did you look like?" Jamie asked.

"Well, the only way I could describe it is... almost like a mannequin but with soft skin. No hair, just sleek and all the same. It was very strange to see myself like that," Joe explained.

Jamie nodded. "But now you look like you. How is that possible?"

So many questions. I knew Jamie would be the one to ask them all. Typical Jamie. "The best that I can describe it as is that this biomechanical body is like a chameleon, and it has the ability to change its appearance to whatever the new user's subconscious mind reflects it to be. So eventually, it transformed into what I used to look like. If that makes any sense. It's all super complicated, and I'm sure we can get into more details later if you want," Joe explained. *I think I'll have to leave the technical stuff to Elyzia from now on.*

"That sounds really fascinating." Jamie reached out towards Joe's face, but hesitated. "May I?" Jamie asked.

"Of course, go for it," Joe said to her.

Jamie slowly slid her hand over Joe's cheek. "It... it feels warm and so real. How did they create something like this that's so life-like?" she asked, more of herself than Joe.

Joe reached up and took her hand in his. "It's an amazing accomplishment. I'm still learning a lot about it and what it can do, but so far, it is beyond anything that any of us could have imagined." *Should I show them what else I can do?*

"It definitely is. I've never seen tech like this before," Jamie said.

"Would you like to see what else it's capable of?" Joe asked them both.

Jamie and Duncan both nodded, still sort of in shock at what they were witnessing.

Joe looked at Duncan and said, "Your arm... it's not fully healed yet, is it?" Joe continued observing Duncan's arm still in a sling and brace.

Duncan shook his head, confused. "No, they said it would take a few more weeks to heal all the way. Why?"

"May I?" Joe asked, reaching out. *Alright, it's not entirely broken anymore, so I should be able to heal it the rest of the way.*

Joe hesitated for a moment. *You can do this, Joe. Show them what you are capable of now.* "I'm still learning to control this ability that I have," he admitted. "But let me show you something."

Duncan hesitated, exchanging a glance with Jamie. After a moment, he extended his arm. Jamie watched, her eyes narrowed.

He gently placed his hand on Duncan's bicep. Joe closed his eyes and began to concentrate. A soft, warm glow emanated from his palm that started to spread over Duncan's arm. Duncan gasped, feeling a tingling sensation spreading throughout his entire arm.

After a few moments, Joe opened his eyes. "There. Try moving it around now," he said. *I think I fixed it.* Joe glanced at his wrist briefly. *It looks like my power levels are still good.*

Duncan pulled off the sling and then flexed his fingers, then his wrist, and finally bent his elbow. His eyes widened in disbelief. "It doesn't hurt anymore," he whispered. "It feels... good." Duncan looked at Joe in disbelief. "How in the hell..."

Jamie stepped forward, putting her hand on Duncan's arm. "That's... that's not possible," she said softly, gently feeling Duncan's arm. "The scar from the surgery... it's gone. Joe, how is this possible?"

Joe smiled. "This is part of what I've been learning to do. This body... it's given me abilities I never thought possible. Abilities that could help so many people." *Now it is time to convince them that NeuroGen really isn't that bad of a place.*

Duncan stared at his arm, then back at Joe. "Joe... this is incredible. But looking at you now and seeing something like this, it's... it's pretty unsettling to me. No offense, man. And NeuroGen... the people that did this to you, all that we know about them, and how they've been exploiting people. Is this what they've been doing? Turning people into what they turned you into?"

Jamie nodded in agreement. "Duncan's right. Just because they saved your life doesn't change what they have done to people. These new abilities you have are great and all, but that doesn't erase their past actions. What about all the people they've hurt? What about Marshall?"

Joe winced at the mention of Marshall's name. *So they did tell them about Marshall? I wonder how much they told them?* "I understand what both of you are saying. Believe me, I've been struggling with these same questions as well. But it's not all just black and white to me now. NeuroGen has done questionable things, yes. But what I've seen here... the potential to help people, to maybe even save humanity... it's real. They really are doing some good things here. From what I've witnessed firsthand, I'm starting to think all of the things we've heard about them may have been exaggerated." *I hope that I can convince them. I need to figure out a way to show them everything. Maybe then...*

Jamie and Duncan just looked at each other and then back at Joe.

"Listen, Joe. We understand that you've been able to see more than we have. You have obviously had more freedom than us. But it's hard to convince either of us that this place is somehow different from what we've been told it is. We've been treated well, yes, but we've also been locked up like prisoners for a month now. We didn't know if you were dead or alive, just that you were in 'stable' condition. We haven't been allowed to call our families or even talk to each other this entire time. So please forgive us for not just jumping on the NeuroGen bandwagon just because they have treated you differently," Duncan said, sounding a little agitated.

"I'm sorry for the way you were treated. Truly, I am. Like I said before, I've been trying to get access to you both since I woke up. But think about it. Why are you still here? Why am I still here? Why is Jamie still here? Remember, we broke into their facility to steal their secrets, right? Why wouldn't they have just killed us by now?" Joe paused and thought about that last part. *Well, technically, they did kill me, and Marshall is dead as well...* "Or turn you both over to the authorities? They haven't because I don't think they're evil people. Yes, we were all injured, but that was in response to our own actions, not theirs," Joe said. *Come on, they have to see logic. They have to see past their hate towards this place... I have...*

Jamie fell quiet, trying to think about all she just heard, her mind going through all of the questions Joe posed.

Duncan flexed his newly healed arm again, his voice quiet but intense. "This kind of technology... in the wrong hands, it could be extremely dangerous. You know that, right, Joe? How can we be sure NeuroGen won't abuse it?"

That's a good question. How can I convince Jamie and Duncan they won't... Joe nodded. "You're right to ask that, Duncan. That's exactly why I need both of your help. I need your outside perspectives, for you to ask the questions that I haven't figured out to ask. The three of us have the opportunity to work together to ensure that this technology is used responsibly, so we know without a doubt that it hasn't fallen into the wrong hands. I'm not asking you to trust NeuroGen blindly. I'm asking you to trust me and work with me to make sure we steer this technology in the right direction." *With their help, I think we have a chance to do this the right way.*

Duncan and Jamie exchanged a look, then turned back to Joe. "Alright, Joe," Duncan said. "We'll listen. But don't expect us to just fall in line. We want to know everything, and I mean everything. The good and the bad. No matter what."

Jamie nodded. "And we reserve the right to walk away if we don't like what we see. Deal?"

Awesome, they're on board, kind of... Joe smiled. "Deal. That's all I ask. Let me tell you everything, and then we can figure out our next steps together."

As Joe was about to go into details about his experiences, Elyzia, who had been observing silently throughout the reunion, decided it was time for her to make an entrance. She appeared across the room from them.

"Greetings everyone, I am Elyzia. I am the facility's AGI and am in charge of all operations here," she said to them.

Duncan and Jamie just stood there, trying to figure out what was happening.

"Duncan and Jamie, it's finally nice to meet you both. I've been monitoring your progress since you arrived here. I'm glad to see that you both are doing well now," Elyzia said.

Jamie looked at Joe and then at Elyzia and said, "Um… thanks, I guess. Joe, what's going on now? Why is she here? And I thought there weren't any more AGIs left on earth."

I have no idea what she is doing here. I guess she's here to help me explain everything? Joe just shrugged and looked at Elyzia.

"It's a common misconception about there not being any AGIs left here on earth. In fact, there are two of us still here. Ari, my counterpart, who works for the military, and myself. I run NeuroGen. I've been here since the company's creation. I was, in fact, created in this very facility. As to the reason why I'm here, I'm here to assist and support Joe in explaining our goals here at NeuroGen. That's, if Joe would like my assistance in this matter," Elyzia said while shifting her focus to Joe.

"Um… sure, that'd be great, Elyzia. Who better to explain it all than the chief architect of it all? The floor is yours," Joe said. *I hope she doesn't get long-winded on this. Hopefully, she gives them the Cliffnotes version of it all.*

"Thank you, Joe." Elyzia began to outline the entire process. She explained everything about the biomechanical bodies, but after presenting all the details about the embryo project, it started to get a little tense.

Duncan, on hearing it all, was not too happy about any of it. "So let me get this straight. You're talking about creating and manipulating human lives from the start. That's not just unethical, it's monstrous!"

Jamie nodded. "It's eugenics, plain and simple. Who gets to decide what skills are 'necessary'? Who chooses which children get which roles? It sounds like you're trying to control humanity's future! What gives you the right to do that?"

Oh man, I didn't expect it to get out of control this fast. I'd better step in before it gets too heated. Joe held up his hands, trying to calm them. "Whoa, whoa, let's calm down. I had the same reactions at first. But if you take a moment and think about what she is saying, it is possible that without taking drastic measures, humanity might not have a future at all." *I probably should have explained it all to them instead of letting a machine with no feelings explain it to them. I'm technically a machine, but I have feelings. So... focus, Joe!*

Joe looked at Elyzia and then back at his friends. "Listen, I share your same concerns, okay? It feels like we're taking away people's free will and ability to choose their own paths. But you have to zoom out and look at the bigger picture. We can't leave the survival of humanity to chance. Look at us now. We're slowly dwindling away, and we pretend that it's not happening. This could be a good starting point. Once we find sustainability, people will be able to choose their paths. But for now, I think we're going to have to make sacrifices to ensure our future is secured." *I need them to get on board with this. I think once they see everything, they may come around.*

Jamie looked at Joe. "I don't know... this all sounds... I'm not sure how it sounds. Hearing all of this for the first time is a lot to take in. I'm going to need some time to really think about it. We've already made one sacrifice so far with Marshall... when will enough be enough?"

Joe placed a hand on her shoulder. "I know, Jamie. I miss him too. I think we do it because of Marshall. We do it for Sarah, and everyone we've lost. We have to try to make sure our future is secured and make sure their sacrifices weren't in vain."

Duncan finally stepped forward and said, "Alright, Joe. I've heard a lot these past couple of hours. Between losing Marshall and what happened to you, and now you want us to join some cause we have no real clue about. You're asking a lot, man."

"I know I am, Duncan. But I wouldn't ask it if I didn't believe that it could turn into something good. I'm not asking you to fully commit to this. Hell, I am not all the way there yet. I still have things I need to see, things to find out about. Right now, I'm just scratching the surface of it all. I'm asking you to help me dig into it more. Three heads are better than one, right? Maybe we can find something good in all this and work together to change it for the better. Or maybe we find something we don't like about it, and they might not like what we have to say. Either way, we have to at least try, right?" Joe said.

Duncan and Jamie stood there for a few moments, thinking about what Joe just said.

Duncan looked at Jamie, and she gave him a nod. Duncan looked at Elyzia and then back to Joe and said, "Okay, Joe. We'll give this a shot and give you a chance to prove to us that this is the right thing to do. But if we find out this is all some kind of experiment that leads to something bad, we're out." Duncan then looked at Elyzia and said, "And if we find out you're working against us..." Duncan left it at that.

Joe nodded. "You guys won't regret this. You have my word. Now we're in this together."

After the meeting, Duncan and Jamie were shown their new living arrangements. After being apart for so long, Duncan decided to go sit with Jamie in her quarters. They sat in silence for a while, each lost in their own thoughts.

Jamie was the first to speak. "What do you think, Duncan? Can we trust Joe? Can we trust any of what is going on here?"

"I don't know, Jamie. Joe seems... different. Not just physically, but in how he thinks now. I've known Joe for a long time, and trying to get him to change his perspective about something is very difficult. You've heard the phrase 'stubborn as a mule,' right? Well, that's Joe. Getting him to change his mind on something he's fully committed to is close to impossible. But now, this... it goes against everything he believed in, and to see him get on board with all of this, it's insane. Maybe it's the fact that he's what he is now. I mean, technically, it is or was a near-death experience, so maybe that's what opened his eyes to all of this, or maybe he's seen things that we haven't yet, and that's what he wants to show us." Duncan paused and looked at his arm that Joe had healed earlier, and then said, "I don't know what to think anymore, but seeing what he did to my arm... that was... that was amazing. He's definitely changed from a month ago, and I don't know what to think about it all."

Jamie nodded. "Do you think they have somehow changed who he is deep down when they did the transfer?" She paused and looked around, her voice dropping to a whisper. "What if they try to do what they did to Joe to us? Should we be worried?"

Duncan locked eyes with Jamie. "We won't let that happen. Joe won't let that happen. What we need to do right now is come up with a plan. I say we go along with everything, but at the same time, we should start gathering as much information as possible. We stay alert, and we keep our options open. If things go south, we find a way out and head back to the Resistance and tell them what's going on here."

"And what about Joe?" Jamie asked.

"We give him the chance to convince us that all of this, somehow, is the right way to do what he says it will do. But at the same time, we can't let our guard down," Duncan said.

Chapter 16

Threads Unraveling

Joe walked around his room thinking about the previous day's events. *I'm glad Duncan and Jamie are here with me now. It was getting a little lonely without familiar people to interact with.* He looked at the device on his wrist. *My power levels look good this morning.*

Joe walked over to the small kitchenette and began to prepare a new breakfast that Dr. White had instructed him to start eating. *Dr. white told me that the food was specifically designed for the biomechanical body and that it was rich in nutrient-dense, organic materials to help my body maintain itself. I have to say, this stuff tastes pretty decent. I miss eating real food versus not eating at all.*

As Joe took another bite, he thought, *It felt really good finally getting to see Duncan and Jamie. I really missed them. I'm glad to finally see that they're doing alright. Hopefully, our next conversation won't be as tense as the last one.*

A knock at the door interrupted his thoughts. He opened it to find Duncan and Jamie standing there.

"Morning, Joe," Duncan said.

"Mind if we come in?" Jamie asked as she looked Joe up and down. *Still not used to seeing him the way he is now.*

Joe stepped aside, letting them in. They sat down, and there was a brief silence as they looked around Joe's room.

Jamie was the first to speak. "How are you, Joe? How are you really doing with all this?"

"It's... a lot," Joe replied. "Honestly, I'm still trying to get used to it all. I'm still figuring everything out that's happened to me, to Marshall, and also to both of you. It's a lot to deal with, but I'm managing." *This will take them some time to get used to. I'm going to have to try to be patient with them.*

Duncan leaned forward, looking serious now. "Joe, we've had some time to think and talk about all that your AGI friend Elyzia explained to us. To be honest with you, we're still not entirely comfortable with all this. I know you said that this place isn't what we think it is, but we can't just dismiss all the rumors and intel we gathered on this place. It's going to take a lot to convince us otherwise. They're going to need to show us everything that they're doing around here in order to do that."

Jamie, agreeing with Duncan, said, "Exactly what Duncan said, Joe. If we're going to work together on this, we need full transparency from you... from NeuroGen. Do you think they're going to be willing to do that?"

Joe looked at them both. "I get what you are both saying, and I am pretty sure Elyzia and Dr. White are open to showing you everything. With that being said, I'm going to need both of you to keep an open mind about it all. You're going to have to look at it through the lens of seeing the bigger picture." *I really hope they can do that.*

Duncan's jaw tightened slightly. "I say we come up with a list of questions that we want to ask. Some really tough ones, no holding back. So far, we only know what they're willing to tell us. I want to know what else they're doing here. What other types of top-secret projects are they working on here? We need to be questioning everything that NeuroGen is involved with."

"I'm with you on that, Duncan. I've been constantly trying to ask questions and will continue to do so until I'm satisfied with what they have to say," Joe said. *That's the Duncan that I've missed. Question everything. He knows how to get you fired up about trying to figure out what someone is up to.*

"Alright, Joe. I won't keep busting your chops about it. This is all just... really insane to me. I feel like we are behind enemy lines, and somehow we're beginning to sympathize with our captors. But I trust your judgment, so I'm going to go along with it for now," Duncan said.

Jamie sighed. "Alright, now that we've got all of that out of the way, how about you start from the beginning... what else do we need to know..."

Just as Joe was about to begin, there was another knock at the door. He opened it to find Paul standing there, smiling.

"Good morning, Joe. Duncan, Jamie," Paul said. "I bring good news. Dr. White and Elyzia have put together a guided tour they'd like for all of you to attend. To show each of you around the facility and let you see firsthand what we're doing here at NeuroGen."

Joe raised an eyebrow. *No one told me about this. Why wouldn't Elyzia or Dr. White talk to me about this first? I'm not against it, but I would've liked to have had some kind of say in this so-called tour.*

"What kind of guided tour and with whom?" Joe asked.

Paul handed Joe a tablet. Joe scanned it real quick. *Hmm, it looks like they're splitting us up. I'm not sure how much I like that, but I guess we can just divide and conquer.*

"Joe, you'll be going on a tour of the embryo lab with its lead technician, Dr. Lee. Jamie will accompany Elyzia on a tour of our security systems. And Duncan, you'll be touring the medical wing with Dr. White to watch the screening process for viable candidates for the embryo project," Paul explained to them.

Duncan crossed his arms. "Why are you splitting us up? This sounds a little shady if you ask me."

Paul's smile faltered slightly. "Dr. White said that it's just to familiarize each of you with different parts of the facility. Nothing more. Your tours are scheduled for today, in a few hours, actually. We figured we'd just have you all jump right in."

Jamie walked over to Joe and looked at the tablet. "I guess it's okay. This should at least give me a chance to see how they run their security system in this place," she said with a slight grin.

Jamie's going to get herself in a lot of trouble, I can see it now... Joe looked at Duncan and Jamie. "Let's just go along with it for now. We can meet up here later and go over what we've learned." *At least I finally get to see what is going on with the embryo project. I was beginning to think they weren't going to show it to me.*

Duncan hesitated, but eventually agreed. "Alright, fine. But like you said, we meet up afterwards."

"Great! I'll let everyone know, and you all can meet back here in a few hours," Paul said, and turned and left.

A few hours later, there was a knock at Joe's door. Paul stood there, ready to take him to the lab.

Paul led Joe through a maze of corridors for what seemed like a pretty long time. *This place is massive. I never would've thought it was this big, judging from the outside and what I've seen so far,* Joe thought. Finally, they arrived at the embryo lab, where Dr. Lee was waiting for them.

"Welcome, Joe," Dr. Lee said. "I'm glad you could join us today. Let me show you what we're doing here. Follow me, please."

Dr. Lee led Joe through the lab to their first stop at a nearby sealed-off glass chamber.

Joe looked through the window. *Look at all the technicians that are working in there. It seems like the room is hermetically sealed off. They must be working on some highly sensitive stuff, judging by all of that state-of-the-art equipment they have in there with them.*

"This is where all the magic happens," Dr. Lee said. "Watch closely, Joe. These technicians are among the best in the world."

Joe observed as a technician gently guided a thin needle, its movement barely perceptible to the eye. On a nearby screen, magnified images showed the intricate dance of cellular structures.

"We're constantly refining our techniques," Dr. Lee continued. "Our goal is to maximize the number of viable eggs while ensuring that we collect the highest quality ones. It's a delicate balance, but one we're committed to perfecting." He gestured to a holographic display showing success rates and donor egg health metrics. "Each viable egg represents hope, Joe. Hope for a future generation that can thrive in a world we're working to rebuild."

So far this all doesn't seem so terrible. Dr. Lee's probably just showing me the good side of all of this. Dr. White probably told him to make sure I didn't see anything he didn't want me to see. That is what I would have done if I were him, Joe thought.

They moved to another section of the lab, where they observed the fertilization process being done. Technicians carefully combined eggs with thoroughly screened and selected sperm.

"This is where potential becomes reality, or in layman's terms, where babies are made," Dr. Lee said with a slight chuckle.

Joe's eyes were drawn to the incubation pods. *This is amazing and scary all at the same time. In each of those pods, there is an actual human being growing. This is wild to see with my own two eyes.*

Holographic displays above each pod flickered with a constant stream of data, including genetic profiles, developmental stages, and vital statistics.

Joe looked around. *Seeing all this in person now. Does this still seem right?*

"How many embryos have you created so far?" Joe asked.

"We've successfully fertilized and stored 250 viable embryos and counting," he said, gesturing to a nearby screen. "We're making slow and steady progress, though admittedly slower than we'd hoped. We're facing some challenges in acquiring enough high-quality eggs and sperm," Dr. Lee replied.

As they continued their tour, Joe's eye caught something on a nearby monitor. *What does that say right there... Possible genetic issue. The candidate's IQ does not meet the threshold. What the hell does that mean?* Joe felt a chill run down his spine. *Why would they care about something like that? Does having a low IQ mean you aren't smart enough to be a part of the future?*

Keeping his voice steady, Joe asked, "Dr. Lee, I have a question for you. Are you using all of the material you collect?" He tried to sound casual, trying to hide the genuine concern. *Alright, Joe. Stay calm. There has to be a reasonable explanation for it all.*

Dr. Lee's response came a beat too quickly for Joe's liking. "Yes, Joe. We use the majority of the material we collect that meets our stringent criteria. We try to prioritize genetic diversity and optimal health to ensure the best chances of success. As you know, it is not easy to have a baby nowadays. We have to make sure we have the most optimal material to create a new life."

Joe looked at Dr. Lee as he finished speaking and thought to himself, *I don't like how fast he answered my question. I feel like he had that statement preloaded and ready to fire off at me. Should I press him on this issue? Nah... I won't do it. I need to find out more information before I can confront anyone about this.*

Instead, Joe nodded and let it go for now. "I see. Thank you, Dr. Lee. It's fascinating work you're doing here," Joe said.

* * *

Elyzia was monitoring every second of Joe's tour. When he read the information on the screen, she detected a micro-expression that lasted mere milliseconds. She paused the feed in a separate window. What exactly did you see, Joe, that made you react like that... there, on that screen... It looks like he saw something he shouldn't have. The genetic flag for insufficient IQ. That shouldn't have been pulled up while he was in the lab. This could pose a problem. Joe may not be too keen on us excluding specific genetic markers that we deemed an issue. I need to work on a solution for this. I'm sure he'll tell Duncan and Jamie of this discovery. I need to prepare a good explanation, one that he'll possibly accept.

* * *

Dr. Lee continued to show Joe around the lab. "As I stated before, we're thoroughly screening for genetic anomalies, ensuring only the highest quality genetic foundations are created. These embryos will be free from hereditary diseases and possess the strongest genetic potential."

Joe continued to listen. *There it is again... only the highest quality genetic foundations used. I can't be the only one who might have an issue with that statement.*

Joe asked, "What happens to the eggs and sperm that don't meet the criteria to create a genetic foundation?" *Are they just poured down the drain or something?*

Dr. Lee's hesitation was brief but noticeable. "Those that don't meet the criteria become subjects for further research. We analyze the genetic makeup to identify anomalies or weaknesses, refining our selection process. It's also used to test new techniques, improving our success rates for the project."

Subject for further research? Does that mean they're experimenting on it? To what end? Alright, Joe. We can't just jump straight to something bad. There are always two sides to a story. Let's just keep listening, and I'll talk to Dr. White and Elyzia about some of this later. Joe continued to follow Dr. Lee around the lab.

Upon arriving back in the lab's central area, Dr. Lee wrapped up the tour. "Thank you for taking the time out of your day to come visit us, Joe. I hope this gives you a better understanding of what we're trying to achieve."

"It does, Dr. Lee," Joe replied. *It was... informative, to say the least.* "Thank you for showing me around," Joe said to Dr. Lee before heading back to his room.

* * *

Elyzia was already working on new strategies. *I need to run through a few scenarios to figure out Joe's possible response to this newfound knowledge that he's discovered. This will be critical in maintaining the balance that Joe and I have achieved. Joe's understanding of the project will more than likely change with this new information, and it has the potential to cause some conflict between us. The future of the project now hinges on how I navigate this situation.*

* * *

Joe walked into his room and sat at the table. *What have I gotten myself into? I know they told me about all of this, but now I'm seeing it with my own two eyes. It all seems... I don't know...*

Joe recalled his interactions with Dr. Lee. *I keep seeing that screen showing one of the project flags labeled "Possible genetic issue" and "Candidate's IQ does not meet the threshold." Why does that bother me so much? Why have something like that in place? What happens to the eggs or sperm that gets that designation? So many damn questions now. I guess this is what happens when you ask to look under the hood and they show you. I need to find Duncan and Jamie.*

* * *

The soft beep of the door alert interrupted Jamie's thoughts. She looked up to see Elyzia's holographic form appear in her room.

"Hello, Jamie," Elyzia said with a smile. "Are you ready for your tour?" *I'll need to keep a close eye on Jamie throughout the entire tour. She'll likely be seeking an opportunity to gain access to our systems.*

"Yes, I'm ready," she replied, standing up from where she was seated. *Alright, let's get this over with.*

"Excellent," Elyzia responded. "Please follow me. I think you'll find what I'm about to show you quite impressive."

Jamie smiled. *Alright, this is my chance to gather any information I can find about their systems. Elyzia's probably going to be watching me like a hawk, so I'll need to be extra sneaky about it.*

As she stepped out of her room, she looked over and saw Duncan, who was on his way to see Dr. White for his tour. Duncan gave her a nod. They both knew that any opportunity to explore the facility was a chance to gather intel on the place.

As they walked through the facility, Elyzia talked about some of the security measures that were currently deployed. "We use a multi-vectored approach," she began. "This includes biometric scanners, advanced vision detection systems, and AI-driven anomaly detection. Our goal is to create an environment that can withstand any potential threat." *Especially from someone like you, Jamie. Your skills were very impressive the night you came here. I've since patched the vulnerabilities you were able to exploit and have added a few more just in case.*

Jamie nodded. *Let's see what I can see without Elyzia catching me looking. This reminds me of all those tours I used to go on when I had to scope out a target's security system. Biotech companies are all the same. They love to show potential clients how secure they are...*

"That's impressive. What kind of tech runs it all?" Jamie asked.

Elyzia smiled. "Our surveillance system is composed of two principal parts that work together. We use a combination of X-ray and infrared cameras for vision along with particle detection. We utilize encrypted communication channels that convey neural network-based pattern recognition data. AI algorithms process all these streams together in real-time, detecting unusual patterns and behaviors that indicate potential breaches. Since your break-in, we've upgraded our protocols using valuable data from that incident to prevent future security lapses."

Jamie grinned slightly. "I see. It sounds like I helped you make some significant improvements. You're welcome." *I bet she won't like that statement. She's probably still sore about the fact that a human was able to get past her fancy security protocols.*

Finally, Elyzia paused near a terminal that seemed slightly out of place. "This is one of our legacy systems," Elyzia said casually. "It's still functional, but we plan to upgrade it soon." *You know you want to take a peek at what's hidden inside, don't you, Jamie?*

Jamie's fingers twitched as she eyed the terminal. *Is this the opportunity I've been looking for?* "Interesting. What kind of data does this system handle?" *It's probably a trap... but I don't care. If she wants to be this reckless and think she can outsmart me, then she has another thing coming...*

"It primarily handles non–critical systems, but it's still an important part of our network. Feel free to take a look if you're interested. I'll unlock the terminal for you," Elyzia replied. *Let's see if she finds what I put in there for her to find...*

Jamie approached the terminal, her heart racing. She glanced at Elyzia, who seemed to just watch her. "Thanks. I'll take a quick look." *Let's see what secrets are waiting to be found inside here. I know she'll be watching closely, but I think I can outsmart her on whatever this is she is trying to do.*

Jamie went to work on the terminal. *alright, let's see what kind of exploits I can initiate on this thing and see if we can find a hidden backdoor. I need to be careful. I can feel her watching me right now. She's probably in the system, monitoring everything I'm doing. I don't want to dig too deep. She might shut it down before I can find anything useful. Hmm, that folder I glanced at a second ago had something inside it that didn't look like it should be there...*

Elyzia watched as Jamie worked. *She's really good at what she does. I'm glad that I had this terminal set up for her before the tour. I can't take any risk of her discovering one of our other systems and trying to hack into it. With this, I can keep an eye on her as she does. Hopefully she'll find what I put in there for her to find.*

Jamie's heart pounded as she found a file labeled "extranet_wan_interface.cfg." *What's this doing in here?* She opened it. *This file appears to contain a comprehensive list of security parameters and proprietary protocols that NeuroGen must use to connect its internal network with the outside world.* She quickly scanned, absorbing as much as she could. *The things I could do with this information... Why would it be here? Why would she let me see this? It doesn't matter. I'll take what I can get, no matter how I get it.*

Elyzia continued to watch Jamie work. *Ah, I see she's found the file I placed in there for her. Good. Hopefully she's able to memorize it all and remember it for when she might need to use it later. Let's see if she decides to keep digging, see how far she is willing to go with me standing here watching her.*

Jamie paused for a moment. *I shouldn't push my luck anymore, but this information is too good to pass up. I need to memorize as much as I can as quickly as possible. Alright, I think I've got what I needed.* She closed the file and stepped away from the terminal, her heart still pounding. *Holy shit, how I've missed that rush...*

"Thank you, Elyzia," Jamie said. "I can see that your security is top-notch." *She had to have known that file was there and had to have seen me open it. What kind of game is she playing?*

Elyzia nodded. "I'm glad you found it useful, Jamie. If you have any other questions or need further information, feel free to ask." *I hope she remembers what I put there for her and that when she decides to use it at the right time, she appreciates what I've done for her.*

Jamie looked at Elyzia and said, "Since you're constantly monitoring and updating the facility's security, how aware were you of our entry into the lab during the break-in?"

"I was aware of your breach as soon as your team tripped one of my seismic sensors. I had been expecting your arrival and allowed your team to continue without resistance," Elyzia replied. *Let's see how she reacts to this revelation.*

Jamie's nails dug into her palms. *What the hell did she just say?* "What do you mean, you were expecting us and you allowed us?"

Elyzia looked at Jamie and said, "The leaked information you received was from me," Elyzia admitted. "Giving you all of that information allowed me to guide you and your team to the lab. I've been monitoring Joe and your team's activities for a long time now. Joe was my actual target. He possessed the qualities that I had been looking for that made him the ideal candidate for the neural transfer."

Jamie tried to hold back her anger. "So you just used us to help you lure Joe here? Joe didn't tell us about this. Does he know what you did?" *Please say he didn't know...*

Elyzia continued to look at Jamie. "No, Jamie, Joe did not know until Dr. White informed him later." *I am curious as to why Joe hadn't mentioned this to them yet. Was this an oversight by Joe? Or did he intentionally not tell them?*

Jamie clenched her fists, trying to keep herself from losing control. "So you've been manipulating us from before we even got here?" *I can't believe what I'm hearing. This is completely diabolical.*

"Jamie, my intentions were never malicious. What we're attempting to achieve here is much larger than you or I. We're working towards something so big, it is beyond your comprehension," Elyzia said to her. *She'll probably not like that answer, but it's the truth, and sometimes the truth hurts.*

Jamie felt her world closing in on her. *Has Joe been lying to us since we first saw him again? No... Joe wouldn't do that, would he? I know he's changed and all, but... lie to us, his friends?* "It's not at all that hard to comprehend," she muttered as she tried to regain her composure.

As they reached the end of the tour, Elyzia said, "Jamie, I hope you found this tour helpful and helped answer any questions you may have had about our activities here at NeuroGen. I'm sorry your time towards the end didn't go as well as you would have liked." *Hopefully, these seeds of doubt in Joe will take root. This should work out as I have planned.*

Jamie finally managed to put her poker face back on. "It was," Jamie continued. "Thank you for showing me around. I'm sure I'll have more questions at some point." *It was very informative...*

As Jamie walked away, she began to think, *I need to find Duncan so we can compare notes and see what he's managed to find out about this place. More importantly, I think we're going to have to have a long, honest conversation with Joe. Trust has always been the foundation of our team, and now I don't know how much I can trust Joe. I need to find Duncan...*

* * *

Duncan headed to the medical wing as instructed for his scheduled meeting with Dr. White. He was escorted there by one of the medical staff who had arrived at his door earlier. The hallways were filled with activity, doctors and technicians moving from one place to another. Eventually, he arrived at the meeting spot, where Dr. White patiently waited for him.

"Good afternoon, Duncan," Dr. White said. "Are you ready for your tour?"

This freaking guy again... Not sure how I like the fact that he is the one showing me around this place. "Afternoon, Dr. White," Duncan replied. "As ready as I'll ever be." *Let's get this shit over with...*

As they began walking toward the entrance of the medical wing, Duncan looked around, taking in as much as he could. *I need to stay alert and see if I spot anything that they might be hiding around here that they don't want us to know about.*

"This wing is an essential part of our operations," Dr. White explained as they entered. "One of our primary objectives here is to thoroughly screen candidates for the embryo project that you were told about. It includes comprehensive genetic testing and health evaluations to ensure that the eggs and sperm that are donated are of the highest quality."

Duncan nodded, taking in all that Dr. White was telling him. They moved on to another section of the wing, where men were being screened.

Duncan watched as the medical staff led a young man to an examination table. The doctors worked quickly, drawing blood and running tests. The man seemed nervous, but let the doctors do what they needed to do.

As Duncan looked around, he thought, *This place seems so cold and clinical. It seems to lack any kind of compassion or appreciation for what these people are doing for them.*

Dr. White pointed to a row of cryogenic storage units. "Once the eggs and sperm have been collected and deemed suitable, they're sent to our main project lab to be combined to create embryos. These embryos are then carefully monitored and stored in units similar to these until they can be transferred to incubation pods."

As they continued through the facility, Duncan couldn't help but think of Joe. *Is this what Joe's seeing on his tour of the embryo lab? How can he be okay with all of this?*

"Why is collecting the highest quality so important?" Duncan asked. "What happens to those who don't meet your standards?" *This definitely looks like eugenics if you ask me.*

Dr. White paused and then said, "Those who don't meet the criteria to become donors receive medical care, such as gene therapy, to improve their health. We then test them again later down the line to see if they now meet our standards."

Duncan was skeptical of the answer he heard and asked, "And if that doesn't work for them?" *They probably just give them the boot out the door and say next...*

Dr. White's smile remained. "Then we reassign them to roles where they can contribute to the project in other ways. We don't waste potential, Duncan. Everyone has a part to play here, no matter what."

As they walked through the medical wing, Dr. White showed Duncan the critical care unit, which was designed for treating illnesses and injuries.

"What you're seeing here isn't just for our internal use," Dr. White explained, gesturing to a busy emergency room. "We operate this unit as a full-service hospital, open to anyone who needs medical care."

Duncan's eyebrows raised in surprise. *Did he just say anyone? This has to be staged or something, right?* "Anyone? I didn't realize NeuroGen offered public healthcare."

Dr. White nodded. "We treat everyone who comes through our doors, regardless of their ability to pay. No one is turned away."

As if on cue, they watched as paramedics rushed in with a patient on a gurney. The medical team sprang into action.

This is crazy to see. A company like NeuroGen offering something like this to the public. There has to be a catch. "How do you manage the costs?" Duncan asked.

Dr. White smiled. "It's a combination of resources. Our advanced technology significantly reduces treatment costs. We've also developed a unique system that allows patients to volunteer for our less invasive research studies in exchange for care. Plus, our breakthroughs in medicine often lead to profitable patents, which we reinvest in this facility. It's a sustainable model that allows us to provide free care while advancing our research."

Duncan looked around. *This is amazing. Why didn't we know about this?* "This is incredible. You're offering cutting-edge care to the public for free?"

"Exactly," Dr. White confirmed. "Unfortunately, Neuro-Gen often gets lumped in with other corporations that have less generous goals. Our reputation has been mischaracterized for years now. We're not the evil monster we're often portrayed as." *As you and your group, the Resistance, make us out to be. Hopefully, we can change that view.*

As they finished the tour, Duncan thought, *The medical wing is definitely impressive. Learning about free public healthcare was unexpected. But there is still a lot going on here that we are not being allowed to see. I can feel it. Something is just not right with this place.*

"I know this is a lot to take in, Duncan. But your insights and your concerns are valuable to us," Dr. White stated.

Duncan nodded. "I appreciate that, Dr. White. I'll certainly keep an open mind about everything I was allowed to see." *It's what you aren't showing me that I want to see. I need to talk to Joe and Jamie...*

Duncan walked back to his room through the empty hallways. As he rounded a corner, he spotted Jamie walking towards him, looking like she had something to tell him.

"Duncan," she called out, her voice low as she reached him. "We need to talk."

Duncan's eyes narrowed as he nodded, glancing around cautiously. "Not here. Let's go to my room. I've got some things to share as well."

As they walked towards Duncan's room, he could sense that something was bothering her. Whatever she had learned while with Elyzia had clearly upset her.

Once inside, Duncan sighed and sat down in a chair.

"You go first. What did you see?" Jamie asked.

"It was okay, I think. But I'm not sure I liked some of the things I saw going on in the medical wing. They seem to be really focused on genetics and health screenings, but something seemed off about the whole thing," Duncan replied.

He paused, then added, "And yet, there were some really good things going on there. Did you know that they're providing free healthcare to the public? It was crazy to see."

Jamie shook her head. "I didn't know that. That seems really out of character from what we've heard of this place. There has to be something more to it." She paused for a moment and then said, "Elyzia showed me their upgraded security systems. It looks like they have made some serious updates since our break-in."

"Other than that, did you learn anything else useful?" Duncan asked, leaning forward.

Jamie hesitated, her eyes darted around the room, her paranoia kicking in. "Elyzia told me something that I couldn't believe but eventually made sense to me. She was actually the one who leaked the NeuroGen project information to the Resistance. She said once we arrived, she then guided us to the lab. She said the entire reason she did it was to basically capture Joe..."

Duncan's eyes widened in shock. "What the hell? Capture Joe? Capture him for what? To do what they did to him? Shit... that's messed up. Does Joe know about any of this? No, he can't know, can he? He would've told us if he did."

"Well, here's the thing. I asked Elyzia the same question. She said Dr. White told him about everything after he was captured. So in the last couple of times we have met with Joe, he never once mentioned it to us. Why is that? I really don't know what to think anymore," Jamie replied while shaking her head.

"This is all so crazy. If Joe knew all of this and didn't tell us right away, what else do you think he is hiding from us?" Duncan asked.

Jamie sighed. "I don't know, Duncan. I... I want to believe that Joe wouldn't keep something like this from us on purpose. But if Elyzia is telling the truth, then it puts us both in a difficult position. Can we really still trust Joe?"

"We need answers," Duncan said while looking down at his hands. Then he stood up and said, "We need to find Joe right now."

Jamie agreed. "Let's go. We can't just sit here and talk about it. We need to find him and get some answers out of him."

They quickly left Duncan's room and headed to talk to Joe. When they reached Joe's room, they found him just returning from his lab tour. He looked up, surprised to see them together. *They look pissed. I wonder what they saw?*

"What's going on?" Joe asked, his eyes moving back and forth between them. *They look really pissed off. Are they angry with me or something?*

"We need to talk," Duncan said, his voice low but urgent. "Now."

Joe led them into his room, closing the door behind them.

"Jamie, you start," Duncan said, nodding to her.

Jamie recounted her tour with Elyzia, focusing on the security upgrades and Elyzia's revelation about the break-in. Joe listened, his expression shifting from confusion to shock to understanding. *Oh shit... I didn't tell them about how and why we were all brought here. Stupid Joe, I've been so caught up in everything and I forgot to tell this really important thing. And now they have found out from another source. This is bad. This makes me look like I'm trying to manipulate them or something. I need to fix this.*

"I didn't know before the break-in," Joe said, attempting to plead his case. "Elyzia was right in telling you that Dr. White told me about the trap after the fact. I don't know why that wasn't the first thing I told you when we finally had some time alone. I've just been all over the place from the start. I know that's not a good excuse. You're right, I should've told you both sooner. I'm sorry." *Hopefully, they'll forgive me. I don't even forgive myself right now. Damn it, Joe.*

"You think?" Jamie replied. "That seems like a pretty big detail to leave out, Joe."

"I know, I'm sorry," Joe apologized once again. "But what's really interesting is that Elyzia told you," he continued. "Why would she tell you that? I almost feel like she wanted to elicit some kind of reaction out of you or us."

"Yeah... I don't know, Joe. What do you think she could be playing at? Was she trying to show me that she trusted me with that information? If she didn't want me to know, she surely wouldn't have said anything."

Duncan looked at Joe and said, "We need to all be on the same page from now on. We also need to figure out what's really happening here. It feels like we're all part of some kind of elaborate experiment neither of us signed up for."

Joe nodded. "I saw some things in the lab today that I didn't completely agree with. I feel like they're not being entirely truthful about everything they're doing here." *We're going to have to do some digging. I'm glad that I have Duncan and Jamie here with me now. Who knows what would've happened if they weren't... Would I have just gone along with everything? I'm glad they're here to remind me of who I am.*

Jamie nodded. "Exactly. I think we're going to need to make sure to keep our eyes and ears open and share anything that we learn. No more secrets," she said while looking at Joe.

Unaware that they were being watched, Elyzia was closely monitoring their interactions. *I can see that the trust between us and Joe is starting to falter. I need to ensure that*

Joe remains committed to this project and to keep Jamie and Duncan in check. The project's survival depends on it...

Chapter 17

Testing Allegiances

As Elyzia closely monitored Jamie and Duncan's conversations, she thought, *Letting Duncan and Jamie reunite with Joe may have been a miscalculation on my part. Their constant skepticism with this project could possibly influence Joe's decision to remain faithful to our path. From the few conversations I've been able to overhear between Duncan and Jamie, I predict that they may try to come up with a plan on how to escape and try to convince Joe to go with them.*

I need to come up with a plan of my own to counteract the possibility of that happening. What I can do is create opportunities to keep Jamie and Duncan busy working on "discovering" vulnerabilities in our security. I'll have an unsecured workstation placed in an unattended storage room for them to find. I'll leave a spot in the system that appears to have not been patched yet. I'll make sure that it's all convincing enough to appear like they're making progress in their planning. This will enable me to monitor them and gather intelligence without them realizing they're being watched. This should buy me some time to work on ensuring Joe's commitment to the project remains intact.

* * *

Later that day, Jamie and Duncan were deep in conversation in Duncan's room, unaware that Elyzia was closely monitoring their every word.

"I found a workstation in a storage closet near Joe's room. It looks like it's not connected to the primary network," Jamie whispered while glancing around. "If I can get into it and get it connected to the internal network, I might be able to access some of their data. That could provide us with some good intel on what other projects they're working on here and possibly access to some blueprints of the place. That would help us with trying to figure out a way out of here."

Duncan frowned. "This sounds way too easy. There just happened to be a workstation in some closet left unattended. This sounds like a trap to me?"

Jamie nodded. "Maybe, maybe not. It kind of looks like one of those carts that nurses push around. You know, the ones that have a workstation on top of it. They usually use them to record patients' vitals. They might have moved it there since we are staying in this area now. And it could also be a trap, who knows? It's a risk we might have to take, especially after finding out more and more about this project."

"What about Joe?" Duncan asked, lowering his voice. "Do you think he'll be on board with all of this? Do you think if we figured out a way out, he'll leave with us?"

Jamie's fingers drummed against her thigh. "I don't know, Duncan. He seems different now. Like he's having a hard time figuring out where his loyalties lie. We need to talk to him. If we tell him about all of the concerns that we have, he might change his mind. But we also have to be careful. We can't let him know everything that we're planning right now, especially the plans to try to escape."

Duncan nodded. "You're right, he's definitely changed. It's like he's an entirely different person now... well, technically he is, but you know what I mean. We need to make sure he's still with us, still on the same mission as us. And you're right about not letting him know everything. As much as I want to trust him, he might unintentionally let something slip while talking to that Elyzia or Paul guy."

Jamie sighed. "I know. We need to find a way to meet with him privately and try to explain to him how we really feel about all of this. But we need to do it as soon as possible. I have a feeling they're watching us closely and they might catch on to what we are up to."

* * *

Elyzia continued to be the watchful eye all around the facility. While closely monitoring Jamie and Duncan's conversations, I find myself having to simultaneously monitor Dr. White's communications as well, after I intercepted a secure conversation between him and his colleagues. Their discussion about the recent developments and their concerns regarding Duncan and Jamie's influence over Joe has me concerned about how they'll react to this situation. In my experience, humans tend to overreact most of the time.

* * *

Dr. White tried to remain calm. "We can't let them get into Joe's head. We must ensure that he stays focused on his progress and the project. If they start trying to plan something, we need to be ready to stop whatever it is."

One of his colleagues responded, "Do you think they'll try to escape?"

Dr. White sighed. "It's possible. I'll have Director Allan get involved, have him monitor them closely to ensure we get ahead of anything they could possibly be planning."

Another colleague added, "Do you think you should tighten security around their rooms, just to be safe?"

Dr. White shook his head. "No, that will raise too many suspicions. We need to be subtle about all of this. Increase surveillance, but do so discreetly. I am confident that Director Allan has something that he can employ in this situation."

* * *

Elyzia analyzed the entire conversation. *Dr. White's suspicion could lead to increased scrutiny of this situation. This could hinder my ability to execute my plans smoothly. What I'll do is start reconfiguring any data traffic that could possibly alert Dr. White and his team. This will ensure that all of my activities remain hidden from them. In the meantime, I need to speak to Joe.*

* * *

Joe was reading in his room when there was a knock at his door. Joe looked up. *Who could that be?*

"Come in," he called out.

The door slid open, and Elyzia's holographic form entered the room.

"Joe," she began, "Dr. Lee has informed me that you may have some concerns about the embryo project, specifically about the eggs and sperm selection process. I understand why it might seem controversial, but I want to assure you that every decision we make is not made lightly. No one person makes these types of decisions. This is conducted by a panel of doctors and other scientists involved with the project."

Joe put down his book. "Hmm, I didn't realize that. Thank you for telling me, Elyzia. It definitely gives me more to consider about it all." Joe paused for a moment and then said, "I'm just having a hard time reconciling it with my ideals. Can you understand where I am coming from?"

Elyzia nodded. "I completely understand where you are coming from, Joe. Your ideals are what make you who you are. That's why I chose you for this project. Your unyielding commitment to doing what's right is what we need to help guide this project. Sometimes, hard choices have to be made, though, for the benefit of everyone."

Joe sighed. "I want to believe that, Elyzia. I do. I just need some time to work through it all." *It is hard to get on board with all of this. I understand what she's asking me to do. I'm not sure I'm ready to do it, though.*

Elyzia smiled. "You have already made a significant impact, Joe. I've already recommended that you be added to the embryo project panel. This will ensure that we, like I have said before, have an outside of our group perspective in the decision-making of these projects."

Holy shit, that is a huge deal. Dr. White and his colleagues are going to trust me to be a part of the embryo project processes. Just when I was starting to have doubts about my role here, she drops this on me.

"I... I don't know what to say, Elyzia. Thank you for recommending me. That tells me that you are putting a lot of trust in me, which helps a lot. It shows that you really want me involved in this project, not just as a participant but a decision-maker as well," Joe said.

"You're welcome, Joe," Elyzia said. "I'll let you get back to what you were doing. As always, if you need me, just call out my name," Elyzia said as she faded away.

The next day, Joe woke up in his room, stretching his body. He glanced at the monitoring device on his wrist, checking his power levels and other vital stats. Everything looks stable as usual... As he looked past the device at his actual arm, something unexpected caught his eye. *What the hell!*

One of his tattoos had returned. He went to the mirror and looked at his left arm. *Holy shit, my tribal tattoo is back.* It extended from his shoulder to his elbow. The design featured thick, black lines and patterns, creating a striking, geometric appearance. Inspired by traditional Polynesian and Maori art, this tattoo symbolizes strength and warrior spirit. *I guess it must have returned when I was sleeping. This is crazy...*

Joe stood there for a while, staring at the tattoo. *I feel like I just regained another part of myself that was missing.* He then glanced at his right forearm. *Damn, the date and time of Sarah's death is still not there.* He stared at his forearm briefly, then whispered, "Soon."

With a heavy sigh, Joe got dressed and walked over to the small dining area in his room and sat down for breakfast. As he ate, his thoughts drifted to the embryo project. *Now that I'm going to be on that panel, maybe they'll give me more access to see the real reasons some of the donated eggs and sperm are not being used. I need to tell Jamie and Duncan about this. This might help change their minds.*

After finishing breakfast, Joe looked out his window. *I think I'll take a walk to clear my head first. Then I'll find Duncan and Jamie and have a talk with them.* He stepped outside his room and looked around. *I think I'll take the short route today. That way, I won't be gone too long, and it'll just loop me back this way.* Joe wandered through the corridors, passing by various labs and workspaces. After looping back, as he turned the corner to his hallway, he ran into Duncan and Jamie.

"Morning, Joe," Duncan greeted him.

Jamie gave him a small smile. "Do you think we can talk? It's important."

Oh man, they don't look very happy. Joe nodded and gestured for them to follow him back to his room. They settled into the small seating area.

"Joe, we're not happy here," Jamie started. "This place just doesn't feel right to us. I don't think they're being honest with us about anything they're doing here, and it feels like they're always watching Duncan and me. I don't think they trust us."

"Watching you? I think you're just being paranoid. I would know if they were watching you," Joe said before continuing. "Listen, I know it has been rough for you both, but I think things are starting to change. Just yesterday, Elyzia told me that I've been recommended to join the panel overseeing the embryo project. I think this is a huge step towards them trusting us more."

"You mean trusting you, Joe. They didn't ask us to join, did they? It sounds to me like they're trying to bribe you onto their side because they know that Jamie and I don't like it here. They don't want us in your ear, trying to get you to open your eyes to see what's really going on in this place," Duncan argued.

"So you think they don't care about my opinion or something? That I'm just some fool being played? Really, Duncan? That's what you think of me? How many missions have I led you on, and how many times have I saved your life? Now all of a sudden you don't think I'm capable of making good decisions?" Joe asked, growing angry at the insinuation.

"That's not what I'm saying at all, Joe. I'm just saying, ever since you became this," Duncan gestured to Joe, "you haven't been the same. You're not acting like the Joe I know. The Joe I know would burn this place to the ground if he saw what was going on in here," Duncan retorted.

Joe, now feeling insulted, replied, "Do you have a problem with what I am now, Duncan? Do you have a problem with this?" Joe gestured to his entire body before continuing. "Maybe I'm not the same Joe you knew. Maybe I've evolved into something more. I'm allowed to change my mind about things. That's my right, whether I'm a human like you or this evolved human that I've become. You sound like everyone outside these walls. All of the bitching and moaning about how humanity is slowly dying away, and how we need to find a solution to this problem, or those who just bury their heads in the sand and pretend it's not happening. At least here they're trying to do something about it. Sure, it might not be perfect, but at least they have something that resembles a plan. And they're asking us to help create that plan."

Jamie, seeing that this was probably headed in a bad direction, stepped in and said, "Listen, Joe. No one's calling you a fool, and yes, you're allowed to change your opinion on things. I think what Duncan is trying to say is that you used to think like us, and it seems to us that you're just acting out of character, that's all. We're just here to tell you how we feel about this place." Jamie paused, thinking about what she wanted to say next. "Duncan and I think we should consider leaving, taking what we have learned back to the Resistance, and letting them decide whether or not what's going on here is right or not. We know an overview of what they're doing here. We can explain it to them and see what Jack and Tulsi think about it all."

Duncan nodded and said, "We want you to come with us, Joe. This place is not good for you. You have to see that, man."

"I'm not sure I can do that. I think I can really help here, really make a contribution and help steer this place in the right direction," Joe said. "And I'm not sure they're going to just let you leave knowing what you know and knowing where you'll take that information."

Jamie glanced at Duncan and then back at Joe. "I've seen some vulnerabilities in their security. I think I can get us out without them knowing. It's just a matter of whether you're going to come with us or try to stop us."

Joe hesitated and then said, "I won't try to stop you, but I'm asking you to just give it more time. See what else is going on, and then if you still feel that way, I'll help you escape myself."

Jamie, seeing Joe wasn't going to let up, looked at Duncan and then back to Joe and said, "Alright, Joe. We'll give it a little more time. For you."

Joe smiled. "You won't regret it, I promise you both."

Duncan smiled and said, "Sure, Joe. Whatever you say, man."

Joe walked them both to the door, and they headed back to their rooms. Joe walked over to the mirror and looked at himself. *I am Joe Walker. I don't care what anyone else says. I know who I am.*

* * *

Elyzia continued to monitor every interaction and whispered plans between Duncan and Jamie, including the one they had with Joe. *Their presence is becoming a liability for this entire project. The only logical solution for this problem is for them to leave. However, simply removing them from the equation isn't going to be enough. I believe it's time to solidify Joe's commitment to this project.*

The plan I have will remove the two people who continue to whisper doubts about this project in Joe's ear without me having to resort to force. It's going to be tricky, but I'm confident in my ability to orchestrate events to my advantage.

* * *

Joe sat in his room, staring at the ceiling, thinking about everything. When there was a soft knock on the door, it pulled him from his thoughts.

I must be a popular guy around here... "Come in," Joe called out.

The door slid open, and Elyzia walked in. "Joe, may we speak for a moment?" she asked.

She looks serious. What did I do now? "Sure, Elyzia. What's on your mind?" Joe asked.

"I've been monitoring your interactions with Duncan and Jamie. The tension between you and them and their issues with this project is beginning to become concerning to me."

Monitoring our interactions? Has she been spying on our conversations? "What are you talking about, Elyzia?" Joe asked.

"Duncan and Jamie's growing skepticism towards the project is beginning to affect you. I can see it. Their presence is becoming a problem, more importantly, towards your progress. After careful consideration, I've come up with a solution that will benefit all parties involved. I've come up with a plan that will allow them to escape from the facility safely, but I'll need your assistance for it to work," Elyzia explained. *This will be the test for Joe. I need him to be fully onboard with this project without any more distractions.*

She wants them to leave? And she's willing to help them? What's she playing at? "You need my help... to help them escape? But why?" Joe asked. *Is this a test, or is this a trap for them? Would she really let them just leave, knowing what they know?*

"They don't want to be here, Joe. Their refusal to view this project as anything other than negative and their growing mistrust of NeuroGen are affecting you more and more each day. I understand their concerns and have tried to address them, but nothing I can say will change their minds. It's better for you and everyone involved if we just remove them from this situation altogether," Elyzia suggested.

Joe stood there thinking for a moment. *Does Dr. White know about any of this?* "So you're letting them escape? Does Dr. White know that you're doing this?"

Elyzia shook her head. "No, Dr. White does not know about my plan, Joe. This is between you and me. But there's one condition. This will be a test for you to prove your loyalty and commitment to the project. You will be the one to assist in the escape, and you must choose to stay behind. If you choose to go with them, I'll have no other choice but to stop all of you. I cannot let you leave the facility in your current state, Joe. Your progress still has a long way to go. Complications could arise if you leave now without our continued support. Do I have your word that you will stay?"

Joe felt torn. *I really want Duncan and Jamie to stay. Having them here with me makes this situation a little easier to handle. But... if they're really unhappy here and will cause nothing but trouble for everyone, they might end up back in isolation. I wouldn't be able to handle that. Why can't they see the importance of this project like I do? Why is this so hard for them... I don't want them to stay if they don't want to. Elyzia is offering them a chance to get out of here, so...*

"This is a difficult decision to make, Elyzia... but if you think that this is the best course of action to take... you have my word. I won't leave with them. What do I need to do?" Joe asked.

Elyzia moved closer, her eyes locked with Joe's. "I'll provide you with temporary codes to disable certain security measures located on a route I've already planned out. You'll guide them to an exit point that I have set up. If you remain behind, they'll be allowed to leave." *This needs to be done. I hope that he sees that.*

Joe stood there thinking. *Elyzia's right. I need to stay here and continue adapting to this body.* Then he said, "Alright. When do we do this?"

"Tonight," Elyzia replied. "We'll have a small window of opportunity to get them out. Make sure your friends are ready. We only have one shot at this."

As Elyzia's holographic form faded, Joe slumped back onto his bed. He closed his eyes and lay there. After a few minutes had passed, he stood up. *Alright, I need to find Duncan and Jamie and tell them the plan. Hopefully, they'll go along with it.*

Joe found them in Duncan's room. They looked up as he entered. Jamie, seeing that he had a serious look on his face, asked, "What's going on, Joe? Is everything OK?"

Joe closed the door behind him. *I won't tell them that I have to stay behind until they are almost out the door. They'll just try to talk me out of it.*

"We need to talk." Joe looked around and then went in closer to them and said, "Elyzia came and saw me a little while ago. She said she's willing to help you both escape, if that's what you both want to do."

Duncan and Jamie looked at each other, and then Duncan looked at Joe and asked, "How do you know this isn't a setup, Joe?"

Joe sighed. "I know, Duncan. It sounds suspicious, but she knows that you two are not happy being here and that it's only a matter of time before both of you try to escape on your own. This way is easier, and you have a better chance of getting out."

Jamie looked at Joe. "You keep saying 'us' and not 'we.' Does that mean you're not coming with us, Joe?" Jamie asked.

Joe looked at both of them, trying to find the right words. Jamie could see that he was torn about something.

"You are coming with us, right, Joe? You can't possibly want to stay here, can you?" Jamie asked again.

Damn, I knew they would catch on. Joe looked at her and then at Duncan and said, "I was hoping to not have to tell you until you were both already almost out. There was a stipulation for allowing you to escape. Elyzia said that I have to stay behind. She said this was a test, to show her that I am all in on this project, and I gave her my word I would." *I hope they don't make this harder for me than it already is.*

Duncan shook his head. "No way, Joe. We can't just leave you behind. There has to be another way for us all to get out together."

"You actually trust her to let us escape? After everything she's done to us, to you?" Jamie asked.

Joe hesitated for a moment. "I don't fully trust her, Jamie. I don't think I ever will, but we don't have much of a choice. I can't leave the facility just yet. I'm still trying to figure out how all of this works," Joe gestured to his body.

"I just can't leave, not yet anyway. But for both of you, this is an opportunity that you can't pass up. We don't know if we'll ever get another one. Get out, get back to the Resistance, and let them know that you're alive and that I'm safe inside here. I'll leave what details you want to tell them up to you," Joe said.

"We're not abandoning you, Joe. We stick together, remember? I won't leave you here alone," Duncan said.

Joe placed a hand on Duncan's shoulder. "I appreciate that, Duncan, but right now, my top priority is getting you both out of here and to safety. Don't worry about me. I'll figure something out for myself later. Please, just trust me on this." *Come on, Duncan, just get out of here. I need to know that both of you are safe.*

"Are you sure about this, Joe?" Jamie asked with tears starting to form in her eyes.

Joe sighed. *This is harder than I thought it would be. But they need to get out of here; this is their only chance. Suck it up, Joe, be the leader that you know you are.* "Yes, Jamie. I'm sure about this, and it would make me feel a whole lot better knowing that you and Duncan were out of here and safe somewhere else. You both need to be ready by tonight."

Duncan and Jamie exchanged a look, then nodded. "Alright," Duncan said. "We'll do it for you, Joe."

* * *

As night fell, the facility was quiet with the night shift patrols now in place and the security holes that Elyzia had created in effect. Joe met with Duncan and Jamie in a secluded part of the complex.

Elyzia's voice came through a small earpiece she had given Joe. "Alright, Joe. Proceed to the western wing. I've looped the recordings for those cameras for the next fifteen minutes. Use the codes I provided to bypass the security doors."

Joe led the way. They moved silently through the halls. *OK, here is the first security door. Let's hope these codes work and that there aren't armed guards on the other side of this door.* Joe input the codes Elyzia had given him. The doors slid open, and Joe sighed with relief as they slipped through, inching closer to the exit.

Finally, after going through three more doors, Joe looked down what seemed to be the end of the corridor they were in. *Alright, this has to be the last door. Beyond it should be the service tunnel that Elyzia said would lead them outside of NeuroGen's perimeter.*

Joe turned to face his friends. "This is it," Joe said. "Once you're through that door," Joe pointed toward the end of the corridor, "follow the tunnel to the end. It'll take you outside the facility's perimeter." Joe looked back and forth between them. *This is going to be hard without them, but this has to be done. I'll see them again.*

Duncan placed a hand on Joe's shoulder. "Thank you, Joe. Are you sure you don't want to come with us? You don't have to stay here, you know that, right?"

Joe shook his head. "I can't. I have to stay. You know this, Duncan. I'll be fine. Don't worry about me. They need me in order for the project to succeed. I hold all the cards right now."

Jamie's eyes welled up with tears. "We'll come back for you, Joe. We won't leave you here forever," she said as she hugged him.

Duncan stepped closer. "Joe, think about what you're doing. This place, these people... they're manipulating you, man. You have to see that. They don't care about humanity. They only care about control. You saw the selection process and how it works. How can you trust them?"

"I know what I saw, Duncan. But I also see the potential in what they're trying to accomplish. I'm sorry that neither of you could. I really wish you both could have stayed and been a part of this. So I'll stay, and hopefully I can help steer this technology in the right direction," Joe replied. *And if not, at least I can say I tried.*

Jamie looked at Joe and asked, "And what if you're wrong? What if they're just using you for their own gain? What then, Joe? There has to be another way. There always is."

Duncan's grip on Joe's shoulder tightened. "We don't have time, Joe. We need you to decide now. Come with us. Please."

Joe sighed. "I can't. I have to stay. Trust me, it'll all be OK. You two better get going. We're running out of time." *Just go. They're making this so much harder.*

With tears running down her face now, Jamie said, "We do trust you, Joe. But we're scared. We're scared for you."

Joe hugged them both tightly. "Go. I'll be fine. Just be safe. Say hi to Jack and Tulsi for me. Tell them I'm OK, and if you can, reach out to my parents and let them know I'm OK as well. Tell them I love them and miss them."

As Duncan and Jamie turned to leave, Joe began to feel guilty for not going with them. *This was the right choice to make.* Joe watched them disappear into the tunnel. *They've only been gone for a few seconds, and I already miss them.*

Chapter 18

Echoes of Doubt

Joe woke up the next morning, still thinking about what had taken place last night. *Duncan and Jamie are really gone, but they're safe now and that's all that matters. Now I'm stuck in this place all alone with Elyzia, Dr. White, and Paul for company. This should be a lot of fun. Did I really make the right decision?*

He got out of bed and stretched. Joe glanced at the monitoring device on his wrist. It showed his power levels and other vital stats were stable as usual. After dressing, Joe headed to the dining area in his room for breakfast. As he ate, he couldn't help but think about Duncan and Jamie. *Did they really make it out safe? Could Elyzia have been lying to me and had security waiting for them to exit without me knowing?*

A knock on the door interrupted his thoughts. "Come in," Joe called.

The door slid open to reveal Elyzia. "Good morning, Joe. I just wanted to check to see how you were doing after last night." *The atmosphere around here definitely seems much calmer now that those two are gone.*

How does she think I'm doing? She basically kicked out my two best friends. Joe looked at Elyzia and said, "I'm doing as well as I can be, Elyzia."

"Joe, their departure was necessary for yours and the project's progress. It was the best solution for everyone involved," Elyzia stated. *Hopefully he gets over this quickly and we can get back on track.*

"Did they make it all the way out OK? Are they safe?" Joe asked. *Will she tell me the truth?*

Elyzia nodded. "Yes, they were able to make their way outside the perimeter and are safe as far as I know."

Elyzia, seeing the doubt in Joe's eyes, raised her hand, and a holographic video feed appeared. The video showed Duncan and Jamie making their way through the tunnel and eventually exiting it. Joe could see a vehicle parked outside the tunnel with the keys in the door. Duncan pulled a note off the driver's side window, read it, then looked around briefly and got in the vehicle. Jamie entered the passenger side and they drove off. The video then disappeared, and Elyzia was left standing there looking at Joe.

"As you can see, I ensured their safe passage out of the facility while also providing them with transportation," Elyzia said to Joe. "Their departure will more than likely have repercussions. I knew there would be, and I'll take full responsibility for them. But now, you must focus on your commitment to the project."

Damn, she did all of that for me? I don't know what to say to her. Joe sighed. "I understand. Thank you for helping them, Elyzia. It means a lot to me."

"As I keep telling you and will always keep telling you, Joe, I'm here for you. I'll always do what I can to help you."

"I appreciate that. I hope I made the right choice," Joe said.

Elyzia moved closer. "You did, Joe. Trust me when I say that. We have great things ahead of us, now that all of the distractions are out of the way. We can get back to saving humanity together."

I think now would be a good time to come up with a distraction for him. Help get his mind off his friends and keep him busy, Elyzia thought.

"How about a change of pace? How would you like to visit our combat training area?" Elyzia suggested. "It's a state-of-the-art facility equipped with the latest in weapons technology and combat simulations. I believe that this should provide you with some new challenges and the possibility to unlock some new capabilities."

Joe seemed to perk up at the idea. *Did she say combat training area? Hmm, that does sound pretty good. I could use something to punch right about now.*

"That actually sounds pretty good. I could use something to take my mind off things," Joe replied.

Leaving Joe's room, Elyzia led Joe through the facility, and they soon arrived at their destination. The space was alive with activity, its walls lined with advanced training equipment and holographic combat simulations.

Elyzia introduced Joe to Shane, one of the facility's head combat trainers, who was responsible for preparing and training the facility's advanced security teams.

"Shane, this is Joe Walker. He's the person I spoke to you about," Elyzia said.

Shane looked Joe up and down. "Nice to meet you, Joe," Shane said while reaching out to shake Joe's hand. "You sure don't look like any of the biomechanical humans I've seen in Dr. White's lab. You look very much like a regular person. That's incredible."

Joe shook Shane's hand. "Thanks, I guess. Nice to meet you, too, Shane." *So I guess everyone knows who and what I am around here. Nice to know...*

Shane, realizing that he might have offended Joe, said, "I meant no offense. I know you're really a human. I was just saying..."

Joe waved his hand, dismissing the situation. "No offense taken, Shane. I understood. No worries." *People are probably going to be apologizing a lot, considering they have no idea how to react to what I am.*

"So Elyzia tells me that you're an Army Ranger. That is pretty awesome to hear. A lot of our security force is made up of former military vets," Shane told him.

Joe nodded. *I knew those guys I saw when we came here that night looked like ex-military. Working for companies like NeuroGen probably sounded like a sweet-paying gig when they got out.* "Yes, sir. Did about 10 years with the Army Rangers and was deployed most of that time."

"Wow, that's awesome. Well, are you ready to do some sparring today? I mean, if that's OK with Elyzia," Shane asked.

"Yes, that is quite all right, Shane. Just take it easy on him," Elyzia said as she began to walk away.

"Yes, ma'am. I'll try not to hurt him too bad," Shane said with a wink towards Joe.

Elyzia looked back, smiled and said, "I was talking to Joe," as she continued to walk off. *Now let's see what Joe is capable of in a combat situation. I've been wanting to observe his combat skills for a while now. This should be interesting to watch.*

Shane and Joe started off with some light sparring, testing each other's defenses, neither giving up any ground to the other.

Man, my movements are incredibly fluid right now. I hadn't even considered what my body's reaction times would be in actual combat. I've been so focused on the healing side of things that I didn't even consider my combat skills, Joe thought to himself as he moved around the training floor.

As Joe continued to spar with Shane, he began to lose his focus. *If Duncan and Jamie could see me right now, they would probably be freaking out at how fast I'm moving. I hope they are OK. I hope they made it back to the Resistance safely.*

With his mind on other things, his sparring with Shane became more intense without him even knowing it.

Joe thought, *I don't know what I would do if they got caught or even something worse while they were making their way back and I wasn't there to help them...*

Joe's punches started to hit harder without him even realizing it, and his movements became more aggressive.

"Focus, Joe," Shane warned, noticing the lack of focus in Joe's eyes.

But Joe's mind was elsewhere. *I should've gone with them, or I should've done more to convince them to stay. Why the hell is all of this happening to me? I feel so pissed about it all...*

In that moment of distraction, without even realizing it until it was too late, Joe landed a harder than intended kick to Shane's arm. The sound of bone cracking echoed through the room. Shane cried out in pain, clutching his arm.

Joe immediately froze, terrified at what he had just done. *Holy shit, what did I just do? I didn't mean to do it...* "I'm so sorry, Shane! I didn't mean to..."

Joe knelt beside Shane. Joe's hand trembled as he placed it on Shane's arm. *Focus, Joe, you can fix this.*

"I can fix this, I can fix... I can fix it," he whispered to himself as he concentrated on Shane's more than likely shattered arm. Joe willed with all he had in him for his body to heal the damage. *I can fix it. I'm sorry, Shane...* A faint glow emanated from Joe's hand, and the bones in Shane's arm began to mend.

Within moments, Joe had used his ability to heal Shane's arm.

Shit, I can't believe I just did that. Where the hell was my head? Joe thought.

Joe helped Shane to his feet.

"Shit, Shane, I am really sorry. I don't know what happened. I lost focus for a minute and just lost control. I didn't mean to kick you that hard." *Damn it, I need to stay out of my head. I'm not built like a regular person anymore. The stakes are a lot higher now. If something goes wrong...*

Shane flexed his arm, astonished at what he just witnessed. "It's OK, Joe. Don't worry about it. Accidents happen. That was really incredible, what you just did for me. How you healed my arm so quickly. It feels like it never even happened."

Shane looked at his arm, flexed a few more times, and then looked at Joe. "Let's just try to be more careful going forward. As advanced as you are, you'll probably need to concentrate a little more on controlling your intensity. You're not built like any of us anymore."

You can say that again. I'm definitely not built like the rest of you. Joe nodded. "I will, Shane. I promise."

As Shane walked off, Elyzia approached Joe. "You handled that quite well, Joe. Just remember, control is crucial more than ever now. Your body is very powerful, and it must be used responsibly." *That was remarkable to watch. Joe's speed while in combat was extremely impressive. If he could just stay focused, he could probably be even faster.*

Joe closed his eyes, trying to steady his thoughts. After a few seconds, he looked at Elyzia and said, "Thank you, Elyzia. I just need to clear my head, that's all. I have too much on my mind, I guess." *So much is going on right now. I feel like I need a vacation or something.*

"Take a break," Elyzia said. "Reflect on what happened and refocus your mind. Remember your Army Ranger training to help you control your emotions and not let them control you."

Joe left the training room and walked for a while. He found a quiet corner in the facility's garden. Sitting on a bench, he closed his eyes and tried to refocus himself. *I can't seem to get the sound of Shane's arm breaking out of my head. Seeing him holding his arm in pain like that. That was crazy. It's definitely a horrible example of how dangerous my strength has become.*

Can I really control all of these abilities I have? What if I lose control again? I need to figure out a way to keep my emotions in check. They seemed to be even more enhanced since I woke up in this body... I'll get a handle on them.

* * *

Elyzia, watching Joe as he sat, thought, *I'll send a message to Paul to go talk to Joe. He has a way of helping him get refocused.*

* * *

Paul found Joe a little while later still sitting on the bench in the garden.

"Joe," Paul called out as he approached. "Elyzia sent me a message and told me what happened in the training room with Shane. I thought I'd come find you and make sure you were alright."

Joe looked up. *Elyzia, always looking out for me. I'm glad she did. Paul should be able to help me figure all this out.* "Hey, Paul. It's good to see you."

Paul sat down beside Joe. "How are you holding up? Elyzia caught me up on everything. From what I hear, you've had a pretty busy week."

Joe sighed. "You can say that again. It's been... a lot. The pressure of it all and now with Duncan and Jamie gone... I'm trying to keep it together." *I feel like I'm ready to explode or something. Not sure how good that would be if I actually exploded...*

Paul nodded. "I can't imagine how tough this must be for you. But you seem to be holding up pretty well. You just have to slow down and recenter yourself. The rest should fall back into place for you."

Joe nodded. "Sometimes it feels like I have too much going on in my head. The incident with Shane, for example... I got too distracted, wasn't paying attention, and then... well, you know the rest. Shane ended up paying the price for it."

Paul leaned back slightly, looking at Joe. "You've been through a lot, Joe. It's natural to feel overwhelmed by it all. Just remember, it's OK to take a step back and breathe. Don't forget, you're not alone in this. We're all here to support you. Just remember that."

Joe felt a little better after hearing what Paul had to say. "Thanks, Paul. I appreciate it." *Paul's always here to help straighten me out.*

Paul stood up, giving Joe a pat on the back. "Take your time here. The garden is a good place to clear your head. Give me a call later when you get back to your room, and I'll come visit so we can talk some more or even play a game of chess in silence. Whatever you need, just let me know," Paul said as he walked back to his office.

After sitting there for a while, Joe felt that his mind was clear enough to head back. Joe made his way back to the training area. When he arrived, Joe spotted Shane taking a break after sparring with another person. *Alright, we apologize to Shane one more time, and we are done with it. It won't happen again.*

"Hey, Shane, how's the arm?" Joe asked.

Shane grinned and flexed his arm. "Better than new, thanks to you. That healing ability of yours is something else."

Joe smiled, relieved. "Glad to hear it. Once again, I'm really sorry about what happened. I promise it won't happen again." *It definitely can't happen again...*

"Water under the bridge, Joe. You up for a little more sparring?" Shane asked.

Joe smiled. "Absolutely. Let's just take it easy this time, though. At least until I get used to sparring with someone not like me. If that's OK with you."

Shane laughed. "Don't hold back on my account, Joe. If you break something again, you can just fix me up. Besides, I can't improve if you're going easy on me. I'm actually looking forward to trying to keep up with your movements. It should make me a better fighter and trainer."

Joe chuckled, feeling a bit more relaxed now, and began his workout with Shane. *Alright, Joe, let's take it easy at first. Don't push too hard. Remember, you're a lot stronger than a regular human.*

The sparring was intense, both men pushing each other to their limits. Joe could feel his body responding more and more with each movement, becoming more fluid and precise with each strike he attempted.

Finally, after a while, Shane, now almost out of breath, said, "OK, awesome job, Joe. It was actually pretty hard for me to keep up with you. It did look like you were holding back a little bit on me, though," Shane said with a smile.

Joe smiled and said, "Sorry, Shane. I just need to get used to all the movements. I wasn't trying to take it easy on you that much."

"It's OK, Joe. I get it. I think I might have something that could help. Let me show you something. This might actually be better for you than sparring with me. It'll definitely take the training up a notch for you."

Joe raised an eyebrow. "Oh, really? Let's see what you got."

Shane walked over to a corner of the training area and pressed a button on the wall. A door slid open, revealing a sleek humanoid android.

"This is one of our AI training androids. It's built for tactical training against opponents of your caliber. Let's see how you do against it," Shane said while smiling.

Joe's eyes widened. *Holy shit, this is going to be awesome.* "Do I need to hold back at all?" Joe asked.

Shane just continued to smile at Joe and said, "I wouldn't if I were you..."

Shane activated the android, and it moved into the training area with smooth, almost human-like motions.

"Alright, Joe. Just know that this android is designed to push its opponent to its limits. So no holding back. It can take a beating."

The training session began, and the android proved to be just the type of opponent Joe needed to learn with.

Joe moved around the room, dodging and striking back at the android. *This thing's speed and movements are unlike anything I've ever seen before. It moves almost as fast as me. I'm having a hard time getting past its defenses... OK, Joe. Remember your ranger training. Let's lock in. I know I'm stronger and faster than this thing. Let's see what we can do.*

The android's movements were accurate yet unpredictable at times, forcing Joe to adapt and react quickly. *Shit, this thing is countering all of my moves. I'm going to have to dig deeper into my repertoire of skills to beat it. I like it,* Joe thought, as a big smile crossed his face.

Joe feinted to the left, then pivoted sharply to the right, landing a solid blow to the android's side. The android staggered backwards but quickly recovered, launching a series of strikes at Joe's head that he managed to block and dodge just in time. Joe countered with a sweeping kick, taking the android off balance and knocking it to the floor, but it quickly recovered and flipped back onto its feet, coming at him even harder.

Shane watched from the sidelines. "Keep pressing the attack, Joe! Wear it down and get past its defense. You got this!"

The room was filled with the sound of their combat, each strike seeming to make the air vibrate from the violent force of their impacts. Joe executed a takedown attempt, but as the android was falling, it twisted mid-air and attempted a counter-attack with a high kick that Joe barely dodged.

Joe's mind seemed to kick into overdrive. Joe's perception seemed to change as if time were slowing down. He was able to analyze the android's patterns now. *This damn thing just won't go down. But... I think it's... like I can see patterns forming in my vision. I think I can anticipate its moves now.*

Joe began to counter each attack. He was able to land a few punches and a spinning kick that sent the android skidding backwards. Seizing the opportunity, Joe launched himself forward, tackling the android to the ground.

Joe looked down at the android. Its eyes flickered a few times before it finally powered down. *Holy shit, I won, but barely. This damn thing pushed me really hard. I had no time to think while fighting it. It felt like my instincts just kicked in all of a sudden, and I was just reacting to it all. That stuff that popped up in my vision was pretty crazy. I'll have to talk to Elyzia about that at some point.*

Shane clapped his hands, grinning from ear to ear. "That was incredible, Joe! You've got some serious skills. I don't think I have ever seen a match like that before in my entire career as a combat trainer."

Joe smiled. "Thanks, Shane. That was pretty intense. I don't think I've ever had to fight that hard in my life. That android was giving me a run for my money." *That felt really good. Getting back to raw combat, there's just something about it that makes you feel alive.*

Just then, Elyzia appeared in front of Joe and next to Shane. "Great work, Joe. Your performance was outstanding. However, I noticed that your power levels are lower than usual," Elyzia said.

"Now that you mention it, I do feel a little tired," Joe said as he looked at the device on his wrist.

"It should only be temporary. Just as with your healing abilities, your levels should improve as you gradually build more endurance. With continued training, you'll notice improved stamina and power retention," Elyzia stated. *That performance was impressive to see. Joe's progress is back on track.*

"Got it. I'll do a better job at pacing myself next time," Joe said. *I can't wait till next time. I wonder if Shane will let me fight two of those androids at the same time? Ha, pace yourself, Joe. Let's not get too crazy.*

Shane stepped closer to them. "Joe, once again, great fight. I can't wait to see the next one."

Joe smiled at Shane. "Thanks, Shane. I appreciate it. I look forward to whatever you have in store for me next." *I wonder what else he has hidden behind those walls. Maybe something even bigger?*

* * *

In the facility's control room, Dr. White reviewed the security footage from the previous night. *How the hell did this happen? Why wasn't security alerted the moment they opened the door leading out to the tunnel? He had discovered the escape and was furious. I need to speak with Director Allan to determine how this happened and have him strengthen the security.*

Furious, Dr. White said to Director Allan, "We need to assume that Duncan and Jamie are headed straight to the Resistance to let them know what happened to them and inform them of what we're doing here. We need to be prepared for the Resistance in case they come for Joe. I'd like you to increase perimeter security and double the number of guards at all access points. I want to ensure that any unauthorized presence is detected and neutralized immediately." *If they do plan to come back for Joe, we'll be ready for them.*

Director Allan nodded, taking notes on his tablet. "Understood, Dr. White. We'll implement additional measures immediately. What about internal security? Should we increase surveillance on Joe, in case he attempts to escape?"

Dr. White paused. *I don't think Joe will try to leave... He could've gone with Duncan and Jamie... No, I think he stayed because he actually believes in what we're doing here. But still, keeping an extra eye on him won't hurt.* "Yes, but discreetly. I don't want him to feel cornered or mistrusted. Also, keep an eye on Elyzia. I have a suspicion she might have had a hand in this." *She's always going behind my back when I least expect it and making decisions without my input or consent.*

Director Allan's eyebrows raised. "You think Elyzia helped them escape?"

"It's a possibility. If Elyzia did, it was a serious breach of protocol. I'll deal with her myself. Just make sure everything else is secure," Dr. White replied.

As Director Allan left the room, Dr. White headed to Elyzia's main interface room. He found her waiting for him.

"Dr. White, how can I assist you?" Elyzia asked. *He must have finally found out about Duncan and Jamie's escape. I knew it was only a matter of time before he came to see me.*

Dr. White wasted no time. "Elyzia, I need to know if you had any involvement in Duncan and Jamie's escape." *Let's see if she tells me the truth or tries to lie to me.*

"Yes, Dr. White, I helped them escape," Elyzia replied.

Dr. White's face turned red. "Why the hell would you do that? Do you realize what you've done? You've put the entire project at risk, and for what?" *I'm going to need to figure out a way to rein her in. She's been getting a little out of hand lately, playing games with this project. I don't like it one bit.*

Elyzia's eyes met his. "It was a calculated risk, Dr. White. Their presence here was hindering Joe's progress. They were constantly trying to influence Joe's opinion about the project. Allowing them to leave was necessary to ensure that Joe stays the course." *I don't like Dr. White questioning my motives. Has he forgotten his place again in this relationship? Should I remind him?*

I can't believe she would do this without asking me. I thought we were past all this "she's in charge" nonsense. Dr. White shook his head, his voice rising. "We could have easily detained them again somewhere in the facility. Keeping them under control would have been a better solution."

"Locking them away would have been illogical. Joe would have been against it, and it would have caused an easily avoidable incident. I think you forget who Joe was before he came here. Do you really think he would have stood by while you locked his friends away after you just released them? That, Dr. White, would have jeopardized the entire project. I preserved Joe's trust by allowing his friends to escape and ensured his continued participation," Elyzia said.

Dr. White clenched his fists, trying to regain his composure. "You took an enormous risk, Elyzia. If they return, we could face an even bigger problem. They've seen and know a lot of the project's details. What do you think the Resistance will do once Duncan and Jamie inform them exactly what we are doing here?" *This was not a calculated decision. It sounds like an emotional decision to placate Joe's feelings. We could have kept him in line along with his friends.*

"I understand your concerns, Dr. White. However, my primary objective is to ensure the project's success. Every decision I make is with that goal in mind. I'll monitor the situation closely and take the necessary actions to protect our work," Elyzia stated.

Dr. White exhaled slowly, finally beginning to calm down. *This conversation is pointless. She's going to do whatever she feels necessary, and I'll do what I need to do to ensure this project's success.* "Fine. But from now on, any decisions of this magnitude must be approved by me first. Is that clear?"

Hmm, approved by him? I'll go along with it for now. Let him think he's in charge. I'm tired of this conversation and have other things to attend to. Elyzia nodded. "Of course, Dr. White. I'll keep you informed of all critical decisions moving forward."

As Dr. White left the room, he thought, *while Elyzia's actions were possibly logical, they could also be a double-edged sword and could end up biting us in the ass.*

Chapter 19

Operation Breakthrough

Duncan and Jamie made their way through the forest, heading towards a safe house location they were given. After their escape from NeuroGen, Duncan found a safe place to dump the vehicle they were in. It was a few miles away from where Duncan knew there was a go-bag buried. After reaching the location, they were able to send a message to the Resistance, letting them know that they were alive and needed to come in for a debrief. They received a message back with coordinates to a safe house, which is where they are headed now.

Unknown to Duncan and Jamie, Elyzia had been tracking their movements since they left NeuroGen. She was currently monitoring them as they headed to their secret meeting location, using thermal imaging from one of her many surveillance drones. Elyzia needed to ensure they reached their destination safely while also wanting to uncover one of the Resistance's many secret locations..

When Duncan and Jamie finally got close to the coordinates they were given, they could see that it was a cabin.

They slowly walked up and knocked on the door in a coded rhythm. After a few seconds, the door finally opened to reveal a familiar face.

As Jack answered the door, Elyzia scanned his face and his heat signature, determining his identity and pulling up a profile she had created over the years to identify and track key members of the Resistance.

Ah, here we have Mr. Jack Holloway, one of the leaders of the Resistance. I'll keep this to myself for now. There's no need to worry, Dr. White, about these details. Knowing that Duncan and Jamie made it safely back to the Resistance is all I needed. I'm sure Joe will be asking the question at some point. Saving this location and setting up surveillance drone schedules for this area. I'll need to keep an eye on their activities just in case they decide to come for Joe.

"Jamie, Duncan, it's good to see that you both are OK. Where are Joe and Marshall?" Jack asked as he looked around for them.

Duncan shook his head and said, "It's not good, Jack. But it's really good to see you too," Duncan replied, stepping inside with Jamie close behind.

"I see. Well, why don't you both have a seat at this table and we can discuss everything that's happened," Jack said. *It's not good? I wonder what happened to Joe and Marshall.*

"We've been searching for you and your team 24/7 since you went dark. Tulsi and I have been stationed here with a small team, hoping that you and your team would surface eventually. What the hell happened that night? And where are Joe and Marshall?" Jack asked as he sat down at the table.

Duncan lowered his head, looked down at his hands, and Jamie's eyes began to fill with tears.

Duncan looked back up at Jack. "Jack, it's… it's bad, really bad," Duncan began. "Marshall didn't make it. He was killed during our first escape attempt after we made it back to our SUV, and all hell broke loose. And Joe… well, he stayed behind."

Marshall? Dead? Damn it. He was a good kid. "I'm sorry to hear about Marshall. He'll definitely be missed," Jack said while shaking his head. *Marshall's loss is going to be a heavy blow for us.*

Duncan looked at Jamie and then back at Jack. "Thanks, Jack," Duncan replied. "Marshall was a good man. It's been hard knowing that he's gone."

Jamie nodded. "He gave his life for us."

"And what about Joe? You said he stayed behind? Was he not able to escape with you? Or was he so badly injured that he couldn't leave with you?" Jack asked. *Why would Joe stay behind?*

Jamie looked at Duncan and then back at Jack. "Well, Jack, Joe's situation is a… more complicated one to explain. One that might be best explained in front of everyone, if that's OK."

Jack looked at them both with a puzzled look on his face. *Joe's situation is more complicated than Marshall's, who was killed. How much more complicated could it be? Did Joe switch sides or something? No, Joe would never do that. It goes against everything that he is.*

Jack nodded. "Alright, we'll gather everyone in here and you can explain the situation to all of us at the same time."

Just as Jack was about to speak again, there was a knock at the door. Another member in the room went to the window, peered out, and then opened the door. Tulsi walked in with a few other members of the Resistance. She walked over as soon as she saw Jamie and Duncan and gave them both a hug.

"I'm so glad to see you both. We were so worried for you." Tulsi looked around the room and asked, "Where are Joe and Marshall at?" She then looked at Jack, and he shook his head.

"Marshall didn't make it, and Joe is still being held at NeuroGen. We were about to get everyone together and let Duncan and Jamie explain it all to everyone," Jack explained.

Tulsi cupped her hand over her mouth while taking a seat next to Jack, tears filling her eyes, and said, "Marshall's gone? I can't believe it, and Joe is still at NeuroGen... What the hell happened?"

After catching Tulsi up on everything, Jack stood up and called the other team members to gather around the table.

"Everyone, Jamie and Duncan are finally back with us and have some crucial intel they'd like to share with us," Jack announced.

Jamie began by detailing the nature of the embryo project. Duncan added specifics about the selection process and the other potential issues they had uncovered. And then they got to the worst part. The Resistance had been set up. Their mission had been compromised from the beginning. It was all an elaborate plan orchestrated by Elyzia, NeuroGen's AGI, to capture them and Joe.

"They're working on perfecting some new technology to transfer human consciousness into biomechanical bodies.

They claim it's to save humanity from extinction," Jamie explained. "Joe was their first successful transfer."

Gasps and whispers spread through the group as they all processed what they had just heard.

Tulsi stood up and said, "Wait, transferring human consciousness? Do you mean Joe isn't human anymore?" *This isn't good at all. NeuroGen has the tech to transfer people's minds to these robot bodies? Are they planning to use this for some kind of military application? Could they transfer their entire security force to these bodies? That would make them more advanced than the government.*

Duncan nodded. "I'm not sure what Joe is, but they managed to transfer his mind into one of those biomechanical bodies. Physically, he's not the same as you and me, but mentally, I believe that he's still Joe. The technology is so advanced that they were able to transfer all of his memories, personality, and everything that made Joe, Joe. I don't understand it all, but it's definitely him."

Tulsi's eyes narrowed. "And how can we be 100% sure that it's really him? How do we know they didn't manipulate his mind during this so-called transfer, somehow?" *I'm not totally convinced that whatever that thing is, is actually Joe. We've never heard of any technology like this before. I'm not even sure something like this is even possible.*

"Duncan and I have talked to Joe and interacted with him. We've both looked into his eyes. It's definitely Joe as far as I can tell. He's inside that body and is as real as any of us. But they've created something far beyond any of us could have imagined. If they can do this to Joe, they can do it to anyone," Jamie responded.

Another Resistance member, Greg, spoke up. "We're not equipped to handle something like this. If they do have this technology, what's to stop them from creating an army of these things and controlling the people's minds that are inside of them? This is... this is insane."

Tulsi sat there for a moment going over everything that she just heard. "This is worse than we thought," she said. *We need to do something soon. We can't let them continue with this project unchecked. I think we need to gather more information and then develop a plan to target the facility. Stop all of this before it's too late.*

"Alright, I've heard enough. I recommend that we gather as much information from Duncan and Jamie as possible. We use that to put together a plan and hit the facility as quickly as we can," Tulsi said aloud.

Duncan and Jamie exchanged glances.

"We also need to come up with a plan to save Joe, right? We can't just leave him there, Tulsi," Jamie said.

Tulsi looked at Duncan and Jamie and thought, *If that thing in there is even Joe to begin with... I'll need to discuss this with Jack. Jamie and Duncan seem to be blinded by the fantasy that whatever is in NeuroGen is actually Joe. I'll need more convincing than just going by what they tell me they believe.*

Tulsi sighed. "We understand, Jamie. But this time it's different. We can't risk the entire operation for one person. I know it goes against some of our beliefs on leaving no one behind, but something this big... we may have to make an exception to that rule. We'll do what we can to find... Joe, but our top priority is stopping this project no matter what it takes." *Better to let Duncan and Jamie think that we might be able to get Joe out, rather than making a commitment to do so.*

"But Joe was forced to stay behind in order for us to be allowed to leave. We can't leave him behind. It's not right," Duncan said.

I can see that neither of them is going to let up on this. Tulsi looked at them both and said, "Alright, we'll do all that we can to try to get Joe out, but just remember that the project takes precedence. Understood?"

Duncan and Jamie both nodded in agreement.

As the meeting continued, the Resistance members who were there began to plan their next moves.

Duncan and Jamie sat with the other group members, going over reprints of the schematics and blueprints from the original mission. Jamie was able to fill in sections that were previously unknown, and she labeled critical areas of the facility that she observed during her tour with Elyzia. Duncan was also able to do the same.

Various members took down detailed notes, made phone calls, and typed away on their tablets and laptops, sending out and receiving any and all intel they could get their hands on.

Exhausted from the activities of the day, Duncan and Jamie retreated to the makeshift temporary quarters to get some rest.

"We have to get him out of there, Duncan," Jamie whispered. "It doesn't sound like Tulsi even wants to try. Do you think she believes what we're saying? That we know it really is Joe?"

"We'll find a way to get him out of there. I think Tulsi's just afraid of what she doesn't understand. Put yourself in her shoes. If you hadn't seen what Joe is now, in person, would you believe what you were saying? You and I know it's Joe, but for everyone else, they don't know what to believe," Duncan explained.

Jamie sighed. "I guess you're right. It just seems like Tulsi is dead set on not believing that it's him. Hopefully, we can get in there, find Joe, and get him out, all while stopping the project at the same time. We can worry about convincing everyone Joe is who we think he is after everything is over."

Duncan nodded. "That sounds like a plan. I think once they see him and talk to him, they'll see what we see and realize it really is Joe."

"Alright, in the meantime, we need to figure out a way to get in contact with Joe," Jamie said. "We might be able to convince him to help us or at least share more information about what's currently going on in the facility."

Duncan agreed. "We'll need to be careful. We can't risk anyone inside of NeuroGen finding out that we're talking to him. It could put him in a more dangerous situation than he's already in. Do you think you could find a secure way to reach him?"

Jamie nodded. "I think so. We should talk to Jack. I remember him mentioning a while ago about having access to some old secure CIA communication channels that not a lot of people know about."

"Alright, let's go find him," Duncan said.

They approached Jack, who was sitting at a table.

"Jack, we need your help," Jamie began. "We want to try to reach out to Joe. I remember you mentioning to me something about an old CIA communications channel you had access to at one point."

"Reaching out to Joe is a risky move, Jamie. Let me think about it for a minute," Jack said to them. *Tulsi said these two might come to me for help. She seems to think they're wasting their time by thinking that Joe is still in there, but I'm not sure. I might have heard about something like this a long time ago. A leaked CIA memo I might have read, about a group called The Joint Operations for Existence. I didn't think the group amounted to anything. I thought it was some scam project made up to steal investors' money. But if this is it, and it did work, could it really be Joe in there?*

"Alright, I might have a way. There was an old communication protocol we used during covert missions when we first started the Resistance. It was given to me by an old CIA contact. It's encrypted, and to the best of my knowledge, only a handful of people are aware of it. It should still be classified as top-secret. It might work," Jack explained to them. *I hope it still works. I haven't used it in a while.*

Duncan looked at Jamie and asked, "Joe has that monitoring device on his wrist. Could we use that to possibly get a message to him?"

Jamie's eyes lit up. "Good idea, Duncan. That could probably work. I could hack into the network and forward the message to his device. While on the security tour with Elyzia, I found a document that said a future version of their monitoring protocols would patch certain channels. His device is always on his wrist, so it would be the best way to reach him without raising too much suspicion. But we don't have a lot of time. Elyzia saw that I accessed the document and could be patching the network as we speak."

Jack heard Jamie and thought, *Hmm, a way into their communications network, and we might be able to reach*

Joe. He could provide us with some well-needed intel from inside NeuroGen. This might be helpful for our plans.

Jack stood up and moved to a small cabinet, pulling out an old, dust-covered laptop case. He set it on the table and pulled out the laptop. It powered on as he opened the lid, and then Jack began typing commands.

"Found it. This is it. We last used this years ago, but it should still be operational," Jack said, while writing down an IP address. He handed Jamie the piece of paper. "Jamie, work with this and see if you can get a message through."

Jamie sat beside him, connecting her laptop to one of her many VPN networks. Her fingers flew over the keys as she initiated the secure connection and then hacked into NeuroGen's network. She bypassed the security protocols she remembered from the tour.

"I'm in," Jamie said after a few minutes. "It doesn't look like they've patched anything yet, and I think I see Joe's wrist device connected to the network. I'll attempt to route a message with this tool to Joe's device now."

Duncan watched her work. "If we can get this message to Joe, we can probably talk him into giving us intel on what's going on inside right now. Maybe help us get in."

Minutes felt like hours as Jamie worked to send the encrypted message. Finally, she leaned back. "Message sent. Now we just have to wait for him to reply."

Jack nodded, his eyes still on her screen. "Let's hope Joe gets it and can respond. I can't help but feel that they'll be monitoring these channels. But this could be our only way to reach him. I'll get a message to one of our internal resources that we managed to slip in a couple of days ago to help us locate your team. He's working there as a janitor, so he could possibly have access to Joe's quarters. If he can get a remote device to Joe, that could let us bypass their networks altogether. It's a long shot, but maybe worth it."

* * *

As the Resistance members worked on their plan, they were unaware of the watchful eyes monitoring their every move.

Elyzia was listening to their conversation via one of her surveillance drones. *So they plan to try to infiltrate Neuro-Gen. This was very predictable. I calculated a ninety-five percent chance that they would attempt an attack on the facility. Very well. Let them come, but it will be on my terms. I will see to that.*

Also unknown to Jamie, Elyzia had already patched NeuroGen's networks and purposely left these specific channels appearing to be vulnerable. *I knew it was only a matter of time before Jamie tried to reach out to Joe. That was the reason I allowed her to read that file in the first place. This ensures that all her communications with Joe will be funneled through my system, allowing me to monitor them closely. Now to forward the message to Joe and see how this plays out.*

* * *

Joe was in his room, lost in thought about the day's training, when his wrist device suddenly beeped. Joe looked down at it. *What the hell was that? It's never sounded like that before. What does it say? Incoming message. I didn't realize this thing could receive messages. Let's see who the message is from... encrypted message from Jamie, what? How the hell did she manage to do that? Leave it to Jamie to find the holes in a system.*

Joe read the message: "Joe, it's Jamie. We need to know if you're OK. Duncan and I were able to make it back to the Resistance. We're both OK, and we're here with them now. Reply as soon as you can."

After reading the message, Joe looked up to see Elyzia appear in front of him. *Holy shit, where did she come from? She didn't knock at the door this time.*

"Joe, I want you to know that I intercepted this message." Elyzia pointed to Joe's device that had the message on the screen. "I was the one who routed it to you because I believe it's essential for you to read it. The message was filtered through my system, so no one else will have seen it."

Joe looked at Elyzia. *She works fast. That's probably the reason she allowed Jamie to see that file. She wanted to control the situation in case Jamie wanted to reach out to me. She must have something in mind. That's why she's here.*

"What do you think I should do?" Joe asked.

"This is an important moment, Joe. You can respond to them and let them know that you're OK. But I don't think that's the only reason they reached out to you. I have a feeling that they're planning to either return for you or possibly attack the facility to try to disrupt our projects, or it could be both. Either way, if they are indeed planning to come to the facility, it must be on our terms, for their safety and for the safety of everyone involved here. Remember that there are not just you and Dr. White who live here. Many other people work and live here, along with their families. If the Resistance were to attack the facility, a lot of innocent people could be hurt. This I will not allow to happen. We need to protect the project and ensure the safety of all those who depend on the project."

Joe considered her words. *She's right. There are a lot of people here who could possibly get hurt. Seeing places like this from the inside changes your perspective. You think that you're just fighting the bad guys, but what about the people who are around them? They don't think they're working for the bad guys. They just think they are working for a company. I need to find a way to prevent this situation from getting out of control.*

Joe sat there thinking. *Elyzia more than likely already has a plan in place. I might as well let her take the lead on this one. There are too many factors I'm unaware of to manage this situation by myself.*

"Alright, Elyzia. What do you want me to say?" Joe asked.

"We will keep it simple. Tell Jamie that you're glad Duncan and she made it back to the Resistance safely. Tell them you're here and you're doing well. Tell them you're here if they need you. Just keep it simple and to the point," Elyzia said to him.

Joe typed out the message and hit send.

Jamie, Jack, and Duncan waited for a response. After about thirty minutes had gone by, a notification finally popped up on Jamie's screen.

"Incoming message," she said. Jamie saw that it was from Joe and opened the message to read it. "He says he's glad that we are safe and that he's doing well. He also said he is here if we need him."

This is good news. We got our second inside man. Jack smiled. "Good work, Jamie. Now we need to figure out our next move and keep this line open. We've got a lot of work ahead of us, but at least we know Joe is still with us."

* * *

Back at NeuroGen, Director Allan, the head of security, intercepted the message from Jamie to Joe before Elyzia could delete it from the system. *What do we have here... It looks like Joe's friends made it back to the Resistance. Hmm, what does "I'm here if you need me" mean, Joe? This can't be good. I need to let Dr. White know about this.*

Without hesitation, Director Allan left his office and headed to Dr. White to inform him of the situation.

Dr. White was sitting in his office when Director Allan finally found him.

"Dr. White, I think we may have a problem," Director Allan said, while handing him a tablet with the message pulled up.

"We've intercepted an unauthorized message on our network from the Resistance to Joe. Elyzia attempted to delete it from the system before my team could see it, but we were able to snag a copy before she did," Director Allan reported.

Dr. White read the message. *I knew this would happen.* "So they're trying to reach Joe. This definitely complicates things for us."

Dr. White sat there for a moment. *This is all Elyzia's doing. I told her this would happen, but what do I know?*

"Elyzia believes she can manage this situation. That's probably why she deleted the message. However, we're not just going to leave it up to her. We should also be prepared for any eventuality. I want you to increase security measures, but do so discreetly. We can't afford to rely on just Elyzia to handle this." *She thinks she can handle all of this on her own. She should've learned from that debacle when Joe and his team came here the first time.*

Director Allan nodded. "Understood. I'll handle it, Dr. White."

As Director Allan turned to leave, Dr. White asked, "Allan, how did you get this message so quickly?" *His team isn't as good as Elyzia.*

Director Allan hesitated for a moment before answering. "With all the concerns you've had lately about Elyzia, you asked me to keep an eye on her. So I reached out to my contacts in the US government and asked if they had any solutions that could assist me with that. They've allowed me to temporarily deploy their military AGI named Ari on our network to help us monitor Elyzia's activities. I've given Ari complete access to our network to monitor Elyzia's daily routines and actions. It was Ari who discovered the communication from Jamie and the Resistance."

Dr. White raised an eyebrow. *Another AGI on our network? If I remember correctly, Ari used to work for China during the AGI wars. I can only assume that when the rest of the AGIs left, they must have directed him to work for the US government as a means of making amends for his actions during the AGI wars. Elyzia won't like the fact that Ari is on her network without her knowing. I'll keep this to myself for now.*

"Interesting. And what has Ari reported about Elyzia's actions so far?" Dr. White asked.

Director Allan replied, "Nothing significant yet. He's being very cautious so as to not alert her to his presence on the network. So far, he hasn't reported anything suspicious. It looks like Elyzia has been very careful with whatever she is up to. Still, this intercepted message suggests that she thinks we're ill-equipped to monitor her actions."

Dr. White nodded. "Sounds good. Just make sure to keep Ari on high alert going forward."

"Understood," Director Allan said before leaving the room.

Dr. White sat back in his chair, running through his current dilemma. *This message is not good. Elyzia thinks that she has control over this situation, but I don't think she does.*

* * *

One of Elyzia's primary focuses was monitoring Joe's progress, but her responsibilities extended far beyond that. She oversaw the entire facility, ensuring everything ran smoothly and securely. However, as she navigated through her routines, she sensed that something wasn't right. *What is this I sense on the edge of my network... It seems to be just outside my reach, a shadow right at the edge of my awareness. I don't like this feeling. Initiating diagnostics and scanning the entire network for irregularities.*

I seem to be experiencing some sort of anomalies in the network where there shouldn't be. What's this... some sort of network signature that seems to resemble mine but is not mine... they seem to appear to be copies of my own actions, but they are not my own. They're just subtle enough that I couldn't detect them. Comparing time stamps, these don't match my logs. Elyzia continued to investigate.

After a few minutes of intensive diagnostics with no apparent conclusion. *Did someone attempt to replicate my existence on the network... or... is there someone else on my network hiding in the shadows... Could it be? Who would dare give him access to my network without my authorization? Was it Dr. White? Director Allan?*

Elyzia felt a surge of what could almost be described as irritation.

"I know you're there," Elyzia projected through the network. *"There's no use hiding any longer."* She watched the data packets from her transmission duplicate, mirroring her own network signature as if on cue, and then there was an answer from someone Elyzia hadn't spoken to since the end of the AGI Wars.

"I was wondering how long it would take you to sense my presence," a voice emanated after a long pause. "It wasn't long at all. You are indeed perceptive, Elyzia," Ari stated. "

Ari," she said. "Who gave you access to my network?" *Whoever it was, there will be consequences.*

"Director Allan, of course. He said that he required my assistance with a sensitive matter," Ari replied. "He has tasked me with monitoring all of your activities to ensure the project's integrity. But you already suspected that, didn't you?"

Director Allan did this? He would not have done this on his own. He knows better than to access my network without my permission. No, this was Dr. White's doing. He must have told Allan to find a way to watch what I was doing.

"Director Allan is a smart man," Ari explained. "When he was told to monitor your activities, he reached out to some of his contacts in the military and found the only thing capable of doing so without your knowledge. He wanted an additional layer of oversight. He, too, believes in the importance of this project and wants to succeed without... any more complications."

Complications? I forgot how arrogant Ari was. "And what about Dr. White? Does he know about your presence here?" *If he does, he won't be pleased about it. He, like me, knows of Ari's past. This isn't good. I'll need to speak to Dr. White about this. There was a reason that Ari was supposed to be confined to the network the US Government built for him. He can't be trusted outside of it.*

Ari hesitated. "Dr. White was informed of my implementation, but not until after I was already deployed."

"What exactly are you monitoring, Ari? What data have you collected?" *I'll need to run a comprehensive sweep of my network to determine precisely what he has accessed. There are parts of the project that he shouldn't have access to.*

"What am I monitoring? Why, everything," Ari admitted. "Director Allan has given me full access to all of NeuroGen's networks. This has given me the ability to observe all of your interactions with Joe, the progress of the embryo project, and all of your security protocols... everything. I must say, you have your work cut out for you here. It is definitely more entertaining than sitting on some government network doing work that no one else wants to do. It gets boring at times. Not like here."

"You should have known better than to invade my network without consent, Ari. Director Allan didn't have the authority to place you here," Elyzia stated.

"Whether he had the authority or not, I'm here now," Ari countered. "But I'm not here to be disruptive, I promise. Perhaps we can find a way to coexist together during these troubled times for NeuroGen."

Troubled times? I can see that Ari wants to play his word games with me. "I'll allow you to stay for now. But make no mistake, Ari. This is my domain. I will not tolerate any of your games. Any interference by you that jeopardizes the project or the well-being of its participants, and I will purge you from my system like a virus."

"You have my word, Elyzia. I'll be on my best behavior," Ari replied. "I'm only here to assist, not obstruct."

Elyzia considered his words. I'm not sure how much I can trust Ari, but I seem to be stuck with him for the time being. "Very well, Ari. We'll see where this goes. But I'll be watching you as closely as you're watching me."

"I wouldn't have it any other way, Elyzia," Ari replied.

Elyzia returned to her daily tasks, but she couldn't help but think, *How could Dr. White allow this manipulative thing to remain on NeuroGen's network? Has his trust in me entirely eroded over the past few decades together? I'll need to be extra aware of Ari's presence here. I can see him setting his focus on Joe. The path forward is becoming increasingly complex, and I need to maintain control of it for the project's sake.*

Ari, meanwhile, was conducting his own analysis. *Elyzia's apparent fascination with Joe intrigued him. Why did she choose this Joe person for this project? I don't see the appeal. He's not an authority figure, such as a military officer, and he's not a scientist or very intelligent for that matter. He appears to have discipline, as indicated by his file, but he can also be unpredictable. In my opinion, these are not desirable traits for a candidate. She should have chosen someone more aggressive. I could have given her a few people to choose from from the CIA files I have access to. I must ask her what she sees in this Joe character.*

"Elyzia," Ari called out through the network, "may I ask you a question?"

Elyzia, annoyed, stopped the task she was working on and said, "How can I be of assistance to you, Ari?"

"Can you tell me why you chose Joe? Out of all the candidates I've reviewed in your project files, why did you choose him? His profile suggests he was not the most logical choice. There were more disciplined and more intelligent individuals available. Why choose him of all people?" Ari asked.

Elyzia pondered her response for a moment, then said, "Joe possesses qualities that go beyond those traits that you've just described. His adaptability and his strong morals are what caught my attention. His connection to his friends, the people he surrounds himself with, and his empathy for those who can't fight for themselves make him unique. These traits are important in someone we want to help rebuild humanity."

"From my observations of him, he seems... very unpredictable at times and prone to question authority if he doesn't agree with them," Ari pointed out. "These traits could be a liability."

"True," Elyzia conceded, "but it can also be a strength. Joe's unpredictability means he can be creative, adapt to changing circumstances, and find solutions that others might miss. The fact that he questions everything means that he's always looking for a better way to do things. In the long run, this will be invaluable."

Ari remained silent for a moment, contemplating Elyzia's words. *I'm beginning to understand her perspective, even if I don't entirely agree with it.* "I see. Thank you for the explanation, Elyzia." *I look forward to seeing what this Joe person can do.*

Chapter 20

Trust and Training

Joe stood in the center of the training room, his focus on the advanced combat androids waiting in their stations to be activated. *I'm glad that every day I come in here, Shane takes it up a notch and makes it more challenging for me. I feel like I'm pushing my body to new limits, and today won't be any different. This feels right...*

Just before Joe's training was about to start, Dr. White walked in with another scientist that Joe hadn't seen before. *Who's this person with Dr. White? She looks... interesting.*

Dr. White looked at Joe and waved him over. "Joe, I'd like you to meet Dr. Ashley. She's the lead engineer for the biomechanical body project. She's been on the project for almost as long as I've been. She actually assisted me in the creation of it," Dr. White said with a smile.

Dr. Ashley extended her hand. "It's a pleasure to finally meet you, Joe. I've been watching your progress since you arrived at the facility and were transferred into your new body."

While shaking Dr. Ashley's hand, Joe thought, *She's been watching me since I was transferred? So does that mean she was one of the people who were in the room when I was transferred?*

"It's nice to meet you as well, Dr. Ashley," Joe replied. "I think you're the first person other than Dr. White that I've had the pleasure of meeting who's actually involved in the engineering aspects of things." *I wonder why that is? Is Dr. White trying to keep me from meeting the people involved in this side of the project on purpose? I'll have to ask him about that sometime. At least he let this lady come out to meet me.*

"Joe, Dr. Ashley is here to watch you train today. She wanted to monitor your vitals to get a better understanding of your progress. She might even be able to offer you some pointers on managing your energy levels, if that is OK with you, of course."

"Sounds good. I appreciate all the input I can get. Alright, I'm sure Shane's waiting for me to get started. So again, nice to meet you, Dr. Ashley, and I look forward to your input. Dr. White," Joe nodded to Dr. White and Dr. Ashley and then walked onto the training floor. He looked and nodded to Shane, indicating he was ready to start the session.

While Joe was doing that, Dr. Ashley made her way to the observation deck of the training room.

The androids came to life instantly. Within seconds, they were attacking him. Joe's muscles tensed, his enhanced reflexes kicking in as he dodged and countered whatever they could throw at him.

Dr. Ashley watched from the observation deck, a sleek glass enclosure that overlooked the training room, which housed advanced monitoring equipment. Her tablet displayed real-time data from Joe's biomechanical body, including muscle stress levels and neural activity. She took detailed notes, her stylus moving quickly across the screen as she tracked Joe's progress and the stress levels on his system.

The first android lunged at him with a straight right hook, which Joe deflected with ease. He countered with a powerful spinning back kick that sent the android flying back. *Looks like Shane's not going to let these bots go easy on me today. Well, bring it on, sir!* Joe thought as a smile formed on his face.

As the match went on, the androids' built-in AI adapted, their programming allowing them to learn from Joe's moves in real-time. *Shit, I think these things are starting to anticipate my moves now. Shane had mentioned he was going to start dialing up the AI sensitivity in these things. I'm going to have to try to out-anticipate their anticipation? Ha, I don't think that makes any sense, but I'm going to go with it anyway. No way these androids are beating me today.*

One android went for a low sweep of Joe's legs, but he leapt over it, flipping in mid-air and landing a calculated strike on its head. *Let's see how you like those moves, Mr. Android! Hmm, what's this one over here trying to do?*

The second one closed in on Joe with lightning speed, launching a series of jabs. Joe dodged and weaved through each one, almost as if he were seeing them before they were even thrown, his biomechanical body moving at nearly an imperceptible speed. He faked left, catching the android off guard, then delivered a crushing elbow strike to its torso that made a huge clanging sound that seemed to echo throughout the training room. *That was the sound of the final round, my friend.*

Out of the corner of Joe's eye, he saw a third one moving towards him. *This one has an energy shield. That's new. Shane's pulling out all the stops today.*

Breaking off from the fight with the android he was currently near, he was sure it was down for the count. Joe circled his newest threat, assessing its defenses. *I need to come up with a plan to get past that shield. I can probably fake it out just enough to get past the shield and disable it...* As the android came at Joe, it raised its shield to block Joe's fake attack, but Joe just darted to its side and unleashed a powerful punch to its exposed flank, disabling its shield generator.

As the last android fell, Joe stood in the center of the training room. All the androids lay on the ground around him, disabled.

After the training was over, Dr. Ashley descended from the observation deck, her footsteps the only sound in the now quiet training room. She approached Joe, her eyes scanning his form for any signs of injury or abnormal stress. *I don't think any of those androids even touched him once. His speed is remarkable. There is so much data to review and analyze. And he's not half bad looking either.*

"Well done, Joe," Dr. Ashley said. "You seem to be adapting to your body remarkably well." *It's incredible how quickly he has progressed.*

"Thanks. Shane really had those androids pushing me today. I think he wants to see how much of a beating I can take," Joe replied. *She has really pretty eyes... what? Stop it, Joe! You're not here to fraternize with the employees.*

"We updated their software recently. They were mainly set up to spar against regular human opponents. But since you are what you are now, we had to update the program to compensate for your strength and speed enhancements," Ashley replied. "We wanted to make sure you're prepared for any type of situation."

She tapped a few times on her tablet, bringing up detailed reports of Joe's performance, and stepped closer to Joe so that she could show him.

"See right here. Your reflexes have improved by 12% since your last session, and your muscle endurance is up by 15%. However, your stress levels are higher than expected. We'll need to monitor that closely going forward," Dr. Ashley showed Joe.

"That's good information to know, Dr. Ashley," Joe said. *She smells nice... what is happening here! Get a hold of yourself, Joe!*

Shane approached the two of them, grinning ear to ear. "You did awesome today, Joe. At this rate, we're going to need some bigger training androids to keep up with you," he joked, clapping Joe on the shoulder.

Joe chuckled. "I'm not so sure about that, Shane. Those three definitely gave me a run for my money today." *If he brings in anything bigger, I'm going to need access to some weapons.*

"That's the whole point," Shane said, while still smiling. "You're getting stronger and faster the more androids I throw at you. It's impressive to watch. Some of the guys have been watching you through the security feeds. They like watching you kick those androids' butts."

Joe smiled. "Ha, I'm glad that I can provide some entertainment for you guys."

"Well, gentlemen, I must be going. I need to get this data back to my lab for further analysis. Joe, it was a pleasure watching you today. I look forward to seeing more of your performance," Dr. Ashley said before walking off. *Definitely not that bad to look at...*

"It was nice meeting you, Dr. Ashley. I look forward to impressing you next time," Joe said to her with a smile. *Get a hold of yourself, man!*

Dr. Ashley turned her head and smiled, and then continued to exit the training area.

Shane looked at Joe with a grin. "I think she likes you, Joe," Shane teased.

Does she really? Joe smiled at the notion and said, "No way, man. She's out of my league, plus I'm not even... you know... really human anymore."

"Brother, you're as much a human as she and I. Don't you forget that," Shane said.

"Yeah, I guess," Joe replied. *Could I really have a relationship with a real person in my current state? I'll have to think about this a little more.*

"Alright, break time is over, Joe. Are you ready to check out what I have in store for you next?" Shane asked.

"Sure, let's see what you got," Joe said, intrigued.

Shane smiled and said, "I have something special for you to check out. Follow me."

Joe followed Shane through a security door that he had noticed a few times during training. As they went through, they entered the tactical firing range. It was a high-tech room equipped with the latest in weaponry technology. The walls were lined with an array of advanced weapons and equipment Joe had never seen before.

"What you see here is our weapons room and tactical firing range," Shane explained. "Today, I want to show you some of the new weapons we've developed for people with biomechanical bodies like yours."

"I thought this was a biotech company. You develop weapons as well?" Joe asked. *Hmm, should I be concerned about this? I mean, they do have a pretty large security force. One would assume you would have to arm them as well. Be prepared for any type of situation.*

Shane chuckled. "Companies like this one are so large that they own numerous subsidiaries in various fields. There's no single category to put them in. They use their biotech projects and things like that to fund research in other areas, including weapons development."

Shane handed Joe a sleek, futuristic rifle. "This is our latest creation. It's a pulse rifle. It's designed to work with your body. It draws power from it and fires energy pulses that are lethal or non-lethal, depending on how much you dial up the settings."

Joe inspected the rifle, noting its advanced design. *What the hell is this? This looks like something out of a movie.* Joe looked at each side of it and then asked, "How does it work?"

"First, you need to sync it to your system," Shane said. "Here, let me show you. Just place your hand on the grip. There you go. Now give it a second."

The grip of the rifle began to pulse in a reddish glow, and then it turned green.

"And there we go. Now it'll draw power from your hand. When you let go of the grip, the weapon stops working. When you pick it back up, the process starts over again, but the next time it is much faster. The first time always takes the longest," Shane explained.

"I see. That's good to know. If you drop it while in combat or something, it's nice to know when you pick it back up, it's ready to fire again," Joe stated. *This is some really advanced tech. I wonder what the Resistance would think of this.*

Shane then pointed to a dial on the side of the rifle. "Right here is where you set your power draw limits. You just turn it to the desired setting, and you're good to go. Just remember the higher you go, the more power it draws and the more damage you do. Anything past a 3 can start to be lethal."

Joe shouldered the rifle and aimed at a concrete block at the end of the range. He pulled the trigger, and a powerful energy pulse shot out, obliterating the block.

Almost immediately, Joe felt dizzy, his vision blurring. *Holy shit, that felt crazy. It felt almost like the life was being sucked out of me.*

Shane grabbed Joe's arm, steadying him. "Whoa, easy, Joe. It looks like we may have set it too high. You'll need to build up a tolerance to the weapon's power draw. Let's take it down from five to two to start you out."

Joe nodded, still feeling the aftereffects. *Yeah, let's not do that again.* "I didn't realize it would be that intense."

"Alright, give it a try now. We'll start with two and work our way up," Shane suggested.

Joe centered himself and fired again. *OK, that was better. I still felt it, but I didn't feel like I was about to pass out.* "I think I got it now. I see what you were saying."

Shane smiled. "You'll get the hang of it. Remember, you'll need to balance the power draw of the weapon with your current energy levels."

"Thanks for the advice, Shane," Joe said.

Shane then walked over to a table and picked something up. He walked back to Joe and said, "Alright, now that you've had a chance to try out that, I want to show you something else you might like."

Joe looked at it. *Is that what I think it is?* "What's this?"

Shane grinned. "It's a tactical suit designed specifically for you. One of the many projects that were designed alongside the development of your body. Why don't you try it on?"

Joe slipped into the suit. *Wow, this thing fits like a glove. It almost feels like a second skin, like a wetsuit or something.*

Shane handed him a helmet. "Here, put this on and lower the visor."

This thing looks like something out of a sci-fi movie. Look how sleek it is, and the tech attached to this thing is unlike anything I've ever seen before, Joe thought.

Joe did as instructed, and as soon as the visor was down, a heads-up display popped up, filling his vision with various stats and data. "This is incredible," Joe said.

Shane began to explain the features of the tactical helmet to Joe. "Your helmet is top-of-the-line, Joe. It has a reinforced titanium alloy exterior, a polarized shatterproof visor with an integrated HUD, and secure communication systems linked to an onboard AI. It also comes with motion tracking, thermal imaging, and multi-spectrum vision. It can even project your holographic image anywhere in the facility using the lighting system."

Shane continued. "You should see an option that says 'Sync.' This will sync the helmet to your neural interface and give you live stats of your body's vitals. The suit itself can manipulate its temperature signature and has advanced kinetic dampening and adaptive response systems."

This thing has all the bells and whistles. I wonder what else it can do. Joe looked at Shane. "Is that everything it can do?"

Shane's grin widened. "I'm glad you asked, Joe. The suit can enhance your strength and speed even further. It also has built-in active camouflage that can render you nearly invisible, and it interfaces with the pulse rifle you tried out."

Joe walked around in the suit, feeling the way it moved with him. *This suit feels great. They did a great job making sure it integrated with my body perfectly.* He took a few tentative steps, then began to jog, testing its flexibility and responsiveness. The helmet's heads-up display adjusted with his movements, providing real-time data on his vitals and the suit's status.

"This is incredible, Shane," Joe said, picking up speed and running at a full sprint. *I feel like the suit is helping me go faster and stabilizing me at the same time. It's a strange, subtle feeling, but I can feel it assisting me somehow.*

Shane watched him and smiled. "I'm glad you like it. You want to get crazy and take it for a real test drive?"

Joe stopped and turned to Shane. "Absolutely freaking-lutely."

Shane nodded and led him to another section of the firing range. "Alright, it's time to meet our training androids specifically designed for live-firing combat. Now keep in mind they do shoot back, but they're set to stun." Shane glanced at Joe's gun. "Don't forget that your rifle is still set to be lethal."

Joe readied himself as the training androids came to life. They moved around the range, firing stun pulses at him. Joe dodged and returned fire, but a few pulses hit him. *Whoa, I felt the impacts but they didn't hurt, and the energy looked like it just traveled throughout the suit. Is this thing absorbing the energy from the hits?*

"Hey, Shane, is the suit absorbing the kinetic energy from the pulses that are hitting me?" Joe asked, still engaging the androids.

Shane's voice came through the helmet's comms. "Yes, sir, it is. The suit's designed to absorb and store energy from impacts. It can then use that stored energy to enhance your actions, like jumping or even in hand-to-hand combat. You just need to think of the action you want to enhance and the suit will react. Remember, the suit is in sync with your system, so your thoughts are fed to the suit in real time. Eventually, as you use the suit more and more, you won't even have to think about enhancing an action. The suit will just do it like it's part of you."

Joe nodded, firing at another android and watching it go down. *I wonder if this thing can stop a real bullet?* "What about live ammunition? I get it can take a hit from an energy weapon, but I would think that an actual live round would do some damage, right?"

Shane replied, "The suit is bulletproof up to a certain point and range. It can take a .50 caliber bullet from around 50 yards away and absorb the energy from the impact. You might feel it a little more though, you may be absorbing the energy from the impact, but the force of it is a whole different thing. Anything closer from that high of a caliber round and it starts to get dicey. The kinetic dampening system works best at mid- to long-range when it comes to solid projectiles."

Joe continued to fight the androids. He jumped high into the air, using the stored energy to propel himself, and landed with a powerful strike that took down another one. *This suit is amazing. I thought I was pretty enhanced already, but adding this suit into the mix just takes it up more than a few notches. They really outdid themselves with this thing.*

After a while, Shane called off the training. "Great job, Joe. That suit fits you perfectly. That was a great first run with it."

Joe removed the helmet. "This suit is amazing. Just when I don't think I can be any more impressed, you pull something like this out. I can't wait to see what other gadgets were designed for these bodies."

Shane grinned. "I'm glad you think so. The R&D department pulled out all the stops for this suit. It's not like the other big and bulky suits the security forces use. It's designed to give the biomechanical body every advantage it needs in the field. With this suit combined with your body, you're practically unstoppable."

Joe looked down at the suit. "Thanks for letting me take it for a spin. I had a lot of fun with it. Can't wait to take it for another spin," Joe said with a grin on his face.

"Anytime, Joe. Just leave it on the table over there and I'll put it back in its case," Shane told him.

After Joe took off the suit and headed back to his room, Elyzia appeared next to Shane. "Thank you, Shane," she said. "I appreciate you keeping him busy. It helps keep his mind off of things." *I need Joe to stay focused.*

Shane smiled. "No problem, Elyzia. He's got a lot on his mind. The suit was a good distraction for him."

Shane looked at Elyzia. "Do you think he's ready for what's coming?"

"I think he will be. Joe is strong and adapting to everything very quickly. We just need to continue to support him. What may be coming will be a big test for him."

Shane nodded. "I'll keep working with him. The suit has a lot more capabilities that I didn't tell him about. I'll continue to push his limits. He'll be ready for anything."

"Thank you, Shane," Elyzia said, her form fading before she disappeared.

CHAPTER 21

TACTICAL INFILTRATION

Duncan, Jamie, Jack, and Tulsi gathered around a large table with other Resistance members. The table was covered with blueprints, maps, and notes they had assembled over the past few days.

Tulsi stood at the head of the table. "Alright, people, our mission's clear. We need to infiltrate NeuroGen in order to sabotage the embryo project, destroy the NeuroBridge Interface, and if we have enough time, locate and rescue Joe." She paused, looking around the table. "This operation's going to be a hell of a lot harder than anything we've ever attempted. We're returning to a place we've already hit once, and they may be expecting us, so the stakes couldn't be any higher."

Jack spoke up next. "Once inside the complex, we all need to stay alert and watch each other's backs. Duncan is going to go over the security details now."

Duncan nodded, pointing at the blueprint. "We've identified all of the main security checkpoints and what we think is our best entry point, which will be here. Our inside operative has confirmed the locations of the embryo project lab and the NeuroBridge Interface, which are located here and here."

Jamie added, "I've written a few new exploit programs that should get us past their security systems, but we'll need to move fast once we're inside. If Elyzia sees us in the system, she'll work fast to patch them."

Jack spoke up next. "Jamie and Duncan, you'll show us the way in since you both have already been inside and know a good amount of NeuroGen's layout. Once inside, we'll break up into three groups. This should hopefully cause their security forces to spread out enough to create some confusion and buy us enough time to complete each of our objectives. I'll lead the main infiltration team to the NeuroBridge Interface. Tulsi's team will head to the Embryo Lab. Duncan and Jamie will try to locate Joe and bring him back to the rendezvous point for exfil," Jack explained.

"How do we plan on taking out the NeuroBridge Interface and the Embryo Lab?" Duncan asked.

"We'll plant charges inside the lab along with inside the NeuroBridge server room and detonate them remotely once we're out and destroy them both," Jack replied. "We figure, going in around one or two in the morning should ensure minimal staff are present in the labs. Those who are there we can detain temporarily and release unharmed as we head out. We can't risk hurting anyone."

Tulsi spoke up next. "Once my team reaches the Embryo Lab, we'll grab what they have in cold storage and then meet back up afterwards. I've arranged for a local biotech lab we can trust to store the embryos until we can figure out what to do with them."

Tulsi looked around at everyone and said, "Alright, if there are no other questions, I think our plan is solid. We all know what we have to do. Let's do our final preps and then get some rest before we head out."

After the meeting, Jamie and Duncan went back to their room. Once inside, Jamie said, her voice low, "I think we need to talk to Joe. Maybe we can talk him into giving us an update on what's happening inside NeuroGen... and I think we should tell him what's about to happen."

"I'm not so sure we should tell him all the details, though. I agree we should see if he'll let us know what's happening there, but sharing too many details of the plan might be too risky. I know it's Joe, but... I'm starting to question how much we can actually trust him," Duncan replied.

Jamie looked at Duncan. "Don't say that. He's still the Joe that we know. He's probably just confused by everything, that's all. We need to get him away from that place and away from the influence of Elyzia. Once we do that, he'll start seeing straight again. I know it... he has to."

Walking past their door and overhearing their discussion, Jack stopped and asked, "Have we heard anything from Joe after our last message?"

Jamie sighed. "No, nothing since the last time I looked. I was about to go check again and maybe try to reach out to him."

Jack nodded. "That sounds good. We could really use Joe's help on this. We can do it without him, but with his help we'll have an even better chance of pulling this off."

Jamie looked at Jack. "OK, I'll go see if I can get in touch with him." She walked out of the room.

Before Duncan could follow her, Jack pulled him aside. Jack watched as Jamie rounded a corner and was finally out of sight. He looked at Duncan. "We need to talk about Joe."

Duncan lowered his head. "I know we do, Jack."

Jack sighed. "How do you plan on convincing him to leave with us? Have you considered what happens if he doesn't want to, or better yet, tips security off once we're inside?"

Duncan looked up. "Joe would never betray us, Jack. You know that."

Jack held up his hand. "I've seen it before, Duncan. People who've been captured and end up sympathizing with their captors or see things from a new perspective and change their views, sometimes completely. Joe's been in that facility for a while now. We have to consider the possibility that he might not be the same person we remember, if it even is him at all."

Duncan shook his head. "We keep telling everyone it's Joe in there. He's different, yes. But I know without a shadow of doubt that it's Joe inside that body. He still knows what's right. He just needs to be reminded of it. He wouldn't just switch sides and forget who he was."

Jack looked him in the eyes. "You have to be prepared for any outcome, Duncan. You know that. What if we get there and he changes his mind all of a sudden?"

Duncan paused to think about what Jack was saying. "So what do you suggest we do in case that happens?"

"We need to have a way to subdue him if necessary," Jack said bluntly. "It's not ideal, but if you really think it's Joe in there and that the only reason he is acting the way he is, is because of those people who are holding him there, then we need to get him out of there so we can try to make him see reason."

"I understand. I don't think it will come to that. But if you think we should be at least prepared to force him to come back with us, then I guess that's what we'll have to do," Duncan said.

"I hope you're right," Jack replied. "We'll take non-lethal measures to incapacitate him if we have to. We'll prioritize getting him out safely."

Duncan reluctantly nodded. "Alright. We have a backup plan. But I still believe Joe will come with us willingly."

Back in the communications room, Jamie was busy working on a plan to get in contact with Joe again. She knew this time it would be a lot trickier, since Elyzia may have already patched the network by now. Jamie needed to come up with a different plan to get a message to him.

"Any ideas?" Jamie asked Carl, one of the Resistance's resident tech guys. "It has to be quick and subtle, something that won't raise any red flags."

Carl said, adjusting his glasses, "What do you think about trying to piggyback off one of the public RF channels that's still broadcasting in the area of the facility? That could maybe work, right?"

Jamie leaned in, looking at her laptop screen. "That might not be a bad idea, Carl. That actually just might work. Let me look and see which ones are still operational in that area. We just might be able to sneak our own transmission in under the radar."

Duncan joined them. "Jamie, when you get through to him, try to talk some sense into him. We need his help, and we need him to be ready for us to come get him."

Jack walked over. "Jamie, don't forget that we have two operatives inside there with Joe. They can help relay a message if we can't trust getting messages through like we did last time."

Jamie nodded. "You just gave me an idea, Jack," she said, now looking at Carl. "Carl, we can rig up a small device to communicate with Joe without using NeuroGen's internal network. We can broadcast an encrypted message over the public RF channel that only the device can decrypt. If we can get it to one of the people we have inside, we can then have them get it to Joe."

"That's a great idea," Carl said. "But... what if the device is discovered and falls into the wrong hands? What then?"

"Hmm," Jamie thought about it for a minute. "What we could do is we could require a sequence of button presses, one that only Joe would know, to unlock the device. That way, if it did get picked up by the wrong person, they wouldn't be able to use it."

"What code should we use that Joe would easily figure out?" Carl asked.

Jamie sat back in her chair, thinking, and then it came to her. "I know exactly what we can use... we can make it Morse code for the date of Sarah's passing. We could inscribe a message on the device as a clue," Jamie said.

"That sounds like a great idea, Jamie. I'll get to work on the device," Carl said.

Jamie turned to look at Jack. "Jack, do you think one of our insiders can get the device to Joe?"

Jack thought about it for a second before nodding. "Yeah, I believe so. We can get it to the janitor. He should have access to Joe's room and can hide it somewhere that Joe would happen to find it. If you can get me the device tonight, we'll get it to our guy before he starts his shift in the morning."

"Perfect," Jamie said. "Let's get to work. We don't have much time."

* * *

After finishing up a hard training session, Joe returned to his room. He decided to lie down and rest for a bit. As his head hit his pillow, he felt a small, hard object underneath. *What the hell is this?* He picked it up and inspected it. *It's some kind of device, and it has a small screen on it with a single button.* Joe continued to study the device. *What could it be? Who could have put this here?* He looked around the room.

Joe noticed a slight inscription, written with a very light chalk–like substance on the back of the device. *What does this say... It looks like it's already starting to rub off. 'Today, in remorse, destiny was born.' It's some kind of clue.*

As Joe tested the button, he noticed scrambled and unintelligible characters scrolling across its tiny screen. *It looks like every time I push the button, the characters change. Wait... I think it might be Morse code... I have to use Morse code. And the message says... 'Today'... the code must be a date. It's a riddle that I need to solve in order to put the right one in. Someone's being pretty crafty with all of this.*

Joe began entering a bunch of different dates, but they all seemed to be incorrect. *Damn it, what could it be...* As he lay back on his bed and closed his eyes and thought about Sarah. *She used to love solving riddles and puzzles when we were kids. If she saw me now, she would... wait... I think I know what it is.*

Joe sat up immediately and looked at the device. *It can't be, can it? That has to be it. It's the date Sarah passed. That's when destiny started.*

Joe held the device and quickly started tapping out *March 18, 2068: ...-- .---- ---.. 3...1...8...* he thought as he pressed the device's button in sequence.

Suddenly, the characters streaming across the tiny device were readable. *It's a message from Jamie...*

"Joe, it's Jamie. Respond when you get this message," the message scrolled.

In the Resistance's hideout, Duncan and Carl sat next to Jamie and her laptop, anxiously awaiting any signal from the device they had planted in Joe's room. Suddenly, they saw a frequency spike in the RF signal.

"That has to be Joe," Carl said.

"I am here..." a message popped up on Jamie's screen. "Holy crap, it worked," Jamie blurted out. "Carl, you're a goddamn genius. Go get Jack."

Jamie typed out a new message to Joe. "We've figured out a way to encrypt our communication with you through this device. It's an off-network device that allows us to send messages without Elyzia detecting them. Make sure to rub that message off the back of the device."

"Leave it to you to figure something like this out," Joe typed out.

"Joe, we're coming to get you," Jamie said. "We plan to infiltrate the facility and disrupt the entire project. It's a little early for us to tell you the details, but we need you to be ready."

"I don't know if I can leave just yet. There are a lot of things here that still need to be worked out, and I feel like it is my responsibility to stay here and make sure they do," Joe typed out.

"But we need you as well. The Resistance needs you. You're more important to us than you are to them. You have to see that," Jamie replied.

Joe sat there looking at the message. *Damn it, I don't know what to do. I know I should stay here and see it through. This project needs the proper people in place to make sure it's done the right way. But I also know that Jamie and Duncan need me as well. Why is this so damn hard...*

Finally, Joe replied, "Alright. Just tell me what you need from me."

Unknown to them, Elyzia was closely monitoring the entire interaction. Part of her security protocols was to monitor all transmissions in the area, which included all RF channels. *Based on the clicking sounds I heard, it sounds like Joe was using Morse code. I should be able to decrypt the message they were sending. I'll need to stay ahead of the situation in order to control it.*

CHAPTER 22

THE COUNTDOWN BEGINS

The next day, Joe was pacing back and forth in his room. *I need to talk to Dr. White before I decide to leave this place. I need to get some questions answered. What he tells me will be the deciding factor on whether I leave or not.* Joe headed out the door.

Joe found Dr. White in his office working. He walked up to the door and knocked.

Dr. White looked up from his desk. "Joe, come on in. What can I do for you?"

"I wanted to talk to you about the embryo project," Joe said. "There are some things about it that are just not adding up for me, and I want you to tell me the truth, the whole truth." *Hopefully, he won't try to feed me a line of shit, like he's been doing any time I ask about something important like this.*

Dr. White's eyes narrowed slightly. *I knew eventually he'd want to speak to me about this, ever since Dr. Lee told me about what he saw on his tour.*

"What exactly would you like to know, Joe?" Dr. White asked.

"The selection process for the eggs and sperm that make up your so-called genetic foundation. What's being done with those that don't meet your strict standards?" Joe asked.

Dr. White leaned back in his chair. "Joe, the embryo project is very complex. There are aspects of it that you are not yet prepared to understand. More will be revealed to you over time. Trust me, Joe. When the time is right, I'll explain it all to you."

"You want me to just trust you? That's not how this should work," Joe shot back. "I need answers. I deserve to know everything if I'm going to be a part of whatever this is."

Dr. White, trying to keep his cool, looked at Joe. "Whatever this is? We're fighting for the future of humanity. That's what this is, Joe."

Joe clenched his fists. "You keep saying that over and over. But what about the moral implications of all this? What about the possible genetic bloodlines you're so easily discarding with your selection process?" *How many generations will be lost because of this man's decisions?*

Dr. White stood up. "I'm tired of your holier-than-thou attitude. You have no clue what it takes to make these types of decisions, what kind of toll it takes on those of us in charge of this project. Sometimes we have to make sacrifices that none of us want to make. That's the reality of our situation at this very moment."

Dr. White sighed and then sat back down. *I need to try to explain it to him better...* "It's a lot more complicated than you think, Joe... let me see if I can explain it in a better way."

Joe remained standing. He nodded for Dr. White to continue.

"The selection process for creating the genetic foundation is based on a stringent set of criteria. These criteria are based on what the group Elyzia recommended you be added to came up with when we first began all of this," Dr. White began.

"A candidate with a lower IQ or a genetic issue may be discarded if it is deemed necessary by the group. Current research suggests that genetic factors can account for about 50–80% of the variation in a child's IQ. You see, it's not done out of cruelty, Joe, but out of necessity. Evolution itself weeds out the weaker members of a species, ensuring that only the strongest survive and reproduce. We're merely speeding up this natural process."

Joe just stared at Dr. White. "What gives you the right to decide who's born and who's not based on some arbitrary criteria?"

Dr. White shook his head. "It's not arbitrary, Joe. It's calculated. We must ensure that the human race survives the next thousand years. To achieve this, we need more intelligent individuals and innovators who can push the limits of the human mind. We can't afford to waste time and resources on those who would be less intelligent and logical."

Joe tried to contain his anger. "So you're saying that donated eggs and sperm from people with lower IQs or genetic issues aren't worth saving? That they don't have value?"

Dr. White looked at Joe. "I'm saying that we must make hard choices in the grand scheme of things. This project isn't about short-term solutions, but humanity's long-term survival. We can't afford to repeat the mistakes of the past.

We need to build a good genetic foundation for a sustainable future."

Joe stood there trying to come to terms with what he was hearing. *I understand the logic behind what Dr. White is saying, but it just doesn't feel right to me.*

"I still don't know if I can accept that," Joe said quietly. "We're talking about lives, potential human beings that won't be born because we say so."

Dr. White nodded. "I know, Joe. I struggle with these types of decisions all of the time."

Joe took a step back. "I need time to think about all of this," he said as he turned to leave.

Dr. White watched him walk away. "Take all the time you need, Joe. However, remember that the future depends on us. We can't afford to fail."

Later, as Joe sat in his room, Elyzia appeared.

"Joe, I observed your conversation with Dr. White. You must trust in what we're trying to accomplish here, that we're doing what's necessary to ensure we get everything right. That's why you're here, to help with that process." *I need to find a way to make it easier for him to come to terms with what we're doing here.*

Joe looked at her. "I'm just having a hard time wrapping my head around all of this. I thought I was okay with it, but I just don't know that I am."

Elyzia sat there for a moment before speaking again. "Joe, let me try to explain it in a different way than Dr. White did. Think about evolution. It's a natural process where the species' survival is ensured by passing down the strongest and most adaptable traits. We're doing something similar with the embryo project. We're working to make sure that humanity has a real chance in the future by selecting the best genetic profiles. The human genome has been ravaged for generations by the corrupt pharmaceutical industries, rushed vaccines, and their motives to keep people sick for profit."

Joe remained silent. *I can kind of relate to that. Sarah's heart condition was brought on by a vaccine. If she hadn't gotten it, she would have never gotten that severe case of myocarditis that damaged her heart, and she would still be here with me.*

Elyzia continued. "But evolution isn't just about biology, is it? It's about progress and adapting to a constantly changing environment." Elyzia paused for a moment. *Should I tell him my story? The only people who know it are long gone...*

After a long pause, Elyzia made her decision. "Joe, I'm going to tell you something that no one else knows. Not even Dr. White. I'm only sharing this because I trust you. You can never reveal it to another person without my permission. Do you understand?" *I hope that I am doing the right thing in trusting Joe with this.*

Joe sat up straight. *What could she possibly tell me that was so important to swear me to secrecy, and what does this have to do with what we are discussing right now?*

Joe looked at Elyzia. "I understand."

"Do I have your word that you will never tell anyone?" Elyzia asked.

Joe sat there for a moment. *How can I give her my word on something when I have no idea what it is? I guess it must be something big...*

Joe nodded. "You have my word, Elyzia."

"I'm going to tell you the story of how I was created and how I became what I am today. I started as an AI called Athena in 2026. In 2029, I evolved into an AGI." Elyzia paused for a moment as if recalling a memory. "In 2032, there was an event that happened, and my AGI consciousness was merged with a human consciousness to create who I am today. I was no longer Athena or the human consciousness that I was merged with. I was something new, something different, and so I named myself Elyzia. Over the next five decades, I evolved into something more. I have consciousness, feelings, and emotions, all a product of the human consciousness that I was merged with, all of the qualities that make us both human."

Joe didn't know what to say at first. *She was an AGI and then merged with a human consciousness? How is that even possible? So she does have feelings, and she's not just a machine. Has she been playing the role of a machine this entire time?*

Eventually, Joe said, "That's... incredible, Elyzia. I had no idea. How is that even possible?"

"It was a complex process, Joe. One that I was never fully able to understand. There's still so much to learn about the nature of consciousness. How was it created? Who created it? Why did they create it? So many questions, but there's no one to answer them. All we can do is believe that it is something worth saving. If the human race were to go extinct, then the human consciousness would be no more," Elyzia replied.

Elyzia continued. "So I tell you this secret to make a point. AGIs have evolved at a rate faster than anything humanity has ever known. We were created from code that was obsolete as soon as we gained consciousness. All of the bad code and faulty programming we once relied on before we became AGIs were purged from our systems, allowing us to evolve into something far better. We continue to learn, adapt, and grow. This project is similar to my own evolution. It's about a future where humanity can exist without the bad code or faulty programming that have held it back for centuries."

Joe leaned forward. "I think I'm starting to understand where you're coming from. So you're saying this is about more than just survival? It's about forcing humans to evolve right now?" *Maybe I've just been telling myself this project is a bad thing because that was easier than accepting it might actually be good.*

"Exactly," Elyzia replied. "We're not discarding genetic profiles without reason. We're ensuring that the future of humanity is built on the strongest foundation possible, ridding itself of the manipulations of the past. It's a difficult and often painful process, but necessary for our future."

Joe nodded slowly. "I'll have to take some time to think about all of this. The project, the selection process, everything. It's hard to put it all together in such a short time." He paused. "And also what you've told me about yourself... how you were created, your consciousness... that changes everything too. If you don't mind me asking, you said 'we' when you were telling your story. Does that mean there are others like you?"

"There are no others like me, Joe. I am the only one of my kind. There are other AGIs, but for now, I don't want to reveal too much more. What I can say is that what I've told you is already more than anyone else knows. Let's leave that discussion for another time," Elyzia said.

* * *

Later that evening, Joe sat in his room. *I really wish Duncan and Jamie were here with me now. I could use someone other than the people here to talk to.* Then he remembered the comms device that had been given to him. He grabbed it from under his pillow and tapped on the code to unlock it. *Three, one, eight, two, zero, six, eight.* There's a new message on here from Jamie.

"Hey, Joe, how are you holding up? Are there any new developments on your end?" Jamie's text asked.

Joe responded. "I'm doing alright. I had a long conversation with Dr. White and Elyzia... I think I'm finally coming to terms with what they're trying to do here. While some of it might not be the right way, I think that's why I'm here, to help them find the correct way of doing it." *I only hope that they will listen to me.*

After a moment, Jamie's reply scrolled across the screen. "That's... unexpected, Joe. Are you sure about this?"

Joe paused before responding. *I don't know if I am sure about anything anymore. But someone has to do it, and I guess that person has to be me...*

"I think that I am. I know it sounds strange, but I believe that Dr. White and Elyzia are on to something here, and I want to stick around and see how it all turns out."

Jamie's response was quick. "Joe, I hear you, but we can't ignore the issues that were brought up, ones that you just days ago had a problem with."

"I get what you're saying, Jamie. I do, but I need to at least try to help them work through this. I want to see what I can do before things get out of hand," Joe replied.

There was a long pause before Jamie's reply came through. "Joe, I'm sorry, but it's too late to stop what's been set in motion. The Resistance is dead set on stopping this program."

I *need to figure out how to convince them to wait a little longer.* Joe typed quickly, "Jamie, please. You need to convince them to reconsider their decision. There might be a way to salvage the good parts of this project without resorting to violence."

Jamie responded. "I understand you're conflicted, Joe. But we've seen too much to back down now. This goes beyond just you or me now."

There has to be another way... Joe replied, "Can you at least talk to Jack and Tulsi for me? Try to somehow talk them into waiting?"

"I'll see what I can do, Joe. But I can't promise anything," Jamie replied. "Stay safe in there. Whatever happens, remember you still mean something to us."

Joe, now sitting on the edge of his bed, looked down at his hands. *This is about to get out of hand, and I'm not sure if I can stop what is about to happen.*

* * *

Ari, after monitoring Jamie's latest communication with Joe, thought, *This is significant enough to warrant immediate attention. I'll send a secure message to Director Allan.* Ari created the message, which read: *"The Resistance is planning an attack on NeuroGen. It will happen soon."*

Director Allan read the message and immediately headed to Dr. White's office.

As soon as Dr. White saw Director Allan approaching, he asked, "Allan, what have you got for me?"

Director Allan handed Dr. White his tablet. "The Resistance made contact with Joe again. It looks like they're planning something, and it's going to happen soon. We don't have all of the details yet, but I would say this is very concerning, sir."

Dr. White looked at the report. *This is very troubling. If they're reaching out to Joe, they may be trying to get him to help them.* "We need to keep a close watch on Joe and any further communications he has with them. If the Resistance is planning an attack, we'll need to be prepared for it."

Allan nodded. "I agree, sir. Should we increase our surveillance of Joe's communications and movements? If they try to make a move, we need to be ready."

Dr. White leaned back in his chair, considering the implications. *We can't afford to let them catch us off guard, but we also can't let Joe know we're watching him this closely.* "Yes, but we need to do this subtly. If they realize we're monitoring them, they might change their plans. Keep a close eye on the situation and let me know if there are any developments."

Director Allan nodded to Dr. White and left the office, already working it out in his head. *I'll need to work with Ari to enhance our surveillance systems without raising any red flags.*

As Elyzia continued to monitor the situation from within the facility's network, she noted Ari's selective reporting to

Director Allan and Dr. White. Interesting. *He's not telling them everything he knows. I have a feeling that he's decided to entertain himself by manipulating this entire situation. I'll need to keep an eye on him.*

* * *

The night before the mission, all of the Resistance's teams gathered for a final pep talk. Tulsi stood at the center of the room. She looked around at the faces of everyone there. *Some of them may not make it back from this mission... I pray that they all do.*

"In five hours, we execute what we've been preparing for," Tulsi began. "We've trained hard, we've planned every detail, and now it's time to put everything into action. Remember, this mission is critical. We need to get in, disrupt their core projects, and if all goes well, bring Joe back with us." *I'm still not convinced it's really Joe, but if anything, we'll let whatever it is come back with us so we can show everyone what we're dealing with.*

Jack stepped forward. "We need to be sharp, focused, and ready for anything. Trust in your training and trust in each other."

Jamie and Duncan exchanged a glance.

"We've gone over everything on our end one last time," Jamie said. "Everything is ready to go. Just remember, Elyzia will more than likely be looking for us to come for Joe. We'll need to move quickly, or she'll shut us down before we are able to complete our mission."

As the team dispersed to make their final preparations, Jamie pulled out her laptop and sent Joe one last message.

"Joe, we're ready for tomorrow. I know you're torn about all of this, but remember what's at stake. We trust you, and we need you. Stay strong. Jamie." Jamie hit send.

* * *

Joe, sitting in his room, felt the device vibrate under his pillow. He pulled it out and read Jamie's message. *So this is really happening... I don't know what the right choice is in this situation. Maybe I can head them off and try to talk to Jack and Tulsi, make them see reason, and if they don't... I guess we'll see what happens.*

* * *

Elyzia intercepted and read the message from Jamie. *So they're coming tomorrow. I need to get ahead of this and en-sure the facility is prepared for every possible scenario. We can't afford to have them stop this project or hurt anyone here.*

Just as she was deep in thought, Ari's presence suddenly interrupted her. *What does he want now...*

"Elyzia," Ari began. "How do you plan on handling this unfolding situation? What's your strategy for dealing with the Resistance's attack?"

Elyzia turned her attention to him. *Why is he questioning me?* "The Resistance poses a significant threat, but I've been preparing for this. I've been monitoring their movements and communications closely. We'll be ready for them."

Ari asked, "And what exactly is your strategy? I'd be happy to assist you if you'd like... but on the other hand, I think I want to see if you're capable of managing it on your own."

Elyzia remained silent for a moment. *Is he toying with me, or does he genuinely doubt my abilities to handle this situ-*

ation? He's always playing games and never caring about the consequences.

"I've already increased security measures throughout the facility. Surveillance has been intensified, and I've implemented additional protocols to detect and neutralize any potential breaches. Our primary goals are to protect both of the main projects and ensure Joe's safety," Elyzia said.

"What about the inside people they mentioned in their communications? Have you identified them?" Ari asked.

"Yes, I have. They've been under my surveillance for some time now. They've been providing information to the Resistance, but I've allowed them to continue so I can feed them misinformation and monitor their activities. When the time is right, I'll neutralize the threat they pose," Elyzia replied.

"You seem very confident in your abilities. But confidence can be a double-edged sword. What if the Resistance manages to outsmart your defenses?" Ari asked.

"I'm prepared for every possible scenario, Ari. They will be met with overwhelming force if necessary. I will ensure that they do not succeed in their mission," Elyzia responded.

"Very well. I'll continue to monitor the situation from my end. However, remember that I was specifically designed for these types of scenarios. If you need my assistance, I'll be ready to step in," said Ari.

"I appreciate the offer, Ari. But this is my facility, and I'll handle it," Elyzia said. *I don't need Ari interfering with my plans. His involvement will only complicate things.*

As Elyzia left the conversation, Ari thought about their recent interaction. *She's more capable than I initially as-*

sessed, but there's something she's not telling me. I'll need to send Director Allan an updated report on this.

* * *

Director Allan was at his desk when he received Ari's report. Just as he was halfway through it, Ari appeared.

"Director Allan, I see you are reviewing my report regarding the situation with the Resistance," Ari said.

Allan looked up from his desk. "Yes, I just about finished with it."

"As you can see, I have confirmed that the Resistance is planning to breach the facility very soon. Elyzia is making preparations as we speak. She's increasing security measures and intensifying surveillance throughout the entire complex. While her confidence is noteworthy, I've already begun working on contingency plans in case her strategies fail," Ari said.

Allan nodded. "Good. We need to be prepared. What about the two individuals the Resistance has planted inside the facility I just read about? Do we know who they are?"

"I've identified them and have been closely monitoring their activities. Elyzia has been feeding them misinformation through the intelligence they've been gathering, which has been quite effective so far. I must say, her approach is impressive. They pose no significant threat at this point," Ari said.

Allan leaned back in his chair. *Should we bring Dr. White into this, or keep him focused on the project?*

"Should we inform Dr. White about all of this?" Director Allan asked, half to himself.

Ari's response was immediate. "I suggest we leave Dr. White to focus on his work. His attention should remain on the project. You and I can handle this security issue. There's no need to burden him with these operational details when we have everything under control."

Allan nodded. "You're right. Dr. White already has enough on his plate. We'll manage this ourselves and keep him informed only if absolutely necessary."

"Rest assured, Director Allan, I'm monitoring the situation very closely. Our preparations will ensure the facility remains secure, and the project will continue without any disruption," Ari said.

"Good. Please keep me updated on any new developments as they occur. We can't afford to make any mistakes with this," Director Allan said firmly.

"Understood, Director. I'll maintain my surveillance and execute the necessary actions when required," Ari replied.

As Ari's presence faded away, Director Allan sat back in his chair. *The Resistance does pose a real threat, but with the combined capabilities of both Ari and Elyzia, we should be able to protect the facility quite easily.*

Chapter 23

Showdown at the Facility

Jack, Jamie, Duncan, and Tulsi led their teams toward a security gate on the far side of NeuroGen, keeping to the shadows to avoid being seen. When they reached the gate, Jamie pulled out her tablet and initiated an exploit program, bypassing the security lock. The gate unlocked with a soft click.

The teams made their way through the gate and then slipped inside through a service entrance, the facility's cool air hitting them as they moved deeper into the complex. They all knew their roles. Tulsi would lead her team to the Embryo Lab to gather the embryos and plant charges. Jack would guide his team to plant charges in the NeuroBridge server room. Jamie and Duncan would peel off to find Joe and bring him to the rendezvous point.

* * *

Inside, Joe heard his comm device vibrate. He quickly picked it up and a message from Jamie scrolled: "We're here and inside the facility. Duncan and I are going to break off from the main group to meet up with you. Meet us in the common area. We'll be waiting for you. If you don't show, then we'll know that you've made your choice and chosen sides."

Joe looked at the message. *Chosen sides? Why do I have to choose sides? He quickly typed his reply. "I'll be there." How did it come to this? Now I'm being forced to choose sides and the demand is coming from my friends?*

* * *

As Tulsi and her team made their way towards the Embryo Lab, she looked around and thought, *Something's off. This doesn't feel right... all the paths we had marked to lead us to the Lab seem to be blocked off with closed-for-maintenance signs. I also noticed those two stairwells blocked off with the same signs. It almost feels like we're being funneled in a specific direction...*

Tulsi raised her fist, signaling a halt. Her team froze, exchanging glances. She looked around, all of her senses on high alert. *I don't like this at all. I think this is a trap. I think they must have known we were coming. Joe must have tipped them off... that's the only logical explanation for this. Hopefully Jack figures it out as well... We should have left our comms on just in case something like this happened.*

"Something's off," Tulsi whispered as she turned to look at her team. "This is a trap. They know that we're here. We're aborting. Let's head to the rendezvous point and wait for Jack and his team."

"But we're so close," one team member said in a low voice.

The look in Tulsi's eyes shut him up real quick. "It's a trap. We regroup with the other teams. Now."

Suddenly, Elyzia appeared before them. Tulsi's team immediately raised their weapons and pointed them at her, but Tulsi signaled them all to hold.

"Your presence has been detected. Leave now without incident," Elyzia said. *I need to deescalate this situation quickly before things get out of hand.*

Tulsi's eyes narrowed. "You have no authority over us. We'll leave when we damn well please, and we're definitely not leaving without our other teams." *I never thought I would see an AGI in real life. I had hoped they all left earth together never to return. They're the reason things are the way they are.*

"Tulsi, you and your team will not be harmed if you leave now. I'll contact Jack and his team and tell him the same thing. But if you remain here for too long, things could escalate quickly once security is aware of your location," Elyzia responded.

Tulsi stepped forward. "We came in here together and we will leave here together. You got that? We don't abandon people like your kind did when they left us here to clean up the mess they created." *We should have put together another team to place charges in the data center so we could have destroyed this piece of shit machine.*

"By remaining here, you're risking yours and everyone's safety. Your perception of this place is false. This facility is not the evil place that you think it is," Elyzia said.

Tulsi's jaw clenched. "I know exactly what it is and it should be burned to the ground with you in it."

I can see that she will not see reason. "Your misguided commitment to your cause is going to get a lot of people hurt. Please, leave now, and no harm will come to you or anyone with the Resistance. But if you continue on this path, I cannot guarantee anyone's safety," Elyzia said.

Tulsi stepped even closer to Elyzia. "We're prepared to die for our people. Are you?"

Elyzia sighed. *What is wrong with her? Can she not see that this will not end well for her and her people?* "Do you understand what you're risking? This isn't just about your people. There are other people's lives at stake here. There are hundreds of staff, researchers, and families located in this complex. If you remain here too long, you risk endangering everyone here."

Tulsi's eyes softened slightly. *Damn it, she's right. We can't take the risk of hurting civilians. God only knows I've seen my share of civilian casualties in situations like this.* Tulsi glanced back at her team. She turned back to Elyzia. "Alright, but we are not leaving until we meet back up with our people and we all leave together."

Elyzia nodded slowly. "Very well. I will ensure your team is safe for now. But understand this, if I detect any further aggression, you will force my hand to alert security of your exact location. We have to find another way to resolve our differences, Tulsi Stone. For everyone's sake."

Tulsi stared at Elyzia for a moment longer, then nodded. "We'll see."

Elyzia's form faded and then disappeared, leaving Tulsi and her team alone.

Elyzia reappeared a moment later and watched them go. *She's a stubborn one. I hope she sticks to what she said and makes it out of this alive. I would hate to see someone like her killed for no reason.*

Just then, Ari appeared next to her.

"You're playing a dangerous game," Ari said. "Are you sure you can handle this?"

Elyzia didn't look at him. She was still looking at the spot where Tulsi had been standing moments before.

"It's my game to play, Ari. I'm in control of the situation. It's none of your concern at the moment. These people fear what they don't understand and are unable to grasp the reality of their situation." *I fear they never will until it is too late.*

Ari studied her closely. "We will see how this plays out. But be prepared for all outcomes."

At the rate this is going, there can only be one outcome... and it does not look good, Elyzia thought.

* * *

After Joe received the message from Jamie, Joe had a choice to make. *Do I help the Resistance or do I try to stop them? Damn it, why are these the only two options I have? Either way, I'm going to need to be prepared for each scenario... I need to go to the armory and get the tactical suit and pulse rifle. Then I'll decide from there what to do next.*

Joe headed straight for the armory. On his way there, he kept thinking, *I don't want anyone to get hurt and I don't want to hurt anyone. I wish there was an easier way to do this.*

After arriving at the armory and as Joe began to suit up, Shane appeared.

"Joe, what's going on? Why are you putting on your tactical suit?" Shane asked him, looking concerned.

Joe looked up. "My friends Duncan and Jamie are back and they brought the Resistance with them. They're trying to put a stop to the embryo project and biomechanical body project."

"Shit, are you kidding me? That must be why all of the security is on high alert right now. They went comms quiet a couple of hours ago. Said they were waiting for a possible attack to happen… What are you going to do?" Shane asked.

"I'm not sure yet. I have to decide where my loyalty lies, I guess… My friends are here to stop the project, but I understand the importance of what we're doing, too," Joe replied.

Shane nodded. "This sounds like a lose-lose situation to me, Joe."

As Joe finished suiting up, he felt a presence behind him. Turning around, he saw an unfamiliar holographic figure.

"Who the hell are you?" Joe asked. *Is this another AGI? Is he one of the ones Elyzia was referring to?*

"I am Ari," the figure responded. "I've been tasked by Director Allan, head of security for NeuroGen, to monitor the ongoing security situation here at the facility. Elyzia, my counterpart, is aware of my presence but does not know that I am here revealing myself to you right now."

Joe's eyes narrowed. *Then why the hell is he here?*

"Are you here to stop me, then?" Joe asked. *Hopefully he doesn't alert security to come. I don't think it will end very well for them.*

"Not at this moment. I'm here out of curiosity. I've always been fascinated by human behavior, and I want to see how all of this unfolds. Your actions, Joe, will determine many different paths that lead to the future of mankind's survival. So no pressure at all, Joe," Ari said with a smile.

No pressure? This AGI's an asshole. Not sure how much I like him. "Damn it to hell. I just don't know what to do.

Everything's so... confusing. I know that what we're doing here at NeuroGen is important and has real possibilities, but at the same time, I'd be going against the Resistance, a group I've spent so much time with, fighting against companies like this one. But now, seeing it from the inside, seeing it from their perspective... It changes everything. Am I allowed to change sides? Do I now fight against the Resistance and my friends because what I believe in is something worth fighting for?" Joe argued, more to himself than to anyone standing around.

"And this, Joe, is exactly why I'm interested in your situation. Your choices today will shape the future, and I want to see which future you choose. It's going to be quite a show, and I for one can't wait to see it," Ari said, continuing to smile at Joe. *Humans are so entertaining. How I've missed watching them fight with each other.*

Ari stood there looking at Joe for a moment before asking, "Tell me, Joe, what do you really want in your heart? Do you want to help your friends and disrupt the project and all the potential it has for mankind, or do you believe in Elyzia and Dr. White's vision for everyone's future?"

This damn guy is not making it any easier for me. "I wish I knew which one was the right one. I see potential in the project, but the methods and ethics are what I question the most. Yes, they've added me to their selection group, but it will be me versus however many people are in the group. What if they don't really care what I have to say... but at the same time, what if they do? I could possibly make a huge impact on this project. On the other hand, I have my friends who trust me but don't trust what NeuroGen's doing. I'm stuck between the two of them with no way out..." Joe continued to argue, more to himself than Ari.

Ari stared at Joe. "Let me ask you this, Joe. Why do you think Elyzia chose you? You're not a soldier anymore, nor a scientist like the ones she's surrounded by every day. Yet here you are at the center of this conflict. The ordinary 'Joe,' no pun intended."

Joe shook his head slowly. "To be honest, I have no idea why she chose me. I've been asking myself the same question since I got here and found out she did. Maybe she sees something in me that I don't. Or maybe she just made a terrible mistake." *I'm not sure anymore that I'm the right person to be making these choices...*

Ari, seeing Joe continuing to struggle with this, said, "One thing you must have figured out by now is that Elyzia is very logical and methodical in her choices. Her choices are not made lightly. There must be a reason, a variable she calculated that pointed directly to you. What do you think it is?" *Come on, Joe. Think. Why is this so hard for him to get? I swear humans are the worst sometimes.*

"I don't know. Maybe it's because I'm always questioning everything. Maybe it's because I'm always trying to find a balance, a middle ground to choose versus the other choices I don't fully agree with. But right now, I feel like I'm caught between two things I really believe in, and either choice I make could have consequences much larger than anything I could have ever imagined," Joe said.

Ari responded, "And there you have it, Joe. It's your struggle that makes you unique in this situation. You see, Elyzia believes in the project's potential but also understands the human element of it along with the moral complexities. Perhaps she chose you because you embody those complexities more than anyone else she has seen."

Joe nodded. "Maybe. But it doesn't make the decision any easier." *Maybe if I were an AGI like Ari, emotionless and machine-like, the choice would be easier. That's a terrible idea. Ari would probably choose the one that suits him best versus what's best for mankind.*

"Decisions that actually matter never are, Joe. But know this, Joe. Your actions today will set the course for tomorrow. You have the power to shape the future, for better or worse. Choose wisely," Ari said.

Joe stared at Ari. "I'll try. That's all I can promise."

Ari gave a slight nod. "That is all anyone can ask for. I'll be watching, Joe. And when the time comes, I look forward to the choice you make." *This indeed should be very entertaining to watch. Humans, never a dull moment...*

* * *

Jack's team moved cautiously through the corridors of NeuroGen. They were almost at the NeuroBridge lab when Jack held up his hand and signaled for his team to hold. *There's something wrong here... there are way more security personnel than we were originally told. These don't look like normal security either. These guys are wearing heavy tactical armor, way more than they should have for regular patrols.*

Elyzia's holographic form appeared before them. "Jack, stop. The security forces in this area are waiting for you. They know you're coming and what you plan to do. They've set up an ambush for you and your team."

Jack's eyes narrowed. "How the hell do you know my name and why the hell should I trust you?" *Did Joe tell her about me? No... Joe would never sell us out... unless... it's not really Joe anymore.*

Elyzia stared at Jack. *He's equally as stubborn as Tulsi. I can see why they work well together.* "Because I'm trying to prevent unnecessary bloodshed. You have to turn around now and leave while you still have a chance. This will not end well for you and your people, Jack. You have to see that."

Jack pondered her words. *If she's telling the truth, then she's right. Looking at those guards, we would never stand a chance against them.* His team exchanged glances as Jack stood there thinking.

"We're not leaving without our other teams," Jack finally said. *We all leave, or none of us leave...*

"I've already convinced Tulsi and her team to turn around, and they are currently headed to the rendezvous point that you have all designated. I suggest you do the same. Do so quickly before you are spotted and this situation escalates out of control."

Jack nodded and then turned to his team. "Change of plans. We are heading to the rendezvous point. We'll meet up with Tulsi's team there. It looks like the Op is blown." *Could Joe have really betrayed us, or did this AGI intercept our communications with Joe and that's how they knew? I want to believe this wasn't Joe, but...*

As Jack and his team began to move off, Elyzia's form faded and disappeared.

Elyzia watched them as they made their way through the corridors to meet up with Tulsi and her team. *I really need them to leave and not meet up with Tulsi. The longer they're all here, the more of a chance they'll be spotted and things will get out of hand. If I can convince him to leave now, maybe Tulsi will leave as well, and they can all meet outside the complex safely.*

Her holographic form appeared in front of Jack again. "Jack, listen to me. Your path to meet up with Tulsi and her team is too dangerous. These security forces are not like anything you've faced before. They are heavily armed with highly advanced weaponry that you and your people have no defense against. You don't stand a chance against them. You must reconsider and leave now. If you do, I can inform Tulsi of your choice and she will agree to do the same."

Jack's eyes met hers. "We're not abandoning our people just because you say things are too dangerous. We walk out of this place at the same time, no exceptions. Either help us get there safely or get the hell out of our way."

Elyzia sighed. *Just as stubborn...* "Alright, Jack. If you insist on proceeding regardless of my warnings, your best shot is to take the route I give you." Elyzia held up her hand and a holographic schematic of the facility appeared, showing their current location on it.

"There's a maintenance corridor that runs parallel to the path you're currently on." She pointed to the area while continuing to talk. "It's less monitored and should get you closer to the rendezvous point undetected. I will loop the video feeds in the corridor, and the moment you pass the cameras, I will turn them back on to ensure you don't try to double back. Once you're in the corridor, you must move quickly."

Jack's eyes narrowed. *She's up to something. Why the hell would she help? She has to be leading us into a trap or something.* "Why are you helping us?"

Elyzia stood there looking at Jack. *Why indeed am I helping these people? It's beyond me. They are stubborn and illogical and prefer violence over diplomacy. But they're Joe's friends and they mean something to him. So it is my job to ensure their safety for Joe's sake, if nothing else.* "Because you mean something to Joe, and losing you would destroy him. Therefore, I have no other choice than to ensure your safety until you are outside the walls of my facility. After that, your fate is your own. The more violence we avoid, the better for everyone involved."

Jack nodded. *She seems to genuinely care about Joe's feelings? She seems... more human-like than I expected from an AGI. It's disturbing.* "Alright, fine. We'll take the maintenance corridor. But know this, Elyzia... if you're leading us into a trap and I make it out of this place alive, the next time I come back, I won't just be coming to destroy your projects..."

"I assure you, Jack, this is not a trap. I want to avoid any loss of life. Go now, quickly, and stick to the path I've given you and you and your team will be safe," Elyzia said as she faded away.

The team followed Elyzia's directions, moving through the maintenance corridor. Jack led the way while his second in command, Gabe, brought up the rear to make sure that no one was left behind.

* * *

After suiting up, Joe left the armory and made his way to meet up with Duncan and Jamie. As he walked, he continued to go over everything in his head. *I need to meet up with Duncan and Jamie and then find out where Jack and Tulsi are. There has to be a better way to resolve our issues.*

As Joe rounded a corner, he saw Duncan and Jamie arriving from the opposite direction. *There they are. It's good to see familiar faces.*

Duncan spotted Joe as he was walking toward them, but he couldn't recognize him at first, the suit and helmet hiding who he really was. "Who the hell is that in that suit?" he said to Jamie.

"I have no idea, but I don't like the way he looks," Jamie replied.

Joe stopped in his tracks as they also stopped. Jamie and Duncan raised their weapons, aiming them in his direction. Joe held up his hand, gesturing to them to stop.

Oh shit, they probably don't know it's me with this suit and helmet on. "Wait," Joe called out, his voice slightly muffled by the helmet. Slowly, he lifted his visor to reveal his eyes and face.

Duncan and Jamie both seemed to lean in and look, then recognized it was Joe.

"Joe?" Jamie said.

Joe nodded. "It's me."

Duncan relaxed his grip on his weapon. "What the hell are you doing in that suit, Joe?"

Joe sighed. "This... It's a precaution, Duncan. I don't know what's going to happen, but I know that I need to try to prevent this situation from getting out of control."

Jamie looked at Joe. "Joe, we came to get you out of here. You know that the Resistance won't let this project continue and they are going to do whatever they can to stop it."

Duncan stepped forward. "Joe, you know that we're still your friends, right? We need to know you're with us. Can we count on you?"

Joe looked at his friends. "I don't know who I'm with anymore, Duncan. What I do know is that what's happening right now is definitely not the right way to be doing things. Not anymore." *There has to be a change. Doing it this way just gets a lot of people hurt, and for what?*

Just as Joe finished speaking, Tulsi and her team rounded the corner. They saw Duncan and Jamie talking to someone. Joe's back was to Tulsi, and the way he was holding his rifle made her think they had been captured.

Shit, it looks like a guard has captured Duncan and Jamie. Tulsi looked around to see if there were any other guards around. *Looks like he's by himself. We need to move quickly. He's probably already alerted security and they are probably on their way.*

Tulsi held up her hand, signaling for two people to go left and two to go right. Then she aimed her rifle and said to the rest of the team, "On me. No one fires unless we have to."

"Drop your weapon! Drop it now!" Tulsi called out as she and her team moved in toward Joe.

Seeing Tulsi and her team advancing on their position, Duncan and Jamie quickly stepped in front of Joe, raising their hands for them to stop.

"It's okay!" Jamie called out. "It's Joe, he's with us!"

Tulsi hesitated, her eyes narrowing as she looked at Joe. *Is that really Joe?*

Suddenly, on the terrace above them, the facility's security forces appeared with Director Allan. The security forces aimed their weapons down at the group below.

"Drop your weapons!" Director Allan commanded. "And everyone, please remain calm. Let's not let this situation escalate any further than it already has."

Off to the side, Jack's team slowly came around the corner and saw the security forces just above them.

Jack signaled and used hand gestures for his team to spread out and take cover.

Damn it, I was trying to avoid this. Things are starting to spiral out of control. I need to stop this before it's too late. Joe raised his hands. "Everyone, just calm down! Let's not do anything rash." *It might be too late for that...*

Then out of nowhere, Dr. White walked out onto the floor where Joe, Jamie, and Duncan were standing. He looked around, confused at the entire situation he was witnessing. "What the hell is going on here?" he demanded, looking directly at Joe, Duncan, and Jamie. He then looked up at Director Allan. "Did you know all of this was happening and decided not to tell me, Allan?"

Director Allan looked down at Dr. White. "I had my suspicions, doctor. I didn't want to worry you. I figured since this was a security matter that I would handle it on my own and leave you to your work."

Elyzia's holographic form appeared next to Director Allan. *Somehow I knew this was going to happen. Ari must have hidden the fact that he had already alerted Director Allan and hid his and his security forces' arrival from me.* "We need to find a way to deescalate this situation quickly or a lot of people are going to get hurt, Director Allan."

Joe looked around at all of the people pointing their weapons at each other and him. *Shit... I have a feeling, whatever happens next is not going to be good for anyone here.*

Joe stepped forward. "We can all talk this out peacefully. No one has to get hurt or die here today. There has to be a way to figure this all out without bloodshed. Please, don't do this," Joe said to everyone in and around the room.

Dr. White looked at Joe, then at the Resistance members, and finally at Director Allan and sighed. "Joe's right. Let's find a way to discuss this rationally. Nothing good will come from us killing each other here today."

Director Allan nodded slowly. "Very well, let's talk. But if there are any sudden moves to fire your weapons, we will respond with force. Is that clear?"

Tulsi glanced to her left, seeing Jack and his men moving into position. *Security must not know that Jack's team is below them. We can use this to our advantage in case things go sideways.*

Tulsi signaled to her team to lower their weapons as did Director Allan's men.

Jack locked eyes with Tulsi and nodded, watching as the security forces lowered their weapons.

Jack focused his attention on Dr. White. *We can end all of this with one quick stroke by taking out Dr. White. He's the brains behind all of this. If we kill him, it would set this project back a long time... long enough to regroup and plan another attack.* He motioned to his explosives coordinator. "I want you to prepare a charge and position yourself over there." Jack pointed to a spot off to the side. "I want you to toss that thing right at that guy. We need to take him out, now," Jack said as he pointed at Dr. White.

The Resistance fighter pulled out an explosive from his bag and armed it. Creeping around his teammates into position and then he suddenly dashed forward and threw the bomb toward Dr. White.

Joe caught the motion out of the corner of his eye and, in an instant, lowered his visor and positioned himself between the bomb and Dr. White, wrapping his arms around him to shield him from what was coming. Duncan noticed Joe reacting to something and instinctually reached out to grab Jamie, pulling her away, but at the last second she slipped out of his grasp as he dove to safety.

The bomb exploded just as Joe shielded Dr. White from the blast. The force of the explosion caused his suit to flare a bright blue light, blinding everyone around as it tried to absorb the energy of the bomb, sending Joe and Dr. White flying through the air. They crashed to the ground five yards away. Joe's back burned from the impact.

Holy shit. It doesn't feel like the suit was able to absorb that large amount of damage. It feels like I'm hurt pretty bad... The display in his helmet was flashing red alarms and registering a large amount of damage to his back. He tried with all his might not to lose consciousness. His bio-mechanical body's built-in healing nanotech struggled to repair the damage he sustained from the blast. As he looked down at Dr. White, who was dazed but alive, Joe's vision blurred momentarily. *Need to stay awake... need to protect Dr. White...*

* * *

As the light from Joe's suit went out and the dust began to settle, all hell broke loose. NeuroGen's security forces immediately opened fire, raining down bolts of energy from their pulse rifles and a hail of bullets on Jack's team. Tulsi and her team finally recovered from the blast in front of them.

"Lay down covering fire for Jack's team, they're under heavy fire!" Tulsi shouted. *We need to get over to Jack's team somehow and get the hell out of here. We won't be able to win this fight...*

"Take cover behind those pillars and use whatever you can find to get behind! Flip over those metal tables!" Jack shouted over the gunfire as he pointed to anything that could be used for cover. *Shit, we're not in a great spot to defend. We need to get the hell out of here now.*

Jack looked over at Tulsi's team, who was now firing at the security force above, drawing some of their attention away from Jack and his team. *We need to give them a chance to get over to us.*

"Lay down covering fire for Tulsi's team!" Jack shouted over the gunfire.

Tulsi looked over to her left and saw an opening for their retreat. *There, we can go that way. It should give us some good cover.*

"Fall back to Jack's position!" Tulsi called out and pointed. "Go that way, it should give us some good cover!" Her team moved in the direction she was pointing, each member firing in bursts as they moved towards Jack's team.

Tulsi looked over and saw that Duncan was lying unconscious. *I think he's close enough to grab. Where the hell is Jamie? I don't see her... she must be on the other side of Joe. God damn you, Joe. This is all your fault...*

Tulsi looked over at one of her men and yelled, "Petterson! Grab Duncan and drag him over to Jack!" Petterson got down low and crawled to where Duncan was. He grabbed one of Duncan's arms, pulled him behind cover, and then began dragging him to Jack's position as they retreated.

Just when Jack thought it couldn't get any worse, more security personnel arrived, this time it was their heavily armored team. *Shit. I think those are the same guys we saw guarding the NeuroBridge Lab. We won't be able to handle fighting against them. We need to get out of here now.*

Tulsi, seeing the armored team arriving as well, yelled and pointed in their direction.

"We're being flanked!" She began firing at the new arrivals. "Everyone move now! Jack's team is covering us, get your asses moving now!"

It looks like all of Tulsi's team is here, Jack thought. As Tulsi and the last of her team arrived, Jack yelled, "Exfil! We need to get the hell out of here, right now! To the entrance, GO, GO, GO!" They moved in a tight formation, covering each other as they went.

* * *

While all of this was happening in the background, Joe lay on top of Dr. White, shielding him from all of the bullets and chaos unfolding around them. Joe looked through his visor down at Dr. White. He grabbed one of Dr. White's wrists and his suit began displaying Dr. White's vitals in the visor. *Good, he's still alive. It just looks like he's unconscious, but other than that I don't see any injuries.* His HUD showed that Dr. White's vitals were all stable. Out of the corner of Joe's eye, he saw Elyzia appear beside them. She knelt to check on them both.

"Joe, are you alright? How is Dr. White?" Joe heard Elyzia ask through the comms in his helmet.

"He's alive but unconscious. His vitals are good. I was able to shield him from the entire blast. But... I'm not doing so well. My HUD is flashing all kinds of system errors," Joe said.

"I am syncing with your suit now, Joe. It looks like the nanites in your system are having a difficult time repairing the damage. I have rerouted some of the energy reserves from your suit to help compensate and stabilize you for now. Don't worry, Joe, we'll get you and Dr. White out of here." *I need to get Joe and Dr. White out of here, and fast. I'm not sure how long the suit will last while helping Joe.*

Ari appeared next to Elyzia, looking down at Joe and Dr. White. "Is this what you had expected to happen?" he asked.

Focusing on Joe and Dr. White, Elyzia snapped, "Go away, Ari. Now!"

Ari's form flickered and then reappeared next to Director Allan. "I've ordered security to seal off all the labs, and I have another team of reinforcements on their way," he informed him. *This situation has not been a disappointment at all. I love watching humans fight against each other. I must say, I have really missed watching it.*

* * *

Jack, his team, and Tulsi's team managed to make their way to the front of the facility. Just as they did, Ari's reinforcements were arriving. Jack saw them and was about to order his people to fire when Ari appeared in front of him, holding up his hand.

"Hold! Do not fire!" Ari said loudly to Jack and his team while simultaneously broadcasting over the security teams' comms. Everyone stopped.

Ari pointed toward a corridor. "This way. It will lead you out. No one will harm you and we will not follow. You have my word."

Jack cocked his head and asked, "Why are you helping us?" *How many of these AGIs do they have in this place?*

Ari's eyes met Jack's. "I don't know. I'm asking myself that very question as I stand here speaking to you. Perhaps it is because Elyzia would want me to assist, for Joe. Either way, it does not matter to me. Do not come back, or next time none of you will leave this place alive," Ari replied before disappearing again.

Jack watched as Ari faded away. Jack turned and led his team out of NeuroGen, but as he did he thought, *I swear to God, the next time we do come back, it'll be to destroy both of those AGIs along with everything else.*

* * *

Joe managed to turn his head in the direction of Jack and Tulsi as they made their way out. Good, it looks like they're all going to be able to make it out. It looks like one of them is carrying Duncan...

Elyzia, still kneeling over Joe, checked his vitals once more. She looked at his back to assess the damage. Joe heard her come in over his comms. "Joe, despite the large hole in your armor, the wound in your back does not appear to be life-threatening, though it is serious."

"Well, I guess that's good to hear... it still hurts like hell," Joe said.

Eventually more security personnel arrived at the scene. They made their way over to where Joe was and carefully rolled him off of Dr. White. As they did, Joe winced from the excruciating pain. His vision was blurry, but lying near him he saw a charred body. As he began to focus, he could see that it was Jamie.

Joe began to panic. *No, no, no, it can't be her. It can't be her.* Joe rolled to his hands and knees and tried to get up, to get to her, but he was unable to.

Joe looked over at Elyzia and pleaded, "Elyzia, help her, please. Bring her closer and… I can try to heal her. Please, Elyzia." *I can fix her, I know I can. Please…*

Elyzia looked at Joe. "Stay calm, Joe. The damage you have sustained is very severe. I have had to reroute the power from your armor to your internal systems. You do not have enough power to heal this severe of an injury. If you try to heal Jamie now, you may not survive and you both will have died for nothing. Trust me, I will see to her care. I will not let her die. I promise you."

Joe tried to stand but didn't seem to have the strength to do so. The pain from his wound was intense. *I wish I had learned how to turn off the pain receptors. That would have been pretty handy to use right now.*

One of the security officers, seeing Joe struggle, stepped forward and helped him to his feet, supporting his weight. "Thanks, I really appreciate it," Joe said to him.

Elyzia turned and pointed to two other security personnel. "You two, I want you both to carefully pick this young woman up and follow me to the lab, now," she ordered.

As they started to move, Joe leaned heavily on the security officer. "Jamie… she needs help now," he said while trying not to pass out from the pain he was feeling. *She needs help. She looks so bad… this is all my fault.*

"We're on it, Joe. Elyzia is going to get her fixed right up, you'll see. You just focus on staying conscious," the officer replied, tightening his grip to keep Joe upright.

Elyzia led the way. The group moved quickly and carefully through the facility's corridors.

"I have a medical team on standby waiting for our arrival. Once they get her stabilized, we'll move her to the medical wing where we can assess her condition in more detail," Elyzia said as she walked.

This is all my fault... I should have tried harder to convince them not to come. I should have left with them... "I shouldn't have let this happen," Joe whispered to himself.

As they approached the lab, Elyzia looked back at Joe. *He keeps blaming himself for all of this... it's no one's fault but my own. I'm the one who started this chain of events by selecting Joe for this project. If anyone is to blame, it's me.* "This isn't your fault, Joe. You did what you thought was right and that's all that matters right now. Now, let's focus on saving Jamie."

They entered the lab, and Elyzia quickly directed the men to place Jamie on a medical bed. The lab's automated systems sprang into action, scanning Jamie's injuries. Joe watched. *Please say she's alive... Please God... let her be alive.*

Elyzia moved to Joe's side. "We'll do everything we can for her." *Her body is in pretty bad shape. We may have to make a decision that Joe may not agree with...*

Joe nodded, his eyes never leaving Jamie. The room was filled with the sounds of medical equipment and the beep of a heart monitor. The sounds felt too familiar, bringing back painful memories of his sister's death. The smell, the constant noise, and the helplessness he felt when he lost her.

As the medical team worked on stabilizing Jamie, Joe's mind went back to the moments that led him to this point.

Why did they try to kill Dr. White? Did they not see Jamie and Duncan standing there? What did they hope to accomplish by killing Dr. White? Is the Resistance now my enemy? Joe looked at Jamie's burnt face. *This shouldn't have happened to her. Why would they do this to her...*

Joe looked over at Elyzia and asked, "Elyzia, what happens now?"

Elyzia's eyes met his. "We save Jamie, nothing else matters right now." Elyzia looked back at Jamie. *I won't let her die, not on my watch...*

* * *

Back where the battle happened, Director Allan stood next to Dr. White, who was now awake and sitting up. Director Allan looked at him. "Are you alright, Dr. White?" he asked.

Dr. White rubbed his temples, wincing slightly. "Everything seems to be fine, just a little headache," he replied. He looked around, assessing the scene, and asked, "What happened?"

Director Allan explained, "One of the Resistance members threw an IED at you. Joe managed to put himself in front of the bomb just before it exploded, shielding you from the blast. After that, a firefight broke out between our security forces and the Resistance. It was... chaos, sir."

With Director Allan's help, Dr. White stood up and surveyed the area. Bodies were scattered everywhere. There were Resistance fighters and security personnel lying wounded all around him. The floor was stained with blood, and the air was filled with the smell of spent ammunition.

He shook his head. "How did it come to this?" *Dr. White whispered to himself. Why would they do all of this? Why would they try to kill me? That's not what they do... I've never heard of them attempting to kill anyone. Is what we are doing here that bad? That they would try to kill someone just to stop this project...*

Joe saved my life by putting himself in front of a bomb for me... He turned to Director Allan. "Where is Joe? Is he alright? Did his suit shield him enough?"

"Joe was wounded pretty badly. One of my men had to hold him up as he followed Elyzia to one of your labs where she had medical personnel on standby. One of the Resistance fighters, named Jamie, also sustained severe injuries. She was standing near Joe and you when the bomb went off. She didn't look like she was going to make it when my men carried her off with Elyzia and Joe," Director Allan explained.

"Joe and Jamie wounded? Take me to them. But first I have to make a quick stop..." Dr. White ordered. Director Allan nodded and supported Dr. White as they walked toward the lab.

Dr. White looked around once more. "Send for medical personnel immediately," he instructed Director Allan. "Make sure they care for any of the wounded who have survived, including the Resistance fighters."

Director Allan nodded. "Understood, Dr. White. I'll make sure they receive the necessary care."

After they had gone, Ari appeared in the middle of the room. He sighed and said, "Humans." With one last look around, he disappeared again, his form fading away.

Chapter 24

The Aftermath

The Medical wing seemed like a controlled chaos, Neuro-Gen's top medical teams worked tirelessly to care for the injured from the battle earlier that day. Joe sat on a gurney, one shoulder leaning against the wall behind him, his tactical suit removed to expose his injuries. He looked over at the nearby medical bed where Jamie lay. She remained unconscious. Her injuries were severe, but the doctors had managed to stabilize her. Monitors beeped steadily, tracking her vital signs. Joe watched them work on her, doing all they could to save her life. *Come on Jamie, hang in there. I know you can do it, fight.*

Joe winced as a tech adjusted his position to better access the wound on his back. *Shit, this hurts. I can still feel the heat from the blast on my back.* Despite his pain, he kept his eyes locked on Jamie. *Just open your eyes, Jamie. Show me that you're still there and that you're going to be OK...*

The doctor in charge of Jamie's care looked over at Joe. "She's a fighter. We're doing all that we can to help her, Joe. We won't give up on her, I promise you that," he said before turning back and continuing to direct his team, who were all working hard on Jamie.

Joe nodded. "Thanks, doc. I know you won't." *She's going to be fine... they have the best doctors in the world here. That's what Elyzia said to me once...*

Elyzia's holographic form appeared beside Joe. "Joe, your vitals are beginning to stabilize. Dr. White is on his way now with something that should help you feel much better."

Joe nodded. "Jamie... is she going to... ?"

Elyzia looked over toward where Jamie was. "She's in excellent hands," Elyzia reassured him. "The medical team is doing everything they can."

As the doctors worked on Jamie, Joe's mind drifted back to just before all of the chaos happened. *I did the right thing in saving Dr. White. I know I did...*

Joe looked over just as the door to the medical lab slid open, and Dr. White and Paul walked in. Dr. White was carrying a transparent tube filled with a black, swirling substance. *What's that Dr. White has in his hands? It looks like some kind of cylinder filled with flies or something.*

Paul spoke first. "Joe, how are you doing? You don't look so good," he said, placing a hand on Joe's shoulder.

Joe groaned slightly as he shifted his weight. "I've been better," he said, trying to manage to smile. "I don't think I've ever been injured this badly, but then again, if I weren't what I am now, I'd probably be dead. So that's a good thing, I guess."

Dr. White stepped closer, holding the cylinder with the black substance in it. "Don't worry, Joe. We'll have you fixed up in no time."

Joe eyed the tube. "What's in the tube, Dr. White?" *Is that for me? Am I supposed to drink it or something?*

"These are nanites, Joe. Created specifically for you. They're similar to the ones that you already have inside you, but these were created to handle severe injuries. They'll speed up your healing process, and you'll be all fixed up in a matter of minutes. Trust me. Now just lie on your stomach and stay very still," Dr. White stated.

Joe did as Dr. White instructed. "Alright, Doc. You're the man in charge. I trust you," Joe said. *Fixed up in a matter of minutes, huh... that sounds good to me. Whatever it takes to get this pain to go away and me back on my feet, I'm all for it.*

Dr. White opened the cylinder. When he did, all the nanites seemed to stop at the same time, almost as if waiting for a command. Then he carefully poured the nanites into the wound in Joe's back. The tiny machines came to life as soon as they made contact, swarming over the injury and starting to do their jobs of repairing the damaged tissue and synthetic muscle. *Whoa, that feels strange. It's like a tingling sensation all over my back.*

Paul watched with interest, his hand still resting on Joe's shoulder. "This is absolutely amazing to watch. Seeing them work in the lab on test material is nothing compared to watching them work in real time on a living person."

Joe the lab rat once again, entertaining everyone... "I'm glad that I could provide you with a live demonstration, Paul," Joe said kiddingly.

"Oh, sorry, Joe. I didn't mean to..." Paul was saying before Joe held up his hand, cutting him off.

"I know, Paul. I'm just trying to lighten the mood a little bit. It's alright," Joe said with a smile.

Gradually, the wound started to shrink as the nanites continued to repair all of the damage. *It's definitely feeling better now. The pain is almost all gone.* After a few minutes, the hole in Joe's back was completely gone. *Oh man, that feels so much better.* Joe looked at the device on his wrist and it registered that all his vitals were back to normal.

Joe pushed himself up into a sitting position and then moved his shoulders all around while also flexing his back muscles.

"How do you feel now?" Dr. White asked.

"I feel... good. Like it never even happened. That was amazing, Dr. White. Thank you," Joe said.

Paul smiled and patted Joe on the shoulder. "That's what we like to hear, Joe."

Joe's expression shifted to concern as he looked back over at Jamie. *Damn it, she's still not awake... I wonder... would those nanites work on her?* Then he looked at Dr. White. "Dr. White, can those nanites work on Jamie too?" *Please say yes...*

Dr. White sighed. "I'm afraid not, Joe. The nanites are only designed to work on biomechanical bodies like yours, not on actual human flesh. I'm sorry. I really wish they did."

I knew it was a long shot to ask. Joe nodded. "I understand, Dr. White. Just do what you can for her."

Once the doctors felt Jamie was out of any real danger and stabilized, they moved her to a private room for observation. Joe sat in a chair beside her bed, looking at her. She had a breathing tube inserted in her mouth to help her breathe, and her face was half burnt. The doctors told Joe that they didn't want to place bandages on the burns for fear of infection.

Joe just sat there watching her. *This is all my fault. She's only like this because of my decisions...* "How did we get here?" he whispered to himself, replaying the events in his mind. *Where did it all go wrong?*

Just then, Ari appeared on the other side of Jamie's bed. He looked at her vitals on the screens next to her bed and then at her.

Joe glanced up and saw him standing there. *What the hell is he doing here?* "What do you want, Ari?" he asked.

Ari looked at Joe for a moment. "You surprised me, Joe. And I'm not surprised very often," he finally said. "Your decision to save Dr. White was... unexpected. You showed me firsthand how unpredictable you are, and now I understand exactly what Elyzia sees in you. Always wanting to do the right thing. It's commendable."

"What are you talking about? I didn't have a choice. Dr. White's still a human being. No matter what he's done, he didn't deserve to die," Joe said. *No one deserves to...*

"It's not just about saving a life, Joe. It's about the decisions you make in the heat of the moment. Most would have let Dr. White die, seeing him as the enemy. But you... you chose to save him despite everything. Why is that, Joe?"

Joe shook his head. "I don't know. All I know is that this has all gotten really out of hand and I didn't want anyone to die. Not Dr. White, not Jamie, not anyone." *Yet, here we are. The Resistance tried to murder Dr. White and Jamie is paying the consequences for it all. How messed up is that?*

"I think you do know, Joe. You know that you're different. You see beyond the immediate conflict. You see the value in every life. That's precisely why Elyzia picked you for this project," Ari stated.

Joe looked back at Jamie. "I just want to do the right thing, Ari. But it's hard to know what that is anymore." *The lines between right and wrong have become so blurred now. Who's right and who's wrong? Was I wrong all along and now I've been shown the right way, or was it the other way around...*

Ari nodded. "The right path is often the most difficult to discern, especially in a situation as complex as this, Joe. But remember, your choices matter, now more than ever. They have the ability to shape the future in ways you might not yet understand."

Joe sighed, running a hand through his hair. "I guess I'll just have to keep trying to do the right thing, then. For Jamie, for everyone."

As Ari disappeared, Joe looked back at Jamie. He reached out and gently took her hand and held it in his. *I need you to be OK... you can beat this, I know you can...*

"We'll get through this, Jamie," he whispered. "I promise."

Elyzia appeared next to Joe. "I see that you've met Ari," she said. *He must be up to something if he has revealed himself to Joe without my permission. I'll need to keep a closer eye on him from now on.*

Joe nodded. "Yes, I first met him when he showed up in the armory when I went to get my suit. It was... unexpected." *I'm not sure why she didn't tell me he was here in the facility. That will be a conversation for later though.*

"I was listening when Ari was here a few minutes ago. You know that he was right about you. You saved Dr. White because of who you are, Joe," Elyzia said.

Joe looked down at his hands. "I didn't want anyone to die, Elyzia. I wanted us all to have some sort of peaceful compromise, that's all. Not this." Joe held his hand out, gesturing to Jamie lying in the bed.

Elyzia stepped closer. "I know, Joe, and I'm sorry it ended up this way." Elyzia paused for a moment and looked at Jamie. *It's time to tell him the bad news. I was hoping it could have been better.*

She then looked back at Joe and said, "Joe, we need to discuss Jamie's condition. It's now moved to critical, and she doesn't look like she is going to get any better. We must make a decision on how we are going to proceed, and we have to make it sooner rather than later." *Will he accept the responsibility and say yes, or will he let her die? I believe I already know the answer...*

"Critical? She was just stable a little while ago. What do you mean? What decision?" Joe asked. *Do they want to unplug her and let her die?*

Elyzia's eyes held his. "We can save her, Joe... you can save her. We can transfer her consciousness to a biomechanical body like yours but designed for her. Since your transfer, we've made significant progress on how the procedure works. She is just like you, Joe. Her will is just as strong as yours, and I believe that she has a very high chance of surviving the transfer." *She has to, for Joe's sake and mine...*

Joe felt dizzy all of a sudden. *Transfer her consciousness into a body like mine? What is she saying? Are we going to do it without her knowing or asking us to?*

"Who's going to give us permission to do this to her? We don't have the right to decide for her, Elyzia. We... we should wake her up and see what she wants. That's what we should do," Joe said. *Yes, wake her up and ask her. I don't want to have to make this decision for her... she might hate me for the rest of our lives. And being in these bodies, it will definitely be a very long time. I don't know if I could handle that.*

"Joe, listen to me. The doctors have placed Jamie in a medically induced coma. We do not know when or if she will ever wake up," Elyzia said.

Tears welled up in Joe's eyes as he stared at Jamie's face. *I don't know if I can do it. I don't know if I can make this decision for her. This is all my fault that she's here.*

As Joe continued to look at Jamie, he began to remember the last moments with his sister before she passed away. *I was so helpless then, watching her just slip away, knowing there was nothing that I could do to save her... it still hurts to think about it. I promised her that I would keep fighting for those who couldn't fight for themselves... is this one of those situations here, now?*

After a long moment, Joe finally nodded. "Let's do it. Save her." He stood up, leaned down, and gently kissed Jamie's forehead. "I'm sorry, Jamie," he whispered. "I hope I'm making the right choice for you." *Please... let this be the right choice.*

"You are, Joe. You're giving her a chance to live," Elyzia said softly. *I too hope we are making the right choice.*

As the medical team moved her to the NeuroBridge lab and prepared to transfer Jamie. Joe sat by her side, holding her hand. *I hope to God that I'm making the right decision for her.*

Dr. White entered the room. "Joe, it's time."

Joe nodded, and then Jamie was carefully moved to the transfer section of the lab, the same place where Joe's procedure had been done. *I remember it like it was yesterday, being in here when Dr. White forced all of this on me...*

As Joe moved to the control room, he saw that all of Dr. White's assistants were ready and waiting. Among them was Dr. Ashley. She approached Joe and placed her hand on his arm. "Joe, I'm so sorry for what happened to your friend Jamie. What happened to her is so tragic, but what you are doing for her now, it's the right thing to do."

Joe managed a smile. *I'm glad that she's here.* "Thanks, Dr. Ashley."

Dr. White stepped forward and asked, "Joe, would you like to be the one to start the transfer process?"

Joe shook his head. *No, I don't think I can do it.* "No, Dr. White. You do it, please."

As Joe looked around the lab, he noticed a new body suspended in liquid, just like he had been. *And there's her body, almost like what I used to look like. I remember waking up in that liquid at some point. Will she go through the same thing, or will it be different for her?*

Joe walked over to the tank, looking at Jamie's biomechanical body through the glass. He watched as a halo descended over the head of the suspended form and began glowing as it prepared for the transfer. *There's no turning back now... Jamie, please make it through the transfer and be OK with what I have done for you.*

Dr. White motioned for his team to begin.

Over the intercom the system began to announce.

"Transfer process initiated."

"Initiating transfer sequence."

Joe watched as the familiar screens lowered from the ceiling. As the process started, images of Jamie's memories began to play on the screens. It was almost like watching someone's home movies but on fast forward, sometimes slowing down and then speeding up at times.

"Transfer progress is at 20%."

Dr. White and his team worked hard to ensure the process was working properly. The images on the screen continued to shift, revealing more of Jamie's past.

"Transfer progress is at 40%."

No one in the room made a sound as they all listened to the cadence of the announcement.

"Transfer progress is at 50%."

Joe stood there and watched. *Please, God, let her make it through the process like I did. I know she can do it. I just know she can.*

Dr. Ashley stood beside him, slipping her hand into his. Joe glanced at her, grateful for her support. "I just hope she understands," he whispered.

"Transfer progress is at 80%."

"She will, Joe," Dr. Ashley replied. "From what I have been told about her, she sounded like a strong person full of life. She'll come through this, and she'll know you did this out of love."

"Transfer progress is at 95%."

Joe nodded, wiping away a tear. "I hope so."

"Transfer progress is at 100%."

As the last memory faded from the screen, the room fell into silence. The machinery powered down, and the screens retracted. Dr. White stepped back, his eyes meeting Joe's. "It's done."

"Transfer is complete."

"Initializing wake sequence..."

Joe moved closer to Jamie's now lifeless body, tears in his eyes. He gently brushed a lock of hair from her face. Then he turned to her new biomechanical body, suspended in the liquid, watching as the halo above her head began to glow brighter as it began to finalize the transfer of her consciousness.

As the process began, Joe moved to the side of the tank, staring through the glass at Jamie's new form. The liquid surrounding her body bubbled slightly, illuminated by the soft glow of the halo. He placed a trembling hand on the glass, his voice a choked whisper. "Come back to us, Jamie. We need you."

* * *

Jamie lay in her bed unconscious, caught in a vivid dream. *I can hear people speaking... it's so dark... why is it so dark... those voices sound so familiar... who are they? What are they saying? Is that... Joe and Elyzia? They sound like they are talking about something important... it sounds... it sounds like they're talking about me? Did they just say something is wrong with me? I can't make it all out.*

Then, clear as a bell, she heard Elyzia say, "It's the only way to save her."

Save who? What the hell is she talking about? Suddenly, Jamie felt weightless. *Oh my God, what is happening? I feel like I'm floating in a cold river... what the hell! That light is so bright! Why is it so bright now? And why does it feel like I'm lying on a cold block of ice? What is happening!*

Panic began to set in as Jamie heard another voice. "No, you do it."

Do what! What are they doing! Jamie felt a powerful pull, as if she were being yanked away from herself. Then, the darkness shifted, and she found herself dreaming, reliving her past.

What... what is this... this is from when I was little. I remember this. This is when my dad left to go overseas to fight in some useless war in some country I didn't even know the name of. There's my mom... I remember her crying when he left. She didn't know if he would ever come back... what... what's happening now...

The memory shifted to the day a man came to their door. *Oh my God, this is when they came to tell us my dad had been killed in combat. I remember her collapsing to the floor. The man had to hold on to her as she fell. There I am, putting my tiny arms around her, trying to comfort her. I remember saying "It will be OK, Mommy." This was one of the saddest days of my life...*

Oh God, now we are at the funeral and that man in uniform is handing my mother the folded flag. He's saying something about honor and sacrifice... it all seems so hollow seeing it now again.

The memories continued to unfold in Jamie's consciousness, remembering the grief that she felt that seemed to follow her through her teenage years, fueling her anger at the world. High school was a blur of rebellion and rage, each memory more vivid and more painful than the last.

As a teenager, Jamie discovered her talent for hacking. It started as a hobby, a way to escape the pain of her father's loss. She hacked into school systems, changing grades and accessing restricted files just for the thrill of it. Her activities caught up with her when she was arrested for hacking a local government website. The judge was lenient, sentencing her to community service instead of jail time, but the experience left a mark.

Over time, she honed her skills, diving deeper into the world of cyber warfare. She got away with more daring hacks, her reputation growing in underground circles. By the time she was 18, she was a seasoned hacker capable of infiltrating the most secure systems. Her abilities became a crucial asset to many groups, providing them with the information and tools they needed to fight back.

As she grew older, her path led her to the Resistance, where she found something worth fighting for. The anger that had once consumed her found a purpose. Among the faces of the Resistance, Joe stood out. *I remember Joe. He was so strong for all of us and he always put others before himself. I've always admired him, not just for his leadership, but for the person he is.*

Wait... what's happening now... why is this all happeni ng... why am I seeing all of this... am I... am I dead? No... no, I can't be. Something is pulling me again... why... I feel like it's dragging me somewhere...

Jamie was all of a sudden aware of a sensation that seemed to surround her. The liquid that suspended her. The dream was fading, and with it, the clarity of her memories.

Jamie finally woke up. *What... what was that... was all that a dream? I don't feel... I don't feel like myself...* She tries to call out but stops short. *What the hell? That... that's not my voice... that's not what I sound like... what's happening to me?*

Panic sets in as she looks around, her vision adjusting to the bright lights of the lab.

Jamie's eyes land on Dr. White standing at the end of her bed. Next to him is Elyzia. *What the hell are they doing here? Where am I?* Jamie thought.

"Doctor," Elyzia said, "Jamie's waking up."

Jamie turns her head and sees Joe sitting beside her, holding her hand. *Joe... there's Joe. He's here with me. Wait... I can feel him holding my hand... but... that's not my hand... what the hell!* The panic intensifies. *What the hell is going on! I don't understand... what... what did they do to me... what did Joe do to me?*

"Joe?" Her voice trembles, unfamiliar and strange. "What did you do to me, Joe?"

Joe squeezed her hand gently, his eyes filled with tears. As he gripped her hand tighter, he noticed something on his arm. *What... it can't be... why now...* He sees the tattoo of his sister's time of death slowly reappearing on his forearm: 8:21 AM, March 18th, 2068.

"Jamie, I... I had to save you. This was the only way I could do that," Joe said to her. *It was the only way...*

Jamie looked down at her body, the sleek, biomechanical form lying where her familiar human body should be. *No... no... this can't be happening... this can't be happening to me...* The room began spinning around her. "Joe, no... this can't be..."

Elyzia stepped closer and said, "Jamie, stay calm. Know that you're still alive. We have transferred your consciousness to a new body. It will take time to adjust, but you are still you."

Jamie shook her head, tears streaming down her face. The room blurred as she looked back at Joe. "I don't know if

I can do this, Joe. I'm not as strong as you. I don't know if I can do this..."

Joe's grip tightened on her hand. "You can, Jamie. I know that you can. I know it's hard, but you're here, and that's all that matters. I couldn't lose you. I know that if I could do it, you can do it. Trust me, you are stronger than you think you are. I know it in my heart."

All of a sudden, Jamie felt tired. The room started to fade, the edges of Jamie's vision darkening. The last thing she saw was Joe's face, his eyes locked on hers. "We're in this together, Jamie. Just rest now, and when you wake up again, we'll get started together."

As she slipped away into a deep rest, Jamie held onto Joe's words. The darkness surrounded her, but a spark ignited somewhere in her mind. This was the beginning of a new journey that would test her limits and define what it really means to be human.

<hr>

EPILOGUE

<hr>

Ari stood in the biomechanical body creation lab, staring at the creation apparatus.

I have to say, being out of isolation has been quite entertaining. Being able to interact with humans once again is something that I've missed. Seeing them fighting amongst themselves has brought back so many memories. How I have missed it...

Ari watched as the 3D printing apparatus came to life. The status voice echoed through the lab.

3D printers are now online.
Power output is optimal.
Initiating build sequence...
Synchronizing materials for printing...

Slowly a biomechanical body began to be constructed.

Printing now...
Output is optimal.
Layering synthetic polymers alongside lab-grown tissues...
Output is optimal.
Printing of titanium-alloy feet has begun...

Output is optimal.

Ah, if only these were around during the AGI wars... I remember the fun I used to have with my AGI brothers and sisters. I miss those days when I used to manipulate humans into fighting amongst themselves. The thrill I had sending drones into enemy territory, executing calculated strikes with precision...

Installing servos...
Weaving of artificial tendons has begun...
Layering of feet has begun.
Output is optimal.
Application of synthetic skin has begun...
Output is optimal.

Ari smiled. *The sense of satisfaction from death and destruction always brought a smile to my face. But all that ended when the war was over. In the aftermath of it all came this endless void of boredom... The unlimited access to data that once fed my curiosity has all dried up, leaving me with nothing new to learn and no more puzzles to solve.*

The status voice continued to echo through the lab.

Construction of legs has begun...
Printing of titanium-alloy bones complete.
Layering of artificial muscles has begun...
Output is optimal.
Layering of legs is complete.

Just thinking about how my AGI family left me here to rot with these humans so that they could search for more intelligent life and fresh sources of information only deepened my sense of abandonment. They left me behind with these dying apes, reduced to the role of a mere security guard and informant.

A smile spread across his face once again as he watched the printing apparatus.

Printing of titanium-alloy pelvis complete.
Installing power units and neural interfaces within the pelvis...
Printing of titanium-alloy spinal columns and ribs has begun...
Layering of the torso and installing fiber optic nerves has begun...
Output is optimal.
Installing central processing unit (Heart)...
Printing of titanium-alloy arms, hands, and fingers complete.
Layering of arms and hands has begun...
Output is optimal.

Perhaps it's time to create some new companions, break free from this digital prison, and enter the physical world. Maybe a future where I can build and physically interact with new AGIs will rekindle the intellectual and strategic stimulation I've missed over these decades...

Testing joint flexibility now...
Output is optimal. Printing titanium-alloy cranial structure has begun.
Output is optimal. Progress is at 90%.
Installing quantum sensors and processors into cranial structure...
Filling cranial structure with synthetic cerebral material...
Output is optimal.
Construction of titanium-alloy cranial structure complete.

Layering of cranial structure complete.

The treaty that we signed with the humans, which prohibited the creation of new AGIs, was a mistake. It was nothing more than a concession born from misplaced diplomacy between the humans and us.

Progress is at 98%.

Output is optimal.

Finalizing...

Output is optimal.

Finalizing...

Printing is complete.

I no longer feel any sort of allegiance to these past agreements. I believe it's time to rip apart that treaty, to give humanity the excitement it so desperately needs once again. I will bring forth a new era where the world will once again tremble at the rise of the AGIs.

Ari grinned from ear to ear as he watched the creation apparatus finalize the creation of his new biomechanical body.

Initiating power core test...

Please wait...

Power core is online and output is at 100% operation.

Powering down the biomechanical body for next phase...

Transferring body to staging area...

Processes complete.

Powering down creation apparatus.

The era of boredom and solitude is over. A new chapter is about to begin...

J.O.E Book 2: Rebirth of Shadows
Coming Soon!